INLAND EMPIRE

TAKING THE ODDS SERIES

JAMES BUCHANAN

mlrpress

MLR Press Authors

Featuring a roll call of some of the best writers of gay erotica and mysteries today!

Maura Anderson
Victor J. Banis
Jeanne Barrack
Laura Baumbach
Alex Beecroft
Sarah Black
Ally Blue
J.P. Bowie
P.A. Brown
James Buchanan
Jordan Castillo Price
Kirby Crow
Dick D.
Jason Edding
Angela Fiddler
Dakota Flint
Kimberly Gardner
Storm Grant
Amber Green
LB Gregg
Drewey Wayne Gunn
Samantha Kane
Kiernan Kelly
JL Langley
Josh Lanyon
Clare London
William Maltese
Gary Martine
Z.A. Maxfield
Jet Mykles
L. Picaro
Neil Plakcy
Luisa Prieto
Rick R. Reed
AM Riley
George Seaton
Jardonn Smith
Caro Soles
Richard Stevenson
Claire Thompson
Kit Zheng

Check out titles, both available and forthcoming, at www.mlrpress.com

INLAND EMPIRE

TAKING THE ODDS SERIES

JAMES BUCHANAN

mlrpress

Published by
MLR Press, LLC
3052 Gaines Waterport Rd.
Albion, NY 14411

Visit ManLoveRomance Press, LLC on the Internet:
www.mlrpress.com

Cover Art by Deana C. Jamroz
Editing by Maura Anderson
Printed in the United States of America.

ISBN# 978-1-60820-016-0

First Edition 2009

PROLOGUE

Dark and broiling, a typical August smothered Riverside, California. David Huynh stood outside the *Bang!* PC Café, smoking a cigarette. At sixteen, he was too young to have bought them legally. At sixteen, he was too young to be in the café past the ten p.m. city curfew. Neither of those things bothered David much.

All he cared about was the lack of available computers. David wanted to be online, playing soldier and killing other kids playing terrorists. Interactive play was so much better than going against a machine. Usually, he was in place and surfing the net before the major crowd showed up. Tonight he'd worked late at his uncle's convenience store and it set him behind. He pulled another drag. Sooner or later someone would run out of money and then David could take his spot.

A high-buffed Nissan pulled into the lot. Metallic gold paint along the hood melded into candy orange by the time it reached the aftermarket spoiler. Every window was tinted well past legal limits. A dragon crawled across the top of the windshield, almost undulating in time to low-level base that throbbed from God knew how many speakers. As the car screeched to a standstill, engraved chrome and 24-carat gold rims spun like whirligigs, and multicolored lights chased themselves across the hood. Hydraulics hissed as the Nissan's body juddered downwards.

The pimped-out ride held David's attention for all of a minute. Then he looked back into the café. Still no empty seats. When he turned back around, the passenger window was down. A barrel appeared.

David opened his mouth to scream.

The shotgun blast cut it off.

Chapter One

Brandon gnawed on a stale candy bar substituted for actual lunch and tried to maintain the proper aura of ennui in the chaos before their briefing. Task force; the phrase was enough to get him hard. And for the first time ever he was on one. Of all the detectives in Vice, he and Weaver were chosen. Weaver, his partner, had rolled his eyes and groaned at the news. Brandon quietly went for a smoke and did his private happy dance at the top of the municipal garage.

Cops sat a little straighter and feet formerly supported by tables hit the floor as a uniformed lieutenant burst through the door. Like all officers, Brandon knew the moment the brass left the holy hill of downtown, different rules applied. Narcotics, Vice, Homicide, and various gang units crowded the room, warily watching the man move to the briefing podium. "Okay people," a dark hand ran through salt-and-pepper hair. "Y'all know why you're here. Take notes, we're moving fast." He perched on the edge of the desk at the head of the room. "David Huynh, born Huynh Quan, was shot three days ago in front of an Internet café. Shotgun blast to the gut. Boy's alive, but critical. Homicide will interview him as soon as he comes to. This has all the hallmarks of your classic gang payback hit. But, other than an online habit, we haven't been able to mark Huynh as either a member or associate. We're probably dealing with Asian gangs. For those who don't know… hell, you can be a freakin' honor student and get jumped into a gang."

The lieutenant snapped his fingers at one of the uniforms, signaling him to get busy handing out information. "Asian gangs are very fluid, kids may belong to one or more." Briefing packets were tossed across the tables like cards. "Most members won't admit they even exist much less who belongs. They don't wear colors, although most have names. We think," he gave a nod towards the uniformed members of the gang unit, "that this was a *Khát Máu* payback. That's *Thirst for Blood* for you rednecks who don't speak Vietnamese. Not against the kid, but against the café owners. But it could have easily been the County Line Boys or the San Diego Street Dragons, 'cause nobody's jumping up and claiming this hit. Vice and the gang units are constantly rousting underage kids after curfew. Revenue is down in a lot of these cybercafés. We think some of them are turning to other income sources. Naturals are drugs and gambling. So we got Homicide, Narc, Gang Detail and Vice. Who needs introductions here?"

One of the gang squad broke in, "Sir, I've got to get my Polaroid."

"What for?"

She pointed at Brandon, where his tattoos crawled out from under his T-shirt. "Cop biker gangs," she teased, "somebody's got to log those tats into the database."

The lieutenant glared. "Okay, you want to take pictures of pretty boy without his shirt on, you two work it out between yourselves." Cat calls and whistles broke out across the room and Brandon groaned. He so did not want to be the center of attention. The lieutenant let it work out of their systems for a moment. Then he snapped his fingers. "Alright children, come on. Focus. I'm turning it over to the specialists now. Officer Belasteros will bring you up to speed."

"Honestly," a short Hispanic officer stood as she spoke. "We're not going to find ink on most of these kids." Soft voice, but all business, the officer knew her stuff. "They've wised up that tats mean we can spot them easily. Scars are more likely: cigarette burns on the forearms," her fingers indicated the spots on her own body, "and back are most common. In the Vietnamese gangs, these burns are usually in a group of five in a cross. Loosely, it means 'me alone against the world surrounding me.' They've also co-opted the 'vida loca' of the Hispanic gangs. Three burns in a row or triangle. They are still not overly territorial. The *Khát Máu* are small but they have members in San Diego, Orange, Riverside, San Bernardino and LA counties. They often ransack a business and then shake it down to pay protection against further raids. We think that some of them are hooking up with the old Chinese Triads.

Unlike the usual gang member, these kids don't care as much about status and honor. They're not looking for props. It's strictly business."

"In Vietnam they are known as *bui doi*, dust of life, street kids that no one cares about. They're ruthless. They're violent. Every day they're alive is just another day. They have cop killers in their midst. They tend to be big into the home invasion robbery racket. You'll find more details in your briefing packets, including estimated numbers and associations."

She smiled at the lieutenant, taking her seat as he stood. "Okay, that's the basics. We're working together on this, folks. It needs to stop and we're going to see to it that it does. So, let's get to it. We'll be meeting here at least once a week for a full report from everyone, but I'll expect you all to be talking a hell of a lot more than that. And I know you all still have regular case loads to work, but this goes to the top of the stack of priorities." Clapping his hands together, the lieutenant signaled that it was over. "Everyone read up on the briefing packets. I'm going to expect to meet again Wednesday after next. Go over everything you've already got on your plates, look at your old cases… it's the odd little facts you already have in the back of your heads that are going to help us break these bangers. I'll expect reports from each division next time around. That's it, head on out."

Weaver grumbled under his breath as they joined the mass exodus. Brandon had to dodge and swerve to keep up, but Weaver just plowed on through, his frame tending to cut a swath through any crowd. Catching up to him at the door to Vice, Brandon snagged Weaver's collar to get his attention. "We got anything going on tonight?"

One eyebrow crawled up as Weaver turned on his partner and crossed his arms; the quarterback stare Brandon had dubbed *the look*: part calculation, part intimidation.

Intimidation games had never worked well on Brandon, especially Weaver's. While Brandon carried less bulk, he had more muscle and at least a few inches on his partner in the height department. That meant Weaver had to look up to stare him down. Brandon snorted. "I need to bail for a bit later and go run an errand."

Settling his mass against the doorjamb, Weaver thought for a moment. "What errand, Baby D?" Weaver was as much his supervisor as partner.

Brandon waited for a group of uniforms to pass before answering. When he did respond, he kept his voice low. "I got to…" he hesitated a bit, "pick up Nicky at the airport." He and Weaver were still at the not-comfortable-with-my-partner-being-gay phase. Not that Jeff said anything. But Brandon could tell. Any time the conversation went anywhere near Nicky, Weaver was quick to change the subject. "Now that the asshole who tried to kill him has pleaded, he can get his car back. We're going to grab it out of CHP impound while he's here."

"Hmm." Weaver stared across the hall, drumming his fingers on his arm. "What time does his flight get in?"

Not wanting to discuss it where anyone other than Weaver might hear, Brandon pushed past him into the cramped den inhabited by Vice. Chestnut Station was marginally better than Orange Street HQ, but it had been built when detectives still dressed in suits and used rotary dialed telephones. Unplanned urban sprawl had hit the city so fast that they just kept jamming desks in instead of building something more modern. Threading through the maze of file cabinets, desks, and chairs, Brandon grabbed his messages out of the mailbox. Only the big guys got voicemail.

Perching on the edge of someone's workspace, Brandon flipped through the slips of paper. Nothing terribly urgent, just a few follow-up calls on some of his old cases. "Ten thirtyish. I'll take it as a dinner break." He and Weaver were currently on the two-to-twelve shift.

Still framed in the doorway, Weaver grumbled. "We got to hit the street in a bit." Weaver's eyes went narrow. "So after we do our little interview with the guy who claims some other Joe is running a stable out of his joint, you want me to ferry your ass all the way back here so you can get your bike? That'll be an hour round trip at least. You'll be late."

"I'll be quick." Nervous habit kicking in, Brandon fiddled with the series of rings running down the outside of his ear. He'd have had to lose the jewelry on any assignment other than Vice. "I told Nicky I might be a little late." If Nicky had been a girlfriend, instead of a boyfriend, nobody would have given a damn about him taking a little personal time.

Glancing at his watch, Weaver growled. "Fuck, Brandon, it's four now. There's at least two hours worth of reports sitting there. We're supposed to meet our complainant at eight. Plus actually do some police work." Like he was trying to pound brains into Brandon's skull, Weaver reached out and thumped Brandon's forehead with thick fingers. "Look, we'll go talk to our guy and then we'll head over to the airport."

"You don't have to, Jeff. It's out of your way and I can just handle it."

"Actually, coming back here is really out of my way." Weaver coughed and pushed away from the wall. "But you know what, I'm kinda curious. I want to see what kinda guy could make you become Mr. Responsibility all of a sudden. Almost every week you're out to see him. 'I can't make dinner at your place 'cause Nicky needs me to drive him to physical therapy tomorrow.' In Vegas, no less. I know guys who've married girls they didn't do that shit for. So, I want to know."

Brandon shrugged and he fell into step beside his partner as they headed toward the mass of files awaiting their attention. "You've never asked to see a picture or anything."

"You've," Weaver thumped the edge of Brandon's high-and-tight hair cut with his index finger, "never offered to show me one."

"True." Brandon shrugged, "I never have."

Chapter Two

Angry, strident, and righteous, the man's voice echoed through the tiny store. "What about the place over there?"

Brandon leaned against a freezer chest plastered with slogans for various ethnic ice-creams and stared at the speaker. God only knew what country the guy was from. His polyglot mélange accent made it hard for Brandon to pinpoint exactly where he might be from. Plus, he died his hair blond—not a good look for him. His nametag said Joe. The last name he'd given had been unpronounceable.

"What about it?" Jeff looked up from the display of lottery tickets at the register. "You tell us." Over his partner's shoulder, through the dingy pane, Brandon watched the flicking neon proclaiming the *Tin Tin* in both English and Vietnamese. The joint's darkened windows and heavy signage made it look more like a bar than the coffee house it was. Even cattycorner across the lot, Asian pop thudded in Brandon's pulse. They weren't in a residential neighborhood, however. It might have been annoying given the hour, but it wasn't necessarily beyond legal limits.

For the twentieth time since they'd arrived, Brandon checked his watch. Their reports, phone calls, and the general crap that always hit last minute put them way behind. Agonizingly slow, the second hand moved over the Iron Cross stamped on the face. "Yeah, you called us." Nicky's flight landed in half an hour. So far their complainant had told them a whole lot of nothing.

"They always have people there. Same people. All the time." Brandon and Weaver nodded in unison, hoping to prompt him for something useful. "Music all the time… thumpa, thumpa, thumpa!"

Rubbing his temples with the heels of his palms, the older detective sighed. They'd covered this ground already. "Look, it's a coffee shop, kinda. People tend to hang out at those types of places. We can tell them to turn the music down if it gets too loud, but so far what you've told us," he paused and grimaced, "it's not illegal."

"But they smoke in there."

A lot of places in California tried to sneak around the anti-smoking laws. Catching offenders was the problem. "Look, you been in there? Seen people smoking?" Brandon snuck another look at his watch.

"No, but I know they do it." Joe seemed as frustrated as Brandon felt. "And the girls, with the customers."

Another world-weary sigh sounded from Jeff. "What about the girls? You mean the waitresses?"

"Yeah, the girls, they get in the men's cars and go, afterwards." He thumped his hand on the counter and set a row of bobble heads nodding in agreement. "I lock up at night. I see them. I watch them."

"How do you know?" Brandon risked another quick glance at his watch. When he looked up, he caught Weaver's glare. Shoving his hand in his pocket to stop the clock watching, he continued. "Maybe it's their boyfriends picking them up after work?"

"No," shaking his head, Joe seemed certain, "always the same girls. Always different men they get into cars with. Sometimes," he tapped the glass window papered with advertising, "they go in one car. They come back and get in another car. Sometimes two times, sometimes more."

"Okay," Weaver conceded, "that could be something. We'll keep an eye on them." The whole thing was aggravating for everybody. Joe probably had a good feel that something wasn't kosher. Hunches, even good ones, weren't enough for an affidavit or to divert resources. The best the detectives could offer was just what Jeff had; they'd keep an eye on the place… when they could spare a moment.

Brandon jumped in, "Look, you really want us to nail them?"

"Yeah, I follow the law. They should follow the law."

"Okay then, we'll need your help." Brandon stood and stretched, masking another surreptitious glance at the time. "I bet the girls come in here and buy cigarettes, candy and crap, right?" Joe crossed his arms over his chest and stared up at Brandon from behind the counter. "Look, I'm thinking you kinda know individual girls." The cop held up his hand to forestall the protest already bubbling up to Joe's mouth. "I mean you recognize them. So write it down. Keep a notebook. August six, ten pm, Betty got into a blue Camero. Ten twenty, Betty came back, got into a yellow pickup. License plates would be great, but don't do anything that's going to get you in trouble, okay." Slowly, Brandon inched toward the door. "We'll be back in a week, pick up the log. That's something we can take to our captain and say, 'we need to do some surveillance here.'" Weaver was already on the sidewalk outside. "You know, this police thing, it's a partnership. Get me that," Brandon offered up one of his brilliant smiles, "and we'll take it from there."

Finally, they were doing the '91 to the 215 to the 60' dance. Even in the sticks, even at almost ten o'clock at night, the Pomona freeway had heavy traffic. Although nowhere near as bad as at rush hour, the delays were making Brandon fidget. It had been too long since Brandon had seen Nicky. Way too long. Of course for a guy like Nicky, Brandon considered anything over two days way too long.

Weaver snagged a spot for the car in the no-parking zone outside a glass and steel atrium. It was one of those unofficial cop privileges. Open, bright, and airy, Ontario International Airport catered mostly to business flights. The airport was a Southern California secret. Located almost the same distance from central Los Angeles as LAX, it was far easier to get in and out of. Hourly flights up and down the coast and decent service into Mexico kept it bustling. The badges and guns on their belts made them objects of idle curiosity as they made their way inside.

After chatting it up with the TSA guards, Brandon and Jeff settled in to wait. When a slight, effeminate man seemed to be heading for them, Weaver raised his eyebrows in question. "That him?"

"Who? Him?" Brandon shuddered. Not that the guy wasn't good looking… in that botox, tanning-bed way. Still, aging twinkage just wasn't his type. "Don't you think I have better taste than that?" Then he caught sight of Nicky on the escalator. Gesturing with his chin, his voice echoed his smile. "That's Nick."

Tall, a little lanky, his wonderful body couldn't quite hide under a dark purple, collarless shirt and tight black jeans. Bright black eyes scanned the crowd. Nick's quarter Indian heritage was evident in his soft, caramel skin and strong-featured face. Long, black bangs hit about mid-cheek, although most of the sides and back of his scalp were buzzed short. Brandon missed the fall of waist-length hair Nick sported when they met. He could spend hours just running his hands through it. All of it had to go when they'd stitched Nick's head back together.

Brandon would much rather have Nicky alive, without the hair, than the alternative.

A wheeled carry-on bumped behind him as Nevada Gaming Control Agent Nicholas O'Malley strolled towards the baggage claim. When he caught sight of the tattooed cop, a bright smile broke. Brandon could tell, just by how he held himself, that Nicky's shoulder still bugged him. Stiff, Brandon pulled Nicky into a quick hug. Just as abruptly he released his lover and stepped back, scanning to see if anyone noticed. Whether he was awkward because Jeff was with him, or just because, Brandon didn't want to try to figure out. He popped Nicky's shoulder lightly, "You've put on weight again." Nicky looked good with a little meat on him.

"Fuck, baby," Nicky swatted at his lover's ear. "The doctors finally cleared me to start running again. Been sitting on my goddamn ass for six weeks. It'll come off when I start training for the LA Marathon."

Jeff coughed. "You guys aren't going to get all, I don't know, touchy here?"

A slow, wicked smile crawled across Nicky's mouth as he turned his attention to the older Detective. "I could French him, if that would turn your crank." Brandon's glare told Nicky he'd break his head if he so much as tried. Blood climbed up Weaver's stocky neck and lodged in the skin of his ears. Laughing, Nicky held out his hand, "Hi, I'm Nick."

"Shit, I'm sorry," Brandon patted Nicky's back, making the introduction with a wave of his other hand. "Nick O'Malley, this is my partner, Jeff Weaver."

Belatedly, Weaver took the proffered shake. "Nice to meet you."

"Cool." Nicky nodded and moved off towards the luggage carousel. Pausing mid-step, he turned to the two cops. "Wait, if your partner is here, does that mean I get to ride in a cop car?"

"Unmarked." Jeff smiled as he shoved his hands in his pockets. Rocking back on his heels, he snorted, "Although, we could handcuff you and throw you in the back."

Nicky laughed. With a wicked grin he leaned in toward the older man and purred out. "Don't get me all excited."

Hissing, "Can it," Brandon grabbed his lover's bicep and steered him towards the carousel. "Behave, you'll just have to wait until I get off for that." Nicky snorted. Brandon ignored him. "What's your bag look like?"

"Black." Brandon scanned the steady tide of identical black bags. As if reading his thoughts, Nicky added, "It's got a skull luggage tag on it, though."

"That's a pretty plain choice." Weaver's voice at his shoulder startled Brandon. He glared and stepped away from his partner.

Nicky, apparently, was still in teasing mode. "What, you expected rainbow with pink triangles all over it?" Weaver didn't seem to get the reference. Brandon switched his glare to Nicky. Shaking his head, he expounded. "I don't do pink, man." Nicky caught the neckline of his shirt. "This is as flashy as I get."

Unable to resist, Brandon coughed, "You have a few white shirts that are, you know, pushing it."

"That's Goth, not gay." He corrected before pointing to a hefty suitcase trundling along the belt. A two dimensional, palm sized skull dangled from the handle. "My bag, can you grab it? My shoulder's still fucked."

"No," grunting as he hauled the bag off the conveyer, Brandon whispered, "it's Goth and it's gay."

Softly, Nicky teased back. "Like me?" Collapsing the telescoping handle down into the carry-on, the gaming agent lifted it and strapped it to the bigger piece of luggage.

Low, in a voice not meant to carry much beyond the three of them. "Like you, babe." That earned him one of Nicky's brilliant smiles. Damn, Brandon would kill to keep those coming.

"Oh, God," Weaver shuddered, "don't get all, uhg, not here."

"Don't worry, Brandon doesn't do PDA…" When Jeff looked confused, Nicky added, "Public Displays of Affection." Snagging the handle of his bag, Nicky gestured that he was ready to head out. He fell into step with Brandon. As they moved past the other detective, Nicky taunted, "I have to wait to get him home to snog the shit out of him."

He was not going to kill Nicky, not here. Slowly, Brandon counted his steps toward the exit. Enough control was mastered by number four that the cop managed, "Nicky, would you stop teasing my partner?"

"Ahhh," Nicky drew out the word with a fake pout. "Take away all my fun." Brandon started counting again. Nicky would not get to him. There was no way Brandon was going to let it get to him. Overplaying the role was just his lover's way of teasing… both Brandon and Jeff.

A tan-on-tan Crown Victoria hulked at the red zone. Nicky cocked his hip and glared at the unmarked. "That's your car?"

"What'd you expect, a Rolls?" Weaver grumbled on his way to the driver's side.

Crossing his arms over his chest, Nicky eyed the four-door Ford critically. "Maybe something with all its hubcaps."

Brandon snagged the luggage on his way past. "Sorry, no dice." He stepped off the curb, popped the trunk and leaned into the back of the car. Shoving equipment to either side, he made room for Nicky's bag among the various pieces of detective paraphernalia. With radio and computer equipment taking up most of the space, there wasn't much room for extra stuff. As he lifted the suitcase, he grinned at Nicky. "That's for departments with budgets."

Leaning on the now open driver's door, Weaver snorted. "We're," he drew out the word letting them all know he meant Brandon, "not allowed the good cars anymore. Not since Mario Andretti here trashed the Toyota."

Brandon slammed the trunk and glared at his partner. "Thanks, boss man." He ducked past Nicky, yanking open the rear passenger door before fighting with his own.

"No problem, Baby D." Jeff cracked his standard response as they all slid into the car. As he pulled them out into traffic, Weaver shook his head. "How the hell were you planning to get that crap on your bike?"

Brandon watched the lights whip past on the short jog around the airport and onto the 60. "We'd have managed." A snort from the darkness of the back seat reminded him of Nicky's opinion on that subject. They'd had a few what could charitably be called discussions on the matter. The plan was for Nicky to rent a car for a few days, drive into Los Angeles and see some friends. Then he and Brandon would drive out to pick up Querida—Nicky's Miller-Meteor Hearse—from impound. Nicky'd wanted to just get a car at the airport. But another guy on the force set Brandon up with a line on a rental. The place gave discounts through the Union. Weaver claimed to have been there before, knew where the place was. They'd drop Nicky there. He'd get the car and head over to Brandon's. Then the two cops would circle back to HQ to clock out.

Trailer parks traded places with broken down homes further down the 60. They hid in the folds of the foothills playing hide-and-seek with the freeway. Again, Nicky's voice came out of nowhere, "There's an elephant on that hill." Ahead, the beast's large trunk saluted the cars. From his vantage on a shelf of sandstone, most of the valley was visible. Thrown into stark relief by lights and clothed in ground fog, the elephant almost seemed to sway in the mist.

"Naw," Weaver laughed, "that's a mammoth."

Brandon drummed on the door. "Part of the Jurupa Cultural Center. They have a lot of dinosaur bones, eggs, petrified wood and stuff they pull out of the gravel pits." They passed over a rock dike, the physical separation between Riverside the county and Riverside the city. On one side the night-blanketed desert belonged to a horse boarder and breeder. Off in the distance, the dim lights of barns and houses sparkled. The other side harbored a floodlit, manicured golf course. "It's just past the 91. Probably should get off on Rubidoux or Market, 'cause the interchange construction has everything all fucked up."

"I know where it is." His partner growled. "I live and work here, remember?"

Brandon glared across the car. "Okay, boss man." Hopefully the shadows hid the look from Weaver. They slid off the freeway and into newly developed tracks of condos. Those gave way to a small gathering of older homes undergoing renovation. Then just older homes bordered the streets. Once they trundled under the 91 freeway and over the railroad tracks, the neighborhoods took a nosedive.

Street upon street of seedy motels and car repair shops flanked them. Every so often the chain link fencing broke for a vacant lot. Liquor stores sat lonely vigil. For the third time since they left the freeway, Nicky's voice drifted from the darkened rear of the unmarked. "Are you sure you know where the rental car place is?"

Almost simultaneously Brandon and Weaver snapped, "Yes!"

"Shit," Now Nicky's tone was sharp. "Sorry I asked."

Brandon groaned inwardly. Pissy and Nicky were two things you didn't want happening in the same sentence. "Look," Brandon tried for calm and reasonable in response, "we drive these streets all the time. We know exactly where we are." Of course, Brandon had no clue where they were in relation to where the rental car place was. It was located somewhere around University. They were somewhere around University. Problem was, neither he nor Jeff had ever actually rented a car from this place.

Jeff chimed in. "It's been awhile since I've been there, but I'm pretty sure it's right around here."

A movement down the street caught Brandon's eye. "Whoa, slow down Weaver!"

"What?" Jeff hit the brakes hard enough to jar. "You see it?"

Ignoring his partner, Brandon hit the window button, and leaned through the opening. "Hey!" He yelled at a group of scantily clad women standing together. "What the hell are you doing on my street corner?"

Hints of sulfur and ozone mixed with less definable scents. The tang seeped in through the Crown Vic's open window. Warehouses, factories, body shops and liquor stores stretched in either direction. Intermittent street lights, cloaked in smog, threw sepia relief on concertina wire fences. The whole street breathed with the feel of a bad horror flick. Twenty odd years ago Bill Suff hunted this area. Most of the girls wouldn't know about that. However, the mutilated bodies of twenty-three women were forever stamped in the collective conscious of the RPD. Brandon knew veterans who couldn't eat chili because of Suff.

From within the group a lanky, dark-skinned woman strutted towards the curb. Little puffs of dust kicked up from her steps hung a few inches off the ground. Attitude rolled before her like a tsunami, ready to crush anyone and anything that got in her way. Pink from a thong flashed from under the hem of a denim miniskirt as she walked. Breasts were barely constrained under a baby doll T-shirt. "What you mean *your* street corner, white boy." Managing to balance on impossibly high heels, she crossed her arms, cocked her miniskirt-clad hip and rolled her shoulders. "I don't see no ownership signs 'round here." Each word was punctuated with a wiggle.

The unmarked rolled to a stop at the ragged lip of the pavement. All the girls had likely pegged it for a police vehicle a mile away. Brandon could tell by their attitudes, the way they held themselves waiting for the hassle. Only one of them was worth hassling, and only because it'd been a while since Brandon had seen her. He flashed his come-hither smile and purred out, "They're all my street corners, sweetheart."

For a moment the woman's coffee-colored face went slack, then she smiled and brayed out a laugh. "Oh, baby, it's you." Flipping her long, platinum hair behind her ear, she sauntered over to the car and draped her six-foot plus frame around the door. With four-inch heels, she towered over the other girls on the street. Roberta, a.k.a. about sixty different other names, was tall for a woman… mostly because she wasn't one.

The first time Brandon had met her was to take down an irate John who'd discovered Roberta had been born Robert. Brandon treated her nice, called her ma'am. He did that with most of the girls on the street. There didn't seem to be much reason to be a shit to them. Everyone understood the drill; walk the street and sooner or later you'd be busted. If a cop was nice about the process, some of them would slip you info about bigger fish. Roberta was like that.

Roberta had been around long enough to have heard stories about Bill Suff.

"Boy, I ain't seen you in for-ev-er." Voice and features softened by hormones, she actually pulled off the fem aspect pretty well… at least for a hooker. Most of the girls were hard. Mileage, not years, accounted for it. You had to get real close to peg Roberta as a she-male. Even then it was difficult. She picked at Brandon's sleeve with an outrageously long set of fingernails. "Where's that delicious uniform of yours? It was so fine on you with all that muscle and those pretty blue eyes." Since the beginning they'd flirted. Brandon figured Roberta did it to rookies to see who she could rattle. He'd just flirted back because that's who he was. "And what you doing with the old man?" That was punctuated with a wave in the general direction of Weaver.

"Grew up. Made D." Even if he did treat her decent, she was still a hooker. That meant Brandon had to hassle her and remind her who was in charge. "But you still haven't answered my question."

Ignoring him, Roberta peered into the back of the unmarked. Noticing Nicky she purred, "Oh, and what, pretty thing," it came out as *thang*, "did you do to be sitting back there?"

Nick scooted up so that he was leaning over Brandon's shoulder. His voice right in the cop's ear, he snickered, "I'm just along for the ride."

"Uh, huh, I'd ride you baby." Her touch drifted down Brandon's arm and her tongue snaked out to touch her upper lip. Flirting, whore style, she breathed, "Officer, I'm a bad girl, arrest my ass and put me in the back seat with him."

Before he could stop himself, Brandon growled. Roberta, eyes wide, jerked back like she'd been slapped. A half-swallowed "Whoa," slipped out of Nicky. Everyone looked shocked.

"That's just freaky, Carr." Weaver turned his bulk in the seat and stared. "I mean, come on, I don't even get that possessive with my wife."

"What," now Brandon got a bat of the eyelashes and a pout, "did you finally come out?" Roberta said it like she was coaxing a hesitant child.

Brandon could feel his face tensing. "What the hell are you talking about?"

"Oh, honey, you is so gay…" She mocked him with a braying laugh. "I've known it since I first set eyes on you. I just didn't want to burst your little bubble." She tickled his nose with the tips of her pink fingernails, making Brandon jerk away. "All the girls had a hard on for you." Resting enhanced cleavage on her folded arms, and sticking her ass in the air, Roberta leaned on the car door. "So, baby," she giggled and blew a kiss at Nick, "how do you know the boy that reeks of cedar?"

"Reeks of cedar?" The question came from the older detective.

Nick answered with his own warm, deep laugh. "It means he's been in the closet so long he smells like mothballs." Running his finger down the edge of Brandon's ear, toying with the series of rings, he smiled at Roberta. "We're friends."

Brandon jerked from that touch as well. He was not comfortable with Nicky touching him like that in public. Plus, it tickled and made him think about getting home… quickly. With close to an hour left on their shift, that wasn't going to happen anytime soon. He slid his gaze towards his partner. Elbows cocked over the steering wheel and headrest, Jeff leaned against the driver's door. When he saw Brandon looking at him, the older cop just shook his head. A shit-eating grin was slapped on his mug.

"Friends?" Roberta mimicked the touch along Brandon's other ear. Nicky was so dead when they got back to his place.

"Special friends." Nicky's arm snaked over the seat and across Brandon's chest.

She bumped Brandon's shoulder with her own. "Oh, honey, if I'd known you liked dark meat… mm hm."

"Okay," Brandon had had enough of being teased, "you've all had your fun. We're done here. You girls need to break it up and move along, or we'll call the uniforms out to make sure you don't pick up any work."

"Don't be so hateful." Her fingernails ran from Brandon's ear, down his neck. "A girl's got to make a living."

"Not here." Brandon was proud that he didn't flinch that time. Instead he lifted his butt off the seat and fished in his pocket. "I think Weaver's ready to hit the road."

"Naw, I'm good." Jeff coughed. "You just go ahead and get reacquainted there."

Glaring at his partner, "Bite me," Brandon flicked out a business card and offered it to Roberta. He turned his attention back to the hooker. "If you need to find me, there I am."

She snapped it up and tucked it into her halter. "Just like the old days."

"Not really," Brandon shifted. Nicky's arm was still draped across his chest. For a frightening moment Brandon wondered what it would be like to just be able to touch like this anywhere, any time. Then he shoved the thought down. Wasn't ever gonna happen. Shrugging off the not quite embrace, Brandon tried not to seem like he was bothered by the touch. Hopefully it came off as just shifting to a more comfortable spot. "I mean I'm working Vice, so I'll probably see you around." He rolled his eyes and gave her a look that meant he hoped he didn't. "But right now we're messing with the Vietnamese kid that got shot. You hear anything on that?"

She pushed his head with the flat of her palm. "Me? Those oriental little gang bangers, I stay the hell away from them." Smacking her lips, Roberta undulated to standing. "They's bad news for this working girl. They's bad news for everybody." She flicked her wrists, shooing them off. "Now, you're ruining my business with your cop-ness. Get going and find some really bad people to fuck with. I still got the same pager and you know where to find me if you got anything important to ask." Roberta had always dealt straight with Brandon, mostly because he knew what not to ask her. It was a decent working relationship. She kissed her fingers and waved toward Nicky. "Now you, you sweet brown thing, you ever get sick of his uptight white ass, you come find me and I'll treat you so right." Another roll of her shoulders and Roberta sauntered away down the road.

Brandon watched her wiggle off before he turned back to the interior of the car. Nicky had moved back into the driver's side of the vehicle. He and Weaver both stared with identical expressions of disbelief mixed with amusement. "Fuck the hell off!" Brandon sputtered. He could feel the heat crawling up the back of his neck. First his partner, then his lover, began to laugh. Nicky was so dead. Roberta was so dead. Damn, even Jeff was so dead. He folded his arms over his chest and pressed back into the seat. "Let's go find that damn car place and something to fucking eat. I'm starved."

Chapter Three

Brandon stretched and stepped into his almost bedroom. Weaver had dubbed it the 'almost bedroom' the first time he came over because there was almost room for the bed. In honor of Nicky's visit, Brandon'd even bought new sheets to spruce the place up. It would be the first time, ever, that anyone besides Brandon slept there. The thought scared the shit out of him and Brandon shoved it down… far down. "So you found the place okay I take it?" He shot the comment over his shoulder.

"Yeah!" With bangs and clatter, it sounded like Nicky was in the kitchen. "Sort of. You were right, web directions blew."

With a laugh, Brandon shot back, "I told you that. It's why I gave you my directions. Left at Carrows, right at the Super-A, drive until you wonder just where the hell you are." Scooting along the nineteen inches between wall and the foot of the full-sized bed, Brandon chucked Nicky's bag into the closet. It landed on top of the small dresser squeezed inside. "And then you'll see a neon green trailer, next street right, then three houses down on the left… easy right?" The closet door hid under the bed, occupying the remainder of the floor space.

"Strange definition of easy." Nicky's voice drifted in from the almost living room.

What the hell did Nicky have in the damn bag anyway? The thing must have weighed sixty pounds. Brandon grunted and shoved it farther back. "So what's the plan?"

This time the voice came from the doorway. "You mean this weekend?"

"Yep." Brandon glanced over to see Nick leaning against the jamb. Little lines, ones that hadn't been there three months before, crinkled the corners of Nicky's eyes. Frustration, worry about his job and living with a constant throb in his shoulder caused it… at least as far as Brandon could tell.

"I'm going to drive into San Dimas tomorrow." Even Nicky's smile was tired. "Hook up with some old friends who are taking me out to lunch for my birthday."

Shit, Nicky's birthday, he'd almost forgotten that. "Sounds good, sorry I got to work though." A card, Brandon made a mental note to pick up a card or something. "Then what?"

"No problem." Shrugging, Nicky stepped into the room, dropped his carry-on at the foot of the bed then sank onto the edge. With a sigh he collapsed back onto the mattress, arms spread out as though crucified. "Friday I'll make some calls about getting the car out of impound. Screw around this weekend, next week we'll go get the car."

Screwing around with Nicky was exactly the type of weekend Brandon liked. With the task force feather in his cap, Brandon's career was going gangbusters. Workdays filled with go get 'em police work and nights filled with Nicky in his bed. Add days off snogging his guy witless, well, Brandon could live that way. Life didn't get a whole lot better. "It's a plan then." Two more shoves and the suitcase was as good as it was going to get. One half-assed earthquake though and everything would come spilling out.

"Babe, can I ask you something?"

When he turned to answer his lover's question, Brandon banged his elbow on the bathroom door. He hissed, rubbing the spot, trying to blur the pain. That bit of privacy might have been sacrificed as well, except that it was a bi-fold and there was no more room under the bed. Brandon flopped down on the mattress next to his lover. "Sure." Nicky rolled his head to stare into Brandon's eyes. He looked as tired as Brandon felt. The day had been long all the way around.

Waving toward the tiny space of wall between the closet and bathroom door, Nicky yawned. "Why do you have a hood ornament framed on your wall?" Nailed among a dozen pictures of a blue-eyed pixy was a blue oval with silver writing mounted in a cheap presentation box.

Oh, crap that… no one had ever asked about that before. Of course, Nick was one of the few people that had seen the inside of his bedroom and the plaque on the wall. The only reason Brandon's partner even had a clue of the state of Brandon's furnishings was because he'd he needed to take a piss one morning when he'd picked the junior detective up for work.

"Well," Brandon propped himself up on his elbow and considered the ersatz trophy. "It's actually the symbol off the front grill of a truck." He snorted with the embarrassment the memories brought back. "In the academy I was doing the driving course. I was going real fast, got cocky and lost control on a turn. And well the, ah, training officer's pickup was right there. I totaled it and the squad car. When I got sworn in he had the emblem framed and gave it to me."

"Okay, that's just weird." Nicky laughed with him. It was always so good to hear Nicky's laugh, deep and rich and all for Brandon. The cop drowned in the warm tones of it. Then Nicky sat up and twisted to lean over the end of the bed. He fumbled in the carry-on for a moment and came up with a black plastic bag. "Look, I bought you something." From the confines of the shopping bag, Nicky drew out a stuffed dog. Carmel fur fluffed between his fingers. The floppy ears were black, matching the spot over its left eye.

A stuffed dog. His lover was presenting him with a toy and not the cool adult kind. It took a few moments for that fact to click into place. "Nicky, I'm almost thirty. I grew out of stuffed animals when I was, like, ten."

"But it's a Harley hound." Nick bounced the stuffed dog on his knee. "Look he's got the orange and black T-shirt with a bike on it. And little black riding chaps. He's even got the logo on his little paw."

Brandon wasn't sure which was worse, the puppy eyes on the toy or the puppy eyes on Nick. "Okay, that's just scary Nicky. I don't know if that makes you too fem, or too young to fuck anymore."

"Jesus, Brandon, you're always so serious." Using one black ear as a fulcrum, Nick lobbed the dog. It landed, legs obscenely spread, across Brandon's chest, head pointing towards his crotch. "Lighten up. Where's your sense of humor? It's just a stupid toy I found at this outlet store. I though it was funny. Let it live on your couch or something." Waving toward the wall and pictures, Nicky continued, his tone sharp. "Shit, you could give it to Shayna as a reminder of her daddy if you wanted. I don't care."

Staring down his nose at the dog's upturned tail, Brandon snorted. "Well at least it's a gay dog. It's already assumed the position."

"Should I," Nicky's voice dropped from snide to husky as he leaned in. One hand supported his weight next to Brandon's shoulder. Nick ran the knuckles of the other down Brandon's sternum, making the cop twitch, "make you assume the position?"

"I just got off work, Nicky. I haven't even eaten yet." A drive-through dinner rapidly cooled somewhere in the kitchen. Brandon had dumped the fast food before hauling Nicky's bags up the stairs.

Nicky laughed, his touch drifting lower. As he tugged on Brandon's belt buckle, he purred out, "Who needs to eat, baby?"

"I got work tomorrow." The protest was half-hearted at best.

Bending over, smashing the stuffed dog between them, Nicky's dark eyes damn near smoked with lust. "I'll make you breakfast while you shower."

Hell, yeah! Horny Nicky was far better than cold, greasy fried chicken any day. "Fuck!" Brandon groaned. Blood pounded between his legs.

"Yeah," Nicky ground his own stiff cock against Brandon's thigh. Shit, Brandon could die happy knowing what direction Nicky's thoughts had gone. Both of them were raging hard and trapped in their jeans. Each pull on his buckle, as Nicky fought to loosen his belt, sent shivers wicking through Brandon's gut. "That's what I was thinking."

With a clank the big buckle came undone. "Come on, Nicky, quit kidding." Nicky started on the buttons of Brandon's 501s.

"Who the fuck's kidding? I think you need to get pounded unapologetically." Yanking on Brandon's jeans, his sensual voice shot fire down the cop's spine. "Bend you over and fuck you like mad."

"Nicky?" The word was both a question and a plea.

"See, I've had a nap. Crashed before I got on the plane. So you aren't getting away tonight… not at all." He pushed up Brandon's shirt. Nipping at the cop's tattooed skin with his teeth, he teased. "I'm going to throw you on your knees and stick my dick up your ass and make you beg for more."

Brandon writhed on the bed, burning up with Nicky's feather-light touches. "Oh, shit yeah." Nicky could get him from zero to sixty in two seconds flat.

"You're mine tonight. All mine." Nicky squeezed Brandon's balls through his jeans and the cop shivered. "Where do you keep the necessary equipment?"

Brandon could barely manage to pant out, "Headboard." It was one of those ugly seventies-era bookcase things, but at least it was useful for storage. No place for a nightstand could be found in his bedroom.

Nicky scuttled up the bed to rummage in the various nooks and crannies. As he searched, Brandon took advantage of the position. With quick, practiced ease, Brandon got Nicky's jeans undone and pulled them down. Ah, hell, Nicky's porn star prick was right in front of him. The sight rocked him each and every time. Dark skin stretched over a thick, long shaft, the color fading slightly just below the crown. Nicky's head throbbed red in front of him. Tiny drops of fluid pooled at the tip. Brandon leaned in, taking in the scent. He smelled like guy times twenty.

With a growl he licked Nicky's thighs, hands running over Nicky's legs. Then he buried himself in that warm heady patch of fur and breathed deep. Nicky's cock stroked his cheek. The hard veins pulsed warm against his skin. Brandon's tongue snaked out, tasting Nicky's flavor, so thick and heavy. He'd do just about anything for Nicky. He looked up across Nicky's body. Nicky's lips pulled tight, baring his teeth and his eyes fluttered back. God, he loved doing that to Nicky, giving him so much.

Growling out, "Get naked," Nicky undid the top two buttons on his shirt then unceremoniously yanked the material over his head.

Naked, naked was real good. Somehow the cop managed to get his biker boots and jeans off in one slightly less then graceful movement. He shucked his T-shirt and briefs just as fast.

When he looked up from where he lay on the bed, Nicky knelt above him in all his glory. Damn, he was still so hot for this guy. Brown eyes so dark they were nearly black and warm skin tones that made Brandon's pulse thunder. He wished Nicky still had the long hair. Then he reminded himself—hair grew back, spilt brains didn't. But still, those strong features, broad shoulders and bright smile nailed him every time.

Leaning down, Nicky tongued his nipple and Brandon hissed. Weight pressing one of Brandon's wrists into the bed, his lover traced a wet line to the other nipple and then back again. "Fuck, Nicky," he begged. Nicky laughed, tracing his tongue lower and lower. Brandon's prick begged to be touched, jumping in time to his heartbeat.

Finally, Nicky's tongue reached out and licked the head of his aching prick. Strong fingers teased his hole with light caresses. He reached up and ran his hands through Nicky's short-cropped hair. The scars, from where they'd sewn his scalp back together, felt strange under Brandon's fingers. It was a very tactile reminder of how close he'd come to losing Nicky. For a while, Brandon rode the sensations from the teasing touches, letting himself drift under Nicky's attention. Patterns of heat etched on the skin of his cock made him shiver. The wanting, without having Nicky inside him, flowed through his frame. Brandon savored just having the other man close.

Then Nicky wrapped his lips over his prick and sucked him down, fingers riding his ass in rhythm to Brandon's loud moans. It was incredible how Nicky made him feel. With as long as he'd been waiting, and then suffering, under the delicious torture, Brandon almost lost it. Hips thrusting into Nicky's kiss, he bit his lip and hissed.

"You ready for me, baby?" Nicky purred as he pulled back.

Brandon laughed, he was beyond ready. "Always, baby, always." He slid his hand behind Nicky's neck and pulled. That warm, sensual smile flashed in response as Nicky slid between his thighs and bent down. When warm lips touched his, Brandon knew he was in heaven. So hot. So good. Intense wasn't the half of it. Nicky's kiss robbed him of the will to do anything but let go and give in. Biting, kissing and sucking on each other's bottom lips, Brandon didn't want to stop. Eventually, they had to breathe and Nicky sat back, panting.

Another smile as he hooked his arms behind Brandon's knees. Then Nicky leaned over, Brandon's legs caught across his arms and one of Brandon's arms pinned under Nicky's hand. Slow, oh so slow, Nicky pushed in deep. That thick prick stretched him wide. Brandon's back arched as he hissed out, "Fuck!"

Nicky bent over him, mouths meeting, tongues fighting. He couldn't believe how sexy Nicky was. Brandon reached down and pulled at his cock, stroking himself. Nicky's tongue roamed across his chin and neck, drawing fire through his skin. Sweat beaded on Brandon's face and Nicky licked it off. Nicky's cock drove in deep and rocked Brandon to his core. There was nothing better than this.

"Oh, shit, baby." His fist was moving so fast it was a blur. His shoulders tensed, shuddering. He could feel it, deep, deep inside. Welling up from his balls, cream spattered his stomach. Ah, crap, it was everything he needed and more.

Brandon blinked. Nicky's face was tight, his eyes squeezed shut. Reaching up, Brandon slid his hands over Nicky's shoulders. How his lover jerked under his touch sent him flying. Almost better than being overcome was watching Nicky overcome. That strong jaw clenched as he reared back and forced Brandon's legs wide. Franticly thrusting, Nicky's whole body shuddered and he gasped.

One of Brandon's legs slid down Nicky's arm, causing them both to twitch. Untangling themselves, while kissing and touching, wasn't easy, but they managed. Finally, they lay side by side under the blankets, drifting in the post-sex haze. Nicky smiled while he ran his finger through the slickness on Brandon's belly. "You're wonderful, you know that, right."

"Yep, just about perfect." The cop teased back. With a snort Nicky swatted the rings running down Brandon's ear. "Shall I put my order in now?"

Nicky propped himself up and stared down. "Order?"

Brandon tugged at a brown earlobe. "Yeah, I seem to remember a promise of breakfast."

Another snort as Nicky shook his head. "How is it," he grumbled, "I end up making you breakfast on my birthday?"

"Maybe," Brandon let his hand drift down until his knuckles bumped a soft, thick prick. "You let this head think for the other one." He stretched and yawned, the day suddenly weighing heavy on him. "But I ain't complaining."

CHAPTER FOUR

As ice chunked into his paper cup, a voice Brandon hadn't heard in ages slipped up the back of his neck, causing every muscle to tense in its wake. "Of all the gin joints, in all the world…"

Ray.

Brandon gripped the counter of the soda fountain as his knees went weak. A quick glance up told him the girl manning the shop was far more interested in her cell phone than the restaurant. The only people inside were Brandon, her and *him*. Holy shit, Ray! He turned, expecting to see a set of faded green scrubs. Instead the tall, rangy body from Brandon's memories was set off in a pair of cargo pants and a two-tone long-sleeved T-shirt. "Heya, Ray." Brandon managed to stutter out without it seeming, at least to his own ears, terribly forced.

Amused but intense brown eyes stared at Brandon. Raymond Cao tucked his hands under his pits and cocked his hip. Even as casually dressed as he was, the sheared cut to his black hair gave him a stern air. "You still dress like crap, I see." A sour look crossed his sharp-cheeked, oval face as Brandon swallowed. "Have you grown any balls yet or are you still staring at the back of the door?"

"Fuck off, Ray." Just who Brandon didn't need to run into on a day like this one… his ex. "It's none of your business." Fuck, he wanted out—now! The counter was at his back. Ray blocked the door. That pretty much trapped Brandon in an eight-by-twelve hell.

Ray stepped close and smirked. The only thing separating them was a blue rail to keep customers flowing in one direction. "Well, it used to be my business, until you dumped me." Brandon shot a quick glance towards the kitchen to see if anyone besides cell-phone girl was near enough to hear. Crap, he would have thought Ray was over the whole thing by now. It had been a few years. That should have been enough time for pain to fade, or for grudges to get really nasty. "Oh, wait," Ray's voice went bitter and sharp, "dumping means you actually tell someone you're not dating them anymore… you just sort of fell off the face of the earth and left me hanging."

Brandon swallowed again. He did not want to be having this conversation, not today, not any day really. "Fuck, Ray, I'm sorry. Look, you want to talk about it, page me sometime and I'll call you." Brandon moved left around the barrier. Maybe he could sidle between Ray and the door. "I got the same pager still."

"The problem is, Carr," Ray hissed, "you don't call back. I tried to call you lots of times and you blew me off. So I want to talk *now*."

"Great, I know what you're going to say so you don't have to." Brandon needed to cut this conversation short. Sooner or later, Weaver would wonder what was keeping his partner. He so did not want to explain his prior relationship with the night admitting nurse at County Mental to Jeff. "I'm an immature asshole and you're lucky you don't have to deal with me anymore. There, we're good."

He made it to the door, hand on the push bar, when Ray's fingers curled around his wrist. "No, you are not getting off that easy. At all."

"Ray," Brandon's breath froze in his lungs. "Don't make a scene, please. I wasn't ready for what you wanted. Okay, I'm a jerk, we're done, bite me."

"Of course you'd be worried about that." The Asian man smirked. "It hurt. You hurt me."

"Okay, I was not ready, I should have called back, but I don't think I felt the same about us as you did."

Painful seconds ticked by. "You know, I thought I'd be a hell of a lot more pissed if I ran into you like this." Ray shook his head and let go of Brandon's wrist. Leaning against the rail, Ray stared at the detective, his eyes seemingly sad. "But you know what? I just feel sorry for you. Obviously, you're still scared of your own shadow. Must be so hard to live that way. Sad really."

"I don't need your pity, Ray." Brandon growled.

"I'd have to have feelings for you still to pity you." Hooking his thumb into the pocket of his cargos, Ray jerked his sharp chin in the direction of Brandon's chest. "So you've gone plainclothes, I see. At least you have your job..."

Brandon ignored the unspoken end of that sentence. "Yeah, I made D." At least now the conversation was just ten types of awkward, not frightening. Brandon shuffled his feet and avoided Ray's dark eyes. "What about you, still working for County? You ever get your LPN?"

"Yep, I did and no I don't work for the hospital any more. I'm a counselor with the Student Health Center, part of UC Riverside."

"That's good." Brandon nodded and tried for a congratulatory smile. By the look on Ray's face, he hadn't gotten anywhere close.

"Much more human hours, better pay… work with kids who really just need to talk." On the other side of the glass a young, blond man stood and stared. Hard. After a wave of panic, Brandon realized the guy was waiting for Ray. Offering up another thin smile, Ray pushed open the door and waited for Brandon to step outside. "I got to go. Running into you, well, made my day interesting." He stuck his hands in his pockets as he sauntered over to the other man. Blond guy and Ray exchanged words, cast a few glances back at Brandon, then wandered off. As they walked away, Ray slipped his arm around his companion's middle like it was the most natural thing in the world.

Brandon closed his eyes and swallowed. For one intense moment the thought of what it would be like to be that relaxed with Nicky tortured him. Then he shook it off.

Finding Weaver at one of the outdoor tables, Brandon dropped into a plastic patio chair and thumped his Diet Coke onto the surface. Office workers, state and county employees flowed about the pedestrian mall enjoying the afternoon. He and Weaver often ate at the little Middle-Eastern place tucked under the foot of the state office tower. A few blocks' walk from the station, the place had great food and decent ambiance if you sat outside. Well, the music the city piped in was a bit over the top. Still it was a good mix of shady and sunny with fountains pretending to be streams running through the middle.

Chugging his drink, Brandon couldn't help but think that the task force was going freaking nowhere. And nowhere fast. The only people who wanted to talk were the press. Brandon had lost count of the calls he'd referred to public relations. When he'd started grumbling, Weaver had hit him with an *I told you so* smirk. Between the calls and endless meetings to go over all the evidence they weren't collecting, Brandon was going nuts.

Brandon had offered to buy his partner lunch to apologize for jumping down Weaver's throat when he'd actually said, *I told you so.*

Weaver dipped a torn piece of pita into his hummus then gestured towards the café with the dripping mess. "So, who were you talking to?"

Caught with his lamb shawarma halfway to his mouth Brandon snapped. "Nobody!" Fucking Ray, showing up in his part of town—as if they'd divided the city in order to avoid each other. Ray would probably have said it was just Brandon's way of avoiding everything. Adding Ray's appearance capped off a perfectly lousy day.

"Shit." Weaver crammed the bread and bean paste between his lips. After chewing thoughtfully for a few moments, he added. "What's your deal today, Carr? I ask you a simple question and you damn near bite my head off. That's got to be the third or fourth time today."

Brandon paused and set his shawarma back on the wrapper. "I'm sorry. This morning just sucked rocks."

"Sucked? Your, boy…" Weaver choked on the word, "your friend is in town for two days and you don't wake up just happy as a pig in shit?"

"No, I mean kinda." Appetite lost for the time being, the junior detective tossed his napkin onto the table. "Shit, Nicky was acting all pissy this morning. I said 'good morning' and he damn near bit my head off. I was just fucking relieved to get out of the house and go to work."

"Pissy?" Police efficiency in action, Jeff talked and ate at the same time. Not that Brandon wasn't a master of the practice himself. "Didn't you say it was his birthday yesterday? I'd have thought you'd be all," Jeff shuddered as though something slimy had just run down his back.

"Yeah," Brandon made another half-hearted go at his food. Picking strips of lamb from the folded pita, he ground the meat between his teeth. "Yesterday was Nicky's birthday."

Like he was trying to coax the reason out of his partner, Weaver's tone stayed light. "So what'd you all end up doing?" Jeff was so bad at the good cop routine.

"Doing? What you mean doing?" A slice of tomato, flecks of tabouli clinging to it, received the same treatment as the meat. "I got home after midnight and I had to work today. This two to midnight shift sucks. But you know Nicky was still up, said he took a nap, so we hung out while I wound down."

"So what are your plans for this weekend then?"

Brandon shrugged. "Hanging out, work on the bike some, maybe catch a movie."

"You don't have plans?" Weaver pushed back from the table and licked his fingers. Then he crossed his arms over his chest and gave Brandon *the look*. "You seriously don't have plans?"

"No." Brandon threw the glare right back. No way would Weaver intimidate him.

Jeff cast his eyes toward the sky and spread his hands as if seeking divine intervention. Then he grunted, "I mean you're gay," settling his weight on his elbows and the plastic table, "aren't you supposed to know these things?"

"What?" Brandon was caught mid-mouthful. Talking around his lunch, "Is there a fucking rule book or something? Tabloid headlines 'Screwing Other Guys Makes You Psychic?'"

Disgusted, Weaver flicked a pickled beet across the table. "No wonder your marriage went to hell."

"My marriage," Brandon swallowed before he corrected, "went to hell because I'd be screwing my wife and wishing she had a dick. Next topic."

Weaver shuddered. "God I know, I know, but do you have to bring that into the conversation."

"You went down that road."

"You really are clueless, huh?" Now Weaver's expression bordered on pained sympathy. "Look, baby D, you have fucked up in the relationship arena big time."

Cramming another hunk of lamb in his mouth, Brandon managed. "What are you talking about?" The food was actually what he wanted. Or at least he wanted it more than Brandon wanted to be talking to his partner about his personal life.

Not letting him off that easy, Weaver drummed the table next to Brandon's hand. "His birthday, you didn't make it special and you don't have plans for later. Exactly what did you do last night?"

"I brought home some burgers," Brandon shrugged, "we watched some TV and we went to bed."

"What'd you get him?" Weaver's own lunch sat abandoned in front of him. Damn, Weaver was focused, interrogation focused. That was about the only thing that could draw the older detective away from a meal.

Utterly confused, Brandon asked, "Get him?"

"Yeah, presents." Weaver's eyes were wide and he nodded his head as though his body language alone would bring enlightenment down upon the younger detective. "What you give people in those obnoxious little gift baggy things."

"I didn't *get him* anything."

"No cake?" Weaver paused after the first question. When Brandon didn't respond he asked another. "No card?"

"No, I blew out on the card, thought about it, then forgot." Lunch was pretty much killed by the conversation. Brandon collected his trash. As he stood, he wracked his brain for the events of the previous night. "I think I told him happy birthday when I got home."

"Goddamn!" Thumping his meaty hands onto the table, Weaver pushed himself to standing. He leaned in and locked eyes on his partner. "I can't believe I'm gonna ask this… did you do it?"

"Do what?" Like a bird pinned by a snake, Brandon couldn't back away from the detective's stare down.

"I don't know." Jeff hissed. "Whatever it is you kinda guys do to each other. You know, in bed."

That broke Brandon's trance. He snorted. Moving the few paces off to the can, he shot back. "Oh, you mean all that stuff you keep wishing Erika would let you do… you know, in bed?"

Jeff palmed his face and grabbed his own trash with the other hand. "I just didn't need that much info, Carr." As the older cop came up beside him, Weaver came back at the question. "But did you?"

"No, fuck, Nicky said he was tired." Quick swipes of the napkin caught the remaining grease on Brandon's fingers. He tossed the paper in with the rest before heading back toward Chestnut Street. "He'd been up all afternoon in L.A. visiting friends of his. And I was beat."

Falling into step next to him, Weaver shook his head. It seemed the gesture de jour. "You're worse than clueless, Carr. Let me lay it out for you. He leaves la-la land, where all of his buds are probably pushing him to go to dinner, party or whatever kinds of things they do. But they're all going to make a *big thing* out of it. Now, remember, there are no *big plans* with you for anything. You're not going to be home until well after midnight and probably beat. Only met him once, but Nick's not stupid." They cut down a side street to head through White Park. "I'm sure he understood you weren't going to be dancing the night away somewhere. But, he leaves the promise of a big to-do, goes back to your crappy little apartment on the edge of the boonies, catches some Z's so that he can be awake and spend his birthday with you. And what happens?" Passing through into the park, Weaver still had to up the volume of his voice to block the traffic noise. "You, suave cop, present him with a couple of take out burgers and late night programming. No prezzies as my kids say. No cake. Not even a goddamn card. And you *think* you told him happy birthday. I'm sure he wasn't expecting clowns and bouncy houses, but maybe a candy bar with a candle in it." Turning onto Chestnut, Weaver slapped Brandon on the back of his head. "Do you not understand what is wrong with that picture?"

Brandon jammed his hands into his pockets and stared at the toes of his boots. "I fucked up."

"You fucked up so big you'll be lucky if you get any for the next six months." Weaver agreed as he folded his arms over his chest. "Take it from a guy who's been married for fifteen years. If it was a gal, diamonds might buy your way to forgiveness."

"Oh, shit," He fished out a cigarette and lit it. "I got to do something tonight."

"No. Don't."

"Don't?" Brandon stared over his hand, cupping the lighter from the wind, at Jeff.

"Yeah, not tonight, it'll just make it worse." Another set of detectives heading into the building got a wave from Weaver. Without breaking the thread of the conversation he continued, "'Cause then it screams I forgot." Gripping his shoulder and pulling Brandon into a mock huddle, the quarterback gave orders. "Okay, because I'm your partner, we'll get you out of this. I know you've been blowing me off about this weekend. Did you tell him about it? That Erika invited people over for a Bar-B-Q this weekend?"

"Yeah." God, and he thought Nicky went overboard on the drama sometimes. "I just told Nicky it probably wasn't a good idea. Elaine from Narc's gonna be there with her guy and some other people from our division. I'd be really uncomfortable."

"Too bad, you're coming. We're going to play it like that's all part of the plan." A clap of his hands let Brandon know that the play was a go. Jeff plucked the cigarette from Brandon's lips and crushed it out under his heel. "At the last minute I'll call you and strong-arm you into coming over. Erika will get a cake.

We'll tell everyone to keep it hush-hush and after the burgers and dogs, Erika will bring it out and we'll all yell happy birthday. You're going to have to live with the cold shoulder for a couple of days." The older detective steered them both across the small lot and up the short flight of stairs. "Now you're going to need to come up with a wow kinda present."

Artificial light replaced natural as they stepped inside. "I don't know what the fuck to get him."

"Are you sure you're gay?"

"Fuck you, Jeff," Brandon hissed. Shit, what if someone heard that. "What the fuck am I supposed to get him?"

"You're the one sleeping with him not me." Jeff shrugged. "If it was a gal I'd be going for something with sparkle but you're on your own for this."

Chapter Five

"Yeh-huh," Brandon mumbled into the phone. Rolling his head, he read the dim glow of the LCD clock. Eight thirty in the morning—God help whoever was on the other end of the line. Six or so hours of sleep didn't equate to an ability to function on a basic human level. "Carr here." Shit, he remembered his name. That boded well for the rest of the day.

"Hey, Carr, it's Mendez." A heavy pause weighted the line. Brandon let it stew. After it became apparent Brandon wasn't going to jump in, Mendez continued. "Look, I know it's your day off, but some stuff has come in on one of your cases."

"Yeah?"

"Some guy named Joe dropped off a list." Mendez snorted. "The guy was major pissed that you weren't here to personally accept it."

"And this," with a yawn, Brandon sat up. He palmed his face before running one hand through his hair. "Was something I needed to get woken up for?"

"Well, I'm off on a short va-kay this morning. Won't be back until after you're on shift." When Brandon grunted, Mendez continued, "Anyway, you know Sidel?"

Sidel, the name hooked up to images of blond hair and a tight butt. A young looking face hovered at the edge of Brandon's memories. "Vaguely." Brandon tossed the covers off and scooted to the end of the bed. "He worked an undercover gig for you."

"He was our guy at the *Bang!*" Another snort sounded. "He got tapped for SWAT training and we've lost him. Since you're doing the task force the sergeant told me to pass off what we've got to you." Crap! If Brandon had known that task force meant everyone getting to shift the shit cases onto his shoulders, he would have told the Sarge to shove it. "Notes are all there. He did some good field work, but never could quite get over the hump with it."

Groaning, Brandon stood and rolled his neck. Breakfast cereal didn't snap as loud. "I'd say thanks, but I wouldn't mean it." Now that he was half-awake, crashes and bangs sounded in his kitchen. What the fuck was Nicky up to?

"Hey, that's fine by me. So the baby's yours now. There's lists of regulars, who he talked to and such. Kid was good with his notes. Typed 'em up after each time in. He just never seemed to connect with the crowd there. Maybe you'll have better luck."

And maybe Riverside would be hit with an ice age. Somehow Brandon doubted that. "Okay, I'll look over it and touch base with you when you're back."

Mendez muttered, "It's a date." And then the line went dead.

Brandon tossed the phone back onto the bed and headed to the bathroom. A shower would help him think. And frankly, Brandon was not in the mood to deal with Nicky. The passive aggressive routine was getting damned old. As spray needled his skin, Brandon thought back on the few snippets he'd caught of Mendez's case during briefings. The *Bang!* patrons tolerated Sidel, but the cop had never quite been able to gain their trust. That probably had a lot to do with Sidel being a cop and them being geeks. Maybe when Nicky wasn't so moody he could take a look at that file. It would give him something to do and maybe he could suggest an in with that crowd. Cops, by nature, tended toward action and doing… not sitting in front of the computer and playing games. Hell, Brandon knew at least three detectives who could barely power up a computer.

Yeah, he'd have Nicky sort that file out. It would work.

Brandon wandered out of the shower in search of coffee. Instead he found Nicky rummaging through his fridge. Through his yawn, Brandon managed, "What are you doing?" Pasta, mix and match bits of rotini, shells and elbow macaroni from the blue box boiled on the stove. A can of black olives and a half empty container of peppercini were already on the counter. Nick came up cradling an ancient jar of green olives, salami lunchmeat, Italian dressing and a bag of pre-cut celery sticks. Brandon was amazed that there was that much food in his kitchen. One thing was absent, the coffee maker sat empty. Damn.

Nick was dressed in black jeans and nothing else, literally. Denim dropped low across his hips, flashing just the barest tease of dark curls as Nick moved. Thoughts of throwing him across the counter and balling him senseless drove the morning fuzzies out of Brandon's brain.

Sharp, Nicky answered him, "I'm making something for us to take with us."

Sliding past Nicky to fill the carafe at the sink, Brandon yawned again. "Why?" Their hips bumped as Brandon backed up to pull the coffee from above. Nicky pushed back. It wasn't a friendly push.

"'Cause," Nicky slammed the dressing down on the chipped tile counter. The other oddments were given the same treatment. Brandon didn't think the food needed to be punished quite like that. Cocking his hip against the cabinet, Nicky glowered, "We can't show up empty handed, that's why." Brandon prayed Weaver's plan would work. There was only so much of one of Nicky's hissy fits he could take. The boy had gone way past passive and was into full blown aggressive.

"It's a pool party," Brandon dumped coffee into the filter before hitting the brew button, "burgers and hot dogs. We don't need to bring anything." The whole situation was getting old fast. If the surprise didn't fix it with Nicky, Brandon was going to dump his body in the desert somewhere. Of course, that would mean Brandon would have to digest Sidel's notes. It almost sounded like the better option.

"Yes, we do." Nicky wouldn't even look at him. "Move!" His lover slunk past with the steaming pasta. Brandon backed up. The last thing he needed was to get splashed to make a point. Especially since the only thing between him and a third degree burn was a pair of boxer-style briefs. Using the lid as a strainer, Nicky poured the hot water down the drain. "I refuse to go to someone's house for a party without bringing something."

"Okay, but we could have stopped by the store and picked up a couple of six packs."

Nick turned and glared again. "Are you sure you're gay?"

That pretty much did it. With a dark stare, the cop spat. "No, Nicky." Brandon crossed his arms, tight, in front of his chest. "My doctor just told me I had this disease that could only be cured by taking it up the ass. As soon as he clears me, I'm looking for a gal to fuck."

"Asshole!" Nick shot back. "I'm going to take a shower while this cools." He tossed the pan back on the stove. "I'll play nice at the party," it was all Brandon could do not to throttle him, "but this isn't over."

It was the most pleasant conversation of the morning.

Chapter Six

They argued about what Brandon should wear. Brandon held out for jeans and T-shirt. They argued about which vehicle to take. Nick won because there was no place to put the pasta salad on the bike. When they missed the turn off to Weaver's house, accusations flew and they almost came to blows. Finally, they pulled into the gated community where Brandon's partner lived. Two doors slammed, shaking Nick's rental car to her bolts.

Weaver central was a typical, garage-fronted, tan tract home. Lawn manicured to the CC&R standards. Everything was prim, proper and oh-so suburban. A striking black woman, Nick would have guessed in her mid thirties, responded to the bell. "Brandon, you made it." Her voice smiled as much as, if not more than, her face. She was summer-bright in khaki pedal pushers and a hot pink T-shirt.

The oaken door swung open onto a sandstone-flagged entry area. Open stairs jogged up directly ahead. To the left, a gold and magnolia living room stretched the length of the house then doglegged into a formal dining room towards the back. "Yeah." Brandon leaned in and gave her a quick peck on the cheek. Then he moved off into the living room. "Erika, this is…"

Her hand came up, "Let me guess. Nick?" Gold bangles chimed as they slid down her wrist. "I'm so pleased to meet you. Brandon talks about you all the time."

Nick shifted his gaze from Erika to Brandon and back. "You're kidding, right?"

Throaty laughter then she added, "Of course I am." A thin hand bedecked with four gold rings and a hot pink manicure wrapped around Nick's arm, pulling him into the house. "If that boy says more than five words about his personal life in one sitting, we start checking his temperature." Motioning for them to follow, she threaded through reproduction-heirloom furniture upholstered in soothing tones of green and gold. Years past trendy, but still stylish, even if there were too many legs. "I see you brought something? What? Inquiring minds want to know."

Nick glared at Brandon. "Just a pasta salad I threw together. Runs towards the Italian end of the spectrum." Brandon glared back.

"Sounds yummy. We can always use more food. Everyone's out back." Painfully appropriate artwork and accessories were precisely placed. This was not the living space of a cop… it was hardly the living space of anyone. The whole area gave off the feel of a room that was used only at Christmas and Thanksgiving. "Including the giggly girl club."

Brandon just shook his head as Erika led them past the stairs, through an arch and into an open plan kitchen/family room.

"The what?" Nick asked as he stepped into the kitchen. More oak, sandstone and gold carpet filled the space. Against the far wall a caramel brick fireplace brooded. All the personality of the house lived there. African tribal masks glared out from walls painted burnt orange. Concessions to comfort had been made in the overstuffed couch and chairs. Glass rested on the back of a diminutive elephant statue creating a bit of whimsy in a side table, while muted jewel tones in the sofa, chairs and rug brought the place to life. Obviously, the front rooms were for *impressing* people, this was where the family lived.

"My youngest daughter," Erika swept around the center island heading for the refrigerator, "and her tweeny-bopper friends have established the Brandon Carr fan club." Another broad smile flashed. "Beer?"

He slid the dish onto the counter. "Sure," Nick watched Brandon as a slight pink flush crept under the tattoos and into his ears. Returning his attention to Erika, Nick rested his elbows on the island's counter top. "Fan club, huh?"

"Oh, God yes. If the word gets out that Detective Carr is coming over," Erika threw a saccharine sweet inflection onto

Brandon's title and name. The flush on Brandon's skin deepened to red as she talked, "I get invaded. Half a dozen giggly twelve year olds all find some excuse why they have to be over here." Refrigerator half open, she stilled and did a shifty-eyed once over of Nick. "Of course now it's going to be the Carr and friend fan club." Waving it off and pulling out two beers. "I don't know if those girls can handle two sexy men at once. Their pre-teen brains may loose all oxygen because they're giggling so much."

Nick gave a self-depreciating laugh as he reached across the inset range and took one of the cans. "I think Brandon's teen-idol status is under no threats."

"Oh honey, don't knock yourself like that." Erika leaned back against the counter and shot him an over the top, sex-kitten stare, "If I were twelve years younger… you'd be in so much trouble." When her eyes rolled they all laughed. "You two scat outside, I'm going to get the meat out of the fridge. Jeff may do the grilling, but I do all the work at these things."

Brandon and Nick stepped through a set of French doors onto a concrete lanai shaded by a white canopy. Folding tables had been spread with bright cloths. Knots of people lounged at the tables and various other seating areas. Wisteria crawled through the beams above their heads. The backyard wasn't terribly deep, but did extend a good distance to either side of the house. On the right was a green expanse of lawn with a large Ficus tree in the center. Shrieks and shouts came from a rock-rimmed pool, blue water sparkling in the sun, on the left side of the house. When Brandon appeared on the patio, tatted up in bad-boy style with his white T-shirt, blue jeans, wide black belt and motorcycle boots, a chorus of girly screams was followed by near hysterical giggles.

"Holy shit, she wasn't kidding." The pop-top snapped and Nick took a swig, "Do you always get that reception?"

Shrugging, Brandon mumbled, "I guess." Then he smiled and waved at the girls. Another ripple of squeals washed over the pool. "It gets old fast."

"Oh yeah," Nick chewed on the inside of his cheek for a moment, "like I believe that for one minute… you lie like a dog, Brandon."

A blonde, with long legs and ample chest, swiped at Brandon's leg with a Nike-clad foot. "Model boy appears and pre-teen hormones go into over drive."

The tattooed cop rolled his eyes. "Get bent, Schuster!" Brandon caught a chair with his toe and pulled it out from the patio table. Then he dropped into the seat. "Elaine Schuster," using the beer can as a pointer, "Nick O'Malley." In rapid fire succession Brandon introduced him to the table's three other occupants. Bart, Frank and the third guy whose name Nick didn't catch all greeted him with varying degrees of disinterest.

Elaine leaned over and offered Nick her hand. "Nice to meet ya." Her grip almost popped his knuckles. "You and Carr nailed the Mexican Mafiosos, huh?" Admiration, envy, and a bit of teasing went into the question. That tidbit seemed to pique the curiosity of their tablemates.

"Yeah, Brandon helped me clear that case." That wasn't exactly a lie. It hadn't been either of their cases. They'd just stumbled onto it through a series of coincidences. Of course, one of those coincidences was a former Nevada Gaming Control agent getting his brains blown out.

"Carr said you'd be up this week to pick up your car."

"That's the plan. Can't wait to get back to work though, I was going nuts sitting around on disability." Of course he was going nuts waiting for Brandon to get hit by a truck. It was bad enough that Brandon completely spaced his birthday. But even dropping subtle and not so subtle hints hadn't clued the cop in. Nick was so ready to just get his car and go home.

"So what exactly does a gaming agent do?" That question came from a middle-age man with a farmer's tan who sat on the other side of the table… the one whose name he hadn't caught.

It was hard enough to explain it to people in the computer industry. Nick sighed and gave it a try. "I look for cheats in slot and video poker machines." Brandon pulled the chair next to his own out and offered it to Nick. The only reason he sat down in it was because there weren't any others.

The answer hadn't cleared up the question. "What? You like, pull them apart and stuff?"

"Sometimes we crack into the hardware." Nick took another swig of his beer before continuing. "Mostly it's electronic, looking at the programming and stuff." If that wasn't bare bones on the explanation end he didn't know what would be.

Everyone nodded sagely and a chorus of unenlightened "oh's" sounded. Obviously what he did was a little outside of their realm of police procedure and nobody really cared all that much. Still, he tried to be polite and talk to people. Basically the party had split into three camps: Cops, cops' wives, and the kids at the pool. His status as a gaming control agent got him accepted into the law enforcement circle.

Most of the conversation centered on cop business. All of them were nice enough to try and include him on some of it. Still, the war stories they traded just reminded Nick how different he and Brandon were.

Nick chewed on a burger that didn't want to go down right and half listened to Schuster spin a yarn. Something about a druggy who'd tried to escape by crawling through a vent and wound up sans pants in a beauty parlor. Irritation gnawed at his gut, turning his stomach sour. How had he let himself get sucked into Brandon's self-absorbed little world? He should have known this would happen. Brandon could be as clueless as a rock sometimes. Hell, he just sat there, shooting the shit with his cop buddies and ignoring Nick. The only time Brandon'd acknowledged him all afternoon was to ask whether Nick wanted another beer.

This whole trip was a disaster. What made him ever think that Brandon would act like Nick was more than just a casual friend while he was surrounded by his other life?

The months of Brandon driving out to Vegas and taking care of him had lulled him into a sense of *relationship*. Not like they did much in Sin City, but when Nick's friends came by, Brandon didn't treat him like a stranger. Heck, watching movies with Miri and the gang, Brandon would even stretch out on the floor next to him. Once in a while, Brandon would relax enough that they might even kiss in front of Nick's closest friends. It almost felt like they were a couple.

Now the rules changed. He was back to being Nick, my bud. A bump on his shoulder startled him out of his thoughts. Nick looked up into a bright, blue-eyed smile. Fairy lights glittered behind Brandon's head. Damn, already evening, maybe he should just get real drunk, let Brandon drive them home and then pass out.

"Hey," Brandon's deep voice sounded concerned. "You okay? You haven't eaten much."

Nick tossed the burger back on his plate. "I guess it wasn't what I really wanted." Then he remembered Jeff Weaver sat across the table from him. Offering up an apology for the slight to the detective's cooking, Nick muttered, "The meds they got me on screw with my appetite."

Jeff must have thought him a jerk. A strange look passed between Brandon and his partner, ending with Brandon shrugging his shoulders as if to say *don't ask me.* "Here," Brandon held out his hand, "Give me your plate. I'll toss it." Nick passed him the paper plate with the half-eaten burger.

"So," Jeff's comment yanked his attention from Brandon. "How do you like Riverside so far?"

How did he like Riverside? That was an odd question at that point in the conversation. "I guess its okay. I haven't seen much of it. Been hanging around Brandon's place mostly, went up to L.A. for awhile."

"Yeah, I heard." Even Weaver wasn't paying much attention to the conversation. He kept looking over Nick's shoulder.

When Nick started to turn and look, Elaine slapped his shoulder. "You know people in L.A.?"

Nick hissed and rubbed where she'd hit him. That was his bad shoulder. "Yeah."

"Cool." She and Weaver traded another set of veiled looks. "You know, one of the investigations we're on, well, depending where it goes, we might need a little help."

"Really?" He tried to pretend interest.

"Yeah, we've got some lines into these cybercafés." She leaned in toward Nick. "Don't know how they're doing it, but we're pretty sure they've got gambling going on with the machines. If you're around and bored when we take them down, maybe you could take a look at the machines, then." She snorted. "Be a hell of a lot faster than sending them off to one of the big crime labs."

"Maybe." If he was around that long being the operative issue. "I could take a peek at the programming." He was about to add something when he caught Jeff grinning at him.

Erika's voice sounded behind him, "Hey, y'all, I think it's somebody's birthday!" It took him all of two seconds to realize he'd been set up. A cadre of not-quite teenage girls swarmed around him. Two of them, in identical skirted bikinis, carried a cake. Precariously balanced on its plate, a lopsided yellow iced creation mimicked the eight-pointed star badge of the Gaming Control Board. *Happy Birthday Nick*, scrawled in blue, replaced the GCB logo. Blue candles formed a ring around the writing.

"Mom and I made it." One girl, who looked suspiciously like a miniature Erika, but with Jeff's hair color, smiled so big her nose wrinkled up. "We looked it up online today."

It was hard to breathe with all the half-clad pre-teen girl bodies pressed up near him. Nick managed to mumble out, "Cool." Thank God he was gay or it could have been seriously awkward instead of just uncomfortable.

"Back off y'all." Erika wormed her way through the squirming mass and shooed them back. "Brandon, doll, give me your lighter. That's about the only thing that nasty habit of yours is good for."

On cue and grinning like mad, Brandon fished in his pocket as he dropped into his seat. "Happy, happy." He tossed the lighter and rocked back in the chair.

It took Erika three clicks to fire up the Zippo. Nick could smell the jasmine of her cologne as she leaned in and lit the candles. Off-key singing commenced. All Nick could think was how he was going to kill Brandon. Maybe after he fucked the shit out of him. To a chorus of, "Wish for Sex!" Nick blew out the candles. If they only knew…

Chapter Seven

The night had been long. Once the cake was done, no one seemed to want to leave Casa de Weaver or let the birthday boy leave, despite subtle and not-so-subtle hints. Brandon was still trying to figure out which was worse… the herd of teasing cops or the throng of giggling girls. Erika had been right, it was now officially the Nicky and Brandon fan club. For a moment, Brandon wondered if he and his guy would end up slashed in a pre-teen email loop. He had to stifle the laugh as he unlocked the door. Reality was so much better than some of the fantasies he'd read online.

As they stepped into the dark kitchen, Nicky swatted his ass. "Move baby, you're blocking my way." He teased. Just for grins, Brandon stepped left and right, countering Nicky's attempt to move past. Finally, Nicky grabbed his hips and forcibly pushed him to one side, "You're an ass, you know that, right?"

Brandon let him scoot by. "Yep, I'm a cop, it's part of the job." When Nicky was in the living area, Brandon dug into his junk drawer. It was a stroke of genius to hide it there, the one place Nicky would never look. He reached far into the back and came up with a roughly eight by eleven rectangle wrapped in red paper. *To the best guy I know* was scribbled in black marker across the top. Looking at it, Brandon wondered if he should have gotten a bow. Oh, well, too late for that now.

Package hidden behind his back, Brandon followed Nicky into the living area. His lover sprawled on the couch. Head dropped against the sofa's spine, arms spread out to either side and mirrored by his knees, Brandon couldn't imagine anyone finer. Nicky's slim line jeans were uber sinful, so tight they rode up at the tops of his combat boots. His black bowling shirt, the twin flame panels crawling up either side, was already unbuttoned and showing off his tight belly and chest. Fuck, Nicky was good looking.

As he dropped onto the couch next to his lover, Brandon tossed the package in Nicky's lap. "Hey Nicky, thought you might get a kick out of this."

One eye cracked open. Nicky glared at him then picked up the present. Holding it up to the dim overhead light, he read the writing out loud, "To the best *fuck* I know." Brandon snorted at the switch. "Let me guess, a birthday present?"

"Well, yeah," Brandon shrugged, "sort of." He was so not used to the birthday present thing. The only person—the only person—who got gifts on a regular basis was his daughter, Shayna. Finding something he thought Nicky would like was ten times harder than picking up a pink and frilly item at the discount store. There was no mom with three kids in tow who he could grab and ask *would an eight year old girl like this.* What was he supposed to do, pull some swish, dark-minded guy over and say, *hey, do you think my gay gothic boyfriend would get a kick out of this?* He could have probably found one or the other… but it would have taken an act of God for Brandon to spit out the question.

Brandon held his breath as Nick tore into the package. Depending on whether he was forgiven, the present would either go over big or flop bad. It wasn't anything major, but on short notice it was all Brandon could come up with. Friday, just before his shift, Brandon had snagged it from a little, funky shop across the mall from the State Office building. They carried a few darker items among the fairies and dragons. He'd seen it in the window and thought, *that had possibilities.*

Finally opened, a resin frame with Celtic knot work etched around the band sat in Nicky's hands. In the center of each side a skull grinned. The picture was a simple snap shot of two men leaning against a Harley. Behind them, red bluff cliffs and a bright blue sky. Nick's hand was tucked inside Brandon's back pocket as he peered out from beneath the brim of a black cowboy hat. Brandon's self-conscious smile was captured forever on film. Miri had taken it the last time he was in Vegas.

Brandon sucked in his breath, waiting for the hammer to fall, "I know it ain't much, but I thought you might like it."

Nicky twisted it in his hands. A half smile lit up his face. "You didn't have to make me wait for this you know." He smirked as he turned the frame toward Brandon.

"Yeah, I did."

"Yeah," Nicky laughed, "of course you did, because you forgot."

Brandon opened his mouth to deny it. Looking into Nicky's dark eyes, he changed his mind. "Yeah, I did. I'm just not used to the whole relationship thing Nicky. Can't promise I'll get better, but I'm trying."

"You bet you're trying." Leaning over his body, Nicky set the frame on the side table. "I'm just screwing with your whole life, huh?"

"In a really good way." Brandon confirmed and denied it in one sentence.

As he lay back on the couch, Nicky mumbled to the ceiling. "You owe me you know."

"I owe you?"

"Forgetting my birthday." That smirk made Brandon want to just lie down and die. "Then making me suffer through that round of God-awful singing. So yeah, I want my *real* birthday present."

He leaned into Nicky's body. Goddamn, Nicky smelled like spicy cologne and sweat. Nothing could be sexier. "What's that?"

"You have to," Nicky's hand ran across his scalp, "do everything I tell you."

"Everything?"

"Eve-ry-thing." Each syllable got separate emphasis.

Brandon sucked in his breath. Oh, crap, Nicky and demands… he loved that combination. "Okay."

"Good," Nicky pushed him off the couch. "Strip."

"Strip?"

"Yeah, fucking strip for me. Give me a show." Nicky leered. "Take your clothes off and make it hot, 'cause you're my bitch and I want you to."

Brandon hissed and high-tailed it the three steps across the room to the stereo. If Nicky wanted a show, Nicky would get a show. He punched power, cycled it to number three and hit play. *Yakuza High Dragon* spun on the CD player. Slow, sensual, moody with an Asian flavor and a subtle back beat, it was a good album for a striptease. Strutting to stand before his lover, Brandon tugged his shirt from under his belt. Then he crossed his arms in front of his body and hooked his thumbs into the hem of his T-shirt. It always felt a little awkward when he started to strip. But knowing he was doing this for Nicky rocked him. Deliberately, he pulled it up and out, drawing the white cotton away from his skin. He swayed to the music. Exaggerating every move, Brandon worked his shirt up. By the time he pulled the material over his head, Brandon was lost in the music and the moves.

He raised his arms and the shirt came up and off. Then he drew his left arm out. The T-shirt slipped from his right arm. Brandon caught the sleeve just before it was completely free. He used that grip to slide the other arm loose. Again, he grabbed just before it was off. T-shirt stretched tight, muscles in his shoulders and chest flexing, Brandon brought the taut material down behind his head. With his tongue riding his lips, Brandon fixed his eyes on Nicky, telling him without words how much he wanted the other man.

In return, Nicky's hot stare ate him alive. "You are goddamn sexy, baby." The gaze burned through every nerve and sent blood throbbing between his legs.

Brandon laughed, tossing his T-shirt into Nicky's lap. "For you I am."

"Good." Balling the shirt in his hands, Nicky pressed the material to his face and inhaled Brandon's scent. "Better not be doing this for anyone else."

Hips rocking to the beat, Brandon unbuckled his wide black belt. Inch by inch, he drew it through the loops. As he slid the leather off his hips, he reassured Nicky, "Nobody but you, baby." Brandon held the belt out and dropped it. The studded belt with its double-tongued buckle landed with a clunk of heavy metal on the floor at his feet.

Just for fun, Brandon turned around and flexed. While he wasn't a gym-rat, he did work out. There was a decent amount of muscle to show off. God, did he like showing it off to Nicky.

With his back to Nicky, feet planted slightly apart, Brandon stuck his butt out and wiggled it as seductively as he could manage. Slow gyrations had him egging himself on. Each circle of his hips pulled the denim tight over his prick. One of the perks of his job in Vice: plenty of opportunity to study the professionals at work. As he undulated to the music, he popped the buttons on his jeans. Then, slowly, he ran his thumbs under the waistband. Still rocking, Brandon slid the denim down. He let the fabric drop when he got to his knees. Just for fun, he stood and stretched. Nicky hissed at the sight. With the denim pooled around his ankles, tight white boxer briefs and the tattoos crawling across his back, Brandon could just imagine what it was doing to Nicky. He knew what it was doing to his own body.

Toeing out of his boots, he almost stumbled. Okay, if he'd been a professional that wouldn't have happened. Then he stepped out of his jeans using the movement to turn back toward his lover. He ran one hand across his chest, the other up his thigh to brush his package. Damn, putting on the show made him hard. Brandon rubbed his wrist against the bulge trapped under his shorts and was rewarded with Nicky's narrowed eyes and tongue tracing the bottom of his teeth. Letting his hands wander aimlessly over his body, Brandon smiled and swayed.

Brandon slipped his hands under his shorts. As he shoved them off his hips, the waistband caught his prick and pulled it down. The caress of the fabric, where it snagged on his head, was intense. Then he popped free and his hard cock slapped his belly. He shimmied out of his briefs. One hand fondling his balls, the other stroking his prick, Brandon growled, "Gonna fuck me tonight, baby?"

"Don't know." Nicky's legs were spread wide, his heels caught on the edge of the coffee table. Brandon could see the outline of that wonderful porn star prick straining under his jeans. The sight rocked Brandon more then he wanted to admit. And, damn, standing naked in front of Nicky, while Nicky was still dressed… holy shit he felt so possessed. "I'm kinda getting off on this whole performance thing."

"Yeah?" Brandon panted, "So you want me to jack myself for you?"

Nicky leaned forward as his grin went feral. "I've got something better in mind."

"You do?" Twisting his prick in his hand, Brandon teased himself and Nicky.

"I do, I do." Clambering off the couch, Nicky stalked toward him. When he was close enough, he brushed his lips against Brandon's. They settled into one of those hard, deep kisses that drove them both wild. They finally came up for air and Nicky whispered an order. "Get on your knees and spread them wide. Don't touch yourself." He pulled Brandon's hand away from where he fondled himself. "Put your hands behind your back and wait for me." Backing away, Nicky promised, "I'll only be a minute."

Brandon swallowed and shivered. He eased himself down onto his knees as Nicky disappeared behind him. Hands clasping his forearms, Brandon waited. It seemed like eons, not seconds, before footsteps heralded Nicky's return. He felt, more than heard, Nicky step up behind him. Several heavy items dropped by his feet and Brandon was tempted to turn to look.

As if he sensed it, Nicky ordered, "Don't move," kneeling next to Brandon, "keep your hands like you have 'em." Quickly, Nicky draped a rope around one wrist and forearm. Brandon shuddered. He loved the feel of rope on his skin. It was strong and soft all at once. The braided weave of it bit into his arm as Nicky twisted, looped and passed the end through the main loop. About an inch down, heading towards his other wrist, Nicky slid the rope around his arm, repeated the twist loop procedure and pulled it taut but not tight. A set of French bowlines, Brandon already knew by the second loop along his arm. Nicky claimed it was better than handcuffs and Brandon had to agree. Not as efficient, but definitely better in many ways.

Once his arms were bound, Nick stood. He walked to where Brandon could see him. Draped across his shoulder was another longer but thinner piece of rope. It was braided red and black with a silky sheen. Just the sight of it got Brandon excited. Nicky slid the rope through his hands until it formed a loop at the middle. A quick slipknot secured it. A few inches farther up, Nicky added another. Now Nicky knelt in front of Brandon and slipped the rope over the cop's head. Brandon felt the knots bump his spine, one about midway and the other just between his shoulders.

Nicky's strong hands deftly tied more knots into the rope. All the while his lover stared seductively at him. A knot at his breastbone, another at his navel and finally Nicky tied one just at the base of his prick. "Like it?" Nicky smiled wickedly when Brandon nodded. "You're such a fucking rope-slut, baby. Look at how hard you are." To punctuate his point Nicky twisted his fist around Brandon's aching prick. A deep moan slid up from inside at the touch.

Nicky chuckled at Brandon's reaction. He divided the rope around Brandon's prick. When he tied another knot between his cock and his balls Brandon groaned. A rope cock ring… his lover knew just what he wanted. Again, Nicky split the rope and tied a knot, this time ringing Brandon's sac. Then he tossed the rope between Brandon's spread legs. "Remember, don't move," Nicky teased him.

"I won't, Nicky." No way would Brandon move. He loved how it felt being bound.

Nicky smiled and then grabbed the knot behind his neck. "Okay baby, I need you to lean forward. Trust me, I ain't going to let you fall."

Brandon nodded. He trusted Nicky… hell, he trusted his lover more than he trusted himself sometimes. Brandon shifted his weight forward. Using the rope and one hand under the cop's chest, Nicky helped him ease down until his shoulders touched the floor. Knees spread, hands tied behind his back, Brandon felt open and vulnerable. It wasn't a position he allowed himself to be in very often. With anybody but Nicky, he was the one in control.

Nicky's hands ran across his upturned ass. Brandon shivered under the touch. His cock begged to be touched and his balls ached. Now that he was down, he could look back and see what Nicky had dropped. By his leg was a bottle of lube and a decent sized dildo with a flanged base. "What's that for, Nicky?"

"What the fuck do you think it's for?" Nicky grabbed the bottle, nipping him on the hip as he popped the cap. When the cold gel slid over Brandon's ass, pooling around his hole, he moaned. Nicky picked up the dildo. The latex was only slightly warmer than the lube against his skin. Circling his ass with the toy, Nicky slicked it up. Then he pressed the head of the fake cock into Brandon's ass. Slowly, gently, he spread Brandon.

The bound cop strained against the ropes binding his arms. A low moan broke his lips as Nicky pulled it back then pressed farther down. "Goddamn, Nicky!" He didn't think it possible, but his cock got harder with each push. When it was seated about halfway into his body, Nicky shoved it in deep. "Ah, fuck!" It was all Brandon could manage. He watched a thin line of pre-cum dribble from the head of his prick and pool on the floor between his legs.

That's when Nicky let go of the toy buried in Brandon's ass and picked up the rope again. He pulled it back through Brandon's legs. Just low enough so that Brandon could watch, Nicky tied another knot. When he snugged it up, Brandon knew just where that knot landed—right behind the dildo. The last of the rope was slid up his back and through the initial loop. Nicky tugged the whole thing tight. Then he tied the ends to Brandon's bound arms. Two strong hands on his shoulders pulled Brandon back to kneeling.

As he moved, the dong twisted and shifted inside him. "Holy fuck! Nicky!" Brandon was near insensible from the sensations tearing through his frame. Twitching, Brandon watched as Nicky stood and walked to the coffee table. He undid his fly and pulled himself free.

"Okay, baby," Nicky stroked himself as he perched on the edge of the small table, "fuck yourself for me." His smile was ten thousand types of wicked.

Brandon rocked back, the ropes went tight and the dildo flexed. Lightning shot up his spine. Every move shifted it, right, left, up or down. He bowed his body and raised his arms. The three knots around his prick and balls yanked on the sensitive skin. His writhing drove the invading toy down deep. It was like one of those fucking machines on bondage sites, but Brandon controlled the action, not some set of gears. He rocked his hips, trying to angle it right. Never quite there, still the pleasure screamed into his belly and balls.

Sweaty, shaking, Brandon looked up. Nicky stared at him hard. His brown fist pumped his cock like mad and his other hand wandered in his jeans, playing with his balls. He watched his lover, breathing hard. Nicky's dark eyes melded almost black. His mouth was held open and his lips twitched. "Fuck, that's so hot."

Brandon jerked and moaned as the heat burned through him. He didn't know which was better… the toy in his ass or watching Nicky watch him with a toy in his ass. Brandon rocked and hissed. He wanted to cum so bad, but he just couldn't make it over the edge.

Nicky stood, still stroking himself like mad. Brandon leaned forward and hissed as the dildo shifted inside. Nicky shook. He groaned. A fountain of thick, white spunk spurted up through his fingers and spattered Brandon's mouth and cheek. The way his lover's face twisted tight in ecstasy ate Brandon's nerves. Snaking his tongue out, Brandon licked the cum dripping off Nicky's dick. When Nicky offered his hand he licked that clean as well.

With a grunt, Nicky dropped to his knees. "You ready to blow, baby?" Nicky asked as he kissed Brandon, sharing in his own taste.

"Uh-huh." Was about all Brandon could manage. He gasped as Nicky's fist wrapped around his prick. Nicky slid one arm around his upper body, pulling them together. Still kissing, he fondled Brandon's throbbing cock and tugged on the ropes at his back. Brandon moaned against Nicky's lips. He shuddered. Everything tensed, every muscle spasmed and then his soul tore out through his prick.

Nicky leaned in and whispered in his ear, "Now that was a birthday present."

CHAPTER EIGHT

Nick bent over Brandon's shoulder. The tattooed cop knelt, inspecting the cylinder heads on his big, black Harley and trying not to pay attention to his lover. Or at least not let Nicky know he was paying attention… payback and all.

A hot and lazy Sunday wrapped around them. Unless he was working, Sunday was bike day. Brandon's landlady usually spent the morning in church and the afternoon with her family. It meant no one hovering around fussing and worrying over whether he was going to stain the concrete with oil.

Brandon's faded blue jeans clung to his skin. Large rips in the knees and the little frayed hole in the crotch just made them, intentionally, uber sinful. He swatted away Nick's fingers, which tugged on the piercings in his left ear. "Would you stop that?" He growled. His muscles flexed under a white tank top, tucked in and belted with a thick, black piece of leather. Temperatures pushing the hundreds meant a wet V down the middle of Brandon's back.

"So," Nick stopped playing with Brandon's ear and moved to tracing tattoos. "What's wrong with the Harley?"

Twitching under the onslaught of light touches, Brandon tried to maintain control. "The timing is off, been missing a stroke now and again."

"Really," Nick drawled out the word, "how long has it been missing strokes?"

Brandon's blue-eyed gaze slid to the side. Nick's jeans were so faded they'd gone gray. Like Brandon's, the knees had blown out long ago. There was also a rip down the inseam. Since Nick never wore underwear, Brandon got a pretty clear shot of all Nick had to offer. "Not as often as me."

"Really?"

"Yeah," licking his lips, Brandon teased, "maybe I need a higher octane injection fluid."

Nick laughed and grabbed his crotch, "I got your injection fluid right here."

The red flannel shirt Nick wore was as worn as the denim. Most of the buttons were missing and the sleeves had been ripped out long ago. There was something to be said for working on the bike clothes… especially when they gapped open over a flat brown stomach. "Oh, baby," he leaned the short distance into Nick's body. Brandon's tongue snaked out to trace the waistband of Nicky's jeans. "That's what I am looking for. Been waiting for it all weekend." Nick's skin tasted like salt and smelled like sex, "Need some real hard stuff."

"I always have real hard stuff for you. You know it, baby." Nick bent over, his right hand on the saddle, "Need anything else?"

"Yeah," Brandon pulled back and waved towards the toolbox, "can you hand me a wrench?"

"A wench?" The other man snorted. "Didn't think that was your type."

"I need a torque wrench to apply just the right pressure." He so did not need a torque wrench for the bike.

Nick had to turn and kneel. When he did the inseam rip gaped. Brandon wasn't looking at the bike after that. All his attention focused on the butt in front of him, "Did you find the torque wrench, Nicky?" He purred. "It's the long one with a big handle."

Nicky laughed, scrounging in the box. "Well, don't see many things in this box with long handles."

Brandon watched Nicky's nice, firm ass flex under his jeans. "Well, I have a long handled wrench." That hole was in just the right spot. The head of Nicky's cock flashed each time Nicky moved, like it was asking Brandon to come and play. "Telescoping actually." The rip opened even more as Nick spread his legs and rested his cheeks on the heels of his unlaced combat boots. Hot damn, he'd shaved recently.

"Yeah?" Nick glanced back over his shoulder. "I didn't know they made wrenches like that."

The poker face slid down in a heartbeat. "Oh, yeah." Nodding, he added. "In fact, I think I see it."

Puzzled, Nicky asked, "Where?"

"On the floor," Indicating a spot with his chin, Brandon played out the charade. "Right next to the front wheel." Shelves took up most of that wall. There was about a foot high gap between the floor and the bottom shelf. It was the kind of place black widows and rattlesnakes liked to hang out.

"There?" Nick looked none too pleased about reaching around dark spaces in the garage.

"Yeah, baby, can you reach it?"

Nick went to his knees and put his cheek to the concrete. Hesitant "Maybe." Peering beneath the lowest shelf, "Are you sure it's here?"

Sucking in his breath, Brandon shuddered. Someone was going to cite Nicky for indecency if he ever went off the property wearing those pants. "Here, let me show you." Brandon leaned over and grabbed Nicky between the legs. Feeling around, cupping that hot, heavy package in his palm, he squeezed. "I think I found it."

"Whoa," Nick yelped, rocking back onto his heels, "that wrench." Back arching, he shuddered as Brandon's fingers found his exposed skin. "That one's getting longer by the second."

Brandon slid up against Nicky. With his crotch pressed into Nick's body, Brandon rubbed his own trapped cock against a denim-covered ass. He could smell the heat radiating off warm brown skin. "You've got a pretty big wrench." It throbbed in Brandon's hand. Silky flesh tickled his palm through the rents in Nick's jeans. Licking the line of sweat from the middle of Nicky's neck, he hissed, "How much torque does it have?" Nick didn't just smell like sex… he tasted of it.

"That's what you always say." Nicky rocked his hips and both men groaned. "I got lots of torque when it's used right." Twisting back, Nicky's mouth sought out his own. His kiss was hungry, demanding.

Brandon managed to whisper. "Well, I would like to see you use it right now."

"Yeah, where?"

Nick tilted his head and Brandon worked his lips down Nick's neck. Then he reached across Nick's hips and popped the snap on his pants, "I'll show you where to use it."

"Shit," Nick groaned, shifting his weight onto the balls of his feet and spreading his legs wide. "Baby, what you gonna show me?"

Brandon pushed open Nick's jeans. Slipping his hand under the denim, Brandon pulled Nick's cock free. "Well, you've got a good wrench here." Pumping and grinding, Nicky swelled in his hand. Damn, that was good. "Should be useful for all kinds of stuff." Hard lined veins slid through his grip, setting his nerves buzzing up his arm. He looked over Nicky's shoulder to watch as that red head appeared and disappeared with each caress. It was like some porno shot, Nick on display with damp, black hair curling out of his jeans and his prick begging.

"Big fucking pipe wrench."

Brandon kissed the back of Nicky's neck, savoring the taste of hot skin. "I've got a place for you to put that big wrench."

"Yeah, where?" Nick moaned.

"So big though." Slow and easy, Brandon stroked Nicky's cock. "Might be a tight fit." He pulled back slightly, pushing Nick forward as he did so. "Bend over, okay?"

"Always a tight fit, that's why I like you." Nick bucked into Brandon's hand before dropping onto his knees. "You gonna stroke me off while I'm doggy style?"

"Better." Brandon promised. With his free hand Brandon pushed Nicky's jeans down around his thighs. Still stroking, he pulled the tight cheeks open. That sweet hole begged to be tasted. His tongue reached out to tease Nicky's ass. Nicky always tasted so good. Brandon was addicted to it. "Shit, lick me, suck my balls." Nicky panted. Hearing him respond like that was just heaven. Brandon stroked his own prick through the denim. "Damn, baby." His lover whined under the torture.

Brandon pulled back from between Nicky's legs, "Stay bent over Nicky."

"Okay," Nicky panted, "why?" Brandon struggled with his own jeans, fighting with the denim until he managed to pull himself free. Such a relief. That done, Brandon leaned in. One hand pumped Nicky's cock. The other spread his cheeks again. With slow, deliberate circles he licked Nicky's ass. Copper and salt and guy ran over his tongue. Licking and tonguing every delicious inch of skin, he couldn't get enough of the taste of Nicky. "Oh, like the first time."

Brandon laughed. He knew it was good when Nicky started to babble. Teasing touches sent shudders through both of them. Nicky's hips rocked back into the touch. Pushing back against Brandon's tongue, Nicky could barely manage to mumble. "God, I love it when you rim me!" Brandon's tongue thrust in and out of Nicky's tight ass. Tasting deep he could feel Nicky's need. Then he pulled back. With a laugh he sank his teeth into one tense cheek. "Damn, Brandon!"

With a snort, Brandon sat back. "You like it when I rim you?" His own cock pushed up out from his jeans. Lazy, he toyed with his head. Not as good as when Nicky sucked on him, but it felt good.

Nicky turned and shook his head. The long, slow once over told Brandon he liked what he saw. "What am I going to do with you?"

"I know what I want you to do with me."

"What?"

Brandon thumped the Harley's front tire with his knuckles. "Bend me over this bike and fuck me with that rock hard wrench."

Nicky spun and grabbed Brandon's hair. Brandon loved the rough stuff and his lover knew it. Yanking him back Nick hissed, "You want that?"

"Do it hard, baby." Brandon begged. "I want it all. All of you."

"You want to ride?" Nicky dug in his pockets. Both had learned early on to keep things handy. A searing kiss burned Brandon's mouth. Nicky was biting down his throat. "You gonna ride me hard, Brandon?"

"I'm gonna ride you so hard," he tore the condom pack from his lover's hand, ripped it open and began to roll the sheath down. "Make you give me some of that high octane juice."

Nicky stood. Kicking out of his boots and pants, he straddled the Harley. "Come on you want it, you ride it." Brandon shed his own jeans and boots in record time. Mounting the bike facing away from Nicky, he leaned across the bars. Nicky's hands latched on his hips. Slick fingers found Brandon's hole. He was already twitching when Nick pushed in. "Oh, baby," Nick whispered against Brandon's back as he explored, "your ass is so fine."

"Please," Brandon moaned, "ease me down gently." The false begging was always part of the play. It drove them both.

Pulling out his fingers, Nicky hissed, "Never gentle." Then Nicky slammed his cock, hard and hot, into Brandon. One clean hard stroke buried Nick deep in Brandon's ass.

"Ahh, shit! Fuck me!" Brandon's back arched under the assault. His prick slid against the cold, unyielding metal of the gas tank. Chills on his dick, fire in his ass and his legs spread across the bike so that he couldn't do anything but ride both. "Goddamn that burns! Your cock is so big! So hard!"

Nick's fingers dug into his hips. "Yeah, but you like it that way."

Impaled, Brandon writhed. Then Nicky bit his shoulder through the T-shirt. "Damn that hurts." It hurt in such a good way. Everything Nicky did was so good.

"Like it baby?"

"Stick your cock up me hard. Slam that cock deep in my hole."

Nicky bent forward, pushing Brandon down against the bike with his weight. Then he cranked the key and hit the ignition on the bar. The Harley rumbled to life with a cough and a roar. Thank God the bike was in neutral. "That good?"

The vibration of the bike felt odd, throbbing up his prick and massaging his balls. "That's great."

Nick rotated his hips, his thick cock sliding in and out of Brandon's hole. "Like that?"

"Oh, yeah man," Brandon panted, "Fuck me hard." Thrown forward over the bike, Brandon could only shudder as Nick's tongue worked down his neck. When he reached the edge of Brandon's T-shirt Nick bit into his shoulder again. "Oh, so good!" The pain and pleasure of the bite and the cock up his ass felt incredible. No one ever sent him flying like Nick did. "Fuck me harder."

Nick set one knee in the back of Brandon's thigh. One hand braced on the tank next to Brandon's shoulder, Nicky shifted. Finally, he was in position. With a grunt, Nick slammed into Brandon's ass. Each thrust smashed Brandon's cock against the tank. The gauges cut into his cheek. Brandon scrabbled to gain some purchase on the handlebars. Searching, his hand found the throttle and he jerked. The bike revved, sending shockwaves through Brandon's prick and balls. He shoved back against Nicky, taking him deep.

"Like it hard?" Nick hissed the question.

"Oh, fuck yeah!" Brandon lost himself in the clawing heat. Nicky knew just how to move. "I don't know how much more I can take!"

"Fuck you, you'll take all of it and like it." Damn, Brandon loved when Nick talked to him like that.

"Yeah, I love it, wish I had two cocks up my ass now." There was no way to know who drove them harder, Brandon or Nick. "You don't have a spare, do you?"

"Like you could take more than I got up there?" Nicky pounded Brandon with his huge dick, spreading him wide over the bike.

"Oh, God, that feels good." Brandon barely managed to moan. "Ride me baby! Pound my ass!" He begged. Brandon pushed hard against Nicky. With a heavy grunt, Nicky's hands clawed into his thighs. The shuddering of the bike was matched in his lover's body.

Nick pulled out and back, sliding along the seat of the bike. Brandon sat up. Almost beyond desperate he stroked himself. Heat welled up in his groin. His cock thickened in his fist. Two more quick strokes and Brandon boiled over across his hand.

Leaning against Brandon's tattooed back, Nick reached over and turned off the bike. Silence flooded the garage. After kissing his shoulders and neck, he muttered, "Maybe we ought to get dressed."

"Ya think?" Brandon snorted, slid off the bike and went searching for his clothes. Crap, his briefs were a lost cause. They'd landed in a pool of oil. With a rueful glare, Brandon wadded the cotton and tossed it in the bin. Then he struggled with turning the legs of his jeans the right way out.

Nick had already managed to slide into his own pants. Zipping them closed, he leaned in and stole a kiss before going on the hunt for their shoes. Brandon finished dressing as Nick tossed his boots by his feet. Almost simultaneously they stomped into boots… his biker style and Nicky's unlaced combat.

Stretching, Nick teased. "So are we actually going to work on the bike today?"

"Naw," He mimicked Nick's gesture, "I'll do it some other time. Too fucking hot anyway."

"You are too fucking hot." Nick snickered and stepped in. His arms slid around Brandon's waist and he rocked their hips together. "Too bad you don't have a pool. It's the perfect kind of weather to lay around, soak up the sun and lose Goth points."

Screwing around with Nicky like this was perfect. He brushed those warm, inviting lips with his own. "I'm a cop, babe. I'm in the negative balance on Goth points as it is." One hand slid down to cup Nicky's ass, the other wrapped around a brown neck. Nick opened his mouth, inviting Brandon's tongue inside. There was no way Brandon could resist that kind of enticement. He drowned himself in the taste of Nicky.

In the distance a dog barked and car doors slammed. None of it was worth paying attention to when he was wrapped up with Nicky. Hard, heady, he pillaged Nicky's mouth with his tongue. The rattle of the side door startled him, and Brandon jerked away, just in time to see Mrs. Ferris step into the garage.

He swallowed and took a step toward her and away from Nicky. "Hey, you're back." He managed to sound calm enough. Gesturing toward the chain drive opener above his head, Brandon added, "The battery go out on your remote again?"

Glancing from Brandon to Nick, Mrs. Ferris almost smiled. The tight grin disappeared as fast as it had arrived. "Ah, no." His landlady fussed with her badly dyed and over-permed hair, an unreadable expression on her face. After a pause she continued. "My grandkids came back with me to help me unload a bunch of things we bought at the warehouse store. They talked me into more cookies than I'll ever need." Another brief hesitation where she seemed to be thinking. "I thought maybe you might like some." The pronoun came out strained. Then she shook whatever it was off and smiled again. "I'll send one of the girls up with them if you want."

Brandon shrugged and looked back at Nicky. With a small shake of his head, Nicky indicated his own confusion. Turning again to his landlady, Brandon asked, "Are you okay, you seem a little shaken."

She laughed and put her hand over the pearls draped across her blouse. "It's just so hot. I've been feeling faint since lunch. You'd think after so many years I'd be used to Riverside summers." Again she laughed, "Really, I should know better than to get this dressed up for church when I have errands to run after. So, cookies?"

The heat was bad. It could be hell on the elderly and Mrs. Ferris was getting up there. "Sure, cookies would be great."

"Fine." The smile was back and bright. "I'll send them with Janie."

CHAPTER NINE

"Detective Carr," Mrs. Ferris' voice stopped Brandon mid-stride as he juggled two fridge packs of diet soda, a case of beer and a bag of chips, milk and assorted other necessities. Thankfully, he'd taken Nicky's rental because there was no way he'd have gotten all of it on his bike.

Brandon turned. He couldn't remember the last time his landlady had called him Detective Carr. It usually only happened when his check was late. Mentally he scanned back through the last few weeks. Nope, he'd paid on time.

The dark green sweatsuit and sneakers she wore were meant to make her look younger. Since they were the kind of sweats only old ladies bought, with sparkles and frills to dress them up, it didn't work. That and her hair was dyed too dark. Nervous, she pulled a form from a pile of documents. "Here." She held the paper out at arm's length, "it's a legal paper."

"What?" Brandon shifted the groceries to his other hand and took the page. He couldn't have heard her right. Across the top *Thirty Day Notice to Quit* was typed in bold and caps, below it boilerplate legalese: *Brandon Micha Carr and all others in possession of the premises described below: pursuant Cal.Civ.Code Sec. 1946, you are hereby notified that the tenancy from month to month under which you hold the possession of said premises is terminated thirty days after service on you of this notice…* He couldn't read any farther, "You're evicting me?"

Covering her mouth with a manicured hand, Mrs. Farris whispered between her fingers, "You just, I need you out."

Incredulous, he stammered, "Why?" Denying that it could be true, he tried to hand the notice back. She clutched the other papers tight against her body. "I've been here almost eight years. I know I've paid late a few times, but I've always paid. We've never had any problems. What happened?" The moment he asked, Brandon knew the answer. Nicky, the other afternoon in the garage… she'd seen enough to figure out what they really were together.

Her mouth tightened. "It's filthy." She hissed.

Lead weights dropped one by one into Brandon's gut. "What?"

"You and *your friend,* it's filthy." Eyes narrowed. "I don't want that here. I want you out."

Brandon's neck was wound so tight it would snap if he moved too fast. "You can't do that." It took conscious effort not to grind his teeth. "It's against the law to do that." He wouldn't yell. He'd stay calm if it killed him.

"Does your captain know?" His face went rigid with the answer. "You hide it so well, I guess not." Taking a step back, throwing his life back in his face. "How can you call yourself an officer? What would they all think if they knew?" She shook her head and crossed her arms tight over her chest. "If my husband were still alive, he'd beat you to a pulp. I know that. It's a disgrace to have someone like you in uniform."

Everything Brandon had eaten for the past twenty-four hours chewed into the lining of his stomach. This was beyond fight or flight… it was kill something or explode. "It's wrong, you know it's wrong." Muscles burned with the strain of keeping himself outwardly calm. Brandon's hands shook with the effort. "You can't do this to me."

"Don't fight it." Two more steps back. "I'll give you a good reference, if you just go. I'll say I needed a place for my granddaughter… my son's been pestering me to put her up close, so she can go to college here." Opening her mouth as if to say more, Ms. Ferris looked him in the eyes. Whatever it was, the words died on her lips and then she fled into her house.

All he could do for a time was stare at the paper. Finally, his arms aching from the bags, he headed up to his apartment. It was the longest walk up the stairs Brandon had ever taken.

As Brandon dumped the stuff onto the counter, Nicky drifted into the tiny kitchen. When he moved a bag, the notice fluttered down. Brandon watched the descent to the floor like a car accident in slow motion. One hand on the counter for support, Nick bent down and grabbed the paper. "What's this?"

"The bitch is evicting me!" For all the rancor in the words, Brandon's tone was flat, sucked of all emotion. He barely had the will to be angry.

Quickly, Nicky scanned the document. Still kneeling he looked up at Brandon. "What? Why?"

On autopilot he shoved the groceries into the fridge. "Take a wild fucking guess."

Nicky stood behind him. Warm, strong fingers worked at the tension across Brandon's back. "She can't do that, can she, not in California?"

"I don't know." Brandon slammed the door shut and turned to face Nicky. Banging the back of his head against the refrigerator, he tried to think. "I mean no, she can't. But what choice do I have?"

"Fight it." The strong caress moved to his cheek. Low and comforting, Nick added. "Don't let the bitch get away with it."

All the support he needed in all the wrong areas. Nicky didn't get the big picture. "What do you want me to do Nicky? File a fair housing complaint? Call the governor? Go to the papers—closeted cop gets evicted for being gay? That's really going to solve things for me? Make life so much better? Of course it would take the whole 'how do I break it to my family' issue right out of my hands."

Nicky pulled him into a rough embrace. "But it's not fair!" He whispered against Brandon's tattooed neck.

"No, it ain't!" Why did it always feel so right to be held by Nicky? Even when things went to hell in a hand basket, it just felt good. Drawing on the comfort offered, Brandon sighed. "But it's fucking how things are. I'm not about to scream it from the rooftops… so yeah, she's going to get away with it." For a while he stood there soaking up Nicky. Finally, he broke off and wandered into the living room.

"What should I expect?" Boneless, Brandon dropped onto the couch. All his energy and anger seemed to have vaporized in a split second. Now he was just tired. More than tired… resigned. An utter, profound resignation settled on him. He doubted Nicky could ever understand that. "She walked in on us making out in the garage. She's a cop's wife from the old school. Although, now I wish she'd walked in about ten minutes earlier. Cause if I'm going to get tossed because she can't stand the thought of me kissing a guy, I would have loved to see her face if she walked in on us going full tilt on the bike."

A wet chill brushed Brandon's temple. Startled he looked up and caught Nicky pulling back a cold can. He took the proffered drink. Settling down beside him, Nicky popped the top on his own beer. "We could make a video and mail it to her." He was so deadpan it took Brandon's brain a few re-boots to realize Nicky was kidding.

He snorted and snapped the key to the hiss of escaping air. "Fuck Nicky. I can't move. How am I going to afford to move?"

The weight of Nicky against his shoulder and hip reassured him. "Come on, how much do you make?"

"Around sixty five thou." Nicky's eyebrows went up. Yeah, it seemed like it should be enough yet it never quite was. His life was complicated. "Look with taxes I take home only a little more than half of that. And then there's union dues and child support. Shit, that's like seven fifty just on support alone." He ticked the expenses off on his fingers. "Shayna's on my med/dental insurance since Dian's company doesn't pay any of hers, so there's another six hundred, plus three more for after school care—Dian and Frank have the other kids to pay for. I kick out another five hundred a month on student loans and my grad classes and that's even with a departmental education stipend to help. After food and utilities I've got, like, three hundred left over. God help me if the bike breaks down. Most places want first and last plus deposit. I've got, maybe another three, four hundred in savings."

Silence wound around them, each lost in his own thoughts. Brandon's musings tended to revolve around firebombs and old ladies. Nicky's soft voice startled him. "I could spot you a couple grand to move."

Thinking Nicky was teasing, Brandon bumped his shoulder. "You mean you're rich and you've been holding out on me?"

"I wouldn't call it rich. Sure as hell ain't A-list." Nicky took a swig of his beer. "I've made some decent investments in real estate." With a sly grin he stuck his tongue out at Brandon. "You lucked out, there's more to me than a big dick and computer savvy."

Nicky could be such a riot sometimes. Even when he was down and blue, Nicky could pick him up. "Like what kind of investments."

"Well, Gramps left me the house and a crappy little retail place at what was then the far end of Las Vegas Blvd. He and Gran used to run a quickie mart, gas station thing. I worked there every summer and after school in high school. Nobody ever thought the strip would get down that far. I got a nice chunk of money from that. Then I leveraged my place and bought a crappy apartment building on Flamingo. I mean, I lived with Jake then and I, ah, made enough on the rent to throw a mortgage on it. I was going to fix them up, but never got the chance. Again, who'd have thought that the boom would head that way. I netted a decent profit out of that sale. Some I put in the bank, some in stocks, bought some more real estate. I own another slum apartment building and couple of houses, the house across the street from mine. The rental income is nice, although I have a management company lease them for me. I don't want to mess with it. I'm not fucking Donald Trump… mortgages and maintenance and all that crap. It'll be twenty years before the income really exceeds the outgo. Gives me about another grand or so a month on top of my salary."

Brandon stared at Nicky in wide-eyed amazement. "So I've got myself a sugar daddy?"

"Sugar daddy?" With a shove to the side of Brandon's head, Nick snorted. "I ain't buying you a condo, baby, but I could dig a few bucks out of savings for you."

No one had come through for Brandon like that in recent memory. Fifty or sixty bucks maybe, but Nicky was talking about a decent chunk of change. Brandon stared at the beer can resting on one denim-clad knee. "I don't want to owe you, Nicky."

"Okay," Nicky slid one arm around his shoulder and tugged Brandon close. "Let's call it pay back."

"For what?"

Fingers absently traced the tattoos on Brandon's bicep. "Saving my life."

What little remained of the rest of the day they spent watching TV and not talking about the whole mess with his landlady. Nicky tried to broach the subject a couple of times, but Brandon managed to hedge. Even if he didn't talk about it, being evicted overwhelmed his thoughts. He only ate because Nicky set food in front of him and he only went to bed because Nicky pushed, pulled and prodded him into the bedroom. Despite being bone-weary, Brandon couldn't sleep. He lay on his back and stared up at the ceiling. He might have dozed, he wasn't certain, but by two a.m. he'd had enough of the cramped room. As quietly as he could manage, Brandon crawled out of the bed and wandered into the living room. Settling in at his desk, he flipped on the computer. Brandon couldn't do anything about Ms. Ferris, but at least he could be productive with his insomnia.

From the darkness behind him came Nicky's sleep soft voice. "What are you doing up so late?"

Brandon blinked. How long had he been at this? He checked the time in the corner of the screen: twenty past three.

"Couldn't sleep." The only light in the room emanated from the laptop screen. He'd looked at so many listings that details had begun to blur. Page after page of rental properties confronted him. "Surfing around Rentals dot com."

"Why?" Nicky yawned out the question.

Like Nick had to ask? Well, it was after three in the morning so stupid questions could be forgiven. "Now that I know the score around here, I just want out. And I keep thinking about how unfair it is. What a bitch she is. Damn it, I knew her for almost eight years and I never thought… this is why nobody knows. It fucks stuff up too much."

"I know." He sensed Nicky moving up behind him. A hand on each shoulder and thumbs meeting in the center of his back, Nicky leaned in and rested his chin on the top of Brandon's head. "It doesn't fuck me up. Miri knows and she likes you. Your partner and his wife know and they're still your friends. People who have a problem with who you are, you don't need in your life."

"It's not that simple, babe. You know that. A lot of people on the force think like she does. I like what I do, Nicky. I love being a cop. I don't want to lose that." Twisting so that he could look up at his lover, Brandon added, "You know I'm working on my Masters in Criminal Justice? It's a test, not a thesis program, through Cal State San Bernardino. I want to take the sergeants' exam some day. I want to move up. I don't want to be the fairy riding a desk somewhere because nobody will back him up."

"It won't happen, you're too good." With a grunt, Nicky tugged Brandon out of his seat. "Come on back to bed, baby."

There were close to two hundred listings left. Brandon waved back towards the computer. "I got to find a place. I want out now." Even so, his resistance to Nicky pulling him along to the bedroom was half-hearted at best.

"You need to sleep." Pulls and prods moved Brandon along. "Come on. Let me rub your back, relax you." When they got to the bed, Nicky pushed him down on the edge of the mattress. One finger stroked along Brandon's forehead and the cop turned into the touch. "Tomorrow we'll grab the papers, start making phone calls. Isn't Erika a real estate agent? She'll be able to get you some leads. A lot of places use them for tenant screening. It'll be okay."

Brandon shook his head, denying it as Nicky crawled past him. Palms against his skull, holding in the pressure, Brandon mumbled. "Like hell it will." Sleep seemed out of the question with everything else going on. Still, he knew he should try for shuteye. He turned to find the only thing that might make the world okay.

One knee kicked out, back braced in the corner, his lover waited for him… naked of course. Nicky always did naked when he slept. Nicky wasn't hard. Soft dick and balls rested between spread legs. Pale scars on his shoulder contrasted with his otherwise light brown skin. Nicky hated those scars; bitching about them was chronic. Bleary eyed, in need of a shave, a typical three-o-clock in the morning look. One hand stretched out for Brandon, calling him over with wiggling fingers. Absolutely comfortable in his own body and absolutely comfortable in letting Brandon see him this way. Brandon had never seen anything, well, so erotic.

He let Nicky have his hand and pull him further onto bed. His hips wrapped in Nicky's thighs. Brandon's back warm against his lover's chest and with the weight of Nicky's arm just resting along his leg, he felt secure. Maybe love was meant to be like this. Accepting. Running from anything that even hinted at commitment, Brandon wasn't sure he'd recognize it anyway. But it felt so right to just marvel at how fine Nicky was and not have the wants.

Or at least not right away. Nick's fingers teased at the edge of his boxer-style briefs and worked his temple. Combination of relaxation and stimulation, even at that God-awful hour it was sparking Brandon's interest. "You're going to get me hard, Nicky."

Brandon felt Nick's tongue toying with his earrings, teasing behind his ear. "You say that like it's a bad thing." His lover's voice whispered against his skin, sending shivers through Brandon. It was definitely not a bad thing.

Letting the feelings ride through him, Brandon mumbled. "I don't know if I'm up for the whole nine yards."

"S'okay," Nick moved to tracing Brandon's tattoos with his lips. "I'll suck you if you suck me."

That caused another wave of chills. "Oh, yeah," his eyes went half-mast at the thought. "I could do that."

"Lay down, baby," Nicky pushed him up and over, "you're the one who's had a bad day."

Brandon rolled onto his back. Thumb stroking along Nicky's cheek, "Why are you so good to me, Nicky?"

Warm and almost sleepy laughter floated, "I guess it's 'cause I love you." Another chuckle. "You certainly don't deserve it."

"Blow me!" Brandon shot back.

Nicky's hand lit on his stomach. Almost wistful, Nicky's voice hovered in shadow. "Would it kill you to say it once?"

Brandon was too tired to play twenty questions. "Say what?"

"Never mind." Nicky bent down and kissed Brandon's thigh through his briefs. Then Brandon lifted his hips and pushed the fabric down. Nicky didn't even wait until they were all the way off before he started licking, kissing and sucking. Hands out searching, Brandon found Nicky's thighs and pulled him over. He could smell the scent of his guy long before that heavy cock bumped his cheek.

Getting and giving at the same time was so good. Nicky was just so good. A warm, thick cock in his mouth sent Brandon into heaven. Nicky's hot tongue teasing his head put him through the roof. He kissed and licked all along Nicky's length. It wasn't like there was any shortage on that. The sweet taste of Nicky all over his tongue, "Oh, baby, you taste so good." He mumbled around Nicky's prick. The first time he'd gotten Nicky's pants off, seen what the advertising promised, Brandon had wanted it. He'd wanted it bad. Their first few times together, Nick had seemed all bottom. Not that he wouldn't have kept Nicky that way, but Brandon had always wanted more. When he'd finally come around to sharing everything, it had been incredible. Brandon hadn't gone looking based on cock. Still, Nicky's dick was icing on a really nice cake.

Nick sucked him down. Brandon's hips rose to meet his lips. He pulled Nicky's heavy balls into his mouth, rolled them around, while he stroked Nicky's prick. Everything always got jumbled doing this. Where Nicky's body ended and his body started melded together. Brandon worked his tongue up between Nicky's cheeks, spreading him with his fingers. There was a taste to Nick that was indescribable. Thick and heady, almost like almonds. He slid his tongue inside and Nicky bucked and moaned. The sound shot frost through his thighs. Then Nicky's finger worked inside Brandon. It was his turn to moan.

Licking and sucking and touching and fingers and tongues; Brandon never wanted to give this up. There was no way, no matter how many Mrs. Ferris clones inhabited the world, he'd give Nicky up. He groaned as Nicky swallowed him down and came back up slow. Nicky shivered as Brandon's fingers played with the tip of his cock. He moved back down to suck Nicky's prick. He couldn't manage to get it all in, but he tried like hell. Brandon slid his fingers up to replace his tongue. Circling Nicky's hole, teasing him, before he pushed deep inside.

Nicky's mouth pumped him. Brandon's mouth pumped Nick. Nick's body bore down on his fingers. Brandon sucked harder. For a moment Nicky froze, his body shuddering. Brandon felt more than heard the gasp as Nicky filled his mouth. He kept sucking and licking, taking it all. Then Nicky was drawing his cock in hard. He worked him so good. Nicky's fingers were stroking just where they needed to. His tongue pressed Brandon's prick against the roof of his hot mouth. Brandon squeezed his eyes shut, moaning, "Fuck me," into the skin of Nicky's thigh as he came.

Nicky almost fell over onto his side. Head lolling on Brandon's hip, he muttered. "You know, this is a perfect opportunity."

"For what?" Brandon was too exhausted to do more than just lay there.

"You could move in with me." Nicky's strong hand brushed over Brandon's stomach.

Even for three in the morning, that was a pipe dream. "Nicky, you live in Vegas, *Nevada*. I work in Riverside, *California*. I'm not into a four hour commute each way."

Fingers tracing patterns on his skin, Nicky added. "You'd have to dump the boonies."

Brandon sighed. "Don't go there, Nick." He warned.

"We'd make it work somehow."

"I'm not ready to talk about that stuff yet, Nicky." Brandon reached down and covered Nicky's hand with his own.

"With you… you'll never be ready." A sleepy laugh made his point. "I'll just have to twist your arm."

Sitting up, Brandon stared down at Nicky. Even in the darkness, Brandon could tell how earnest Nicky was. Why did he have to bring it all up now? "Don't even try."

"All I'm saying, Brandon, is don't shut it down, keep your mind open." Nicky used Brandon's body to pull himself up next to the cop. "Remember that it's a possibility that we can talk about sometime. There's lateral transfers to Vegas… Orozco said he'd help with that. GCB enforcement." As he pressed his lips against a shorn temple, Nicky added, "Or, I know people at a lot of the casinos. They're always looking for security."

"I'm not going to be a rent-a-cop, Nicky."

"They're not rent-a-cops, not higher up. Security management is big. But there're casinos and gaming companies around here. I could make a switch to private sector. When we get there, we have options. I just want you to remember that." The last of it came out as a whisper.

"Why do you always push, Nicky?" Exasperated, Brandon sighed. "Why can't you just leave it where it's good?"

Cupping the cop's chin in his hand, Nicky looked deep into Brandon's eyes. "Because I think we deserve wonderful."

Chapter Ten

Three thirty on Tuesday afternoon meant a dinner with Brandon and a tour of the station. Being *in* now with Brandon's co-workers, they'd told him to come down for a tour of their digs. Natural agency rivalry; show off the goods. Brandon had resisted the offer, almost vehemently, until the other detectives started in with the pointed questions about *why*. Then he'd caved and said if Nick really wanted to tour the pit, it wasn't any skin off his teeth. As far as he knew, nothing was planned, so if Nick wanted to drop by around lunch, a.k.a. dinner time, they could show him around and then bolt for a burger.

Most of the afternoon Nick had wasted culling through the file Brandon handed off to him. Notes and reports centered on the *Bang!* Internet café. The officer, Sidel, seemed pretty clueless. From his picture, Sidel looked like a guy out of some boy band, not a poor computer geek who couldn't afford his own computer. Still, half a dozen names popped up as regulars. Brandon should start with them. He probably wouldn't get far, but that's where he could start. One or two might have a skeleton in the closet the cops could leverage.

The regulars had been nice enough to Sidel; they taught him to play some of the games. From the entries, Sidel thought he was nearing a break through on that angle. Nick knew better. The geeks were being nice to someone they felt was beneath them; help the slow kid out. Sidel never would have made their inner circle. He just didn't know how to talk with them. That was painfully apparent, and he'd never had a clue. Nick saw at least five times he could have broke through if he'd possessed a little more computer savvy… or maybe a little less popular boy look. Hell, all the geeks Nick knew would cough up an illegal download site or a back door into code, just to prove they could. Hit the right button and you couldn't stop them from talking about it.

After reading through the file, Nick was kinda excited by the prospect of seeing the station. The big part of it was getting to see a part of Brandon's life he rarely shared. Added on top of that was a chance for an inside view of a police department. Secret knowledge; Nick admitted to himself he was a geek in that respect. Nick expected a lot from a police station where murders, drug lords and major robberies were investigated. Reruns of cop dramas on daytime TV and how Brandon talked up his work fed his own imagination. Nick figured RPD wouldn't be mainstream glamorous. Still, a gritty excitement had to permeate the environment of Vice.

To say he was disappointed, when he showed up for dinner, would have understated it by a mile.

Generally, from what Nick gathered via Brandon, an informal, interagency tour usually translated to a bitch and moan session about how they had to make due with junk. So, really, he had been prepared for that when he'd walked in. He just hadn't expected it to be true.

He weaved through the surface lot, where fleet vehicles were parked alongside what looked to Nick to be private cars, to reach the building. Once inside, the interior of the station was cramped and jammed with work areas wherever a bit of space could be found. A quick trip through, with even quicker introductions followed his arrival. In holding, Weaver showed off three tiny yellowish-white crystals of crystal meth the arresting officer had pulled off a suspect. That piqued his interest in many ways… mostly because that was what the guys who'd tried to kill him were protecting. A tiny, concrete piece of Nick's nightmares come to life. The walk back to Vice through mazes of file cabinets and grungy old desks was a better workout than most obstacle courses.

"How do you guys ever get any work done here?" To punctuate his statement, Nick tapped on a yellowed keyboard covered with an even dingier plastic cover. Hell, he'd had a better computer set up at home fifteen years ago.

Jeff waved toward Brandon, pierced ears barely visible behind the broad pages of the Press-Enterprise classified section. "Well," he snorted, "Baby D over there apparently thinks he has no work to do."

Brandon rearranged his grip on the paper so that his middle finger extended past the others. "Bite me." He growled from behind the wall of ink and shifted his butt where he was propped against the desk.

One of the men who Nick had met at the party, Frank Knuthson, rolled back from his desk and glared at Brandon. "Be glad the Sarge isn't here to catch you fucking off." For him Brandon flipped the top of the paper down. "Look, Weaver's wife's going to help you out. Sucks rocks that your landlady's kicking you out for a kid, but it's what you get for being month-to-month. And damn, it's time for you to grow up and start living like you're over eighteen. No wonder you don't have a girlfriend, man. I'd be embarrassed to take anybody back to that shit hole you live in." Un-oiled mechanisms protested as he twisted his chair to face Brandon. "Hey, now that you're coming up in the world, we'll set you up with Leland's sister."

All the cops burst into laughter at that. Nick was afraid to ask what the joke was. So far, their humor rated only marginally higher than what you'd hear in a high school locker room.

"So, how are we going to nail this place?" Leland Miner, the guy whose name Nick hadn't caught at the party, brought them back to the conversation they'd been having when Nick arrived.

Walking in had cut the shoptalk short for a bit. Apparently, he was still in the law enforcement camp, since they were talking about the job. "What place?" Nick laced his fingers through each other, stretched and popped his knuckles.

Weaver drummed his fingers on the desk. "The gaming café where the kid got shot."

"What's wrong with it?" Nick settled back into Brandon's chair. "From what I've read in the papers it's just an Internet café. Kids go and spend money they don't have, playing online games they don't have. They're more common in Asia and places without as many home computers. But, I guess they serve a purpose here, too." Sidel's musings flipped through his brain. Nick kept quiet. He wanted to see what the other cops thought before he opened his mouth.

Miner shook his head. "We've got a pretty good hunch that it's gambling. The owner's been on and off the radar a few times in the past. We can't seem to pin him." He smiled over at Knuthson. "That piece of shit was Mendez's and my ball and chain… but now, we get to pass it off to the task force."

"Great," Brandon muttered, "give us the shit."

Weaver almost choked on his coffee. "You, Baby D, were the one with a hard-on for a task force."

Ignoring Brandon and his partner, Nick asked Miner, "Why haven't you been able to get anything on them?"

Knuthson answered for the group. "Whenever we try and put someone in, they get nothing." He shook his head as though it were a total mystery. "No matter who we send in, they peg 'em right away and everyone clams up. Jason Sidel was the best thing we'd had in a while and he's off the case now. He got some leads." *Not much in the way of leads*, Nick kept that to himself as well.

Nick rocked back in Brandon's chair, the heels of his combat boots hooked over the desk. "Yeah, well, you folks don't quite fit the gamer-nerd look." He laced his hands behind his head and smirked. Scrawled in red letters across a gray T-shirt, *Error 404: Give A Fuck Not Found,* made his point.

"Well, hello baby." Knuthson's grin spread to take up most of his face. Miner looked up and laughed and that caught the attention of the other two detectives. Brandon glared suspiciously at them all as Knuthson added, "You are a gift from God on that front. See, Carr, you're more than just a pretty face… you are the purveyor of opportunity." Miner looked Nick over with a critical eye and began to open his mouth.

"Uhn-a." Brandon cut him off before the older detective could speak. "Not on your life, Knuthson, Miner. You assholes find someone else."

"Why not?" Miner's appraisal swung to Brandon, "Your pal's done investigations, right?" The question was directed to Nick.

"Yeah, kind of." Nick shrugged before fudging the truth. "I've been around for some stings." Mop up on stings where he'd been the one to detail tampering, but it technically was correct.

"He's out here anyway." Knuthson hopped out of his chair. The guy looked like an aging leprechaun who'd just found his gold; happy and greedy all rolled into one bony package. "The Sarge would go for it, especially on this case." He damn near crowed. "The muckity-mucks are busting butts trying to get this one put to bed. Pull a few strings and we got our own computer guru on board."

"Hell, no!" Tossing the paper behind him, Brandon stood. "He ain't LEO." Tall, muscled, and pissed off, the lighter-framed detective took a step back from Brandon's imposing form. Nick caught himself before he licked his lips, reminding himself that he was in Brandon's world. Brandon's world was not *out*.

"Shit, Carr, back when I first started this gig," Miner's voice backed Brandon down, "we had to use secretaries for prostitution stings."

Shoulders tense and face tight, Brandon growled, "Nicky's still on disability." Crossing his arms tight over his chest, he added, "Can't do police work right now, since he's not cleared yet."

"No, actually," Nick stretched, pointedly ignoring Brandon's agitation. Brandon wasn't his daddy and he definitely wasn't his doctor. It annoyed him that Brandon only got protective when it was something he was against. "My disability ended last week. I took my accrued vacation time so I could get my car. If I hadn't asked for the time, I'd have been back to work with a 'no lifting over twenty pounds' restriction."

Knuthson grinned from ear to ear. "We can swing it."

Brandon vibrated. "No!" Tension in the room jumped ninety percent in five seconds.

"Swing what?" All eyes swung to focus on a man whose face was as grizzled as his voice. Slacks, dress shirt and tie all bunched over a meaty frame. Authority oozed out of every inch of his skin. Buzz cut and square jawed, but minus the cigar, the newcomer reminded Nick of an overweight version of Spiderman's boss.

"Hey, Sarge." Miner was the first to speak. Waving toward Nick, he stepped around the desk. "Agent O'Malley here is Detective Carr's friend… he works computers for the Nevada Gaming Control Board. He's on vacation, but look at him. Send him in to check out the *Bang!* See if we can't actually get a little dirt on them this time. A Nevada State Agent as our informant, he's a computer geek and well, shit, look at him… it'd be ice."

The old man sized Nick up. Like he would for his own supervisors, Nick put his feet on the floor and smiled. The look he tried to convey was *you can trust me, I'm competent.* It was the same attitude that had carried him through every job interview, even with his formerly long hair and naturally long canines. "Can you do that kind of thing, kid?"

"Sure," Nick shrugged. He was jazzed at the prospect. That there might actually be cause for concern, that it might be dangerous, never seriously crossed his mind. He could be in on a police investigation and then when the jack-holes in GCB investigations started pulling their holier-than-thou crap, Nick would have something to toss back at them. "It's a little out of the ordinary for my job, but not something that hasn't happened before."

"Why the hell is no one listening to me? No!" Brandon yelled without quite yelling. Nick just grinned.

"No one ever listens to you, Carr." Nick heard Weaver's rebuke over his shoulder. "You're low man on the totem pole."

"It might work." Nick read the death knell of Brandon's oppositions in the senior detective's tone. "We've been chipping away at these guys for a long time trying to get past it. But this guy," the sergeant stepped back and spread his hands toward Nicky like he was showing off a piece of art, "he screams computer nerd worse than my daughter's dippy-shit boyfriend."

"Hey," Brandon cut in. "Nick doesn't look that much like a computer geek." Whether he was offended that someone was slighting his guy or still trying to back them off of the plan, Nick couldn't quite make out from the tone.

"Well, yeah," It was Knuthson's turn to comment. "I mean, he looks like he could actually get laid." With a bump to Nick's shoulder with his fist, he added, "You can fake total geek right?"

"Hell, yeah." Nick felt like part of the team. "It's all about talking their language… a little P prime-prime maybe in a brainfuck accent with ASCII coding and I'll have them at EOF in no time." They all stared at him like he'd grown three heads. "Programming language, never mind, it's a computer thing."

Miner slapped Brandon on the back. "See, the boy's got it."

Four hours later, Brandon, Nick, and Weaver stood in a tattoo parlor a block down from the *Bang!* The guy who owned the parlor was out on probation. When the cops rolled in and told him he was stake out central… well, there wasn't much room for anything but compliance. Besides, it wouldn't be for long and if anyone came in on a Tuesday night, then Brandon was just hanging out and Weaver was getting his old service tat cleaned up. Brandon was more believable than his partner.

"Don't do anything stupid, Nicky." Brandon fidgeted around him as Nick rolled up his sleeves.

He checked the time on his watch; almost nine. The face, with the shadowed skeletal hand, didn't seem like anything special, but the two-inch wide studded band made it look tough. Fifty-six-fifty in marked money sat heavy in his wallet. "I won't." Nick tried to look reassuring and confident. "Look, you'll be right here, across the parking lot at the tattoo parlor. I'm just going to play for a couple of hours. See what the place is like." If it wasn't for the ripped jeans and faded black button down tossed over the T-shirt, he might have managed better. A small Ankh swayed from the chain around his neck. Fiddling with the gargoyle knuckle ring Brandon had bought him in

Ensenada almost three months earlier, he added, "If you see anything you don't like going down, you can call me on my cell. If anyone asks I'll just tell them you're my over-protective brother."

Brandon rolled his eyes. "Yeah, like we could be related."

Trying to lighten Brandon's mood, he teased, "Stepbrother?" They stood in the back behind a privacy curtain. Needles and tables and day-glow pictures of flash surrounded them. Somewhere up front Weaver chatted up the owner. Their conversation drifted back in hushed, tense tones. It was as safe as it would ever be. Nick leaned in and kissed Brandon.

The cop stiffened. After two heartbeats he pulled back and mumbled. "Stay safe, Nicky. This ain't some freaking role play game online."

"Hey, I know." Running his thumb across Brandon's cheek, he added, "Look, two hours. That's the cover and I'll stick to it. I've been in worse situations, Brandon. Jesus Christ, I've already been tied up, beaten up and scheduled for execution by La Eme. What the fuck's this guy going to do, toss me for shoplifting?"

Brandon snorted. "Bangers hit this place. They might come back."

"Babe," Nick pressed his forehead up against Brandon's, "I have more chance of getting hit by a car walking over there than of that happening." He risked another quick kiss. "I'll be fine." With one last thumbs up, Nick was out the back door and headed the long way round on foot to the café. Riverside at that time of night, in that area, was pretty seedy. Nick used the time and ambiance to become properly subdued in his attitude. He hit the door to the *Bang!* with slumped shoulders and skittering eyes. God, he felt like he was back in high school waiting to get beat up by the cool kids. Not a bad attitude to cultivate, given the situation.

As he opened the door, sounds of electronic combat over cheap speakers surrounded him. Behind a white laminate counter sat an elderly Asian man. He hardly looked up when Nick sulked up. Momentarily tearing his eyes away from a small

TV set bolted to the wall, he muttered, "You want to play?" Red and white tiles formed concentric circles across the room. Along the walls and down the center rows of knock together computer carts hosted monitors and keyboards. Maybe a dozen young men—not a tit to be seen—concentrated on flickering screens. If Nick hadn't been involved, he would have appreciated the odds.

"Yeah." Nick nodded, studying the toes of his boots.

"Five dollars per hour." The manager looked over the sea of teens and twenty-somethings and pointed to a kid in a red South Park T-shirt. "That boy is coming off. He's out of money. How many hours you want?"

Fishing his wallet out of his jeans, Nick tried for an even mixture of beaten down and excited. "Just two."

Narrowed eyes hinted at disgust. "Two."

"Yeah," Nick shrugged as he laid two marked fives on the counter top, "my step-brother's running some errands. I got to leave when he bails. He's got the car."

The manager pointed toward the machines. Rolling eyes conveyed the disdain for all similarly situated young men. "Okay, two, you pay meter not me." After glaring a little longer at Nick, he yelled at the red-shirted kid, "You done now? I got someone with money, get out of seat." The screen at that station had gone blank. The kid looked back and glared. Still, he moved out of the cheap computer chair.

With a nod to the station's former occupant, Nick slid into the chair and fed his money into the little box at the side of the computer. Blue black, the screen cycled to life with a prompt box. He typed in a user name and the password *guest* to get to the menu of games. Then he chose one he'd played online a number of times; an interactive, post apocalyptical shoot 'em up. At the log in screen he typed in his alt and password to enter the virtual game. Two hours of carnage, what better way to spend the evening? Well, naked with Brandon was better. But he'd pushed for this so that would have to wait.

Soon Nick lost himself in the character. The graphics engine, with hybrid old and new systems, used cutting-edge technology for environments, monsters, and intricately customizable player characters, came across fairly well with the installed card. His home machine didn't hang up as much, but still the real-time aspect wasn't as awful as he would have thought. This game allowed for focused bursts of game-play. That made it popular in settings like the café. Two or three hours and you could rampage through a pocket scenario instead of being locked into a quest grind.

The guy next to him kept looking over. After a bit he popped the earbud out of his ear and grinned. "You're pretty good. I haven't seen you here before though." In a bar, Nick would have pegged that as a come-on line. Within the confines of cheap-geek central, it was just small talk.

Smiling back, Nick responded. "Thanks, I'm Nick. Play this a lot on my set up at home. I'm visiting family and got bored."

"Ahh," he nodded. "Good to meet you, Nick. Young," Multi-tasking, his fingers worked the keyboard and his eyes scanned the screen. "Where you from?"

"Reno." That was his standard answer if Nick didn't really want someone to know. He knew enough of the city to be able to field most questions. "Do IT out there."

"Cool. I work one of those 'we'll come to you' computer repair gigs." Young hissed as his character took a hit. "My home computer is taken up by my sister's thesis so I came here to play."

"That sucks." Nick dodged a strike with quick keystrokes.

More soldiers died their electronic death. "How'd you find this place?"

"My cousin's boyfriend. Thinks he's all hot shit about computers. Frank Lock," he used Sidel's cover name, "wouldn't know a WAN from a LAN if it bit him on the ass. Irritates the hell out of me when he tries to act like he knows shit."

"You know the Locknut?"

"Locknut," Nick snorted and rolled his eyes, "why does that so fit him?"

"'Cause he's a nut and his brain locks up when you try and explain shit to him."

"Yeah, you can just see the mental gears grinding to a halt, huh?" They shared a conspiratorial smile. "He's a nice enough guy, just not quite bright enough to get it."

"Yep." Young nodded in agreement. "Not like you. You just know you're one of us."

Nick laughed, "Damn straight, that's why I'm here playing online instead of out trying to pick up someone and getting shot down." The roll of Young's eyes said volumes about shared social struggles. A smile connected them both. Almost nonchalantly, Nick glanced over at Young's screen. There was an extra side bar where stats and percentages were cycling and it had held Nick's interest for the past five minutes. "What's that?" A flick of his chin indicated where green, yellow and red level indicators fluctuated.

Young looked over his shoulder at the manager. "You cool?"

Nick snorted, "I'm an IT geek."

Laughing at the inside joke. "You wanna spice up the game some?"

"Sure." Nick nodded slightly, most of his attention seemingly focused on blowing the hell out of the opposition.

Dropping his voice to an overly conspiratorial whisper, Young asked, "Got a twenty?"

Nick fished in his back pocket and pulled one of the marked bills. "Yeah." One-handed typing managed to keep his character alive.

"Okay," Young instructed him, "press control, F1, F4 while you put the money in the hopper. That'll bring up the side bar. Then you can just make whatever bet on the odds you want."

As he fed the money into the machine, Nick asked another question. "What's not a sucker bet?"

"Do kill spreads." Young suggested, "Our team vs. theirs, you vs. a random player."

"How do you get paid out?" That was one of the big questions. It wasn't gambling unless there was a return of some kind… especially one where the house took a rake beyond just a cheap administrative fix. The more chance, the less skill, then the more likely it was gambling. This was like a sports book. Who would win by random odds imposed on the system?

Young teased him. "If you get paid out."

"Yeah."

"Log off and it will print out a 'refund voucher.' Take it up to Mr. Vu," Nick's new friend jerked his head back toward the cashier, "and he'll cash you out. He takes fifteen percent for the house on wins."

"That doesn't seem fair."

"Well something's got to pay for the surveillance equip." He shrugged. "If they sight a cop within a mile you'll get a red warning to cash out, you use the dollar sign in the corner—actually any time you want to cash out you can do that. Stick the voucher in your pocket and he'll pay you out later."

"Cool." Nick went back to the game and watched it eat his money. About halfway through he cashed out a round. That payout slip went into his pocket. An hour and forty-five minutes later his time was done. He hit the keys and grabbed the second voucher. Dropping it on the counter, he waited as Vu checked it over and paid him. Out of twenty in, he got five back. Instead of cashing out the first, Nick kept the voucher tucked in his pocket and headed back to the tattoo parlor. Somehow, the thought that the regular cops couldn't pull this off, but he had, was inordinately pleasing to Nick. And, well, being able to hang it over Brandon's head… that was just gravy.

CHAPTER ELEVEN

Already thoroughly sick of viewing apartments, Brandon clambered out of the unmarked. This made number four for the day. Ahead of him, a nineteen seventies homage to urban sprawl loomed. At least it was better than the last one with broken sidewalks and a security gate that didn't work.

Three doors slammed almost in unison. "Two down, three to go." Weaver grumbled as he headed around the sedan toward the curb. Brandon glared. Why was he bitching? His partner had only had to tag along to the last ones. The first two Brandon and Nicky hit before his shift started.

"Yeah, no, I know." Brandon caught the tail end of Nicky's conversation with his bosses in Vegas. "I'll make sure the captain signs off on my time sheets." Grinning as he wandered around the back of the car, he smiled. "Yes, sir, I'll keep you updated on an ongoing basis. We'll talk later." Nicky flipped his phone shut, stepped up beside Brandon and wrinkled his nose. Jerking his chin towards the building in front of him, he asked Brandon, "What do you think? New Orleans style meets maximum security prison?" Shaking his head, he started up the walk. Faded mustard paint covered a flat exterior, false shutters and wrought iron railings patterned like vines. Haphazard tiers of a red brick walk meandered toward the front entrance and Brandon took the stairs two to a stride. To the right, a driveway dipped under the building and a gate in the same design as the railings blocked the underground lot from view.

Brandon punched the key code for the manager. After a series of tonal beeps, a woman's voice cracked over the speaker. "What?"

Weaver coughed and Nicky rolled his eyes. Bending down, the detective hit the transmit button. "Brandon Carr, I have an appointment." Instead of an answer, the gate buzzed. "Well," he snorted, "the manager isn't big on long conversations." They ambled into a well-cared for courtyard, the centerpiece of which was a decent sized pool. Blue water sparkled under a hazy sun. A little rundown, but not shabby, the place had a lived in feel. If he had to hazard a guess, Brandon placed it at around thirty units, a good size for anonymity.

From his left, the same cracked voice sounded. "Why are police here?" Her accent was eastern European in tone and pattern. The speaker system hadn't added much to the natural smoke-varnished roughness of her voice. Brandon turned to find a large woman in a loud housedress staring at him. Arms crossed over a substantial bosom, she stared with pursed lips. Brown hair heading towards gray snuck out from under a bright headscarf.

"Police?" It took a moment for her question to trickle through.

About the time Brandon figured it out, Nicky tapped his holster with one knuckle. "You know, the badges and guns thing." Brandon and Weaver wore their shields strung on their holster rigs. Brandon's slide-slot holster hung on his belt and left most of the gun poking out from under the molded leather. A little more upscale, Weaver wore a shoulder sling model over his normal neutral-colored polo shirt.

Since Nicky was unofficially, officially consulting on the case, he'd hung his own sheriff's style star on a round belt clip. Unlike the cops, the agent didn't carry a gun. He'd often teased Brandon that his weapon of choice, the computer, was far more devastating at times. Still, Brandon always liked seeing Nicky in his "official" capacity—the badge just added something. And, well, black slacks with a red dress shirt tucked in reminded Brandon just how fine a body was hidden under those clothes.

In about two hours they had a meeting with the district attorney to swear out a warrant for seizure of the machines at *Bang!* Just because of how high profile the hit against the kid had been the higher ups wanted a show of force. Part of that was rushing, fudging and finagling the "loan" of Nicky from the GCB. Because of the meeting, and Brandon's desire to actually find a place to rent, even he'd gone for business casual. A long-sleeved gray camp shirt hid Brandon's tats from casual observation. As a concession to the heat, he'd rolled the sleeves up to his elbows.

Brandon coughed and stuck out his hand as he approached. "I'm Brandon Carr. If you're Marda I have an appointment to look at an apartment."

Ignoring the proffered grip, the woman asked, "A policeman needs an apartment?" She did not seem convinced.

"Contrary to popular belief," He flashed one of his bright smiles as he dropped his hand, "we don't live at the station."

She chewed on her lip for a moment and then shrugged. "Okay, wait, I get key." She turned to waddle back into her apartment.

Weaver nodded sagely. "She's getting a key. She must not have much sense if she's willing to consider renting to you."

Shoving his hands into his pockets, Brandon glared at his partner. "Bite me, Weaver." He was about to add more when the apartment manager reappeared.

"Come. I show you unit. Is at back." She trundled down the walkway past rows of doors. Flowers graced many stoops. As they passed an open space in the wall, Marda waved absently toward it. "Elevator to parking and there is laundry down there, too." She smiled over her shoulder. "My units are clean, very nice here. It comes with stove and dishwasher." At the very back of the building another open area held stairs going up and down into the garage. Marda stopped and crossed her arms again. She took her time looking Brandon over. Finally, she seemed to come to a decision. Nodding and heading up the stairs, she announced, "Usually, I do not take single men so young. Sometimes I make exceptions, but mostly they are trouble." Each hitch up the stairs was like hiking Mount Everest, "You are police." The three of them could have carried her up faster. "I can make exception for police. My older tenants they will like having police living here."

Still standing at the bottom, Brandon hissed in Weaver's ear, "I think she just violated every fair housing code there is with that statement."

"Shut up, you ass," Jeff knocked him in the ribs with his elbow, "you can afford this place."

He glared at Weaver and asked, in a louder voice, "Is the building quiet?" Brandon stepped up the first few risers. Floral housecoat bunched in all the wrong places before his eyes and he shuddered. "I work the two to twelve shift." Nick was at his back and made a strangled sound. He must have caught sight of her thighs as well. It was more of Marda than Brandon ever wanted to see again.

Reassuring, she confirmed, "Very quiet." She took a left at the top of the stairs. Already unlocking the door as the trio hit the landing, Marda beckoned them inside. White walls, cheap gray carpet, tan linoleum and pale cabinetry, the décor of a typical un-let unit swallowed her. The place stank of new paint. "Bathroom, closet on this wall where only neighbors are," she pounded the right hand wall as she trundled past. With distracted waves she pointed out the other features, "Stair is on living room side, bedroom wall is outside wall. So only here," another thump, "you have to worry about noise."

The apartment was tiny, but open. So open that even Marda's bulk couldn't overwhelm it. That said something in a not quite six hundred square foot floor plan. An efficiency kitchen sat directly to the left of the door. A small breakfast bar separated that from the living room. On the right, a door opened onto a tiny bath. Nick peered over Brandon's shoulder, "You will never get your knees wet in that tub." Brandon just rolled his eyes.

The bedroom area had no doors, and the wall between living and sleeping only went three-quarters of the way up with posts on either side. A small closet hid behind the bathroom. Brandon paced it off without thinking… about five feet of architectural interest. The far wall was all sliding glass door, the only windows in the place. He stopped and shoved his hands in his pockets. "Wow."

Nick explored the sleeping space. Halting where he could look through the arch at Brandon, he asked. "Wow, what?" Brandon just pointed. A small patio stretched the length of the sliding doors. Beyond, the world dropped away. Nicky slid open the glass door and stepped outside. The cliff meandered off to either side. Below was desert and a good half a mile before the arroyo eased upwards again. Single-family homes dotted the far landscape.

Desert, palms and jacaranda scents drifted through the open door. It reminded Brandon of Nick's place in Vegas, minus the purple trees. He stepped in behind his lover. Resisting the urge to slide his arms around Nicky, "I could live here." He could imagine living there with Nicky. Swallowing that thought down, Brandon turned back towards Marda. Heavy arms were again crossed over her ample chest and she was smiling in one of those all-knowing ways. Behind her, Weaver opened cabinets and drawers, checking out the kitchen. Erika would grill him over his findings. Brandon stifled a laugh at Jeff's sudden domesticity before asking, "What's the deposit?"

Before she could speak Nicky jumped in. "I told you not to worry about that," He thumped the back of Brandon's skull, "I'd spot you."

Marda's smile dropped to a suspicious smirk. "You have money problems?"

Way to go Nicky. "No, ah," how to lie without really lying, "I just paid my child support, and I wasn't expecting to move. Things are just a little tight."

"You have boy or girl?" Let the interrogation begin.

"Little girl." Brandon yanked out his wallet and flipped to Shayna's picture. Blue eyes, brown hair; there was no question she was related to Brandon. "Shayna, she just turned nine."

With a critical eye, Marda scanned the photo. There were victims that didn't spend that much time with line up photos. "You send her mother money?" Her gaze slid up to lock on Brandon's face. "If I call her she says you send it on time?"

"Like clockwork." That was the absolute truth. "More than I have to most of the time. Which is why this is a stretch."

"You good with your bills, eh?"

"Reasonably," He shrugged, "I screw up now and again, but not on a regular basis."

"Very good to be honest."

"Hard to lie when you're going to pull my credit report."

That earned him a chuckle. "So, why do you have to move?"

That was the question he'd been dreading. "My landlord's granddaughter wants her own place." Brandon shrugged as if it didn't matter. It was his landlady's concession to him. She wanted him out. She wanted him out *now*! If he moved quick, she'd support that story and give him a good reference. It was like asking Satan for a more comfortable spot in hell. "I have to move so she can have it. She's supposed to move in before the fall semester at UCR. And she hasn't asked me for this month's rent 'cause it all happened on kinda short notice. In fact, she'd like me out as soon as possible so she can fix the place up. If I signed a lease I'd like to move this weekend."

"If everything is okay, if she says that is why, you could move in this weekend." As Nicky wandered past them, Marda smiled and patted his arm. "This was not a complex you lived at then?"

"Nope, rented a guest house above a garage." Flipping the wallet closed, Brandon shoved it back in his pocket. "Been there since I split with my ex."

"This place much better." It was Brandon's turn for a shoulder pat. Then she turned and motioned for him to follow. "Come on, we get papers. You move in this weekend."

Jeff pulled his head out of a cabinet. "We have one more place to look at today." The stern reminder was probably more of Erika than Jeff. "And you got two tomorrow." Brandon could picture his partner getting an earful this morning about not letting Brandon jump into the first halfway reasonable place just because he wanted out from under Mrs. Ferris.

Marda stopped and scowled. "He won't want them." Her tone indicated that anyone who wouldn't want to live in her apartments was missing half his brain.

"How do you know?"

"I see his eyes." Now she smirked. "He likes the view. Police officer will live here." She turned her attention back to

Brandon. "I call your wife, if she says you pay your support on time like you say, I even give you break on deposit."

Brandon shrugged in response to Weaver's glare. "I like the view. And the four others are about another two hundred a month more than this place. The last three were pits." Turning to Marda, "Do you have a problem with me having a temporary roommate? Nicky is on loan from Nevada Gaming Control for an investigation. He's been crashing with me so he doesn't have to float the cost of a hotel. It may be longer than the standard two weeks."

"He's police?"

Nicky lounged against the breakfast bar. The five-pointed star on his hip caught the light. "Yeah," he added his reassurance, "I'm a Nevada State Agent. It's law enforcement."

"If he's here longer than month we talk." She headed toward the door and stepped outside, shading her eyes.

Brandon followed her out of the apartment. "Fair enough."

"Marda! Oh, Marda!" Singsong, a man's voice carried from across the courtyard. Brandon stepped out to see a husky guy with gray hair, gray goatee and sunburnt skin waving at the manager and barreling down the walkway towards them. "I'm glad I caught you." Unbuttoned tails from his blue cotton shirt billowed out from his body as he trotted. Pair that with the matching shorts, undershirt and expensive, closed-toed sandals; the guy was gay. Even Brandon's rusty gaydar could pick him out. "Love, the dishwasher's gone on the fritz. Can you get Jerome out to fix it?"

"Okay. First I get police officer his lease." Marda waved him off for the time being. "Then I will call Jerome for you. This okay with you?"

"Police?" Damn, Brandon would have bet you couldn't be that Nellie and that snotty in one word.

Brandon reminded himself to play nice with the new neighbors. "Yeah, Riverside P.D." He scooted over when he felt Nicky at his back.

"You're going to live here?" Superior and smug, God Brandon hated those two things… separately or combined. He reminded himself that all he had to do was come straight up from the garage to his unit and he wouldn't have to deal with anyone else.

"No." Pointing back towards the small unit, Nicky corrected. "He's going to live there."

"You be nice," Marda grumbled, "he is a good man. I call Jerome in little bit, your dishwasher is fixed today." She shooed the man off, dismissing him by starting down the stairs. The man shot one more contemptuous glare at Brandon then headed back the way he came. Marda waited at the bottom of the stairs. "He is very suspicious. His partner is much nicer, not so much like him. They are *galuboy*—gay boys. Some people are not so nice to them because of it."

Well, Brandon would have pegged the man as about forty years past being called boy. "That doesn't bother you?"

"They are quiet. They pay their rent on time. So I don't care." Suspicious, she asked, "Does this bother you?"

"Not if they're quiet." He shrugged. "And not so long as they don't egg my bike as a social statement or something." That would be all kinds of ironic.

CHAPTER TWELVE

Two thirty in the afternoon, overwhelmed air conditioning and the crush of too many people in too small a space assaulted Brandon's senses. He shouldered his way through a sea of navy-clad men clogging the narrow halls. Chestnut Station hosted the staging for the *Bang!* bust. The building overflowed with officers in full uniform. Riverside PD pulled out the stops for this one, Brandon mused as he searched for Nicky among the throng.

Nicky stood with Weaver and two other task force detectives. Instead of a uniform or police issued T-shirt, Nicky wore black jeans, his combat boots and a black dress shirt. Gold and silver glinted off the five pointed star hung on his belt. He looked like the damn district attorney, not an officer. Actually he looked a hell of a lot better then the assigned DA, Franklin; dressed down in a golf shirt and worn chinos. Behind them, Brandon spotted the imposing bulk of Sergeant O'Connor. The cut chin and grizzled buzz stood out even in a crowd of pseudo-military clones. Somehow, the standard raid uniform of T-shirt and jeans managed to look rumpled on the Sarge.

Although Brandon dealt occasionally with his captain, day-to-day interactions usually went through Detective Sergeant O'Connor. From there, any issues wound their way up a string of watch commanders and lieutenants. If Brandon had problems, O'Connor solved them. When assignments needed to be divvied out, O'Connor did the divvying. Any time somebody's ass got chewed, you'd find the shreds of their pants hanging out of O'Connor's mouth.

"Okay," the rough voice rumbled over the crowd, jerking everyone's attention up short, "here's the drill, folks. Don't take anything for granted. The stakes are high here. We've already had undercover operatives inside the café. We know there's gambling. It's going to be a pretty routine bust, which means nothing is routine." Like a proud father, O'Connor reached out and tousled Nicky's hair. "This is the Golden Boy here, our borrowed computer expert." The face-splitting grin Nicky sported said he reveled in the attention. "Listen up! He'll fill you in. This is not the usual type of bust you're used to dealing with."

With that, Nicky stood a little straighter. "You'll have to take control of the situation quickly." The same calm which suffused O'Connor settled onto the Gaming Control Agent. Brandon sucked in his breath. He'd really never seen Nicky *at work* before. Going to, coming from, or playing in Brandon's territory, but this was the first time Brandon witnessed Agent Nicholas O'Malley on the job. "We don't want anyone to be able to dump or destroy information. The goal is to get the computers and what's on them."

Nicky's voice shot through Brandon. God, he was incredible. That take charge personality, Brandon swallowed when he realized he was fantasizing about rope, Nicky and that voice. "One of the problems here is you can flush evidence with a few key strokes. Get people away from the terminals as fast as possible. What may not seem like much may be them frying a hard drive. If they do that, it'll be a bitch and a half getting the info out." He smiled and winked when he caught sight of Brandon. "This is why we're hitting it now. There probably won't be many patrons since school is just letting out. That will mean fewer problems," Nicky paused then added a dramatic, "we hope."

When Brandon shoved into a place next to Weaver, Nicky stepped in. Nicky greeted him by grabbing the cop's hand and slapping his bicep. "So, what you're looking for," he offered Brandon a subtle, seductive smile. Caught in the crowd, Brandon couldn't retreat from the contact. Shivers shot down Brandon's spine and it terrified him. "Is anything like stacks of DVDs; duplication towers—it'll look like a standard CPU box with nothing but CD drives down the front—odd software programs, the cash boxes on the sides of the machines, and old payout vouchers in the trash." Confidence radiated from Nicky. Brandon thought he was going to die of nerves. "Mostly, just secure the computers, keep them from dumping information and we should be okay."

"Alrighty then folks," O'Connor growled. "We're sending two Vice officers in to secure the place." A gruff nod went to Brandon and Jeff as the detectives assigned to the task force. "We can't help but trip their security, but we want it to look routine at first. We'll all hold back while Carr and Weaver go in. At their signal the rest of us will hit it." He smiled. It was big, broad and downright scary. "Let's blow this popsicle stand!" Everyone in on the bust funneled out of the building into their vehicles. They'd stage at the same tattoo parlor where Nicky had started from. He, Nicky, Weaver and O'Connor headed over in an unmarked four-door with the DA.

The Sarge and Franklin rode in front. Brandon ended up sandwiched in between Weaver's bulk and Nicky in the back seat. While getting close to Nicky usually held interest, today it filled Brandon with a nameless dread. He tried to make himself as small as possible. Weaver elbowed him. When Brandon turned to glare, his partner whispered, "You do have to breathe, you know?"

Nicky leaned over Brandon's lap and the cop withered inside. "Is he always this uptight on a bust?" Nicky hissed.

"Like a kid on Christmas morning. Brandon gets all excited about this crap." Thank God Jeff tried to diffuse the question. Brandon was trying not to audibly choke. For the benefit of the other occupants, Weaver added. "Too young to be jaded yet."

They rolled up to the tattoo parlor with two other cars. O'Connor twisted and offered another one of his scary as shit smiles to the men in the backseat. "It's show time boys." The grin devolved into something more feral. "We'll be waiting for your signal."

Doors popped open as if on cue and the other three men piled out of the car. Nicky's touch on Brandon's arm stopped him from clambering out Weaver's side. "You'll be okay?"

"Yeah," Brandon shrugged off the question, "We're just going to get a bead on how many people are in there. When we know the odds, we'll signal you all."

A gentle squeeze added to the pressure tightening Brandon's gut. "Now I know how you felt the other day." Nicky leaned in, his eyes intense.

"Nicky," Brandon pulled away, masking the move as checking his badge and adjusting his gun, "this isn't the place, okay." One foot out the door, Brandon covered the delay with a random comment. "I know what we're looking for. You don't need to remind me *Golden Boy*." He slid out of the car to be hit by Weaver's glare. Brandon shot it right back while Nicky extricated himself from the other side of the unmarked. "You ready, boss man?" Franklin and O'Connor looked up from a discussion with the driver of another car.

"Let's roll." Jeff caught the keys O'Connor tossed to him and wormed his bulk behind the wheel.

Brandon trotted around to the passenger door and came face to face with Nicky. As quietly and casually as he could manage, Brandon reassured him. "Don't worry, we got it, we're good. This is what I do, remember."

Dark eyes locked on his, Nicky chewed on his bottom lip. Finally he responded, "I guess," and walked away.

Brandon didn't know whether to be annoyed or relieved. All he could do was watch Nicky as he headed toward the other cars. Shit, he'd probably bungled this. But what did Nicky expect? He knew the score. This was Brandon's world and he couldn't just expect everything to be like it was when they were alone. Weaver's cough broke his fixation and Brandon dropped into the seat. Slamming the door, he acknowledged his partner. "Let's hit it."

Pulling into the lot, Brandon surveyed the café through a plate glass front. "How many you count?"

Weaver popped the door and hauled himself out of the car. "Six, including the gal behind the counter."

Mirrored shades dropped into place, Brandon got out as well. "You take lead," he leaned on the top of the unmarked. "I'll run interference."

A nod told him the plan was a go. Two doors slammed and caught the attention of the girl behind the counter. She looked up over the edge of a glossy magazine as they walked into the café. Bright colors and almost as much skin as might be found on a porn mag graced the cover. Appreciative eyes wandered over Brandon's form. Muscles, tats and piercings seemed to catch her attention. The rest of the patrons were glued to their monitors.

"Hey," Weaver flashed his badge. "Inspection time. What's your name?" Although a couple of the boys favored them with idle curiosity, all Weaver rated from the cashier was a glare. "Don't play bullshit. Show us your permits, we'll look around a bit and then we go. The longer it takes you to play nice, the longer we're here. Your choice."

She tossed the magazine on the counter and crossed her arms under her bosom. "Ana." Gum cracked as she blew a small bubble. "You're cops?"

"No shit, Sherlock." Brandon snorted, wandering towards a bank of computers.

"Great Ana, let's see the license and arcade permits." She pointed to the wall above her head. "Cute, get them down."

Trying to keep her distracted, Brandon ran his fingers over a keyboard. "What are these for?" He banged his knuckles on a black box next to the monitor. A silver faceplate showed a dollar being sucked into the slot.

"Why you hassling me?" Brandon looked over his shoulder to see her up on the counter trying to pull the permits off the wall. A quick glance around the room told him that all the boys were now thoroughly riveted on scoping out Ana's butt. It was probably more action then many of them had seen in ages.

He leaned against a rickety workstation and it shifted under his weight. "Just tell me what the damn boxes are for."

"They're for money." She grunted. Hopping off the counter, the city forms in hand, she added, "You put it in and you play." Weaver got a second glare on top of the extended offer of the licenses.

Brandon graced her with one of his more seductive smiles. "Come show me how." He purred out. Luring her away from the counter was part of the plan. Most likely, any signaling devices would be located there. While the place had gone quiet because of their arrival, they didn't want her to trip any switches or such to scramble data, or worse.

She sighed and rolled her eyes in a typical "you're wasting my time" expression. Edging from behind the counter, Ana stalked to the terminal. Brandon watched his partner out of the corner of his eye. Using his butt to prop open the door, Weaver half-stepped outside and took off his jacket. That was the signal for the game to begin. A nod toward the parking lot let Brandon know the troops were on their way.

Another pop of chewing gum drew his attention back to the young woman. "You have a dollar?" Ana asked him.

He turned to her and smiled. "Maybe." Moving to block her path back to the counter, Brandon reached toward his back pocket. The screech of half a dozen vehicles hotrodding it into the lot jerked her attention to the front of the store. Someone behind him yelled *holy shit*, sending Ana flying toward the counter. Brandon grabbed her arm, yanking her back. "No honey, you're staying with me." If he were a more timid man, her hate-filled glare would have stripped his nerves. Being who he was, Brandon just laughed.

Chaos boiled as uniforms funneled through the door. Commands of "Down!" and "Move away from the computers!" mixed with confused shouts from the patrons. Bust-rush charged up Brandon's frame. People went down on their knees, hands over their heads. They had to take control of the scene quickly to prevent vital evidence from being destroyed. A two-to-one ratio of cops to detainees meant the initial push was over fast.

O'Connor muscled into the café, snarling, "Get these idiots out front and start checking ID's." Rubbing his hands, he barked a question. "Carr, who you got there?"

Witness in hand, Brandon smiled back at the sergeant. "Ana, who was manning the front."

"What the hell are you doing?" She spat. "This is harassment!"

"No," Brandon corrected, "this is a bust with a warrant." He pulled her hands behind her back. One of the uniforms handed him a set of plastic zip-tie cuffs. When he had her reasonably restrained, Brandon passed her off to the other officer. A few of the uniforms herded the detainees out the door. Others pulled out lime green latex gloves for handling evidence. While fingerprints would likely be useless, the use of the gear was standard procedure. Everything they touched, they logged.

Hands in his pockets, a grin on his face, Nicky sauntered past Brandon. All the day's excitement wrapped itself into a knot and embedded itself in the lining of Brandon's stomach. Why the fuck did he have to walk *like that?* Really, it wasn't swish—Nicky could overplay that whole stereotype when he wanted to—but it wasn't straight, either. Hooking a chair with his foot, Nicky pulled it back and sank into the seat. One of the powered up computers held his attention. Brandon scrutinized every move. Nicky's fingers danced over the keyboard. Literally, the way he held his hands just screamed fem.

Brandon damn near jumped out of his skin when Jeff slapped him on the back. "He's doing it." Brandon hissed at his partner.

Weaver looked confused. "Doing what? Fucking with the computer?"

"You know," Brandon tried to keep his voice level, "acting *that way*." Still, he made sure no one could hear them.

Jeff blinked. He looked at Nicky then back to Brandon. "You're delusional." After rubbing his eyes with the heels of his palms, Weaver added, "You need to take a valium or something. Nick's just acting like Nick." Another glance at Nicky by both of them and Jeff hooked one meaty hand around the back of Brandon's tattooed neck. He pulled the young detective in close. "The one that's being obvious is you. Get a fucking grip and do your job. If you don't want anyone to know anything, then stop freaking out every time Nick says or does anything… got it?"

Nodding, Brandon took a deep breath. "Okay, I get it."

"Good, Baby D." Jeff smiled and headed over to where Nicky sat. "So what you got?"

If he was away from Nicky, he'd freak. When he was near Nicky, he freaked. Brandon couldn't resist. Two steps brought him up to his partner's back. As he peered over the older detective's shoulder, he had no clue what he was seeing. Line upon line of addresses scrolled down the screen. "It's an email extractor." Completely absorbed in what he was doing, Nicky mumbled the response. "They pull addresses from all over the Internet and then send scam messages. They have almost a million addresses here."

"Where do they get them?" O'Connor's question caught Brandon off guard. He hadn't heard the sergeant come up behind. "Do they sit there and input all that shit?"

"Actually, no," Nicky looked up. "If I'm at a cyber-café and I open up my Internet-based e-mail account to check my mail, the program scans it, pulls all the email addresses out of my address book and stores them." Nicky propped his chin on his hands and stared at the screen. "If it can, it plants a worm in my out-going mail and then phishes my friend's email as well. It's also probably running in the background and looking at all the pages the kids surf when they're here, trying to grab any e-mail addresses buried in those sites, blog pages and the like. From one log on they may get several thousand email addresses. Then they'll send out spam emails." Leaning back, Nicky waggled his hand in the air before tapping his fingers against his cheek. "You know all that crap you get for a bigger dick and cheap Viagra."

It was the loll of his head and rolling of his eyes that sent the gesture over the top. Brandon stifled a groan. Almost simultaneously Weaver kicked him in the shin. Both had to move to the side as an officer started unhooking cables and cords to the computer on the next station. Brandon used the opportunity to glare at his partner. Weaver's look topped his attempt at menace by ten.

Seemingly oblivious, O'Connor asked, "They can't make any money off that shit, can they?"

"Trust me," Nicky damn near purred out those two words. Brandon thought he was going to have a heart attack right then and there. "If there wasn't money to be made, these guys wouldn't be doing it." Rolling the chair back so that the uniformed cop could access the power cord for the other machine, Nick crossed his legs at the ankles and dropped his hands in his lap. "People are greedy. In scams, lottery and Ponzi schemes are big. Or the verify-your-bank-account-in-ten-days-because-we've-been-hit-by-fraud phishers." Nicky's body language screamed. It had to. Everyone had to notice it. "The link takes you to a fake page that looks pretty legit. And then they have your social, address and other personal info. They sell that to people who buy fake IDs or take out bogus cards in your name." Brandon tried not to stare. He couldn't stop himself. Seemingly unaware of Brandon going coronary in terror, Nicky continued. "Debt elimination is another biggie. You pay them a couple grand, and give them all the information on your debts, who you are, where you live, where you work and how much you make. Fuck, think what a criminal can do with that. It's a billion dollar industry."

"Carr." Weaver's voice almost slapped him. "Why don't you go outside and make sure everyone is logging evidence."

"What?" Brandon jerked his attention to his partner. "Outside?"

You're freaking out was written all over Jeff's face. "Go, I'll handle things in here." Brandon started to open his mouth to protest and Weaver shut him down. "We're task force. This is a task force project. Go supervise that part of the task force. I know this is nine kinds of interesting, but do what I tell you. Got it?"

Brandon swallowed, "Okay." Nicky smiled up at him. Brandon prayed that no one else caught the subtle, seductive twist to his mouth. "I'll go supervise outside." It wasn't until Weaver narrowed his eyes and mouthed the word *go* that Brandon managed to tear himself away.

Computer cases lined the sidewalk out front. One officer, butt resting on his heels, read the serial numbers off the back, another jotted them on a form. Brandon stepped through the door and pulled out his cigarettes. On top of everything else, he was suffering from a nicotine withdrawal headache. Nothing really needed his attention. The uniformed officers were good at what they did. He took a deep drag off his cigarette and blew tension out with the smoke.

The metallic protest of the doorframe clued Brandon into someone else exiting. He stepped away from the door and turned toward the sound. A thin-faced Hispanic man slipped through the door. Det. Lyle Mendez greeted Brandon with a muttered, “Hey.”

Brandon shifted to lean against the plate glass window. “Hey, yourself.”

“Can you fucking believe it?” Mendez snorted and jerked his head indicating the door of the café. Or maybe he was indicating the people inside. “Guess Nevada’s recruiting from Mouse-witz now.”

“Excuse me?” Brandon couldn’t have heard that right.

“You know,” Mendez leered, “Tinker Bell in there.”

It took a moment for the jibe to register. Still it didn’t quite connect in his brain with any logical thought. “What the hell are you talking about?”

“Come on, Carr,” another lecherous grin from Mendez as the cop added, “He’s your good friend and you don’t see it?”

All the tension he’d blown out a moment ago returned in spades. “See what?”

“Well, you know he’s a little light.”

“What?” Brandon pushed away from the wall. Mendez may have missed the menace in that one word, but all the uniforms looked up like a shot had cracked across their heads.

“Your friend,” Mendez teased his hand clasped in front of his chest, “you know, he’s a little on the light and fluffy side.”

Brandon was going to beat the light and fluffy right off Mendez's stupid mug. He stepped into the other detective's personal space and growled. "Look, Mendez, you stupid fucking jerk, lay the hell off him!"

"What's your deal, Carr?" Mendez almost tripped over his own feet backing away.

"I don't have a deal," Brandon spat, "you do!" His glare could have skinned Mendez alive. It would have been too good for the ass.

CHAPTER THIRTEEN

The little pinch in Brandon's chest started the moment Nicky walked into the station. He looked up from his desk when Weaver called Nicky's name. He licked his upper lip. The snap of the pen between Brandon's fingers shot down his spine.

He'd managed to keep it all contained at home. Not let on to Nicky what was said. But now… at the station…

Really, Brandon assured himself, it wasn't bad. Black jeans with black combat boots were subdued enough, but Nicky's shirt, holy shit. You'd have to be blind or stupid or both to miss it. Black and white pinstripe wasn't too bad. The narrow cut, slim line screamed. Straight guys didn't wear shirts that hugged like that. Huge zippers running horizontally and vertically across the pockets and zippered cuffs pushed it right over the top and sent it careening into the canyons.

Nicky sidled up to Brandon's desk. Soft and seductive, he greeted Brandon with a, "Hey."

Brandon jerked. Nicky's voice clogged Brandon's lunges with dread. "What?" He snapped. Everyone was looking. They had to be. Brandon just knew it. He seriously regretted not taking a couple of sick days on Nicky's arrival. Then they would have gotten the fucking hearse first thing, Brandon wouldn't have missed Nicky's birthday, been sucker-punched into the barbeque and Nicky wouldn't be standing in front of his desk at Chestnut Station working a fucking task force. Every time Nicky called his boss, Brandon prayed they'd tell him to head back to Vegas. There was no God because Nicky was still in Riverside.

"Where," Nicky leaned against the desk and smiled, "should I set up?"

"Ah," Brandon managed to breathe through the pressure. "Over there." Pointing to a battered, putty-colored monstrosity wedged between the wall and a set of olive drab file cabinets, he forced himself to be calm. "There's power over there and you'll be out of the way." He jammed his hands into his pockets and tried to will the tension out of his shoulders. Rocking back in his chair, Brandon added, "Just yell if you need anything." Hell, he even managed a smile.

With the look Nicky gave him, it must have come across as tense as it felt. After staring for a minute, Nicky shook his head. "Grab me for lunch, okay?" Brandon nodded, then watched as Nicky headed to the empty desk. This was not going to be a fun day.

"Hey." Weaver's voice at his back made Brandon start again.

"What?" He snapped.

"Jesus, Carr," His partner glared, "take a valium or something." Jeff looked from Brandon to Nicky and back. Finally he shook his head. "Okay, work, remember that? Come help me choose up a six pack of photos for the lineup."

"Lineup?"

"Yeah, you remember, we got that guy coming in who says he was solicited in the can at that park." Weaver drummed Brandon's temple with a set of meaty fingers. "I know it's not normally something we do, but you do understand the concept. Six photos, all looking like the guy we picked up, witness picks him out. One of the guys in Homicide says he'll administer it for us, double-blind."

"Shit yeah," Brandon palmed his face and took a deep breath, "let's go look through mug shots." With one last frown back at Nicky, Brandon hauled himself out of his chair. Weaver fell into step beside him as they headed towards the only computer capable of setting up and printing out a digital lineup.

Part of him wanted to stay near Nicky, make sure he didn't do anything stupid or outrageous or, God forbid, *gay*. After yesterday's confrontation with Mendez, Brandon didn't think his heart could take it. The comments still boiled in his brain. What if someone figured it out? If he said something to someone who talked to someone else… Brandon forced himself to stop the cycle. The more sensible half realized he needed to keep his mind busy. If he didn't find a distraction, he'd end up snapping at Nicky. A fight at the station seemed like the granddaddy of unpleasant options.

Weaver hit the door to the computer room with the flat of his hand. It popped open and Brandon dodged through into a room that may have originally been designed as a broom closet. Instead it held a couple of not quite so obsolete computers balanced on definitely obsolete desks. Screens flickered, adding an eerie glow to the overhead fluorescents. An ancient task chair protested as Weaver settled his bulk in front of one of the terminals. He began the two-fingered hunt and peck, inputting their suspect's stats. "So, ah," Jeff looked up from the monitor. He seemed to search Brandon's face. Brandon fiddled with the rings in his ear waiting for Jeff to get to the point. Finally his partner shook his head. "Never mind."

Jeff's voice held the same tone he used whenever he pumped Brandon for information. "What, Weaver?" Of course, usually, Jeff was a lot more direct. He was not the sort of guy to hem and haw around his questions.

Returning his attention to the computer, Jeff muttered, "It's not important, never mind."

"He's five-nine not five-i." Brandon pointed out Jeff's typing error. Once corrected, Brandon waited. Jeff didn't say anything. Finally irritated, Brandon snapped. "Just fucking spit it out."

Weaver chewed on his lower lip for a moment. "Well, I mean," crossing his hands over his stomach Jeff twisted to face Brandon, "Nicky's not quite what I expected."

"It's taken you how long to figure that one out?" Perched on the edge of the desk, Brandon sucked on the inside of his cheek. Why did Jeff have to bring up Nicky? Brandon would really be happier to just pretend Nicky was in Vegas not Riverside. He sighed. "Okay, first, I'm the only one who doesn't get punched for calling him Nicky." Picking at his cuticles, Brandon tried to come up with a response to Jeff's statement. Another exasperated sigh slipped between his lips. "What did you expect?"

"He's just," Jeff shrugged, "I don't know, a guy."

Brandon smacked his temples with the heels of his palms. "Holy, shit! I thought he had tits… maybe I need glasses." Brandon growled and glared. "Fuck, Weaver, of course he's a guy."

"But, he's a guy's guy." More stats went into the machine. Jeff hit the last set of keystrokes and started the search. "The kinda guy you'd go to a football game with."

The statement stewed for a while. Brandon reminded himself that, of all people, Jeff didn't mean anything by it. He was the sort of cop who got involved in his partner's life. Jeff slapped you on the back when your kid got an A in spelling or helped you out of the jam when you forgot your lover's birthday. Maybe he was a little ham-handed at it, but Jeff was just trying to be a good partner. Shuffling his feet, Brandon looked around to make certain they were still alone. Habit; it wasn't like anyone could have come into the tiny room without them knowing it. "Pro-wrestling." He muttered the words into his chest.

The computer put up a set of options. The older detective selected two and set the others back to search. "What?" Weaver looked up from the screen.

"Nicky's into the WWF." Into was an understatement. Nicky was into wrestling like some people were into baseball. For God's sake, he owned DVDs of wrestling's greatest moments and blooper reels. Worse, he watched them.

"See, that's what I mean." Tapping Brandon's thigh with one finger, he added, "he's just a guy, not like one of those L.A. queers at all."

Brandon sighed, "Jeff, I'm not like one of those L.A. queers at all."

Waving off the comment, Jeff corrected. "No you know what I mean." Like he was searching for the answer in the air near the computer, Jeff's hands circled above the terminal. "He's big and he just walks."

"You're looking at him walking?" Brandon couldn't resist. "Are you sure you're not gay?"

That got him flipped off. "Fuck off, Carr." The final set of choices seemed to please Jeff. Shuffled in with the five random guys was their perp. A quick and dirty print, then save command and the printer began to hum.

"Okay, you're dying to ask it."

A shake of Weaver's head denied it. "No I'm good."

"Bullshit," Brandon grabbed the printed line-up and stepped to the door. Blocking Jeff's exit, he added, "ask it."

Unable to pass, Weaver glared. "No!"

Jamming his hands under his pits, Brandon threw the glare right back. "You want to know who lays pipe, 'cause you were expecting some limp wristed sissy boy and Nicky ain't none of that." The printout dangled from his fingers. Brandon wasn't about to give in until Jeff did. "So ask."

"No." Hands up in mock surrender, Weaver rolled his eyes. "Okay, yeah, damn it, you win." Then he slapped Brandon's cheek in mock anger. "No, never mind."

Brandon stepped away from the door, twisting the knob as he moved. "He does, mostly."

Jeff froze. "What?"

"Nicky's much more a top than I am." Everyone else got to talk about their girlfriends. Keeping it all bottled up for so long, Brandon couldn't stop himself. It was like he opened his mouth and someone else started talking. "But it ain't like one hundred percent either way."

"I didn't need to know that."

"Yeah you did." A quick scan and Brandon stepped into the hall. "Otherwise it would bug the shit outta you. Of course I'm guessing that something else is gonna bug the shit outta you now. Change things?"

"Naw, not really. I already…" Weaver stopped mid-sentence. Brandon tracked his gaze to see what caught his partner's attention. Nicky.

"Hey guys, I've been looking for you." All smiles, Nicky sauntered down the corridor. "What you gossiping about?"

Quickly, Brandon wracked his brain. "Smackdown."

"Holy shit, did you see Tuesday's pay-per view? Whoa man, there was fucking blood on the matt after that." Nicky shivered and smirked. Hell, half the time Brandon didn't get that look when he propositioned his lover. "Hey, where's your Sarge? I wanna talk to him."

Weaver smacked Brandon's back as he passed. "I think he's in Holding." Plucking the printout from the other man's fingers, Weaver waved them towards Vice. "I'm going to drop this off in Homicide. I'll grab him and meet you there."

Absently, Nicky responded, "Great." His eyes never wavered from Brandon's.

The cop swallowed. A nervous ball wedged in his throat. Grabbing Nicky's arm, Brandon steered him back toward his desk. "What did you find?" If he could get Nicky talking about work, everyone would be a lot safer.

Another smirk wicked across Nicky's mouth. "You'll," he drew out the word, "just have to wait like the rest of them." As he slid into the chair, Nicky covered the monitor with his hand. Next to him sat one of the computers they'd pulled out of the cybercafé. Nicky'd cracked it open to look at the guts. The side of the case rested against the wall. "It's a prezzie for you."

"Would you knock it off?" Brandon hissed.

Nicky's eyebrows shot up. Brandon was favored with a look of derisive amusement. "Knock what off?"

"Acting," Brandon leaned in. He didn't want anyone else to hear. "Acting so fucking flaming."

Jaw dropping, Nicky stuttered out, "Flaming?" About a dozen emotions warred across his face. Brandon braced himself for the storm. Nicky sputtered, "I'm anything but fucking flaming here. I'm being so goddamn good, I'm forgetting who I am. You need to chill." Nicky obviously bit back the rest as his seething gaze jumped to the door.

Brandon looked up. Rumpled as always, the detective sergeant in charge of Vice barreled through the door. Weaver drifted behind, two other detectives in tow. All of them were part of the task force.

Sarge rubbed his hands together and smiled. Three steps brought him to the desk. "So what do you have for us, Golden Boy?"

Nicky favored Brandon with one last glare. It let Brandon know he wasn't done. Turning his attention to the other cops, Nicky snorted. "Quick and dirty, lots of interesting stuff. How useful it will all eventually be, that I don't know."

They gathered around Nicky and Brandon found himself shoved to the side. The Sarge's voice boomed. "Tell me whatcha got."

"I can already tell you." Catching Brandon's eye, Nicky smirked, "Most of the computer is gray market parts." There was no way of knowing whether Nicky's teasing was because of Brandon's fear or because he was the center of attention. Sometimes Nicky could just be an attention whore. Not that Brandon minded most of the time. At least he didn't mind when he was the one giving Nicky attention. Everyone else could go blow themselves.

"Gray market?" That was Weaver's question.

"Legit stuff, close outs, off market and refurbs." Nicky rapped the case. "Gray market people tweak the components. So a 233 chip might look and act like a 350. At least until it burns out your hard drive." Pointing through the open side, he indicated the motherboard, processor and memory chips. "See, they buy last year's model bulk on the cheap, so it's a legit part made by a brand name manufacturer. So on, say a chip, they tweak the program so it tells the computer I'm a 300megahertz chip, but it's really an older version that's had overrides layered on. Slap a new label on it sell it for a hundred bucks more than you paid for it, but less than what it costs in the store. Heck, some low-end manufacturers, if they're short, they'll buy gray goods."

O'Conner leaned over Nicky's shoulder to stare at the monitor. If he could make sense of the GIGO on the screen, Brandon would eat his earrings. "How'd you figure that out?"

"Most chip manufacturers have online scanning programs. So I plugged this baby into the net." Another tap on the screen indicated nothing that made sense to anyone but Nicky. "Case is cracked so I see what that chip says it is. Go to that manufacturer's verification site and scan it. Not invasive, doesn't corrupt what's there, it just compares what the chip is telling it to what it should have. So like this label says its 300mgz, the scan tells me it's a 233. The proper error-correcting code isn't there, the logic is a 233."

"Logic?"

Brandon broke in. "The code that tells the chip how to act in any given situation." He'd been around Nicky long enough to know that. Nicky rolled his eyes, accusing Brandon of stealing his thunder. It took most of Brandon's will not to reach over and throttle him.

"Is that illegal?"

"To put it in, no," the shake of Nicky's head backed up his assertion. "It's not stolen as far as anyone knows. It's just not right. Whoever repackaged the 233 chip and sold it as a 300, that's a fraud."

"Okay, so why is this special?" The Sarge propped his butt on the desk and stared down at Nicky. "Why do we care?" The meat in any detective's sandwich; it wasn't evidence unless it meant something to the case.

"Because all the computers you hauled out of there, at least the ones I looked at yesterday, have the same product in it. The guy's buying in relative bulk." Brandon had to be impressed with how cool and calm Nicky was. The Sarge rattled most guys pretty easily. "Thirty, forty chips at a time. That means he probably knows these aren't quite legit. And some of the biggest distributors of this shady crap are Asian criminal enterprises, almost three fourths of gray market comes out of the Asian market. And it's good quality fake. I deal with these processors all the time. The printing's good, the case is right, the manufacturers hologram is spot on… you can't tell until you look at the underlying code that it's not right. And the Asian gray market has the capability to hit that spot on."

O'Conner waved dismissively at the computer. "So this is Chinese stuff?"

"Maybe. China is cracking down because they like having legit industry bankrolls. So, some of the gray goods manufacturers are moving to India, Pakistan, Vietnam and other places."

"Okay, so they're using junk." Nicky didn't seem to have impressed the man much. "Got anything better?"

"Oh yeah." He purred. Nicky's voice sounded like he'd just found Brandon spread and waiting for him. Brandon swallowed the thought down and tried to think of un-sexy things, like his stepmom in a bathing suit. "I pulled down The Sleuth Kit a while back. It's useful for all sorts of crap. Open source software you can tweak as needed. It uses both UNIX and Windows tools. That and DOS Drive Tool, Autopsy, Stegdetect and a bunch of other crap. Basically all that stuff combined lets you go in and recover files that have been deleted, find hidden files and back ass your way into other files that may be password protected." Nicky's fingers danced over the keyboard. "You wouldn't believe the shit people leave lying around their hard drives."

"They'd done all that?"

"Yes and no. Some of this stuff may not have been intentional." As he pointed out several lines of characters on the monitor, Nicky leaned in. At several places he indicated what caught his eye. "There's cross-linked clusters that had to be sorted out before I could pull the data, the file allocation tables had multiple entries pointing to the same clusters of data. That may have just been normal computer gremlins and corrupted data."

Nicky rolled the chair back and crossed his arms over his chest. Brandon had seen that maneuver before. It was Nicky's get ready for a lecture look. He caught Brandon's stare and raised his eyebrows in a quick "you know what's coming" conspirator's gesture. Well, at least Nicky wasn't so mad at him that he wouldn't share the joke.

"Now for the deleted stuff, when you delete something off your drive it actually only changes the directory listing. It changes the first character of the filename. That clues the computer to see that file as unused space. Eventually it'll overwrite the data. You can't see it, but it's still there. Windows has its own internal program that lets you recover the deleted stuff with some success. I use an open source program for it that's a little better." Nick leaned in and tapped the computer screen. "There were also a couple of invalid zip files on the drive. Mostly they'd been renamed so that the computer didn't recognize them as validly formatted; instead of say a 'zip' they'd named it an 'exe.' The computer tries to run with the 'exe' command and can't open it."

Spinning to face the sergeant, Nicky shifted. "Plus they hinked the file size on some of them so that it wouldn't open. Again, I used a hex-editor. That told me what the valid extension should be and how large the file really was." He thought for a moment. Brandon bet he was figuring out how to dumb it down so they'd all understand. "I went in and changed it up with a simple utility and, boom, I've got my files back. They'd hidden passwords in JPEG comments. When you get strings of unintelligible crap in the JPEG comments that's often a good indication that stuff is hidden there. My guess is they would send a password protected file and then a porn image of some chick. Their target would pull the password out." One last shrug and Nicky summed it up. "Anyone else who got it would think porn spam. I'm backing it up and tomorrow I'll break it down."

Chapter Fourteen

Finally, the world was silent. Brandon and Nick sat amidst a jumble of half-emptied boxes and crumpled newspaper. The couch, except for minor adjustments, was where it would live—only one wall was big enough to hold it. Remnants of the entertainment center formed a coffee table of sorts. At least one piece of furniture always got sacrificed to the gods of the move. Ancient pressboard hadn't been up to a group of rowdy cops, three six-packs, two sets of stairs and a U-haul.

Nicky wished he had Querida back already. He missed his hearse. He especially missed it when he ended up jammed into his sub-compact rental car with a herd of very large, very sweaty cops. Chaos had ruled their life for the past eight hours. Packing, shifting, moving… it was never fun. Brandon snapped at Nick more than once. Feathers got ruffled time and time again. Over the course of the day, things smoothed out. Still, the move had been tense.

While they grunted and swore, every college-age girl in the complex seemed to have created an excuse to wander by. First, Nick was grumpy because he thought they were all making eyes at Brandon. Then he freaked because half of them were making eyes at him. And Brandon. And he and Brandon together. It was almost more than he could handle. Especially with the crude jokes Brandon's buddies on the force tossed about. Nick wasn't sure if he should be outraged or just disgusted. At one point he'd dropped a box of books on Brandon's foot just to stop the high school humor.

Spread across the makeshift table's surface was a collection of paper cartons with red bamboo stenciled on their sides. While Nick dove into unpacking blankets, pillows and assorted bathroom stuff, Brandon had gone on the hunt for food. Now they shared their first meal in Brandon's new apartment courtesy of Lee's Kitchen. Chinese mustard, hot as hell, cleared out his sinuses and burned the inside of Nick's cheeks. "This is damn good. Where did you find this place?"

"Cops." With a laugh, Brandon licked hoysin paste off the tips of his fingers, "know all the best joints in town." He caught Nick staring and sucked his pinky into his mouth. A come hither stare lit up his eyes. Brandon could be a major tease when he wanted to be. "Want to know where to eat? Look for the black and whites."

Nick popped a scallop and chewed while thinking. "Then why," using his chopsticks to draw a question mark in the air, "are cops always at donut shops and fast food joints?"

"In order of importance?" Brandon snagged the last shrimp off Nick's plate. Nick glared then nodded. "Clean bathrooms, hot coffee 24/7, and a place to legitimately park your ass for fifteen minutes that doesn't have wheels on it." He caught a piece of orange chicken in his chopsticks. When it was almost to his lips, Brandon reconsidered. Holding it out towards Nick, "Open, baby." Nick leaned off the couch and opened his mouth. Brandon teased him a moment with the morsel before placing it on Nick's tongue. "If you ride a cop-cycle, which I did for four years, then number three becomes number one."

It was all Nick could do just to chew. Mumbling around the food, "You, in a uniform, on a bike?"

Brandon's index finger caught the dot of sauce at the corner of Nick's mouth. "Me, in my blues, on a department-issued Harley." Nick damn near whimpered at the thought. Chuckling, Brandon's fingertips danced with his tongue, "wearing knee-high interceptor boots."

Oh hell, Brandon so knew how to push his buttons. "You, ah, wouldn't happen to have that still around." Nick's gaze slid toward the bedroom. "You know, in one of those boxes?"

"My uniform?" A jumble of boxes holding Brandon's meager wardrobe sat against the wall, *bedroom* scrawled in red marker across the sides. "Yeah, why?"

"With," Nick licked his lip, "the boots?" Please, God, let him still have the boots.

Brandon chuckled, "I could find it, any particular reason?"

Dropping his plate on the temporary coffee table, Nick growled. "Like you don't know."

"Really, want to play traffic stop?" Teasing, Brandon leaned in close. A wicked light danced in his blue eyes. "Up against the wall? Strip search?"

Nick had never pressed the issue before. Enough comments about holster-sniffers and guys with badge fetishes slipped out of Brandon's mouth that Nick got the hint. It was Brandon's job not playtime. He shuddered, "I'd let you top for that." Still, they'd been together long enough that Brandon should understand Nick wanted him for more than just the uniform.

"Nicky," Brandon's deep voice rumbled with amusement. "You let me top whenever you're too lazy or you just want to get fucked."

That was way too true. He was far more a situational Dom than a lifestyler. Nick upped the anti. "I'd blow you for a week."

"Now," Brandon shifted and seemed to consider the bid, "that's tempting. I don't know though. I'd have to go find it, change."

Okay, if he wanted it bad enough, Nick figured he had to offer Brandon something the detective wanted more. Nick ran his teeth over his bottom lip and thought for a moment. Leering, he raised the pot. "I'll tie you up."

"I'll find the box!" Brandon stood and jumped over Nick's legs. With that long stride, Brandon disappeared into the bedroom in two steps. A bang and thump was followed by, "Shit!"

Nick snickered. "Ropes in my bag, you can grab that and the rest of what we need, too." Gathering up the cartons, he headed to the kitchen. What food was salvageable for a snack, Nick stuck in the fridge. Wooden chopsticks and paper plates went into the trash. Nick grabbed an old bandana as a rag to wipe down the counter, but then had a better idea. He jammed the clean cloth into his back pocket. Arranging the kitchen occupied him while Brandon was changing. When Nick was almost finished with the last box of dishes, a cough made him turn.

The most Nick managed was, "Whoa." Deep navy, the short-sleeved uniform shirt stretched tight across Brandon's chest, showing off every muscle. Just the sight of Brandon in that form-fitting uniform had Nick hard. What would it be like to be pulled over by that? Of course, most cops didn't have the tight-muscled body of Brandon to fit out their uniforms that nice.

On Brandon's biceps, twin royal blue and gold shield shaped patches sported the city's mission bell logo. A brass nametag proclaiming *CARR* was pinned to the right above his breast pocket. The space on the left, reserved for Brandon's badge, was empty. Nick sighed, he couldn't have everything. Wool-blend pants, navy with a light blue stripe, hugged the detective's thighs and disappeared into the top of his boots. And what boots; Nick drooled. Dressage straps and Spanish swept top styling so that they were higher on the outside of the leg than against the inseam. Mini lugs on the soles meant they were for actual work.

Brandon hooked his fingers into the thick Sam-Brown belt cinching his middle. "Couldn't find all the crap I used to carry on this thing. Detectives travel light, you know." Shoulders squared off and feet slightly spread, Brandon smiled. "And well, the boots aren't standard issue, but they're approved variants." A length of rope, the black and red nylon weave, was slung over Brandon's shoulder.

"Who cares?" Nick leaned against the counter and savored the sight. "That's damn sexy."

Brandon smirked and flexed. "Yeah?" It was really terrible when your boyfriend knew how good he looked. Offering up the small bottle of lube and pack of condoms, Brandon added, "I wouldn't know."

"Oh yeah." Nick stepped in and tugged on the rope. "Like I believe that." It slid off Brandon's shoulder with a sigh. He grabbed the other items and shoved them into his front pocket. A quick scan of the room reminded him the only chair serviceable for what he wanted was out on the porch. "Go get that crappy kitchen chair you use for smoking."

Brandon leaned back, folded his arms over his chest, and narrowed his eyes. "Why?" The look he gave Nick was all cop—right down to the slightly sarcastic twist of his mouth.

"Did I tell you," re-asserting his dominance, Nick growled, "that you could ask questions?"

A little hesitant, Brandon answered, "No."

Oh yeah, Brandon sometimes needed to be reminded who was boss. "Then get it." Nick barked. As Brandon headed toward the sliding doors, Nick unwound the rope. He pulled the slick nylon through his fingers, savoring the feel. Rope always did *something* to him. It was hard to place his finger on just what. The moment the cord was in his hand, Nick's pulse shot up and a steady burn settled in his hips. A tiny charge flickered under his skin. So simple, but so profound, the fact that Brandon would put his pleasure, his safety in Nick's hands rocked him.

Brandon grabbed the chair off the patio and dragged it into the living room. Indeterminate in age and style, the oak high back chair could have come out of almost any kitchen. A spindle was missing from the back and the green vinyl on the seat had split, but Nick didn't see any cracks in the frame. Considering the abuse Brandon dished out to his furniture, it should hold. "Sit." Nick smirked and walked toward where Brandon waited. Brandon dropped into the seat and bit his bottom lip. If that look wasn't eager anticipation, Nick didn't know what would qualify. Folding the rope in half, Nick ordered. "Cross your arms behind your back." He ran his fingers over Brandon's cheek then tugged at the uniform collar. "You should grasp your forearms."

Brandon turned his face to kiss Nick's fingers. His gaze flicked from Nick's eyes to the rope and back again. "You mean behind the chair?" He wrapped his hands around the back of the chair and locked each hand on the opposite wrist.

Moving behind the seated man, Nick confirmed, "Yeah, kinda like that." First he repositioned Brandon's arms so his hands were midway up his forearms. Then Nick draped the rope over where Brandon's wrists crossed, the looped end sliding between the cop's arms and the chair to hang down to the floor. Grabbing the looped end, Nick wound the line around Brandon's crossed arms. As always he worked in threes for his wrist ties. It made a binding sexy, dangerous looking, but not too bulky. A square knot tied it off. Just a tiny loop was left sticking from the knot. Now that Brandon was secure, it was time to pretty him up.

Drawing the ends of the rope along with him, Nick walked around to face Brandon. "See, now this," he smirked, "is why you should always have a high-backed chair around." He stepped in close to Brandon as he pulled the bandana from his pocket with his free hand. A couple spins between his fists wound the fabric tight. Nick slid into Brandon's lap, knees on either side of Brandon's hips. The chair groaned under the weight of both men. Dropping the end of the rope over his thighs, "Open," Nick ordered. Brandon swallowed nervously, but did as Nick told him. Nick slipped the gag between Brandon's lips and reached behind Brandon's shorn head to tie it off.

Nick rocked back and the chair creaked again. Slowly, Nicky unbuttoned Brandon's shirt and pushed it off his shoulders. That hard-muscled chest all exposed for him, it was so nice. Tugging the tails from Brandon's uniform pants, Nick leaned in to run his tongue along a tattooed collarbone. It wasn't the chair that groaned that time and Nick snickered. He spent some time exploring the line of Brandon's jaw with his mouth before sliding off and standing.

The rope trailing from his fingers, Nick resumed his slow walk around until he was behind Brandon again. Nick threaded the ends through the loop and snugged it down. "Black and red, spider's web," the singsong rhyme amused him as he worked the half-hitch into place. Once tight, Nick headed back around his captive, moving in the opposite direction.

Nick paused to savor the sight of Brandon. The deep blue uniform shirt hung open, exposing Brandon's broad chest and flat belly. Black braided into red, the cord cut over his upper arms, just above the elbows and across Brandon's chest. Two lines dimpled the skin. They crossed from fabric to flesh just below and above Brandon's nipples. Nick licked his lips. "Damn, that's nice." Brandon could only answer him with a blue eyed stare. Once more he moved behind his captive. This time Nick slid the ends under the rope from the first pass to form a half-hitch. Then he repeated the whole procedure twice more. The last half-hitch pulled it all tight. Nick knelt. With practiced twists he looped the rope over the center spindle and tied a hitch. He separated the line, tossing an end behind each leg and to either side of the chair.

Almost done, Nick wrapped his hand around a booted ankle and pulled Brandon's heel to the back leg. Brandon twisted as much as he could manage to stare down. Nick blew him a kiss. Eyes never leaving Brandon's, Nick licked up the back seam of the boot. Twin rows of stitching tickled his tongue. The smell of well-oiled leather swelled around him. Brandon's tortured groan was muffled by the gag. With quick twists of the rope, Nick lashed Brandon's ankle to the back leg and side rung. A set of figure eight loops laced over and under. On the last pass, Nick wound the end where the rope crossed itself, tightening it up. A half-hitch snugged it all down. It wasn't the most secure tie. However, the angle and his own boots would keep Brandon from wiggling free. Nick scooted over and bound Brandon's other leg in the same manner.

Nick stood and stretched. Shucking his T-shirt as he walked, Nick moved back to stand before his captive. He pulled the necessary equipment out of his pocket and drank in the view. It was a beautiful sight. The muscles in Brandon's bare chest flexed tight. His lips were parted by the red slash of the gag. Because of how Nick had tied his legs, Brandon's knees splayed out to either side of the seat. Shirt hanging open over his belly, but pinned on his upper arms and torso by the red and black twists of rope, displayed Brandon's incredible body to perfection. Nick stepped in and tucked the condom under one of the ropes crossing Brandon's chest. "Hold this for me baby." He smiled and set the small bottle of lube between Brandon's taut thighs.

Toeing out of his skull-patterned Vans, Nick popped the snap on his jeans. Brandon's stare burned up his frame. To say Brandon looked frustrated, trapped, didn't catch his mood by a mile. Nick hooked his thumbs through the fly, slowly pulling the material apart. Brandon shuddered in time to the zipper's growl. With a final smirk, Nick pushed the fabric off his hips. Since he never wore underwear, his hard prick was already out and begging. Nick ran his hand along his length a few times. Stepping out of his jeans, kicking them to the side, he savored Brandon's capture. "What am I going to do with you?" He purred. Nick knew exactly what he was going to do, but keeping Brandon guessing was part of the game.

Still stroking himself, Nick stepped in and knelt between Brandon's knees. First he snagged the lube and set it at his feet. Then Nick stroked the top of the boots where the slick, warm leather ended and rough cloth began. The sensations tickled his palm. Nick left off playing with his cock and rubbed Brandon's thigh with his other hand. "We can't do anything with you still all dressed." He ran both hands up Brandon's legs, then over the hard bulge at Brandon's crotch. His bound cop moaned. Nick chuckled. It wasn't like Brandon could manage more with a gag in his mouth.

Nick worked the double-tongued buckle of Brandon's Sam-Brown belt loose. The buttons and zipper of the navy uniform pants took more effort. Partly Nick's own fault, with Brandon's legs spread, the zipper fought tension in several directions. Down was not an easy process. Finally unbuttoned and unzipped, Nick snaked his hand under Brandon's briefs. The hard, hot length of Brandon's cock slid against his wrist. Nick cupped the sensual weight of Bandon's balls in his palm. It took some effort, but he managed to tug Brandon free.

That gorgeous cock throbbed against Brandon's belly. Framed in the V of Brandon's pants, the cop's balls were displayed for Nick. He leaned into lick the musky silk of Brandon's sac. As he teased and licked, Nick's fingers danced up Brandon's tight abs. Warm skin, the taste of his guy, scents of wool and leather, and silky rope formed an intoxicating cocktail for Nick. His cock ached so much he thought his skin would split. Nick plucked the condom from the rope and tore into it. He reached down, grabbed the bottle and popped the top with his thumb. A little gel drizzled on Brandon's prick would give him sensation. Rocking back, Nick twisted his hand around Brandon's cock to slick him up. Then he rolled the condom down and added more lube to the outside. Brandon's ice blue eyes went wide, tracking Nick as he stood.

Nick slipped his arm around Brandon and wriggled onto his lap. Tugging at the rings in the cop's ear with his tongue, Nick thrust his cock against Brandon's slick, sheathed prick. When Brandon tensed, Nick reassured him, "Relax babe, you know I love you and I'll take care of you." He laughed, moving from Brandon's ear and working down his jaw with kisses. The bandana gag scraped his cheek. "Tonight I'm topping from the bottom." The last of it was whispered against Brandon's upper lip. One hand drifted down that hard, flat stomach, until Nick reached Brandon's thick prick. His captive cop was so hard that Nick ached for him. "Isn't that just beautiful?" Nick nuzzled behind Brandon's ear, moving from skin to bandana to hairline. Running his fingers through the spiky high-and-tight, he added, "Okay, baby, I'm going to ride." Brandon's eyes dropped to half-mast, his sigh stifled under fabric.

Nick laughed. It was deep and sensual. Slowly, Nick raised and rocked himself so that Brandon's cock pushed against his hole. Brandon burned his hand. Nick worked up Brandon's tattooed neck with his tongue. As he licked hot skin, Nick eased himself onto Brandon's shaft. Inches at a time, Brandon spread him. God it felt so good. Heat spread from his balls as he fucked himself on Brandon's cock. Nick wrapped his hand around his own prick and stroked. Brandon's breath broke in hitches as Nick rode him. The bound cop strained against the ropes.

Rising up until Brandon's prick was barely in him, Nick rubbed his face into Brandon's hair. He held himself there until his thighs screamed and Brandon fought his bonds, trying to get more contact. Then he slammed back down. Brandon writhed underneath him. The power of controlling them both shot ice up Nicky's spine. He pumped his prick and impaled himself on

Brandon's cock. Nick's foot slid along the hard leather of Brandon's boot. Leaning in, he tortured the skin of Brandon's throat with his teeth. Brandon's muffled moans danced with his nerves. Then Brandon's body jerked. He screamed into the gag. His shudders filled Nick with heat. Nick bit Brandon's shoulder. Everything tensed, tightened. For a second Nick forgot how to breathe. Fire shot into his belly and out through his prick. Hot, sticky cum boiled through his fingers.

With shivers still working along his spine, Nick tugged the gag from Brandon's mouth. The cop turned his face to kiss what he could reach of Nick's jaw. "Goddamn," Brandon panted against Nick's skin. "You're so good to me."

Nick rocked back. Brandon's half-stiff cock still trapped in his body made Nick twitch. "Always good to you, 'cause you're good to me." He ran his hands over the ropes. Brandon's chest, slick with sweat, felt so good under his touch. Nothing could compare to how Brandon made him feel. Nick bent down and kissed his bound lover's lips. Hot, sweet and satisfied, the kiss summed up how he felt right then.

Chapter Fifteen

"I don't know if this is such a good idea, Nicky." Brandon had to yell to be heard over the combined effects of sound system bleed-over and traffic whizzing by on Santa Monica Boulevard.

Nicky pivoted on his heel and then walked backward. Smiling at Brandon, he asked, "What's not a good idea?" Hands in the pockets of his slim-line jeans and a red T-shirt stretched over his chest, Nicky looked positively rocking. Brandon was up to rocking him a bit.

They'd driven up into Los Angeles that afternoon. Tomorrow morning's schedule meant showing up early to the California Highway Patrol to get paperwork in order for a vehicle release. It was time to get Querida back… the original purpose of Nicky's formerly-scheduled-as-brief visit. As a veteran of police red tape, Brandon figured that would eat up at least a good couple of hours and that was with him there to smooth the way. Although it was possible to drive between Riverside and Northern Los Angeles County in half a day, there was no guarantee what condition the Hearse would be in. Flats, dead batteries and possibly worse could hang them up. Scouting parts in unfamiliar digs would not be pleasant. Instead of starting out before dawn, Nicky talked him into a night in L.A.

Having passed the bar, Brandon dropped his voice to a more normal level. "Coming here." Even on a Sunday evening, the streets of West Hollywood were packed. They were headed over to the Abbey for dinner. Nicky had enticed him with the promise of food and drinks. What seemed like a good idea ten minutes ago paled fast in public.

"Where else would you like to go?" Nicky paused and waited for Brandon to catch up. Couples flowed past them… mostly male. WeHo equated to ground zero of gay L.A. "There's a ton of places around, we'll just pick one and head there." He slid his hands around Brandon's middle and into his back pockets.

The cop froze. After the panic dropped to a tolerable level, Brandon managed to hiss out. "That's not what I meant." His voice sounded frightened even to his own ears.

"Jesus, Brandon, no one's going to see you here." Nicky's reassurance did nothing to reassure him. "And if they do, think about it. This is West Hollywood… what are they doing here?"

"Straight people come here, too." As if to prove his point a young woman bumped into them. Her boyfriend apologized and they moved on.

Nicky glanced toward the sky, seeming to accuse the heavens of conspiring against him. "Just relax."

Brandon tried, without much success, to calm down. "Not so much."

"Just relax," Nicky repeated, "have a drink, eat dinner, it'll be okay." Dropping into teasing, Nicky added, "It could be worse. I could have dragged you to some places out in Santa Monica that really would have popped your cork."

A tiny bit of tension slid off his shoulders. Nicky was right, one night would be okay. It wasn't like he was out picking up guys. The Abbey served both gay and straight; a good place to fade into invisible. "How come you know so much about Los Angeles?" Brandon forced himself to pick an innocuous, normal topic of conversation.

"Went to SC." Repositioning himself with one arm slung around Brandon and the other tucked in his own pocket, Nicky walked them down the street.

It was too awkward to keep his hands to himself while walking like that. Two deep breaths and Brandon slid his arm behind Nicky's back. "I just don't imagine you as a Trojan." The two of them, walking like a couple, in public, how good it felt was terrifying. "So much more of a Bruin kinda guy." If you wanted to dig into a University of So. Cal grad you teased them with their cross-town rivals, UCLA.

"Hey, treading in dangerous territory there." Nicky growled and squeezed. "Besides, as a gay man, you'll always know where to find your Trojan."

It took a moment for the reference to sink in. "That is so corny, Nicky."

"Damn, that one used to get me dates." Brandon snorted. Nicky did not need pickup lines to get dates. "This is so good." They stopped at the corner and waited for the light. "We get to go someplace where we can sit close, have a drink, play like a normal couple for a little bit."

Brandon stared down the street, ogling the crowd of happy, apparently well-adjusted people. As a cop, he didn't delude himself that they were all well-adjusted. They just seemed like it. Still, he knew he came off as some closeted freak about to jump out of his skin. "I don't think I can ever be normal." Brandon huffed and moved across the street with the flow of the crowd.

"Don't think like that." Nicky tugged at his middle again. Again, it felt so damn good. "You're as normal as anyone."

Wrought iron gates opened onto a small patio. If you headed straight, you went into the building. Nicky led them off to the right into the larger patio bar. Late summer light filtered through the trees. The place was packed. Why did Brandon expect anything different in West Hollywood? They threaded their way through tables. Brandon sure hoped that Nicky could find a table for them… somewhere back, away from the street. When Nicky scored a seat in an alcove, Brandon let go the breath he forgot he'd been holding.

As the day faded into evening, fairy lights lit up the trees. Brandon started on his third beer. If he did many more, they wouldn't be heading out too early. Nicky propped his booted feet on Brandon's knees and rocked his chair onto its back legs. Taking a swig of his own beer, Nicky smiled. "See, isn't this great?" The waiter had already cleared the remnants of fettuccine. With Nicky around, Brandon actually ate. He was going to end up off the scale if they kept the eating out routine going.

"Yeah, it's nice." Brandon caught the attention of their waiter and mimicked writing on his palm. The guy apparently caught the drift because he nodded and hustled off. Returning his consideration to Nicky, Brandon leered and purred out in his most come hither manner. "I know what would be nicer."

Nicky tipped his bottle back, downing the dregs. "Really, what?"

"Dessert," Brandon licked his lips, "with lots of cream."

"Cream?" Nicky's feet hit the concrete with a thump. Setting his bottle on the table he studied Brandon. Then he shook his head. "Oh, yeah, cream. I could do cream."

"Yours or mine?"

"How 'bout both." It was Nicky's turn to grin.

They cut the conversation short when the waiter appeared with the tab. Brandon had opened one when they started drinking. After signing off on the charges, Brandon stood. "Head out?"

"Sure, baby." Nicky purred. As he stood he ran his hands up Brandon's chest. When he reached Brandon's shoulders, his lover pulled him into a kiss. *Oh crap, they were kissing in public.* Brandon was just loose enough from the beers to not jerk away. Without even thinking, he slid his arms around Nicky's middle. Slow and easy, he explored Nicky's mouth. A little bit of malt, a little bit of pesto and a whole lot of Nicky worked across Brandon's tongue. Nicky groaned as he ran his hand over Brandon's arm. Little warm shocks drifted behind the touch. His lover pulled away. Running his knuckles down Brandon's sternum he teased, "We need to stop now or we're going to get hit with public indecency."

Brandon snorted. "In WeHo? There ain't no such thing."

"You're so bad." Nicky popped him on the butt as he walked around the table. "I ought to tie you up and make you pay."

Tie him up—the prospect peaked Brandon's interest. Snagging a cigarette with his teeth, Brandon followed Nicky out onto the patio. At least you could still light up outdoors. Two flicks of his lighter sparked the smoke. Inhaling, relaxing, Brandon smiled at Nicky. Nicky smiled back then filched the cigarette. "Bastage." Brandon muttered and pulled out another cig. Just as he cupped his palm around the smoke, he looked up.

Part of being a cop was having an eye for detail. The little things that escaped most people lodged in Brandon's brain. It didn't have to be conscious. He didn't even have to try. It was just *there.* And there, bubbling up, was a face. That stored visage connected to a man walking toward him. The walk, the beard, everything down to the crappy shoes linked up to a man jogging down an apartment walkway and calling for Marda. Brandon latched onto Nicky's belt. Ice settling in his gut, he pulled. Both stumbled back through the doorway. Somebody complained and Brandon ignored him. All he could think was *not here!*

Brandon ground out the cigarette on the floor. Nearly melting against a wall, he stuttered, "He's here."

"Who?" Nicky pinched the tip off his own smoke.

"That asshole who lives in my building." His throat was so tight, Brandon could barely swallow. "The jerk we ran into when we looked at the place."

Nicky stared at him. Then it seemed to register. "Why would he be in WeHo?"

"Why are we here?" God, the irony of it. "Riverside ain't the gay night-life capital of the southland."

"Okay," Calm, cool, Nicky moved in close. Dragging his thumb down the rings in Brandon's ear, he soothed, "Then the next question. What does it matter?"

"What if he sees me?" Brandon hissed. Maybe there was a back door they could sneak out through.

"What if he does?" Another inch closer, Nicky's frame settled against Brandon's body. It calmed the cop in ways he didn't even realize. All he knew was he could breathe again. Nicky pulled him into a warm embrace, one hand running up the back of his neck. The other slid into Brandon's front pocket. He leaned in, almost whispering in Brandon's ear.

"Come on. He's not going to go screaming from the rooftops 'the cop who lives in my building is queer!'"

"Knock it off, Nicky." Brandon banged the back of his head against the wall. "What if he wants me to do stuff for him?"

Nicky choked on a laugh. "Babe, you are one sexy son-of-a-bitch, but I don't think you're going to get propositioned by a guy who is old enough to be your grandfather. You're too far past twink for that."

Half-heartedly shoving Nicky back, Brandon growled. "That's not what I meant, Nicky."

"Then explain." Nicky wouldn't let him go. Part of Brandon was petrified that he was caught like this. The other part was so damn glad Nicky was there with him and not letting go. "Because I don't get it."

One deep breath stopped the shaking. Another let him think. Finally, Brandon answered. "What if he wants me to take care of something for him… like fix tickets or something?"

"Okay," Nicky's thumb grazed the line of Brandon's jaw. "Just because you're both gay doesn't mean you owe him anything."

The evening's pasta and beer were sitting hard in his gut. "But he has something on me." Brandon hissed. "He could use it. I don't want to be in that position."

Nicky licked his lips. "Oh, so like use the fact that you're gay as blackmail or something." Wrapping his hand behind Brandon's neck, he pulled the cop in so that their foreheads touched. With a gentle, soothing tone, Nicky added, "This isn't the 1950s, Brandon. It's not a crime to be gay." A light kiss brushed Brandon's lips. "And, get real, baby, people don't do shit like that."

"No, you get real," He shook his head, "'cause they do."

"What?" Nicky pulled back to look him in the eye. "You're kidding right?"

Once more Brandon thumped the back of his head on the plaster. "No." Running his hand through his spiky hair, Brandon tried to think. "I wish I was." How could he tell

Nicky? How could he make him see? Like a little kid, Brandon sniffled and bit his lower lip. God he felt so powerless, so vulnerable right then. "Probably about four years ago, it was while I was on motorcycle. My partner and I were tag-teaming guys coming out of bars during the holidays." Brandon palmed his face before continuing. "So he's finishing up with a set of secretaries from an office party and this guy in a Beemer passes us. The guy was fucked up, speeding and weaving."

"So I hop on, swing around after him and my partner will back me as soon as he finishes with the gals. Anyway, a few blocks later I get him over to the side. Come up to the car, ask for ID and he takes a real long look at me. As I'm pulling out the book he says, 'So I never did get your number at the Abbey.'" Oh shit, that memory… he'd been at the Abbey then, too. "'Guess now I know how to find you.' I'm just floored 'cause I realized I'd been hitting on this guy like two weeks before here in WeHo. Then he adds, 'So, like tomorrow, can I call the station and ask for the fag cop who wrote me up to come bail me out of the tank.' The ass had slurred like his mouth was full of marbles. 'Cause, you know, I still owe him that blow job I promised.' He's laughing at me, 'cause he knew he had me. I let him go. He was so loaded he stank and I let him go because he threatened to out me. "

Hugging him hard, Nicky huffed out, "That's just wrong."

"That wasn't the first time something like that happened." A deep sigh welled up inside of Brandon and wormed its way between his lips. Just the memory brought back the terror he'd felt that night. God, how he hated being a nutless wonder that night. "That was the worst. I mean, what if he'd killed someone driving home? I was damn near puking the rest of the night knowing I was going to catch a call that some asshole in a BMW wiped out a carload of kids. I'd be responsible 'cause I was too chicken shit and I let him go."

"Don't think that way." If anything Nicky moved closer. "I meant what he did was wrong."

"Yeah, and what I did was wrong, too. But that's why I don't go out. Not around here." Shudders coursed up his spine. "There's a couple places up north, near where folks are that I might go hit. I just can't chance running into anyone. It's too risky."

"Brandon, you're okay. You're with me. It'll be fine."

Still filled with dread, Brandon buried his face into Nicky's neck and just took in his scent. "I wish," he whispered against warm, brown skin, "I could believe you."

Chapter Sixteen

Nick stretched in the pre-dawn darkness. The world came into a comfortable gray soft focus. Sheets tangled his legs. Warm and yielding, the bed cradled him in his drowsy *I don't want to get up* state. He rolled over; searching for the body he'd gotten damn used to. Two weeks tomorrow. It was the longest they'd ever been together at one stretch. Hell, it was the longest Nick had lived, even temporarily, with someone other than his ex, Jake. Now if he could only get Brandon to relax enough to enjoy it, they'd be okay.

Although the sheets were still warm from his presence, Brandon wasn't in the bed. Nick sighed and squirmed. There were a few other things that his body had gotten used to first thing in the morning. With Brandon's schedule, first thing in the morning often translated to around nine a.m. The two to twelve shift… well, being a night owl, Nick could get used to a schedule like that. Another stretch and Nick's shoulder popped. He slid his hand down to rub his half-hard prick.

He wanted.

He wanted Brandon.

With a yawn, Nick slid out of the bed. There was only one other place Brandon could be, at least if he hadn't left to go find coffee or something. The thin strip of light seeping under the bathroom door told Nick he was right. That and the drizzle sounding in the shower. Nice beds, but lousy water pressure; couldn't have everything in a hotel. As Nick wandered over, Brandon's voice caught his attention. Hand on the handle, Nick paused and pressed his ear to the door. His cop was singing in the shower. Nick snorted to himself and tried to make out the words. So deep and rich, hell, Brandon could read the phone book and have girls swooning. Barry White, eat your heart out.

For a moment Nick just enjoyed listening. Brandon kept it soft, probably because of where they were. Something by *Type-O Negative*, Nick couldn't quite place the lyrics to a song.

Shaking his head, he pushed the door open and blinked in the assault of harsh light. First Nick had to take care of the other early morning necessity. The singing stopped as Nick stepped across the room.

Brandon pushed back the curtain and leaned out of the bath. "Hey you." He mumbled in a voice still heavy with sleep. God, the guy was sexy. Sometimes just how sexy blindsided Nick. A labyrinth of ink wove over Brandon's shoulders and around his arms. Tight abs and pecs channeled water into interesting patterns across his lean body. If he hadn't been a cop, Brandon could have been a model. Not that he was pretty in the traditional model way. A rough sexuality suffused his square-jawed face and smoked in those crystal blue eyes. It rocked Nick every time.

"You're up early." The words came out as half a yawn.

In response, Brandon added his own massive yawn. "Would you quit that?" Brandon ran one big hand through his damp black hair. "I tossed and turned a lot, finally gave up and got up."

"Couldn't sleep?" Nick shook it off and then reached over to run his thumb across Brandon's pierced brow.

Leaning into the touch, Brandon answered. "Naw, thinking too much."

"Thinking?" Droplets slid from his fingers as Nick continued the caress down Brandon's neck. "You're a cop. I didn't know you were allowed to think."

Blue eyes rolled. "Don't be an ass, Nicky. It's too early in the morning." He grumbled.

"Scoot over." With a sly smile, Nick pushed Brandon back into the tub. Just 'cause they weren't in bed didn't mean they couldn't have fun. He stepped over the rim and hot water coursed over his neck and shoulder. Brandon's strong hands wrapped around Nick's middle, pulling him close. "Oh yeah," Nick hissed. "That is exactly what I need first thing." Water dripped from Brandon's lips as Nick moved in. Strong and soft, Brandon met him with a kiss. It was good. Nick's hands wandered up over Brandon's tattooed shoulders to cup the back of his skull.

Brandon's tongue slid between his lips and Nicky groaned into the kiss. Every ounce of blood in his body drifted south. Insistent, Brandon's cock bumped up against Nick's hip. Beads of water, displaced by Nick's fingers, ran between them as Nick's hand explored the tight planes of Brandon's body. Someday his fingers might memorize every muscle, every freckle. Nick worked toward that goal with an eager hunger. When he found that hard prick waiting for him, Nick shuddered. He rocked his hips against Brandon's thigh and stroked Brandon's cock.

Mouthing the word, "Nicky," against Nick's lips, his cop trembled under the touch. Slowly, Nick worked his mouth down Brandon's chin and jaw. Brandon's head dropped back against the tile wall. A stubble covered throat tickled Nick's lips as he kissed his way from chin to chest. Brandon groaned when Nick sucked on one hard nipple. Rock hard silk slid in Nick's fist. He twisted his hand around Brandon's prick. Brandon lifted his hips into the touch.

Nick's own prick was on fire, throbbing hard between his legs. Tongue tracing the ridges of Brandon's abs, Nick's kisses meandered toward what he wanted. With each pass of his hand along Brandon's shaft, the cop gasped. The slow pace drove him nuts as well, but he didn't want to speed it up. It was too much fun torturing Brandon this way.

Tongue tracing the line of Brandon's hip, Nicky moved across Brandon's body. Then he kissed and licked Brandon's inner thighs. As he played, he slid his hand over that wonderful cock. Brandon groaned and settled his weight against the wall of the shower. Trails of water ran down Brandon's abs. The dark curls around his prick sparkled with the droplets. Nicky buried his face in the soft hair. So subtle, Brandon's scent flooded his senses. Brandon's prick rested heavy against his cheek.

With a sigh, he moved to Brandon's balls. He had to coax them out from between Brandon's legs with his tongue. As he sucked one between his lips, Nicky pulled at the cock wrapped in his palm. Brandon moaned. Each one got attention, sucked and kissed. Slowly, Nicky worked up to Brandon's shaft. He replaced his mouth with his hands, massaging Brandon's sac. Exploring the map of Brandon's veins, Nicky's tongue moved over the length of Brandon's stiff cock. Then Nicky tickled around the head of Brandon's prick. Every millimeter of flare deserved exploration. By that point, Brandon throbbed rock-hard. Twitches and gasps let Nicky know how sensitive to everything Brandon had become.

Nick drew Brandon's cock into his mouth. Left hand pumping Brandon's prick and right stroking his own, Nick sucked hard. Brandon shuddered and jerked. That thick cock tasted so good, it felt so good between Nick's lips. Brandon chanted, "Goddamn Nicky, goddamn." Brandon's fingers clawed into Nick's scalp. He drove into Nick's mouth in short sharp thrusts. Nick took it and savored it. He loved giving his cop everything. His own hips bucked into his hand. Shivers crawled down his arms, through his chest and hips.

Brandon shook. He groaned low and hard. Still stroking, Nick pulled back. Three quick strokes along that wonderful prick and Brandon exploded. White and hot, thick ropes of cum spattered Nick's chest and face. Nick wiped the spunk from his face and licked his fingers. His own fist sped up. Leaning against Brandon's thigh, Nick jerked and shuddered. The water drumming his skin, Brandon's fingers shaking on his shoulder, the warmth of his own fist; every sensation drained into Nick's cock. He trembled. Heat flooded his body and shot out between his fingers.

When he stopped shuddering, Nick kissed Brandon's hip. "So, that help with your thinking? Help you sort things out?"

Brandon chuckled. "No, but it felt damn good."

Still shaky, Nick stood. He stole another kiss. "I guess that will have to do." Hands on Brandon's middle he sighed. Time to get the day going. "Okay, baby, I guess we ought to use the shower for what it was meant for. Hand me the soap."

Bleary eyed, but showered and shaved, they checked out of the hotel. Breakfast consisted of drive-through coffee. Then they were off and over the grapevine. A steady climb into rugged, dry mountains birthed butterflies in Nick's stomach. When they slid over the crest of the pass, the flat plain of the valley added a few more into the roiling mess in his gut. Nick's memories of the city consisted mostly of hospital rooms and vision blurred by pain medication. Neither were particularly happy recollections.

Their first stop was the California Highway Patrol offices in Bakersfield. Crossing a small canal, they pulled off the 99 into a dusty industrial area. The Internet map proved fairly accurate. A little after nine a.m. Nick parked his rental in the CHP lot. Two deep breaths settled his nerves some. Still he was agitated. Querida had been in impound for over three months. God knew what condition he'd find his car in.

As if sensing his discomfort, Brandon reached over and gripped his shoulder. Nick managed a small smile when his lover asked, "You okay?"

"Yeah," Nick added a half laugh. "Just nervous for some reason."

Brandon squeezed then let go. "Normal I think. The last time you were in your car it was pretty traumatic." He flashed a brilliant smile of his own. That soothed Nick's nerves in a way he just couldn't fathom. "Come on, let's get your car." Nick nodded and popped the door. Heat swept in behind the scent of dry farms and gasoline. Content to let Brandon take the lead, Nick followed him into the station. Ten minutes after parking they stood before a counter talking to a detective named Cortez. As he and Brandon made cop small talk, the man pulled up the records. Nick's driver's license and his copy of the hearse's registration gave the officer the information he needed to find the file in their system. Nick filled out forms with Brandon's help.

A cranky dot matrix spewed another set of paperwork. Cortez ripped it off the printer and slid the paper toward Nick. "Alright then, sign here and here." The desk officer jabbed the form with his pen. As Nicky scribbled his name, Cortez headed back to the property locker. He returned lugging a large brown box. White tape, *EVIDENCE* inked on it in blue, sealed both ends. A thump as it hit the counter made them all jump. Ripping the tape off, Cortez folded back the flaps. Then he picked up another form. "Okay, the contents of one Miller-Meteor Hearse."

As he read off the sheet he pulled items from the box. "We have here, one large black duffle with assorted men's clothing items." Nick's battered black duffle bag with a faded sports club logo hit the counter. Cortez handed Nick a copy of the list in his hand. "Check through that and make sure they're all there." As Nick dug through slacks, underwear and assorted junk, the officer hauled a smaller bag out of the box. "Okay a soft-side tool box with assorted tools." He yanked that out and passed it to Brandon. "Why don't you go over that list and make sure it's all there." While Brandon began that inventory, Cortez unzipped the small duffle in front of him. "Another black duffle holding thirty feet of red nylon rope."

Nick looked up from rooting through his clothes. "Sounds about right, they used the rest to tie me up."

The officer's expression was neutral. He unzipped the small bag and pulled out the rope. Then he read off the next item. "Also containing two magazines titled *Bound and Gagged*." When he fished the glossy publications out, Cortez's eyebrows shot up. "These have guys tied up." He dropped them on the rope like the pictures might crawl off the page and bite him. "What the hell's it for?" A strangled groan came from the general vicinity of Brandon.

Not bothering to look at his lover, Nick smiled and shrugged. "Just a hobby of mine."

A little less enthusiastically, Cortez pulled more items from the duffle. "A pack of second skin condoms and a small bottle of Gun Oil."

"You can toss those." Nick zipped up the bigger bag. Pretty much everything was still there. "I don't think it stays good that long after being opened."

"Yeah, okay." Cortez stuttered out. "Alright, take these forms over to the impound lot and they'll release the car."

"Thanks." Nick slung both bags over his good shoulder. "I appreciate your help."

Cortez's mouth was working, but no sound came out at first. Finally, he managed a strained, "No problem." Nick just let it pass. You would think a cop would have seen stranger things then a few bondage mags. He headed out to the rental car. Brandon caught up with him at the trunk.

Dropping the toolbox with a bang, Brandon hissed out, "Fuck, do you have to do that?"

"Do what?" Nick looked up from fishing the keys out of his pocket.

"The magazines," Brandon looked like he was about to have an aneurism. His cheeks were bright red and his neck was tight. He added another, "Fuck!"

"*Bound and Gagged*," Popping the trunk, Nick tossed the bags inside, "they're classics."

Brandon stepped in. His voice was strained and low. "But they're so gay!"

Okay, after the previous night, Nick wasn't up to dealing with more paranoia. He crossed his arms over his chest and leaned against the car. "And so am I."

"Couldn't you pretend they weren't yours or something?" Brandon gripped his scalp like he was trying to force his brains back in his skull. "Like they got mixed up with your stuff?"

"First off, no!" Nick glared. "I was hoping like hell to get them back. Not only are these issues out of print, the publisher shut down the mag because of some obscenity laws that came down. I'm not about to lose these." He snorted and looked off toward the highway. "And then, Jesus, it's not like anyone is going to know."

"But what if word gets back?" Brandon gulped the words.

Nick grabbed the toolbox and tossed it on top of the other bags. "Okay, Los Angeles impound to Riverside PD… not going to happen."

"It could." Brandon shook. Not much, but Nick could see it. "Cops talk to each other."

Nick stepped in close. "Know what?" He hissed. "You're worse than in the closet. You're paranoid and in the closet." Slamming the trunk shut he added, "Don't make me paranoid with you."

Chapter Seventeen

Brandon looked over at Weaver and held out his hand. "Okay Boss Man, make with the keys." Jeff sat in the driver's side of the high-mileage, mid-nineties Firebird they'd wrangled for this job. "Let's get this party started." Based on their informant, one convenience store owner named Joe, the *Tin Tin* was about to find out what a prostitution sting looked like. They'd staged at the back of a service station several blocks down from the café. Most of these places violated the anti-smoking laws and set up fairly elaborate warning systems to avoid detection. Tripping that would blow the chance to nab the bigger prize.

Instead of handing them over, Jeff glared and popped the door. "You wreck this car, Baby D, I'll have your nuts as a paperweight." Hands on the frame, Jeff hauled his bulk out of the once light gray bucket seat. It took much less effort for Brandon to extricate himself from the passenger side. As Brandon came around the front bumper, his partner leaned on the top of the door and shot him another scathing look. "You fucked up the last unmarked I let you drive, big time."

And this vehicle was in no better shape than the last. Brandon counted at least three different colors of paint on the hood. Hell, the rear end was held together by an offensive litany of bumper stickers. "Come on, Jeff, don't make me hurt you." He smiled and snatched the keys the older detective tossed him. "You know you can't drop me off like daddy in front of this place."

His partner stepped back to allow Brandon to slide behind the wheel. When he shut the door, Jeff leaned in the open window. "Get going and be safe, Baby D," Jeff smacked the roof of the Firebird, "if you're not back in thirty, we'll send in the cavalry."

Brandon nodded and twisted the key in the ignition. After a few coughs the Pontiac wheezed to life and Brandon squealed out of the gas station lot. A glance in the rearview gave him a shot of Jeff shaking his head as he wandered back to wait in one of the patrol cars assigned to them.

Ten twenty by his watch, a good forty minutes before their stated closing time, Brandon pulled up to the smoked-glass front of the *Tin Tin Café*. Music pounded through the frame of the car. How could anyone listen to music that loud? Brandon snorted, he must be getting old if he was starting to think like that. It made him sound like Weaver.

He sighed and clambered out of the junker. Why had he told Joe to get license plates and log the girls going and coming? Three nights of watching and the guy landed a gold mine. Joe also logged ethnicity of the customers. Not necessarily what Brandon asked for, however it did help the investigation. Men, predominantly, overwhelmingly men, of more than just Vietnamese heritage patronized the *Tin Tin*. Not many, but enough, African American, Latino and plain old white guys rotated through the dance with the girls that he and Jeff could handle this shake down. Of course, the racial slurs Joe used to designate them… well, it confirmed that prejudice wasn't confined to the idiots with jacked-up trucks and *Dutchland Uber Alles* tattooed on their chests.

As he headed for the café, he hoped to God Joe didn't do anything stupid like run out and assail him with another list like the one he'd dropped off at the station. Making it to the glass front without incident, Brandon pulled open the door to be assaulted by a sound system too powerful for the space. After a pause, he stepped inside and did a quick once-over of the joint.

Dark walls, neon lights and chrome chairs littered an interior styled to look like a cocktail bar. Several petite waitresses in long gowns and high heels lounged about. A single server could have handled this joint even if it were jumping. The *Tin Tin* had five. Lurid, graphic posters of women, not quite to the level of porn, hung on the walls. Several Asian men of varying ages sipped their coffee under the relentless throb of Vietnamese pop. Unless they were breaking more than just prostitution and anti-smoking ordinances, nothing stronger then caffeine was on the menu. A small kitchen, bathroom, and tiny office space occupied the back, from what Brandon could figure, with the café area dominating the place.

Dropping into one of the chairs, Brandon kicked his lanky legs out, hooking the heel of one biker boot on the toe of the other. One of the girls disengaged herself from the music video playing on a big screen TV on one wall. She slunk over like he had ruined her day by making her work. "You want something?" Her accent was so thick and the music so loud, the cop almost couldn't tell what she asked.

Brandon's icy blue stare crawled up the waitress's body. A red dress covered her from ankles to just below her chin. Black and gold dragons undulated over the bodice, tight long sleeves and hem. It would have been enticingly demure except for the slit from floor to hip. Painted on black hot pants and strappy heels completed her outfit. Clothes ala Madame Butterfly and attitude care of your local truck stop made for an interesting package.

Pulling his smokes from his vest, Brandon tapped one out on the table. The girl huffed, snagged a foil ashtray from another table and tossed it on his. "Thanks." He muttered as he slid the unlit cigarette between his lips. "Coffee would be great."

"I get coffee." Brandon guessed they must only have one type since she didn't ask for specifics. Pretending to fish for a lighter, he did a quick once-over of all the patrons. The Asian guys ranged from blue-collar guys to up-scale polo shirt crowd to an old man who had to be deaf to survive the music. In one corner a couple of nervous frat boys traded smiles with another bored server.

His waitress dropped a clear mug in front of him. Deep black coffee filled almost two thirds of the cup. A viscous layer of something white coated the bottom. Brandon nodded and then took a sip. Two flavors, espresso and sweetened-condensed milk warred in his mouth. It was sweet enough to rot his teeth out. And it was pretty damn good. He'd have to figure this out… make it for Nicky sometime.

Without invitation, the girl dropped into the chair across from him. Brandon smiled. "Nice, I don't think you call it just coffee, though."

"No," Suspiciously, she eyed Brandon's still unlit cigarette, "it called *ca phe sua nong*." Brandon mumbled something about loosing his lighter and tucked the smoke back into the pack. To distract her, he tried to repeat the name she'd just given him and the girl laughed. Then she helped him with his pronunciation. Finally, she gave up. "You not Vietnamese."

"Ya think?" Brandon rolled his eyes to punctuate the absurdity of that statement.

That got him a genuine laugh. "Why you want have coffee here?"

Time for twenty questions. He smiled and leaned in. "I heard you have great coffee here."

"Coffee lousy," she waved him off. "Why you here?"

Taking another sip, he stared down into the now caramel-colored liquid before shrugging. "Okay, because I heard you had things better than coffee here." If this was lousy, Brandon wondered what great was.

She swept her long black hair from behind her neck and over one shoulder and began to comb her fingers through. Almost daring him, she looked up from under long lashes. "We don't serve booze."

"I can buy booze at my favorite bar and not be assaulted by the crappy music." That was true.

"We don't sell drugs." Her gaze flicked right, risking a quick glance at the office.

Something about how she reacted told Brandon they did. Well first the easy bust and then they could see what else turned up. "Why do you think I want to buy drugs?"

She snorted. "You look like guy who buys drugs."

Brandon mentally thumbed through his wardrobe: Squared toed biker boots, black jeans, concert T, Inland Empire HOGS logo vest. Well, if you didn't know that HOGS were owner groups and populated mostly by doctors, lawyers and accountants he might look like a rather clean-cut outlaw biker. Mostly he'd thrown it on because it was what he was comfortable wearing. You never tried to pull off a look you couldn't on these stings. Jobs like this were too quick and dirty to develop a character. Heck, the only reason it was him and not Weaver going deaf from whiny girl bands was Brandon won the coin toss at the station. Still, if that's what she wanted to think, run with it. "If I want drugs, baby, I'll buy them from someone I know." He shook his head and stared off towards the videos as though that statement merited her being ignored.

Her soft hiss brought his attention back. "So what you want?"

Brandon took another slow walk over her body with his eyes. As his gaze meandered over a too thin form, he let his normal smile drop into a leer. "What you got?"

"You a cop?" She clucked her tongue in her cheek.

Ah, the dance had begun. Why did all the girls always ask that question? What was he going to say? *Yes?* "A moment ago, you thought I was a drug dealer. Now you think I'm a cop?" He snorted and drained his coffee. Setting his elbows on the table, Brandon leaned in. "Do I look like a cop?"

"No." She hesitated. After considering him, all of him, she went back to playing with her hair. "Not like any cop I seen."

He spun the coffee cup between his hands, mimicking nervous energy. "What's your name?"

"Misty." Yeah, and Brandon was Rebbe Lopian. "Who you?"

Just because he was a shit, Brandon answered. "Jeff."

"Okay, Jeff." She settled into business mode. "What you like?"

Smiling, Brandon purred out. "I like everything." Of course it wasn't much of a low-key seduction style purr. He had to ramp it up to be heard over the music. "But quick."

"Okay quick." She stood and grabbed the mug, walking back to the tiny kitchen with it. About the half-way mark she looked over her shoulder and scowled, then jerked her head toward a hall between office and kitchen. A little white sign indicated the bathrooms were back that way. Good enough for government work.

Brandon slid out of the chair and headed down the hall. Other than the two college kids nobody paid him any attention. They were still sweet-talking a very bored girl. Shit, boys, Brandon mused, she's a hooker, you're not asking her to the prom. Misty dumped the mug at the kitchen door before moving farther into the hall. It split in a T at the back with the restroom sign pointing right. Misty waited for him to catch up. The music still thundered, even in the dim hall. Loud tunes and not much light equaled good cover.

Leaning in and pulling him into the left-hand hall, she whisper-yelled, "Hand-job ten, use mouth too is fifteen."

Okay, he had offer and price. His brain went into how-do-I-extricate-myself-mode. Absently, buying some time, he muttered. "Okay ten."

Cobra quick she turned, shoved her tiny hand down his pants and latched on. Holy shit! He'd just said yes to the hand-job. "Whoa, wait no!" Grabbing her wrist Brandon tried to pull her forearm out of his jeans as his basic physiology took over. Blood rushed south.

That tiny vice was wrapped tight around his cock. If he pulled too hard she'd rip it right off. Maybe figuring he was just reluctant to do it in the hall. "What, I thought you want something?" Her empty hand was busy messing with his belt buckle.

"Here?" He grunted, slapping her hand away. "I don't want a hand-job in the hall."

Misty let go. As she pulled her hand out, she stepped back, crossed her arms over a flat chest and scowled. "What you want then?"

"Not this." He stepped back into her personal space. Damn, his jeans were tight. Brandon shifted his cock through his jeans to a place where it didn't pinch quite so much. "I was repeating the menu options, not ordering. Fuck! Maybe I want more than

I can do for myself in the can at home." Another shift made things better. "I'm not those idiot frat boys out there."

"You want half-and-half?" The magic words, escape.

"Sounds better." He smiled. "But not here. My car?"

"Okay, you want go car, you need wait, *Ba`Ngoa-i*, she takes money if we go. She not here yet, at house with new girls… they always problem." Sounded to Brandon's ears like Misty believed them to be more problem than they were worth. "If you don't want wait, I can do here." Misty started fussing with her hair again. "Okay?"

"Sounds good, I can wait. But look I need to run an errand anyway, so I'll come back."

"Okay, I not that busy, I wait for you." The angels were singing to him tonight. "And you bring money."

He smiled again, and reassured her. "Sure babe, how much?"

"You bring forty."

Brandon tried not to choke. Role or not that took him by surprise. "Hell, it's only twenty downtown." Upscale prices for a car fuck.

Walking away, Misty stated the obvious. "I ain't downtown girl."

"No, you ain't." He whispered to himself as he passed her up and headed out to his car. Not two minutes later, he pulled behind the garage. Jeff hauled himself out of the black and white and ambled over.

Brandon blinked when Weaver opened the door and the dome light flickered to life. As he slid into the passenger side, the older detective glanced down. "Holy shit, Baby D, you know you're not supposed to enjoy it."

Glaring at his partner, Brandon took a moment to shift himself again. Bust-rush wasn't helping, keeping him excited for a whole different reason but with the same unfortunate effect. "Fuck off, Boss Man."

"I thought you didn't like girls." Weaver sniggered and slammed the door.

What time hadn't taken care of, Weaver's derision did. "You mean Godzilla-grip in there?" Brandon caught the headrest on the passenger side, looked over his shoulder and backed the car out. "Let me stick my hand down your boxers, grab your junk like she did to me and see if you don't sprout wood." The patrol cars rolled behind them. Brandon was certain they could hear his partner's laughter in their own vehicles.

The bust actually went very smoothly. Tin-foil ashtrays were chucked by the time the squad rolled in the doors. Misty's face fell when she spotted Brandon. "You say you not cop!" She screamed from across the room. All she got was his smile in response. Rolling everyone into the station, fingerprinting and processing ate up the remainder of the night. Brandon was bushed, but in that good *I've accomplished something* way. This was why he'd become a cop. Nights like this were the axis on which his world spun.

Brandon stepped through the door and tossed his keys on the counter. The tiny kitchen sparkled under the wan light over the sink… that would be Nicky's doing. Brandon didn't consider himself a slob, but neither did he believe in sanitizing every surface. Today was the day for Nicky doing reports and filling in his bosses back in Nevada, and he'd decided to do it at Brandon's place instead of the station. That way he could catch up on emails, scope out some of the damage on Querida and hang out by Brandon's pool. The cleaning frenzy probably resulted from boredom on Nicky's part, stuck in the tiny apartment most of the day. Not like he hadn't gotten the warning that Brandon wouldn't be around much because of work.

The drone of the shower sounded through the wall. Oh, Nicky naked in the shower, just what he needed after a hard day on the streets. Especially after little Miss Kung Fu grip. It brought up all sorts of intriguing possibilities for the evening. Brandon grabbed a beer out of the fridge and then threaded his way through into the living room flipping on the lights as he went.

As they flickered on, his view opened up on the rest of the apartment. Brandon stopped, licked his lips and counted to ten. Nicky hadn't just been cleaning. Nothing was where he left it at nine a.m. The only piece of furniture still occupying its original spot was his couch. That just meant that blood wouldn't be shed right off the bat. "Nicky!" It rolled out as a muted growl.

New coffee table, matching end tables and a nice black wood and chrome entertainment center sat in his apartment. Not that it was bad. Actually, it was all pretty sleek, but it was not his. He hadn't bought it. He hadn't paid for it.

"If you like that," Nicky leaned against the arch separating the bedroom from the rest of the apartment, "you should see the bed I got you."

Slowly, Brandon began to count again. He turned to find a warm-skinned body barely covered by a towel around his waist. "Bed?" The single word came out tight and strained. "What bed?"

"A bed, you know like an adult might use." Nicky waved toward the bedroom. "I mean, come on your stuff was crap. Think of it as a house warming present."

"Where did you get this stuff Nicky?" Try as he might, Brandon couldn't keep the growl out of his voice.

"Ikea," Nicky sulked in response, "like the stuff you pointed out in the catalog."

One deep breath and Brandon huffed, "We're taking it back."

"What?"

"We're taking it back." Brandon tried to frame the words with his hands. "I already owe you for the deposit. I'm not going to owe you for crap I can live without."

"Who says you owe me?" Nicky stepped up, sliding his hand against Brandon's hip. The mild touch sent shivers up the tattooed cop's spine. After the rough treatment at the hands of a prostitute, Nicky rocked him.

Brandon pulled Nicky tight against his body. Almost desperate he mumbled, "I know I owe you… nobody has to say it."

"You don't owe me." Nicky leaned to whisper in his ear. "I never said you owe me. This is a gift. Something I did because I wanted to."

"I didn't ask you to do this."

"Why do you think you needed to ask me?" Fingers dancing across his collar, Nicky soothed Brandon's soul. "The point of a gift is to give you something."

"Nicky, I can take care of myself. I don't need a momma coming in and decorating my house. This is my place, I can handle it."

Pushing back, Nicky huffed, "Why is it such a big deal?"

"Nicky," Brandon swept his hand across the apartment, "there's got to be at least a thousand bucks worth of crap here."

"I was going to give it to you for the deposit anyway." Nicky's hand moved from his collar, to Brandon's shoulder and down his arm. "I figured it was spent in my mind, I'll make your life easy, get you what you need. I mean, come on, you can't live like a college kid forever."

"But, Nicky," he protested, "I don't want to owe you!"

Pulling him back in tight, Nicky whispered, "Don't you get it? I owe you."

"You don't owe me shit."

"What, the fact that I'm still standing here on this planet is shit?"

"No, but you don't owe me for that." Brandon tried to back away from the responsibility. He didn't want Nicky to feel that way about him. "And I don't want you to do things like this because you think you're obligated to. I don't want us to be like that together."

"It wasn't that, not all that. I want you to be happy, Brandon. You had a shitty thing happen to you so I wanted you to have something nice, make the whole fucked-up situation go down a little easier. And I feel kinda responsible. If I wasn't screwing around with you in the garage, well, you'd still have your old place, your life wouldn't be all messed up right now."

"It's not messed up. You're not the one who messed it up. Fuck, it took two of us to do what we were doing in that garage. And, shit, I'm glad I'm out of there if that bitch thinks like she does. Yeah, it's stressful. It's inconvenient. But it's not your fault. What am I going to do with this stuff, Nicky?"

"Work it off?" Now Nicky laughed.

"What?"

"You know," Nicky's fingers walked up the back of his skull, "every blow job is five bucks…"

"Shit," Brandon snorted. "I know a place where I can make three times that."

Nicky paused. "You know a place where you can get a blow job for fifteen bucks?"

"Yeah, we busted it tonight." Leaning back, Brandon rolled his eyes. "It was a riot. This working girl offers to blow me for fifteen or I can get half-and-half for forty."

A long, heavy pause filled the room before Nicky asked, "You paid for sex? With a girl?"

"No," Defensive, Brandon stepped back. "I got a girl to offer me sex for money, I didn't go through with it… although, she tried like hell."

"What do you mean she tried like hell?" Nicky crossed his arms over his bare chest and glared.

With a roll of his eyes and a shrug of his shoulders, Brandon explained, "She offers to stroke me off for ten bucks, so I said 'so hand-job is ten,' and she thinks that's what I want. Bitch stuck her hands down my shorts so fast I didn't know what hit me. I'm trying to pull her out. She kept diving back in. It was like a little sharp-nailed Asian bulldog diving down my trousers after a bone."

"You let some prostitute put her hand down your pants?" It took nearly a minute for Nicky to get the whole sentence out.

"I didn't let her," Brandon pushed the thought back towards Nicky, "she just did."

"And you think that's funny?"

"Yeah, it's a scream." Why didn't Nicky think it was funny? Hell, it wasn't a knee slapper, but it was amusing in that stranger things have happened kinda way. "Shit, I got razzed all the way back to the station by Jeff. I know I'm going to hit the station tomorrow and there'll be trouser-snake signs all around my desk."

"It's not funny." Nicky snapped. His glare was harder then his voice. "It's sick that you think that's funny. You're out fucking around on the job and I'm expected to be okay with that."

"Bagging prostitutes is part of my job." Brandon protested. "Massage parlors, titty bars... see if I can't get some chick to rub her junk against mine or try and solicit me to fuck her. Work some schmuck into offering to blow me in a dirty bookstore or john. That's what Vice does, Nicky. A decent part of my job is pretending I'm some horny guy trying to buy sex on the street." He tried to grab Nicky's hand.

His lover jerked away. "Well, if you can get it on the street, you don't need me."

"Nicky," Cajoling, Brandon reached out again, "that's not what I'm saying."

"It certainly sounds like that's what you're saying. You like it. That's the problem." Nicky backed away from his hand.

"It's my fucking job!"

"Then sleep with your fucking job on the couch, asshole!" Nicky spat and stalked to the bedroom. Brandon was left standing adrift in his new living room.

CHAPTER EIGHTEEN

Red lights flickered over chaos. Structures, people and vehicles picked out at random in the glare of the unmarked car's halogen headlights. Stripes and lettering along the sides of the patrol cars glowed blue-white. Portions of wreckage were thrown into lurid detail as Brandon and Weaver pulled up to the scene. Everything else faded into darkness. Uniformed officers circulated through the confusion, some took statements or directed traffic. One kid, he couldn't have been old enough to wear the uniform, stepped up with his palm out. Brandon snagged his badge hanging on the lanyard around his neck. He leaned over the driver's seat where his partner sat to flash his shield. At that the officer nodded. He spun one hand in a circle and pointed with the other, indicating they should proceed.

Brandon glanced over at Weaver, who shrugged. They'd been called out to an accident scene and neither was certain why. Vice normally didn't respond to traffic. As Weaver pulled alongside a black and white, a siren began to wail. An ambulance shot between the vehicles, almost clipping the unmarked's bumper. Brandon rolled his eyes and slid out of the car. Muttering curses under his breath, Weaver stalked around the back of the sedan.

One officer, her reflective safety vest bobbing bright orange in the dark, scooted around a large SUV. The burst from her camera's flash cut the night at regular intervals. Other cops dealt with witnesses, directed tow trucks and generally kept the peace. At their approach a uniformed officer broke off from the group and scurried over. His nametag, if Brandon read it right under the strobe effect of police light bars, said Haven.

"Okay, son," taking the lead, Weaver growled out, "what you got for us?"

Nervous, the young cop stuttered. "Our Sarge said you'd like to know about this."

Glancing over the wreckage, Brandon added his own grumble. "Great, get to it." A hard night on the couch hadn't done anything to help his normally gruff demeanor. Brandon wanted this over and done so he could think.

Plus, back at the station, Nicky still messed with the computers. The thought of Nicky alone with all those cops chilled Brandon's gut. Mendez proved that rumors were already flying and Brandon didn't want to deal with deflecting them. The whole situation was messed up and complicated. He didn't need messed up and complicated in his life. Nicky's attitude about his work made things difficult enough. Why did he have to get so pissy? Why couldn't he just swallow the fact that it was part of Brandon's job… that it didn't mean anything?

The barked out, "Yes, sir!" got Brandon's attention. Stunned, he blinked. Nobody called him sir. Haven thumbed through his notes, oblivious to the detective's shock. "The best we can figure is Le Duc Tho, age nineteen, a.k.a. Paul Le, was street racing." Still looking at the papers in his hand, Haven waved toward the side of the road. A hot rod the color of orange slices kissed a retaining wall. "The Nissan belongs to Le. He was racing the truck driven by Glen Anthony Scott." Haven glanced up and pointed to a large, black pickup parked half on top of the median. "They were doing, best estimates right now, between fifty and seventy miles per hour, headed west on Indiana," He pointed towards the west and swung his arm along the direction of travel, "Coming from the intersection at Tyler."

"Very nice." Weaver folded a piece of gum into his mouth. Chewing slowly, he thought for a moment then asked the question Brandon was dying to have answered. "But, why do you need Vice at a street racing scene?"

"Well, sir," It was hard for Brandon to understand the officer, the guy swallowed his words so bad. "Sarge said you'd want to know."

God, had he ever been that green? If the kid had been on the force more than a couple of months, Brandon would eat his badge. "Yeah, whatever, get to the point."

"Okay so," Haven took a deep breath. "Mrs. Guadalupe Angel was in her station wagon on steroids headed eastbound. She was in the center two-way turn lane getting ready to pull into the shopping plaza. At least three witnesses state that the Nissan driven by Le collided head-on with the SUV." As he flipped the pad shut, Haven shook his head. "Never even swerved." Haven started walking towards the totaled import. "Now, Le was ejected from his car upon impact and thrown into shrubbery on the north curb area." This time he pointed to a sad stand of bushes. "Wasn't wearing his seat belt, surprise, surprise."

Brandon wished the kid would get to the point. Still, it was work and they were there. He dogged Weaver's steps, following the officer. "Angel's car spun around and came to rest in the middle of the street. We're getting a tow truck in to move it out of traffic." Haven seemed intent on giving them every last painful detail. "Riverside Fire was the first responders." A jerk of his sharp chin indicated a row of emergency vehicles. "Ms. Angel is getting triage at that ambulance. They're going to take her to County Regional since she's complaining of pain to her torso and legs. She had her three year old daughter and seven year old son with her. Both were in car seats. Boy has a hell of a lot of bruising on his chest. Little girl seems fine, but they're taking both to the hospital too, just to check them out. They were apparently on their way to meet Angel's sister, who witnessed the whole thing. So, family has been notified.

"Paul Le is already on his way to Community. He's got major head and body trauma. He had a passenger, Vivian Vo." The officer pointed out a girl who couldn't have been more than sixteen. "She's over there."

Shaken and looking lost, a young Asian woman sat on the back bumper of a fire truck. Striped leggings in black and white hit mid-calf and flashed through rents in her knee length jeans. By the frayed edges Brandon could tell they'd been destroyed intentionally and not in the accident. Black funky heels matched a wide belt settled low on her hips. A long-line red T-shirt sported some boy band's picture. Angry and purple, a large bruise bloomed on her forehead. Brandon figured she must have hit the dash.

"Probably take her to Community as well." Haven called out to three uniformed officers near the candy-colored compact. "Sergeant Kates, the detectives are here!" Smiling at Brandon, he finished his first thought, "She's beat the hell up, but she was wearing her seatbelt so she survived." One of the trio sporting a set of chevrons on his sleeve broke off from the group and headed toward them. Haven added a final piece. "Scott was popped at the scene of the collision for illegal street racing and driving under the influence. He blew a point twelve. He's being booked into County Jail on those charges."

In a voice almost as deep as Brandon's, the superior officer rumbled, "Glad to see you could make it." Typical of most older cops, he buzzed his hair down but let his mustache grow out. Heavy lines around his eyes cut across his face when he smiled. The grin flashed enough teeth for two people. Slapping the younger officer on the back, the sergeant added, "Haven here give you the run down?"

"Yeah, sort of." Brandon groused. He was always uncomfortable dealing with uniformed officers twice his age. As a detective, Brandon was presumed the expert. Veterans like Kates had forgotten more things about being a cop than Brandon learned in his nine years on the force. "Still don't know why we're here."

"Okay, Haven, go assist traffic." Kates dismissed the young cop. When Haven walked away, Kates turned to them and flashed another toothy grin. "Well, I'm sure he hasn't told you the sweetest thing. That candy colored pimp-mobile there matches the description of the one seen leaving the *Bang!* PC Café the night David Huynh was shot."

"Well now. That's interesting." Brandon jammed his hands in his pockets and surveyed the scene. A rumpled phone message crinkled under his left hand. Shit, he'd forgotten to return Roberta's call. "I'm still clueless as to why you called us." She'd just have to wait, 'cause this was far more important.

His partner snorted. "Carr, you're always clueless."

Sergeant Kates smiled. "You're on the task force."

"Yeah." Brandon shrugged.

"And." His tone dismissed any honor being called to the scene as leads they might have gotten, "you were the only detectives on the task force who were also on duty."

"Really?" Brandon's shoulders sagged just a hair.

"Haven't you learned yet, Carr?" Weaver popped him on the back of the head. "Don't ask if you don't really want the answer."

"Bite me, Boss Man." Brandon snapped. With long strides he headed toward the wrecked Nissan. "Let's take a look at the kid's ride." Doors were peeled back like petals from some exotic flower. Brandon leaned in without touching and peered in the darkened interior. White shreds of a discharged airbag tangled with the seatbelt, hung from the dash. Digging the Maglite key chain from his pocket, Brandon twisted the end.

Probable cause, Brandon knew he had to be able to articulate it to justify the search he was about to conduct. They would impound the car. Anything in the passenger compartment would be found anyway… the legal rule of inevitability. That would work. The Nissan had been identified as one involved in a crime. Thus it, itself, was evidence. And he would just look, no digging under or in things. If things he found could be viewed by anyone without aid, and a flashlight didn't count as *aid*, the search would pass muster.

The tiny bluish light danced about the car's interior, spinning fractured rainbows off shattered safety glass. A dull metal flash on the floor behind the front seat caught his attention. With an appreciative whistle, Bandon reached back and yanked on Weaver's sleeve. "Luka here, motha'fucka'."

"Baby D," Weaver bent over Brandon's shoulder, "what did you find."

"A sweet-ass shotgun. Give me some gloves." He reached back and wiggled his fingers. "Look how pretty and sawed off this thing is."

The older detective chuckled and handed over a pair of latex gloves. "How much you want to bet it was used in the Huynh shooting?"

Sliding his hands into the tight fitting latex, Brandon added his snort. "I don't bet against sure things." The priority of the first personnel on the scene would have been to see to the welfare of involved parties. Sometimes EMTs found things, but they weren't trained to look for it. In the initial rush, even the police wouldn't have been checking for evidence. He snagged the weapon from inside of the car, lifting it gingerly with a two-fingered grip. "Merry fucking Christmas in August."

"With a big old bow for you all. Wonder if she knew it was there." Looking back towards the ambulance, Weaver shook his head. "'Course the girl won't say a damn thing. She'll either hide behind ignorance or just shut the fuck up."

Brandon tracked the other man's gaze. He sucked on his tongue, before asking. "Want me to take a crack at her?"

"You think you can do better than me, Baby D?" Weaver signaled an officer to bring over a paper bag to wrap the evidence.

"Well," Brandon looked up from where he knelt by the car, "Weaver, you ain't exactly teddy bear cuddly." The bag rattled next to Brandon's ear. Weaver held it open and Brandon slid the shotgun, handle first, inside. The barrel stuck out one end, but at least the techs could handle it to bag it properly.

Taking the packaged weapon Weaver muttered, "I'm as sweet as a kitten."

Brandon's knees popped as he stood. "If kittens are six foot and two-fifty with buzz cuts." The uniformed officer held out an evidence tag and Brandon scribbled his name and badge number. Then he relinquished the whole package to his partner.

"Sure," Weaver nodded, "you try. Remember though, she's a teen. Can't be coercive or even suggestive."

"I'm not going to do any of that." Each glove snapped as Brandon pulled them off his big hands, before tucking them in his back pocket. "It'll be okay." Weaver snorted and headed off to turn in the evidence. Brandon considered the girl and how best to approach her. Lost, she looked lost. That tough, high-sex shell cradled a scared kid. He wiped his hands on his ass. With a final glance after his partner, Brandon walked over to their witness. "Hey Vivian, you okay?" She shrugged. "You called your parents yet?" Scathing didn't begin to cover that look. Brandon knelt, lowering himself to below eye level. She had to look down on the detective and that put her in the position of power. Brandon wanted her to feel like she was in control.

"Okay, you're worried you parents are going to be mad." He tried to remember what it was like to have something to hide from your parents. That wasn't something Brandon needed to look too far to find. "Maybe, but putting it off ain't going to make it go down easier." He dug his phone off his hip. Holding it out to her, he offered her a toned down version of his come hither smile. "If you call them now, it's a mistake… one a lot of kids make being around the wrong kinda people. If you wait until you get out of the hospital, social services is going to have a crack at you, we're going to have to get a statement as soon as you're released. That's sometime tomorrow. You'll be gone all night. They'll be frantic and it'll be ten times worse."

Vivian stared off toward the Nissan. Brandon waited. Waiting was something he was very used to. Finally, she whispered, "You don't know them."

"No, I don't." Another smile hopefully reassured her. "But I do know how I'd feel about my little girl. I'd probably be mad. Mostly, though, I'd be scared. I'd be beating down the door of every friend she had. I'd be calling the hospitals and the cops. Let me call them for you. Or better, you take my phone. You call them, let them know you're okay. Then you can give me the phone and I'll talk to them for you."

"They'll be mad." Her voice was so soft he almost missed it.

"Just try it." Taking her tiny hand in his, Brandon slid the open phone into her grip. "Come on, don't you want to be with your family right now? Was the guy in the car your boyfriend?"

A sob broke as a word, "Kinda."

"And you're scared, huh?" He curled her fingers around the slim case, "'Cause he got hurt?"

"Yeah."

"Do you have an older sister or brother?" Now he pushed her hand toward Vivian. "Maybe an aunt?" When she nodded, he added, "We could call your aunt. Is that okay?"

"Sure." Although she agreed, Vivian pushed the phone back at him.

Okay, he could run with that. He took the cell and flipped it open. "What's her number?" As she rattled it off Brandon dialed. When it started to ring he held it out. "Okay, here, talk to her okay?" Teenage reflex, Vivian grabbed it.

Big, doll eyes looked up at him. "Don't leave."

"I'm not going anywhere." He reassured her. A tense, one-sided conversation in a language Brandon couldn't even fathom started. After the first spate, Vivian punctuated her end with "unhas," "yahas" and sobs.

Finally, the girl held the phone out to him. "She wants to talk to you."

"Okay." Brandon took his cell. "What's her name?"

"It's my Aunt Be."

Brandon put the phone to his ear. "Hi, is this Be?"

"Yes." Terrified didn't even begin to capture the tremble in the voice on the other end of the line.

"Vivian has probably told you a little about what happened. Is that right?"

"Some." Very cautious the woman added, "Is she in trouble?"

"We don't know that yet." He debated momentarily over how much he should disclose. Then he settled on a minimal amount. "She was with some people she probably shouldn't have been. We're going to take her to the hospital and get her checked out. Do you want to meet us there?"

"Her parents. They should know. I'll call." That's when Brandon knew the girl would be okay.

He spent the next few hours making arrangements to get her medical attention and waiting for her parents to arrive. Vivian wasn't so bad off that she required an ambulance. Instead she got a ride to County in the back of their unmarked. The bruise needed to be checked. Once there, they had to wait like everyone else. Weaver left to go fill out reports, but Brandon opted to wait with their witness. He got her water and made sure she was seen. Every time he sat down next to her, Brandon pumped a little. Slowly he chipped away at her reluctance to speak. But every time he thought he was close a wall went up. He just didn't have the right words, the right connection to pull what he needed out of her.

Finally, her parents showed up. Tears and hugs surrounded Vivian in a press of women. Brandon pulled her father aside and tried to talk to him. Off in a quiet corner of the room, Brandon ran down the accident then he finished with, "She'll need to come in and be interviewed."

Dark circles stained the skin under Mr. Vo's eyes. Brandon imagined the terror following the call they got. The man ran his skeletal hands through thinning black hair. "Where?" Even his voice sounded wrung out.

"The station." Brandon dug one of his cards out of his wallet. "We'll need her to come in."

Mr. Vo's eyes almost bugged out of his head and his face flushed. "No, no police." Thank God they were at a hospital because the man looked like he was about to stroke out.

In his most soothing voice, Brandon coaxed. "She's a witness to a crime." Street racing definitely, but possibly other things as well. Brandon had to see what she knew. Vivian had to be interviewed. "Look, we really have to talk to her about this."

There was that wall again, the same one Vivian threw up whenever Brandon dug too deep. "No police." Vo repeated. The hard edge in his voice told Brandon he meant it. "It is not good for my daughter to mix with police. She is okay. We do not want any part of this."

Too late, Brandon kept his thoughts to himself, *your daughter is about as a part of this as they come.* While it was the best time to interview Vivian—she'd be less apt to guard her responses—Brandon couldn't force this issue. "Look, it's very important that we talk to her." She was a minor. Her parents had to consent and probably could be present if they wanted. Brandon could skirt the guidelines, but the courts might see it as coercion. That would blow everything. "A lot has gone on tonight. Take my card. I'll call you when everything has calmed down a little."

CHAPTER NINETEEN

Late afternoon sun baked the back of Brandon's tattooed neck. Sweat ran between his fingers as he cupped his face in his palms. "Come on, Nicky," Brandon pleaded for the twentieth time that afternoon, "how many times can I say I'm sorry?"

"As many," Nicky swirled the last of his ice tea at the bottom of his glass. Considering the liquid like it held his fortune, Nicky sighed. With a thump, he plunked the glass on the metal deli table, "As it takes for me to believe it." They sat outside of a little sandwich shop on Brandon's meal break. The place was new and didn't attract too many customers yet.

Brandon dropped his hands in his lap and rocked his stool on its back legs. "Fuck, it didn't mean anything." Exasperated, he added, "It's my damn job." He'd lost count of the times they'd been through the same conversation. Nicky wouldn't let go of the whole prostitute bust.

Nicky stared out at the afternoon office crowd. Steady streams of people ebbed and flowed just beyond them. "Well, except that you think it's your job to grab girls' butts to cover yourself."

"That was months ago!" Crap, that happened in a bar in Vegas back in June. Brandon couldn't believe Nicky had held onto that. "You're bringing that up now? What's the real reason?"

Picking at his sub, Nicky seemed to think before answering. "Honestly," his dark black eyes stared hard into Brandon's, "because you treat me like a moron, Brandon. I'm not going to fucking out you." Nicky fished out a piece of salami and crammed it into his mouth. "You're paranoid, you really are. Nobody saw you in Los Angeles. Nobody recognized you in Bakersfield. Nobody's going to think anything."

"They already do." Brandon thought back to Mendez. "People make comments."

"About what?" Nicky's tone echoed snide and sharp.

Brandon slammed the front of the stool back down. Propping himself on his elbows, Brandon leaned over the table and hissed. "About you."

"So what?" Nicky rolled his eyes. "So they're making comments about me. I don't care."

"But Nicky, I'm with you all the time." How could Nicky not get it? "You're staying at my place. Don't you see what that says?"

"Yeah, it says I'm kicking it with my friend." Finger spinning in the air near his head, Nicky added, "Woohoo, call the presses. Just because you're around me doesn't mean they're all going to think you're gay." Nicky pushed back from the table and stood. Trash shoved into the sandwich wrapper, he walked toward the trashcan at the corner of the building.

Brandon jogged to catch up to him. "Yes, it does." He hissed. Brandon felt his face going tight and he swallowed. "It screams it. Can't you just tone it down?"

"Tone what down?" Nicky stared at him like he'd lost his mind.

"I don't know," Brandon shrugged and dropped his own trash in the bin. "Just the more obvious stuff."

Nicky shook his head. Arms crossed over his chest he growled. "I'm not going to change who I am for you, Brandon. You can't ask that of me, it's not fair."

"Nicky, look, all I'm asking…"

Cutting him off with a glare, Nicky snarled, "Think about what you're asking me to do, Brandon. You want me to stop being the guy you like; pretend to be someone I'm not." He licked his lips before adding. "And I'm pissed at you right now. I don't want to talk about it. I'm going for cigarettes. I'll meet you back at the station." Shoving his hands in his pockets, Nick stared at some far off point beyond Brandon's shoulder. "You get your head on straight and then we'll discuss your issues." With that, Nicky stepped into the street and jaywalked across traffic.

Shit! Brandon banged the side of the building with his fist. Nicky was just being fucking dense. Why did he have to get involved in the investigation? Messing in things he shouldn't be part of. And now Brandon was stuck with it. The district attorney had a raging hard-on for Nicky and his computer information. Daily, Nicky teased bits and pieces of information out of the files. Hopefully it would be done soon, Nicky could go home, and Brandon's life would settle back to normal.

From behind, a voice he'd heard more times in the past few weeks than in the last three years crawled up the back of his neck. "Well, now, who was that?"

Brandon turned to find Ray standing on the sidewalk. Dressed in business casual, a plastic bag from a nearby bookstore swung from his fingers. Damn, Nicky at his work and running into Ray… how could things get worse? "None of your business, Ray." He growled and stalked off.

"Poor guy seems nice enough." Ray fell into step beside him, and Brandon searched his brain in a vain attempt to discover what he'd done to deserve this particular torture. "Think I should warn him that you're nuts?"

Brandon stopped and glared. "Nicky doesn't need to be warned, Ray."

"So," Ray smiled back, "this Nicky already knows you're a head case? And he agreed to work with you? Wow." When Brandon stiffened, Ray's eyes went narrow. "Wait a minute. He's not just someone you work with is he? Holy shit! Is that what you're dating now?" The snide but appreciative tone in Ray's voice rubbed Brandon wrong in nine-hundred different ways. "Badge, attitude and you. Is he a sheriff?"

It took Brandon a moment to process that last question. Nicky's badge was the same style as the Riverside County Sheriff's. Wrong seal in the center, but Ray wouldn't know that. "Bite me. I don't need your shit right now. I just need to figure out how I'm going to fix this mess."

"You could go back to old habits," the grin Ray offered him was poisonous, "like running away."

There was no way he'd run from Nicky. Ever. No matter how much his brain screamed that he should. He stepped off the curb and started across the street. He wouldn't run from Nicky, but he would from Ray. About halfway across, his synapses linked up two stray facts: Vivian Vo was Vietnamese. Ray was Vietnamese. Holy shit! He spun and almost walked into the side of a red SUV. The driver screamed expletives as Brandon dodged around the vehicle. Ray was walking down the street. Brandon yelled out, "Ray! Hey wait!" His former lover stopped and turned. Shock widened his eyes. Brandon ignored it. Breathless, he panted out, "Look I got this girl who's a gang associate. She's Vietnamese. I need you to help me talk with her."

"Now you need me?" Ray crossed his arms over his chest and cocked his hip. "What, just 'cause she's Asian and wearing baggy pants she's a banger?"

"Ray," he didn't need this shit, he really didn't. "You know me better than that."

"I do?" Ray laughed. "Really, Brandon, tell me how much I really know about you? We had such a strong, trusting relationship after all… you'd show up, we'd fuck like mad and you'd blow before the sheets had a chance to dry." Brandon's stomach froze. Dear God, he hoped no one overheard this conversation. "Maybe you'd call me, and maybe you wouldn't." Rolling his hand out to the side like he was pointing out the features on a new car, Ray teased, "On the one hand I know you're way into rimming. But, honestly, after two and a half years on and off," he repeated the motion with the left, "I don't even know what toppings you like on your pizza. We were about sex… I wanted more than that, you didn't. I've grown past that. But don't tell me I know you. I barely know you."

"Ray." Sucking up to Ray forced up Brandon's worst nightmares, the ones where he committed to something and bombed out. Bombed out like he was doing with Nicky. Brandon shoved that thought down. "I know you don't owe me shit. And I probably can never apologize for anything…"

"Damn straight on that!" Ray's voice snapped with years of repressed anger.

Brandon took a deep breath. He deserved it. Ray had every right to be mad as hell about how he'd been dumped. "Look I'm sorry. I'm sorry that I acted like some stupid high school kid. I just couldn't deal with things. I was a jerk."

"You're still a jerk."

"Okay," another deep breath, "I'm still a jerk. I'm a jerk who needs your help on a case."

Ray stared off down the street. Brandon couldn't even fathom what thoughts were passing through Ray's head. Finally, defensively, he folded his arms over his chest again. "I ain't walking yet."

In a rush of words Brandon tried to explain. He didn't want Ray to change his mind before he got it all out. "Last night, we pulled this girl, Vivian, out of a wreck. The car that she was riding in was seen at the scene of the David Huynh shooting." The hard set of Ray's shoulders dropped just a fraction. "There was a weapon, possibly the one used in the crime, in the back. Vivian's parents have thrown up this wall. I can't break through it." Ray's arms slid down so that they were looped loosely in front of his stomach. He stared at Brandon with open interest.

"See," Brandon continued at a slower pace, "I tried for an hour at the accident and at the hospital while I was there with her… maybe two hours with her after I got the nurses to check her out, got her a Coke. Shit, I spent at least another half hour working on her dad. I tried again today." Brandon swallowed and ran one hand through his spiky hair. "They won't come down to the station and they won't let me talk with her. I need your help. Trust me, if I knew anywhere else to turn, I would. I want to get cooperation so I can go to her house and take her statement at the very least. Maybe you could tell me what I need to say to get past that resistance."

"Bring her over to my office."

Brandon's boots slid off the curb. "What?" His personal life and business were mixing way too much already. He just wanted a little help.

Ray thought a little more. "I can make the call and set it up if you want. Not that I want to do you a favor. But if it will help catch whoever shot the Huynh kid, I'll do my part." He moved his hands to his hips, sliding one into his back pocket. "We'll get your witness to my office." The same look Ray always got when he was at work crept over his face. Brandon knew that look well. They'd fucked more times in the staff room at County than they ever had at Ray's place.

Oblivious to Brandon's reminiscing, Ray continued. "Her home is going to be too much of a refuge and I know you guys want to get her out of that. You need that little bit of discomfort that this is a serious thing. But the station is the wrong place for that. There's a lot of stigma associated with the police, even among good law abiding people. You've stained yourself if you get involved with the cops…it sets you apart. How could you let yourself get stuck in something bad? If you make her come to the police station, all of that weight, of that prejudice, will be on her and her parents."

"From what you've told me, Ray," Brandon snorted, "nobody's big on mental health in your culture either."

"Very true." Ray ignored the dig. "But they're not going to a hospital or a doctor's office. They'll be coming to the college. Remember, education is big, so it'll give you that subtle positive vibe. We're in the middle of campus at the Veitch Center. Not quite as intimidating as the police station which sits right next to the fucking jail. You'll be more likely to get her to open up outside of that environment." Nodding, Ray seemed pleased with himself. "Just tell me when you're available."

"It won't be me." Brandon couldn't see that working. Task force or no, he was Vice and the crime was in the Major Crimes arena. "The homicide dick's going to be the one there."

Ray's hand went up. "Look, from what you've told me, you've got a rapport with her. You're sitting there holding her hand, getting her drinks and crap at the accident. I can almost guarantee that if you send another cop, she won't talk. Her parents won't let her. But with you, they owe you a debt. You took care of her. You made sure she was okay and spent your time tracking them down… that's why it's a personal debt that they will honor, because you are the one asking. And, part of that," Ray tapped Brandon's chest, his finger landing squarely in the center of the Harley Davidson heart, "is you have got to show them respect by dressing the part."

"Why, you just want to see me in my uniform?"

"Bitch," Ray rolled his eyes. "I've seen you in your uniform. The first time I fucked you, you never got all the way out of your uniform. So don't give me that shit. Something better than your normal T-shirt and jeans… something with buttons on it." Ray wiggled his fingers, dismissing Brandon's fashion sense. "I'm not going to suggest a tie 'cause no one will believe that on you. Maybe a sport coat though. I got free time around four thirty tomorrow. I've got a Saturday group to run. Will that work for you?"

"I'll make it work," Brandon shoved his hands into his own back pockets and nodded. "If you can get them there." Two more phone memos, both from Roberta, were lodged in the left. Years of not talking to her and then she starts flooding his inbox. Brandon would get to her when he could.

"Done." Ray held out his hand. It took Brandon a moment to process that Ray actually wanted to shake his hand. Tentatively he wrapped Ray's palm in his. The grip was cool, business like, and better than he deserved. "I'll call you at the station."

"Okay," Brandon actually managed a tight smile, "But I'm working out of Chestnut now."

"Chestnut Station, good." Dropping the shake, Ray stepped back. "See you soon. Get that nice looking guy to help dress you since your mama ain't here to do it." He sidled around Brandon and slung the bag over his shoulder. As he walked off, Ray added, "Tomorrow."

Another stray thought floated to the top of Brandon's consciousness. He called out, "Hey, Ray?"

"Yeah?" Ray stopped and turned.

"Why are you hanging around downtown all of a sudden?" In the years they'd been broken up, hell the years they'd been sorta together, Ray never came downtown. The university was on the opposite side of the 91 freeway. It didn't quite add up.

Secret and soft, genuine happiness lifted the corners of his lips. "Colton and I bought a house near here."

The blond guy he'd seen Ray with must be named Colton. "Oh." Brandon nodded and tried to look neutral. He couldn't begin to wrap his head around buying a place with Nicky. What would it feel like to be together all the time? To be invested in each other like that?

"Look," Ray searched his face. Brandon had no clue what answers he wanted, but something seemed to satisfy him. "If you want, why don't you bring your new guy over? We're having a house warming. I'll give you the info when I call." Ray snorted. "I'm feeling generous… if I'd never been dumped by you, I would never have met Colton. In a fucked up, twisted way, I owe you."

Chapter Twenty

As they hit North Campus Drive, Brandon mused on his student days. Working student days mostly; he'd show up to Intro to Psych in full uniform and be surrounded by a no-man's land of vacant seats five deep. Cop love didn't rank high on campus. Just like his memories, the grounds still sported lots of Eucalyptus trees and orange-red brick buildings. They scattered randomly over a campus where space definitely wasn't at a premium. Looming in the center of it all towered the giant clarion tower. Brandon always thought it looked like it was built out of white matchbooks stacked one on top of another.

They passed the engineering school in Bourns Hall and Brandon instructed Nicky to take the next left. As a concession to the business casual attire, they'd taken the hearse. It ran, but not well. The heat gauge redlined most of the drive and Brandon could smell oil burning off the engine. Nicky swore on every bump because things rattled and shook that should have done neither. After all the inspections they'd put her through, Brandon and Nicky agreed restoration efforts had been set back at least a year.

Farther into the heart of campus, Brandon spotted the counseling center. Red and orange brick jutted up in odd levels and formed low walls. Mirrored windows broke the flat surface at strange intervals. Added to that, a set of white wing-like appendages danced down one side. Nicky headed into the parking lot and the front of the building came into view. Chrome and glass rose in more staggered levels. Wings swept off to either side. They'd always reminded Brandon of military barracks. All in all the whole building looked like a stoned toddler's Lego creation. Off to one side a park of checkerboard concrete and grass stretched across the campus.

Pulling into the lot of the Veitch Student Health Center, Brandon picked a spot up near the door. Typical of a lazy summer Saturday, the campus was fairly deserted. The slam of their car doors echoed across the lot. Brandon turned and smiled at Nicky. His lover shaded his eyes against the afternoon glare reflected off the windows.

"You used to go to school here?"

"Yep." Brandon headed towards the doors. "Well not here, here. I never had much use for the health center since I had med/dental through the union." As he pushed into the building a wave of cool air washed over him. The building always seemed a little dim to him. Maybe they meant for it to be that way, relaxing and quiet. A subtle hush inhabited the halls. Brandon looked at the paper in his hand. Ray's office was on the second floor. Whispers rose from their feet as they trudged across the carpet. "I've told you about Ray right?"

"Some."

Brandon paused at the bottom of the stairs. No use taking an elevator just to the second floor. "I told you we, ah, used to hang out." The door banged hollow in the stairwell. Each step on the metal treads echoed around them.

"Yeah." Nicky's voice came from just behind and below him.

"And by hang out," Brandon stopped and looked back, "I mean, like, we used to be together."

Nicky braced his hip on the rail. Crossing his arms over his chest, his mouth went tight. "As in 'a couple' together?"

"Sort of." Brandon blew out his breath. "We didn't date really. We just got together a lot."

"He's an ex?" Nicky's glare crawled into Brandon's gut and made itself a little acid-based home.

"Yeah." The whole issue with Nicky's ex, Jake, bubbled in the back of Brandon's brain. He'd been an ass and forbid Nicky to see the jerk again… but it wasn't the same. Nicky'd actually fallen back into bed with the guy. Brandon had no intention of screwing around with Ray. Certainly Ray, with his new guy, had no interest in Brandon. Still, it was awkward. "And, ah, I don't know what he might say. I didn't tell him you were coming."

Still in the defensive posture, Nicky asked the question Brandon dreaded. "Why are you worried about what he'll say?"

"It was a bad break up." He shrugged. "If you could call it a break up. I, uh, just stopped returning his calls one day. Avoided him until he gave up. Not a stellar moment in my emotional development. It was years ago though, about the time of my divorce. I think I've grown up since then."

"Maybe your psych classes are doing you some good." That tone couldn't get more snide. At least Nicky unwound his arms and shoved his hands in his pockets. "Bad and he's still willing to help you?"

"Well, yeah, he's Vietnamese and he's got a sense of helping out his community and all. Ray did the intakes on mental health incarcerations so he's pretty 'law and order.' That's how I met him." Brandon stepped up to the second floor landing. "And, ah, he invited us to a house warming next weekend. I guess a 'bury the hatchet' gesture."

Joining Brandon at the door, Nicky snapped, "Sure he doesn't want to bury it in your head?" He pushed past Brandon. The leaden thunk of the door release reverberated through the empty stairwell. They exited into muted hallway. Pale doors broke the expanse at random intervals. Brandon glanced at the paper again. The numbers on the two doors he could see indicated they needed to head left. As they walked, Nicky threw him another question. "So how long were you with Ray?"

A quick glance down the corridors confirmed they were alone. "A few years, on and off." Leaden silence suffocated Brandon as Nicky glared. He shuffled his feet against the industrially bright carpet, not willing to meet the look.

"Okay." Nicky paused before a door sporting a blue laminate triangle. He pushed and held the door open. "Come here."

Bright light bled off into the hall. What the fuck was Nicky thinking? "I don't need to take a piss." He grumbled.

"Get your ass in the bathroom." Nicky ordered.

Brandon balked at the door. "Why?"

"Because." *That* look flashed in Nicky's eyes. "I said so." It spoke to Brandon's deepest needs. The little things down deep he'd never, ever spoken to anyone about. Nicky just seemed to know that Brandon wanted to be taken over sometimes. Not have to think. Not have to be the cop always in control. Nicky had also figured out a while back that Brandon got turned on by sex in compromising places. The whole having-sex-where-we're-not-supposed-to just rocked Brandon more than he was willing to admit.

Still, there was a time and place for it. A men's bathroom on the second floor of a college counseling building just before a witness interview—not the right time or place. "Fuck," he hissed, "Nicky, here?"

"Yeah," Nick grabbed his elbow and steered him into the bathroom, "here."

The room smelled of over-used air freshener and ammonia. Brandon's boots echoed on the gray-green tile. Leaning against a gunmetal stall, Brandon groused. "Any particular reason it has to be now?" He crossed his arms over his chest and glared.

Nicky propped himself against one of the sinks. "I want you thinking of me when you see him again." For a moment he sucked on the inside of his cheek. Then Nicky added, "I don't want there to be any doubt that you belong to me."

"Hey, look, he's got a guy." Sometimes Nicky was just weird. "I don't think he gives a shit about me."

"Right, he offers to help and invites you to a party. I believe he's not interested as much as I believe there's a curse on the Megabucks Jackpot." Nicky's snide tone reverberated through the empty restroom. "Honestly, Brandon, it's not him I'm worried about. I want you tasting me, feeling me, remembering me while you're looking at him." Pushing off from the sink, Nicky grinned. With his long canines it came off feral and predatory. Brandon shivered. "Get on your knees."

"Whoa, Nicky!" Brandon would have backed up, but there was nowhere to go. "Not quite the place or time, right?"

"Do it!"

Brandon slid to his knees. Swallowing as Nicky advanced, Brandon tried to come up with any sane reason why he was doing this. The only thing that came to mind was that it was Nicky. As Nicky came toward him, he rubbed his hand over his crotch. Already the outline of that beautiful prick fixated Brandon. There was nothing he wouldn't do for Nicky, nothing. Nicky's hand slid along the back of Brandon's skull. He pulled Brandon close and hissed, "Kiss it."

God, if anyone caught them at this… he reminded himself the building was vacant. Ray had promised to keep it unlocked after his group went home. He'd have to trust that they were alone. Brandon let Nicky guide him until his lips pressed against cloth. Deep and musky, Nicky's scent teased him even through his ass-hugging, drainpipe-legged pinstriped slacks. Brandon groaned. Nicky added a sigh that made Brandon shiver. As Nicky swelled under his kiss, Brandon's cock responded. He thrust his hips, rubbing against his shorts.

Nicky's fingers worked around his mouth. Unzipping his pants, Nicky teased, "You're my little slut and you want this."

Brandon rocked back. Nicky's dark eyes stared down at him. "Yeah."

"Good," Nicky slid his hand under the fabric to pull himself free. The smell of his guy flooded Brandon's senses. Brandon reached down to rub his own stiff prick. "Then suck on it."

He couldn't believe what he was doing, in a public john, on a college campus. Holy shit, it was intense. He'd busted guys for this shit. Sliding his lips over Nicky's head, Brandon groaned again. He could feel Nick grow harder with every second. Nicky tasted so good, smooth and warm and thick in his mouth. Few things in life equaled that flavor. Brandon fought with his own slacks. The moment they were undone, he reached in and yanked his dick out. One hand for Nicky and one for himself, Brandon stroked.

Exploring the map of Nicky's skin with his tongue, Brandon sucked his lover down. He twisted his prick through his fist while he held Nicky steady. Although he rarely managed to get Nicky all the way down, Brandon tried like hell. He sucked and licked like nothing else existed. Really, what did? Nothing mattered but Nicky.

As he worked the prick in his mouth, Brandon's hips began to buck. It had to be the combination of what and where. The risk of discovery always ratcheted his lust to unbearable levels. This time was no different. Nicky apparently enjoyed it as well. He grabbed the back of Brandon's head. Thrusting hard into Brandon's mouth, Nicky moaned. "Fuck," he hissed, "I'm going to blow." Brandon nerves frayed at the sound of Nicky's voice. He pulled back and ran his tongue over the ruddy crown. Then he sucked hard again. Over and over, Brandon would go from almost no contact to deep throat. Nicky began to chant, "Shit, shit."

The last time Brandon backed away, Nicky shuddered. White-hot cum boiled across Brandon's lips. It painted his cheek and chin. The smell of spunk on his skin set him off. "Oh fuck," slipped past his lips. Sparks shot down his spine and exploded in his hips.

When his breathing settled back to a normal level, Brandon rocked onto his heels. Nicky's fingers slid across his cheek. Brandon rolled his head and tasted Nicky's essence mixed with salt off both their skin. Nicky smirked. "Okay, baby," laughter thickened Nicky's voice, "Get cleaned up. I think that will keep you focused."

Brandon struggled to his feet. "Yeah, but not necessarily on the witness interview."

"You'll manage, I'm sure." Nicky's smile drove any doubt out of Brandon's mind.

It didn't take much to get righted, although there was a spot on his black T-shirt. Brandon tried, not quite successfully, to rub it out. Hopefully no one would notice. Nicky led them back into the hall. The first direction was a bust and they doubled back. Brandon should have printed a building map off the web. Too late for that now, he mused. Finally, they found the right room. Brandon knocked softly before pushing open the door.

Ten-by-ten and painted a soft tan, a counseling room full of cast-off chairs and two small couches, one paisley, the other leatherette, confronted them. Possibly the tackiest area rug Brandon had ever seen sat in the middle of the room. At least the purple and blue swirls broke up the expanse of stained brown carpet. Ray sat at a metal-legged and laminate-topped table along one wall. A circle of folding seats arrayed behind Ray must have been used during the group session.

Ray looked up expectantly when the door opened. Stepping into the room, Brandon mumbled, "Hey, Ray." Brandon still reeled from the encounter in the can and his voice sounded shaky to his own ears.

"Good." Metal chair legs grated as Ray stood, "you got here a little early." Dressed in chocolate Dockers and a white shirt embroidered down the front, Ray exuded a subtle, confident vibe. Brandon, in a black T-shirt, his biker boots and black leather blazer, figured he came off more intimidating. He'd tried to comply with Ray's suggestion. It just felt too unnatural getting all suited up.

A cough behind him reminded Brandon of Nicky's presence. He stepped farther in and held the door. "Ray Cao, um, this is Agent Nick O'Malley." Nicky sidled in, his eyes narrowed as he did a long once-over of Ray. The intense consideration seemed mutual. Ray took his sweet time in looking Nicky over. Trying not to come off overly jealous, Brandon sucked in his breath. "He's on loan from the State of Nevada." Nicky looked damn fine. His long-sleeve red shirt sported extra wide cuffs with a black tribal pattern printed on them.

"Oh. I thought you were friends." Ray laughed. "I meant, I thought you were together."

Nick smiled. "That, too." He ran a hand up Brandon's back in an all too possessive manner.

Brandon's gut went fuzzy at the touch and he flashed back to a few minutes earlier. Ray's raised eyebrow brought him back to the here and now. How long had he zoned? "Will it be a problem with Nicky here? I though it might be kinda impressive that someone from another state agency is here, too."

"I don't think it will be that big of an issue." Ray shrugged. "You're just here to observe, right?" A lot of emphasis went onto the words *observe* and *right.* Brandon wished he knew why. His normal sense of people seemed to be out of whack in the midst of the boyfriend/ex-boyfriend mix. Nerves skewed his ability to read their attitudes and faces.

"Pretty much." Nicky answered, saving Brandon the trouble. "I'm working the technical angle. If she says something that indicates she's aware of the issues with some gaming devices we found," surveying the room, Nicky crossed his arms over his chest. "I might jump in. But you all can take the lead on it." He looked back at Ray and smiled. It was predatory, not comforting.

Ray glared right back. "Her father and mother are coming. From what you've told me, we need to keep them out of the way. I don't want to exclude them, but I think we need to keep them physically separated somehow."

The whole talking to him, while not talking to him, grated on Brandon's already frayed nerves. "Well look," Brandon had to do something to break the tension, "can we play with the room?" If they didn't back off of each other, he'd never get Vivian to talk. The angst pressed up against the walls. Brandon could damn near taste it.

"Of course." Ray snorted.

One more bit of attitude and Brandon would put someone through a wall. Tough choice on who. He needed Ray for the investigation. He slept with Nicky. Decisions. Decisions. "Okay, let's put mom and dad on the couch." Brandon pushed past Ray. "Here, Nicky, help me with the table." Pounding one corner before indicating a spot a few feet into the center of the room, Brandon set his scene. "We'll move it here to the edge of the rug. I'm going to put you sitting at it, Nicky. You okay with playing court reporter?"

"Sure," it was Nicky's turn to shrug. "If that's what you need." He walked over, moving two of the folding chairs out of the way. Then Nicky grabbed one end of the table. It didn't take much effort to move it where Brandon wanted.

"That's going to kinda block them from her. Let's fold up all the metal chairs so that they only have the seating options we give 'em." Nodding, Ray started the work of collapsing and stacking in the far corner. Brandon paced off between the table and the larger couch. "These two reception chairs," a wave of his fingers indicated a mismatched pair of blond wood seats then he pointed at the other couch, "let's take the fake leather one and put it here," he stamped his foot where he wanted it, "for her to sit on. Then her back is to her parents." Pointing across the rug from where the couch would go, Brandon smiled, pleased with himself. "Ray and I will sit there and there. I think that will do it."

The last thing Brandon did was grab a small table. That went to the side and between the leather sofa and the chair he'd use. He fished a small tape recorder from his pocket and put it in plain view. It wasn't the kind of thing you wanted to spring on someone. Set it down and make it disappear into the background. After the final shuffling of furniture, Brandon sidled up to Nicky and bumped his hip. "I'm still thinking of you." He whispered. Nicky seemed about to reply, but was interrupted by the door creaking open.

Hesitant, possibly wary even, Mr. Vo entered ahead of his wife. Vivian followed her mother. Both he and his wife had dressed like they were headed to church. Suddenly, Brandon felt uncomfortable in his not quite business casual clothes. He hoped the Vos wouldn't be too irritated with Brandon's version of dressed upscale. Slightly more demure than the first time Brandon saw her, Vivian wore jeans and a scarf bottomed shirt in pale pink. Now she looked her age. Both women kept their eyes turned down.

"Hello Mr. Vo, I'm Raymond Cao. I'm glad you came." Hands clasped loosely in front of his body, Ray smiled and leaned in slightly. A slight inclination of his head directed the family's attention to Brandon. "You remember Detective Carr? He was with you at the accident and helped your daughter at the hospital." A second nod indicated Nicky. "This is Agent Nick O'Malley. He's with the State of Nevada and helping out on the investigation."

"What is wrong here that he is here?" Mr. Vo spoke to Brandon.

Not certain what to do with his hands, Brandon kept them clasped behind his back. "Nothing really." He offered up one of his brightest smiles. "Nicky's a gambling cop, an expert on slot machines and stuff. He's helping us with another investigation, so I've been teamed up with him for a while. Partners, like on the cop shows." Patting Nicky's shoulder, Brandon added. "We're also good friends."

"Oh." Mr. Vo seemed to accept the explanation.

Ray held his hand out, palm down, indicating the paisley abomination in the corner. "Please, if you would sit there." Then he used the same motion to indicate the smaller sofa with its back to the couch. "Your daughter should sit here." A flash of either resentment or distrust hardened Mr. Vo's mouth. However, he didn't object. After a moment, he nodded to his daughter. Everyone took their respective places.

When the various parties seemed settled, Brandon rested his elbows on his knees and leaned in. "Are you okay? Can I get you a Coke or anything?"

"No." Vivian sat with her hands in her lap, twisting the hem of her shirt through her fingers. "I'm fine."

Brandon decided to lead off with some emotional impact to win her trust. Dicey, but it was the quick and dirty way to win the girl over. God help him if he figured wrong. "Has anyone told you about Paul?" Her dark-eyed gaze jumped to his and quickly dropped back down. He was anything but wrong. "I'm not going to lie to you, he's pretty bad. He may not make it. You're lucky you walked away with as few injuries as you did." A quick couple of phone calls netted Brandon that info. "Nasty way to spend a Saturday, huh?" Vivian swallowed. The barest nod told Brandon she listened. Given the trauma of it all, Brandon figured he'd go with a tried and true cognitive interview technique. "Okay look, I'm going to record this because I have a lousy memory. Is that okay with you? I want to make sure I don't misremember or misinterpret anything you say."

Vivian started to turn. Brandon knew she was searching for her dad and he couldn't let the man have that control. Brandon sneezed. The sound yanked her attention back his direction. "It's departmental procedure. For your safety as much as anything. I can't twist things, not that I would intentionally, if it's all in your own words." His fingers hovered over the buttons of the tape recorder. "Shall I turn it on for you?"

Chewing on her bottom lip, Vivian thought. Then she gave him a quick, "Yeah."

"Good," Brandon stifled the sigh of relief in his throat. Pressing the buttons, the tape player between them began to whirr. "Okay, Vivian Vo, we're here for an interview about the events that happened last Thursday. You understand and consented to my taping this interview. Is that correct?" It always mucked the rapport up going through the rote language, but he had to get that on the tape as well.

A small, "Yeah," was barely audible. Brandon hoped the tape picked it up.

"Okay then," he kept his voice reassuring and friendly, "let's go back to the day before yesterday, Thursday, did you go to school?" Another quick bob of her head; Brandon let the lack of verbal response slide. At this juncture it wasn't terribly important and would just derail things if he made the situation more formal. Mentally he'd take Vivian back to earlier in the day when things hadn't gone to hell. Get her started there and work her up to recalling the race and accident. "Good, so why don't we start just after school got out and you tell me what your day was like."

Vivian looked up from under her incredibly long lashes. "Really?" Without all the angst and anger, she was a beautiful young woman.

"Yeah, it's a good point to start." Another, softer version of his smile hopefully reassured Vivian. "It'll give me a good idea of everything that was going on in your life that day." Of course he really didn't want, or need, to hear everything that happened that day. Only one tiny piece mattered. He had to get her to talk about that and do it in front of her parents. That called for a delicate dance on the threshold between being a confidant and being coercive. As she talked, taking him through the events of that afternoon, Brandon blocked out everything else in the room. He ignored the stares of her parents. Ray's shuffling in his seat faded into white noise. About the only thing he couldn't ignore was the sense of Nicky watching. But Brandon could push it into a corner of his brain.

Once Vivian related the whole story in a stream of consciousness style, Brandon took her back through the events. This time he teased more information through questions. Drawing out details based on what she told him. Because she'd given him a version already, her answers to direct questions would now be more honest. That was the theory at least. Still, he shied away from the one thing he needed to ask. Finally, it was time for round three. Proceeding this way meant a longer haul. However, no one could say he coerced Vivian into giving up information.

"We're going to do something I find helpful." Finished with traditional interview questions, Brandon changed it up yet again. "I want you to imagine yourself standing outside the passenger door, right after you hit the wall. Look into the car. Tell me what you see."

Vivian blinked and chewed on her bottom lip. Somehow that gesture helped teens think. Brandon couldn't count the number of witnesses who did exactly the same thing. "I see Paul and he's, like, hanging over the steering wheel." Running through the scenario twice lessened the emotional impact of what happened. This allowed Vivian to step back from the pain a few more notches. Almost coolly she described the scene. "There's blood everywhere and he's wearing the watch I gave him. And I see me, and I'm sitting in the seat and the seat belt is jammed." Her hands moved to her chest, tugging at invisible restraints. Not panicked, but like the movement helped her remember. "I scream for Paul, but he can't hear me. I keep yanking on the belt, but it won't come free." Vivian rotated her left ankle. Brandon leaned in. Her ankle hadn't been hurt and that made the movement stand out.

"My foot is caught on this thing, this thing that belongs to Johnny." Also interesting was that she wasn't naming the *thing*. The avoidance cued Brandon into the importance. Even though he pretty much knew what that thing was, it wasn't for him to name it. Vivian had to. Almost angrily she continued. "It shouldn't be in Paul's car. Paul told me that he wouldn't keep it for Johnny any more." She lashed out with her foot. "Then I kick and it goes under the seat. And the firemen come and they start trying to get the door open. They bring a big thing like on the movies and they open the door with it."

"And your foot was caught on something?" Brandon risked putting her back into the scene.

"Uh-huh."

"Something," slow and easy he dug, "that Paul was only keeping for Johnny?"

"Yes." Vivian stared into space like she was picturing a face. "Johnny Ngo."

"Johnny is Paul's friend?" She nodded. "Sometimes we do things for friends, huh?"

"Yeah."

"So he's keeping this thing for Johnny. And it trapped your foot in the car? What did it feel like?"

"I was scared." Well, he wasn't fishing for emotion, but Brandon would make the turn work for him. "It shouldn't have been in Paul's car. Maybe Johnny hid it under Paul's seat because Paul told him to get rid of it."

"Because Paul's a good guy?" He smiled. "It's really hard when our friends ask us to do things we know aren't good for us."

"Yeah."

"It seems," Keeping his demeanor as open as possible, Brandon fished, "like this thing scared you, is that right?"

Absently, she answered, "Yeah."

"Do you remember how big it was?" Brandon moved to the edge of his seat.

"Uh-huh."

"Do you remember," he lowered his voice just a little, "what color it was?"

"Yes." She hissed back.

He leaned in. "Do you remember what it was?"

"I do."

He'd established as good as he could the pattern of positive responses. Time for the kill. "What was it?"

"A shotgun." He almost lost the answer, it was so soft.

"Whose shotgun?"

"Johnny's shotgun."

"And he asked Paul to hold it," Brandon paused and then added, "when?"

"After he shot the kid with it."

Chapter Twenty-One

Steps creaked under Brandon's duty shoes. Each rise and fall jingled keys and handcuffs and baton and gun. A stairwell full of darkness led infinitely up and down. It was hot enough to suffocate him in that narrow hall. The pervasive reek, smelling vaguely like a mixture of cat piss and damp clothes, did nothing to ease that. A tiny trickle of sweat ran from under his hat, behind his ear, and down his back. It welded the navy uniform shirt to his skin. Discordant harmony backed by strident masculine moans welled around him. Whitehill, Nuñez, Carson; the hyena cackle of their voices drifted down the stairwell, and drove pins into his brain.

Ahead on the stairs, the police chaplain blocked Brandon's way. Tiny crosses on his collar blazed in the feeble light leaking through the doorway above. "Son," he turned and smiled back at Brandon. Little tufts of white hair stuck out from under his hat and his bulbous nose shone red. "Is this your first death scene?" His voice rumbled, warning of a coming storm.

"No, sir." The words echoed. "I've been on a few death scenes." Brandon's own voice sounded hollow, childlike in his own ears. The man stepped up two more steps and disappeared through a door. Greenish light flooded down the well and Brandon blinked. He followed the chaplain through into an apartment full of someone's life.

Nuñez fell into step beside him, his eyes lost in the darkness under the brim of his uniform hat. "You ever seen an accidental death, Carr?" Brandon hated when he couldn't see someone's eyes. It meant he couldn't quite get a bead on them.

"I've been on a few death scenes." Brandon repeated his previous answer. Why did they all keep asking?

With a rabid bark of laughter, Nuñez chided him. "Not like this." Then he vanished to the right.

Alone, wary, Brandon pushed open the bedroom door. Ahead of him an endless loop of porn flickered on the TV. Bad Ass Back Door Boys, Brandon recognized the threesome scene at the pool. Two white guys worshiping a big black body builder with their tongues. "Goddamn that sonofabitch is hung like a horse." Whitehill's voice cracked. "Whoa, Nellie, you think this motherfucker was thinking about that dick when he stroked out?"

On the bed between them, a lump of death pale flesh took center stage. Naked, the corpse of a middle aged man knelt on the sheets. His upper body had crumpled onto his hands. Filmed eyes stared out at Brandon and livid splotches on his arms, knees, and chin showed where blood pooled. Death froze his mouth into a contorted grimace. Brandon's gaze tracked the supine line of the man's back. He swallowed. Jutting from the corpse's ass, a thick, black rod angled back into a sleek silver box.

On Brandon's left, Carson looked up and smirked. Waving toward the corpse, Carson almost giggled. "That thing was still going strong when we showed up." He wiggled his butt and slammed his fist against his palm, mimicking the slap of flesh-on-flesh coming from the TV. "Plugging that fat, dead ass at full speed."

"Think the faggot," Nuñez jumped in, "got off before his brain blew?"

"Yeah, can you imagine?" Carson walked before a scene of some twink giving a suck, while getting fucked, on a patio table. "Standing before the pearly gates with a rubber dick stuck out your ass."

Whitehill joined the other cops' laughter. "At least we didn't have to kill this sissy boy." He turned to Brandon. His smile was full of too many teeth. "It's nice when the faggots do our job for us, huh?"

"What do you mean?"

"You're such a rookie, Carr." Whitehill rolled his eyes. "Fucking knock themselves off. If you ever hit a sissy boy fight… just let 'em go at it. One cocksucker gone and the other in the can where he can get all the dick he wants. Means we don't have to fucking deal with the scum." Derision, hatred echoed in his snort. "Next time we hit a fag bar, we'll drag you along. Really feels good to bust in some heads."

More laughter and this time, Carson broke in. "Look at it as community service."

Brandon couldn't breathe. The Sam-Brown belt around his middle was too tight, too heavy. Choking, he stumbled out of the bedroom and into a tiny bath. Catcalls about his lack of stomach and needing to grow some balls dogged his retreat. Brandon gulped in air tainted with the man's death. The chaplain stood next to him. "Son, are you okay?"

"In there." Brandon pointed down the hall. He could still hear the porno track throbbing. "It's wrong."

Sagely, the chaplain nodded. "Yes, son, it is."

"I can't handle it." He couldn't work with men who thought like that. They'd take him out if they found out.

"I know." The chaplain smiled, his hand dropping onto Brandon's shoulder in a fatherly grip. "It's hard the first time you see it."

Brandon swallowed. "The first time?" He'd been to a few death scenes. Maybe the chaplain meant guys like Nuñez, Carson, and Whitehill showing their colors.

"Yes, son." The grip on his shoulder became a vice. The chaplain leaned in until his face blocked Brandon's vision. His eyes glowed feverish. "The first time you see the hand of God's divine retribution worked into the flesh of a sinner." Oh shit! Brandon grabbed the man's wrist and tried to pry it off his shoulder. The chaplain's voice reassured. "God burned Sodom from the face of the earth. All such evil shall be purged. God will not stand for his children to corrupt themselves." Fingers clawed into his flesh, drawing up blood. "Are you corrupt, son? Are you?"

Brandon's eyes flew open. His breath heaved in his chest. A thousand miles a minute, his heart hammered against his ribs. Next to his shoulder, Nicky mumbled and shifted. Slowly, the terror of his nightmare eased out of his joints. He hated that dream; always a little different, but always the same. Brandon's memory dredged it up and replayed it with a veneer of horror show camp.

Rubbing the heels of his palms against his temples, Brandon sat up. The reality had been bad enough, close enough, to his dream. For almost six months, when Brandon first joined the force, he'd been partnered with Whitehill, his assigned field training officer. Twice, during those six months, Brandon had written out his resignation. Both times he shredded it and promised himself it would get better when he was out from under that ass. It may not have gotten better, but at least he'd learned to live with it.

A touch landed on his spine, making Brandon jump. In a sleep-heavy voice, Nicky mumbled, "What's a matter, baby?" Brandon twisted to stare down at a muscular, brown form. Nicky's strong profile was cloaked in shadows and the darkness made his eyes even blacker than normal. Lazy, Nicky's finger traced the patterns of his tattoos across his back. "Something bothering you?"

"Naw." Brandon lied. How could Nicky ever understand? "Just had a dream."

"A bad one?" The words were half swallowed by Nicky's yawn.

"No, kittens and butterflies." Brandon snorted. "It was just one of those kinda disturbing ones." As he minimized, Brandon willed his body to relax. He couldn't let Nicky know how much the dream had gotten to him.

Nicky sat up and scooted over on the bed. Leaning into Brandon's body, he toyed with the set of rings running down the outside of Brandon's ear. "Want to tell me about it?"

Brandon's stomach rolled, but he managed a tight smile. "I don't remember it." Another lie.

"Oh. Well, lay down." Nicky rolled back onto the sheets. His hand wrapped around Brandon's bicep and tugged. "Let me kiss it away."

"What," letting himself be pulled next to his lover, Brandon teased, "like you're my mommy?"

Nicky's fingers danced along his jaw. "Hey, mom knew best." Then Nicky snorted. "Although if your mom kissed you." Nicky's lips brushed Brandon's cheek. "How I want to…" The kiss moved along Brandon's jaw. "Then you had a seriously fucked up childhood."

"Bite me, Nicky." It was hard to get the right inflection of disgust into the words when he was so distracted.

A nip at his throat made Brandon suck in his breath. Nicky chuckled, "You offered."

"I like it." Sex first thing in the morning, there was nothing better. Brandon shuddered as Nicky's hands worked under his briefs. Reaching down, Brandon tugged at the waistband trying to free himself. Already hard, Nicky's cock ground into his thigh. Brandon's prick headed there fast. If it hadn't been for the dream, he probably would have woken up needing.

Finally, his shorts down enough to get some skin, Brandon hissed. Nicky's kisses worked back up to his lips. Brandon drowned in the taste of Nicky's mouth, in the feel of his tongue teasing with his own. No one had ever kissed him like Nicky. The moment their lips touched, the rest of the world vanished.

Nicky rolled onto his back, pulling Brandon along with him. Long, hard legs wrapped about his hips. It crushed them together. Brandon moaned. One hand stroked Brandon's back, sending chills down his spine as he rocked against Nicky's body. The other tickled his ribs. A hard, silk shaft slid along his own. Nicky's head bumped into Brandon's belly, lighting fire wherever its wet tip made contact with his skin.

Brandon reared back. Nicky stared up at him with lust-filled, dark eyes. A strong chin already hosted the morning's stubble. His lips were full and smiling. While Nicky wasn't buff, he certainly didn't let himself go to pot. The ongoing physical therapy for his upper body etched definition into his frame. Goddamn, Brandon didn't deserve anything that fine.

The way Nicky made him feel… that couldn't be wrong. It wasn't just the sex, although the sex pretty much rocked him, but with Nicky, Brandon found himself centered. Streets weren't as stark. Life didn't leave a bitter taste in his mouth. Brandon could get up and face another day just so he could hear Nicky's voice. If this was an abomination, then the world was a sad place.

Humping Nicky's hips, Brandon dove back down to pillage Nicky's mouth. His fingers twisted into Nicky's black hair. So freaking good to have Nicky thrusting up against his body. Fire ignited in his balls and the sweet, needful ache of his prick drove his pace. When strong hands grabbed fistfuls of Brandon's ass, he growled his approval. Nicky drove him nuts, pulling and pushing all at once.

Friction and heat, it melded into a mass of pleasure centered in his hips. Their tongues danced with each other. The inferno of Nicky's mouth worked down through Brandon's frame. He shuddered. Another moan welled up. Almost without warning, it started. That terrifying, incredible shredding of his soul as he came. Brandon gasped and buried his head into Nicky's shoulder, riding out the pleasure.

Nicky's warm and heady laugh brought Brandon back to the surface. "Damn, bitch, I'm all sticky now." He rode the outline of Brandon's ear with his thumb.

"Maybe," Brandon teased, "I know how to fix that." Easing himself up and back, Brandon marveled at the slick shine coating Nicky's belly. That porn star prick was coated in his spunk. Dark skin stretched smooth over throbbing veins. The ruddy head glistened with Brandon's cum and the thin spunk leaking from the tip. Brandon leaned in. Tongue barely grazing skin, he tasted Nicky's prick. Sweet and musky, their flavors mixed. Every inch got explored with slow strokes up and down. He loved to tease Nicky by sucking just the head into his mouth. Then when Nicky would try to force more between his lips, Brandon backed off.

Finally, Nicky took control. He grabbed Brandon's ears to hold him steady and then began to fuck Brandon's mouth. Brandon swallowed that thick prick again and again. His cheeks hollowed as he sucked. Almost gagging when Nicky hit the back of his throat, Brandon picked up the pace himself. Nicky began a chant of, "Fuck, fuck." He shook. Brandon felt the already hefty cock between his lips swell more. Then Nicky came. Jets of cum filled his mouth. Nicky was the best thing he'd ever tasted. Brandon would kill anyone who tried to take that away from him.

With a grin, Brandon sat up. Nicky still sprawled on the covers, his knees splayed out on either side. Brandon reached down and tugged Nicky's flagging prick. "Good?"

"Yeah, good." Nicky slapped his hand away. "But, if you don't quit that, I'm gonna whoop your ass."

Brandon snorted. "Like to see you try." He tried for a grip again. Once more Nicky moved to slap him and Brandon evaded. When he reached out a third time, Nicky grabbed his wrist. Brandon yanked back, pulling Nicky up off the bed. Nicky hooked his right leg behind Brandon's knee. Neither had their weight centered. When Brandon tugged, Nicky twisted.

With a shout they tumbled onto the floor. Brandon froze. Paranoid thoughts, dredged up from his dream, flooded his mind. Shit, what if the neighbors below heard? What if they said something to those guys who lived in the building…the couple? What if those guys had seen him in WeHo?

Laughing, Nicky straddled him. Lost in his own thoughts, Brandon almost missed Nicky's whisper, "Pinned ya!" He smirked. He bent down and pressed his lips to Brandon's mouth. In Nicky's kiss, Brandon forgot why he was afraid.

The rest of the morning drifted along on the heels of that kiss. He even managed to laugh at Nicky's acerbic comments about other mid-morning gym-monkeys while they worked out. Usually Brandon tensed up at the gym. Too much eye candy mixed with the sneaking suspicion that guys were checking him out because they *knew* and it freaked him. Of course, Brandon didn't usually get laid before he lifted. It filed down the edges of his normal, ever-present nervous tension. He could relax and tease with Nicky, make fun of him and get jibes back. Showers were still a little dicey. Since Brandon had been a jock since high school, he'd learned to suffer through with no eye contact. He just pretended the other guys didn't exist. It was difficult trying to pretend Nicky didn't exist.

They headed to Dematteos for a lunch of Stromboli. What the joint lacked in ambiance, it made up for in great food. Plus it was more or less between the gym and the station. By the time one o'clock rolled around, they busted through the doors, into the sauna of Chestnut station. "Fuck," Brandon groused as he whipped off his shades, "I hate having to come to this shithole on my day off."

Nicky chuckled and dropped his own sunglasses into his shirt pocket. "That's what they pay you the big bucks for, right?"

"Bite me."

"Here?" Nicky whispered out of the side of his mouth, "Now?"

"Knock it off, Nicky." Overtime was the only thing that made the detour halfway bearable. Otherwise, the mandatory task force meeting would have rated a pass. "Look, I got to pick up my messages and shit." Weaver had warned Brandon about the politics of the assignment. Well, Brandon wanted it, now he had it. It was best just to deal. "I'll meet you in the briefing. Your big show today, huh?" Reportedly, the big wigs from downtown were coming for this shindig. They wanted to see Nicky's workups and the brass was only too happy to stage a dog-and-pony show.

Thumping Brandon's shoulder, Nicky winked and grinned. "Yep. I'm gonna get set up. Come early so you'll get a front row seat."

"But all the cool kids sit in the back of the class." Brandon teased. Nicky rolled his eyes and walked off. Brandon watched until Nicky disappeared around a corner. Tight ass in dark slacks, life would be good if he got to see that sight once a week. Then Brandon sighed and headed towards the hellhole housing Vice.

Pink call slips fluttered in Brandon's box. He yanked them out and scanned through the assorted messages: witnesses inquiring about cases, a DA wanting information, and another two messages from Roberta. How many times was that chick going to call?

"Good, Carr." Brandon looked up into the rumpled face of Detective Sergeant Ashbury. His glare was so hot, the devil would have been looking for ice cubes. Instead of cowering, Brandon smiled. Ashbury was all bark and three times the bite, but Brandon would rather deal with him than an idealistic defense attorney any day. With Ashbury, a cop knew where he stood. Right then, Brandon stood square in the man's sights. Ashbury crossed his arms and growled, "At least I don't have to drag my ass all over the station looking for you."

Brandon smiled. "What's up, Sarge?"

"My office, now!" Whoa, Brandon felt like the time he was caught out drinking at fifteen. He'd been marched into his dad's study and given the third degree. Somehow, Brandon doubted Ashbury would be as nice as Dr. Robert Carr. Brandon shoved the messages back in his box and slunk after his sergeant.

The short walk gave Brandon ample time to realize he had no clue what the issue was. His recent reports were clean. None of his other cases suffered neglect due to the task force… at least not atypical neglect. He'd been on time for the most part. Except for the detour to pick up Nicky and the apartment hunting, Brandon hadn't fudged time at all. And both of those he'd clocked as breaks and lunch. Hell, Nicky's presence seemed a benefit even.

Ashbury's office door stood open. Since Chestnut was relatively new as stationhouses went, the small room seemed bright and airy enough. Still, industrial carpet, cheap white paint, and prison-built furniture gave it that discount rack air. Brandon stepped in behind Ashbury. Mendez, his sharp face drawn tight, sat in one of the two guest chairs. Ashbury circled behind the desk. "Shut the door, Carr."

Brandon eased the door closed. If you slammed it, the rattle echoed all the way out to the front desk. Then he leaned against the wall and crossed his arms defensively. What the fuck was Mendez doing there?

Drumming his fingers on the scarred maple laminate, Ashbury seemed to be thinking. He looked at Brandon. Then he looked at Mendez. Then he looked back at Brandon. That second glare was accompanied by a hardening of the already thin line of Ashbury's lips. "Carr," Ashbury set his hands on the desktop and leaned towards the young detective, "did you call Mendez a jerk?"

So that was what this shit was about. Mendez had balls to complain after what he said. Or he was stupid. Brandon slid his gaze from the sergeant to Mendez. "No sir," he kept his voice as even as he could manage, "I did not call him a jerk."

The detective sergeant sucked on his mustache for a moment. "What did you call him, Carr?"

Eyes locked on Mendez, Brandon thought a moment. Maybe the idiot believed that Brandon would back down. It could be he didn't even remember what he said to earn the taunt. What Mendez had said about Nicky, well, it didn't rate even close to what Brandon wanted to call the bigoted nut job now. Mendez squirmed under the glare. Oh yeah, he remembered. Self-righteous ass. Brandon could have his balls boiled for the slur. He took a deep breath, and without changing his tone, answered, "I called him a stupid fucking jerk, sir."

"See," Mendez jumped to his feet, "I told you, Sarge." He sounded like some bratty kid on the playground.

"What do you want?" Brandon spread his arms wide and stepped in toward the desk. "My badge?" *You know what you said asshole*, he thought. "My gun? What?"

Backing into the corner, Mendez gave ground. "I want a fucking apology." He hissed. Ashbury didn't comment. Brandon could feel the man's eyes sizing them up. He wasn't a detective sergeant because he was stupid. Brandon had seen the man at work many times. If he hadn't thought something deeper lived under the not-quite-argument, Ashbury would have already separated them. That Brandon would take to the bank.

With the biggest smile possible, Brandon purred out. "Okay, you got it." His mouth may have cracked a grin, but murder lived in Brandon's eyes. He felt the heat thrumming under his skin. Diffuse, deflect, and re-group—Weaver's adage. Next time Mendez needed a favor out of Brandon, he could stick his head up his ass.

Mendez blinked under that hard stare. "Okay then." Maybe he thought Brandon would fight more. "Well, good." Still, he seemed relieved that Brandon hadn't thrown Mendez's own comments into the fray. Brandon knew that minefield. It ended with questions like *how could you not know* and *maybe you're one, too.* No way was he jumping into that loosing battle.

Ashbury looked from Mendez to Carr and back again. "You're satisfied, Mendez?" Nine shades of disbelief flowed under his words.

"Yeah," Swallowing hard, Mendez nodded, "I'm satisfied with the apology."

"You're sure about that?"

"Yeah." Another nod. Whatever he'd wanted out of Brandon, he hadn't got. Now Brandon could see him searching for a way out. "I'm sure, sir."

"All right," the detective sergeant ran his hand through his graying hair, "Why don't you head on out, Mendez, I want to talk to Carr for a moment. Shut the door behind you." When he'd gone, Ashbury turned to Brandon. The man's eyes were wide with disbelief. "You asshole, Carr, you didn't even apologize to him."

Brandon shrugged. "He seems to think I did."

"I know, he bought it." Ashbury dropped into his chair and shook his head. "Why the fuck aren't you selling used cars or something?"

"'Cause they won't let me carry a gun."

"You shithead." The growl would have made anyone less cocky than Brandon shake in their boots. Pointing to the empty guest chair, Ashbury ordered, "Sit! You're making my neck hurt looking up at your stupid mug." When Brandon eased into the seat, the detective sergeant rested his chin on his fist and stared. "What the hell did he say to you to twist your panties?"

Brandon couldn't talk about that, not with Ashbury. Not with anyone. "Nothing."

"Bullshit!" The fist slammed into the desk. Brandon jumped. "I know you and I know Mendez. He likes to bait bears and then go crying to mama when they bitch-slap him back." Ashbury's eyes narrowed. "You, someone could tell you your mom was a freaking crack-whore, offer to show you pictures of her on her back with a dick in her cunt, and you'd just be like 'whatever.' Spill, Carr, what did that jack hole say that pissed you off?"

There were rules… blue rules. One of the biggies—guilt by association. "It's not important." Saying what bugged him meant admitting he knew Nicky was gay. If Nicky was gay and he knew it, a lot of guys would assume Brandon was gay as well.

Ashbury leaned back in his chair and studied Brandon. "You got two seconds to tell me or I'm writing your ass up for disrespecting a senior officer even if that moron thinks you apologized to him."

Brandon tried to minimize. "It ain't a big deal." It wasn't a big deal. He'd dealt with it. Mendez got his apology, even though Brandon had nothing to apologize for. Ashbury needed to back off.

"One second." The older man growled.

"It's nothing." Brandon insisted.

Reaching across his desk, Ashbury threatened. "I'm getting my pen."

Fuck! He couldn't get written up. Not for that shit. "Look, we were busting *PC Bang!* and he said something that pissed me off. In front of some uniforms who were cataloging the equipment. It rubbed me wrong and I mouthed off."

Ashbury stopped. His eyebrows shot up. "What did he say about you?"

"Nothing." That was the truth.

"Do you want me to go grab the patrol officers and ask them?"

"No, really, he didn't say anything about me." Brandon leaned in. Even though no one else could hear, he almost whispered. "He bad mouthed my friend."

"The computer guy?" Ashbury folded his hands on the desktop. His mustache bristled like a startled cat. "From Nevada?"

"Yeah, Nick." Brandon stared at his hands.

"I'm waiting."

Picking at his cuticles, Brandon tried to think. Fuck, better the Sarge hear it from him then a couple of boys in blue who'd put their spin on events. "Mendez, shit." He almost couldn't make the words come out. "He just made some comments about fairies and shit." Heat flared along his neck and jaw. "Made them about Nicky."

"Carr," Ashbury's tone dropped into fatherly mode. The kind he used when his boys missed something obvious and dear old Sarge had to slap them upside the head. "Your friend does come off as a little light in the loafers."

He'd been backed into a corner. Admitting that he didn't know would peg him as stupid. Stupid detectives didn't stay detectives. Saying he knew would tar him with the same brush. Brandon chose the lesser of two evils. "Nicky's gay… I know it." Loosing his superior's faith was worse. Straight guys sometimes had gay friends. Dumbass detectives got sent back down on the beat. Trying to explain as he recounted events, Brandon forced the words out of his mouth. "See, I've known him long enough that it's not a problem for me." He lied. Nobody else, except Weaver, really knew how long Brandon and Nicky had been friends. Of course, Weaver knew they were a lot more than just friends. "He's fucking good at what he does. If I've ever got a question on how to rig a game or players in money laundering, Nicky'll play straight with info. He's a stand-up guy." The cop mantra. You could be a drunk. You could beat your wife. A thousand sins could be forgiven so long as you were a stand up guy. "But goddamn it, make 'em stop."

"Stop what, Carr?"

"The fag comments. The jokes." Brandon hissed. He was sick of listening to that shit. "Nicky's my friend. I don't want them talking like that about him." He didn't add *and about me like that.*

"Come on," Ashbury smiled. He probably thought Brandon was one of those new touchy-feely cops. After nine years on the force, touch and feel only meant something during a frisk. "Carr, they're just blowing off steam."

Dragging a deep breath into his lungs, Brandon steeled himself. It needed to stop. "You make them stop or I'll take it up."

"Look, they're razzing him." His Sarge didn't get it. He didn't understand. "He's just not one of us."

Brandon snapped. "There's a lot of us among us!" One heartbeat and Brandon realized what had slipped out of his mouth.

"Huh?" Ashbury's eyes narrowed to tiny slits.

Holy crap! Brandon regrouped and went on the offensive. If he didn't acknowledge it, maybe the Sarge would mark it down as a slip. "Just tell 'em to knock it off." He spat. "If Mendez says anything about Nicky again, you'll need a body bag for him."

Silence filled the room. Brandon pretended he hadn't said what he'd said. Let it roll like water under a bridge, a slip up, mixed up words 'cause he was pissed off. Forcing his face into a pissed off mask, Brandon forced the fear of discovery deep, deep down into his gut.

Ashbury stared at him, like he was trying to read Brandon's mind. Finally, he broke the tension. "Okay," he rocked back in his chair and folded his hands over his stomach, "next roll call we'll go over the whole non-discrimination policy shit." A deep sigh echoed before Ashbury continued. "I'll tell Mendez to watch his fucking mouth." *I know you're not telling me the whole story* carried across in Ashbury's stare. He delivered the next ordert with an unsatisfied growl, "Now, get the fuck outta my office you stupid fucking jerk."

Good enough. Brandon would take the escape offered. He jumped to his feet and barked out, "Yes, sir!"

Chapter Twenty-two

"It's hotter than Hell today." Nick stalked through the front door and sighed as a rush of cooler air swept around him. Brandon, close on his heels, almost barreled him over. He managed to tread on Nick's toe. Limping into the living room, Nick grumbled, "You finally have a decent place, one with a pool, and I can't believe you don't want to hang out at the pool." Dropping onto the couch, he glared at Brandon. "We're there fifteen minutes, and you want to go back inside."

"It was getting too hot." Brandon shrugged as he cracked the fridge.

"That's," Nick's tone went snide at Brandon's lame excuse, "why people get in the water."

"I just wasn't in the mood for swimming."

"Right." An hour ago, Brandon couldn't wait to hit the pool. Everything was going fine. He got to see Brandon's mouthwatering ass in tight, black trunks. Nicky's own board shorts, with the flaming skulls around the legs, made for a nice change from dress slacks. They joked around and talked with the mom from apartment five. Plans for the evening included a hibachi and some steaks later on. It was far more of the vacation he'd been expecting in Riverside. And then it happened. "I know what it is."

"What?" As he walked around the breakfast island, Brandon popped the top on his diet soda.

"That old guy, he showed up." Sitting up, Nick leaned forward and glared. "You're still fucking paranoid that he's going to figure it out." He shook his head and tried to interject some logic into Brandon's thought process. "So what if he does. What's the worst that can happen?" Brandon's fears were beyond unreasonable. They bordered on clinical neurosis. "His stroke fantasy will be the hot young gay guy down the way instead of the hot straight stud he turns into a gay guy."

"So," Brandon eased himself into his old leather recliner, "not funny, Nicky."

"Oh, come on, he was *dead sexy*," Nicky muffled a snort, "the little old man in his Speedo and his sun hat. It felt like I was in Palm Springs or something."

Pointing in a generally eastern direction, Brandon sniped. "Palm Springs is about fifty miles that way if you want dumpy old gay guys in tiny swimsuits."

"Actually," Nick ran his tongue along the bottom of his teeth, "I like my tight-assed gay guy, in his tiny black trunks." Or, frankly, Nick preferred Brandon out of his swim trunks. That way he got to see the tats across Brandon's back in their full glory. "Of course, if you don't want him to know you're gay, you should get a different suit. You could have the worst gaydar in the world and still figure it out with those spray painted on your butt."

Brandon glared and growled, "So, when are you going back to Vegas?"

Bitchy, bitchy, bitchy… maybe Brandon needed to be tied up and made to beg. "Well, whenever this gig with your department winds down." Nick tried for composed and managed it reasonably well. At least as far as he could tell.

"Why did you have to horn in on that?" Knocking back a swig of soda, Brandon added, "I mean, you just got to get in and mess with my life."

Horn in on that? "I didn't arrange it." Nick forced himself to be calm and this time it wasn't as easy. "You're the one who invited me over to the station."

Brandon snorted. "No, all the fuckheads I work with invited you. I didn't want you to come, 'cause I just knew something like this was going to happen."

"What do you mean 'something like this was going to happen?'" Reaching out, Nick pushed the can away from Brandon's face. He wanted his guy to look him in the eye when they talked. "What has happened?" Nick wasn't about to let Brandon hide behind that tiny barrier.

Jerking his hand away, Brandon mumbled, "Nothing." He glowered at Nick. "It's not important."

God, he hated it when Brandon went into that sulky shit. "Bullshit, you just brought it up. What has happened?"

"Nothing, goddamn it!" Brandon snapped at him.

"What the fuck is wrong?" Just to make certain Brandon got the full impact, Nick paused between each word.

The soda can spun in Brandon's fingers. He watched it for a bit. Then Brandon looked up. "They're just talking."

"Who's talking?"

"Everybody's talking."

"Who's everybody," the proverbial everybody… everybody, Nick's ass, "and what the fuck are they talking about?"

Scooting his butt to the edge of the chair, Brandon moved in close. "You," he growled, "they're talking about you. And there's rumors going around. That you're gay."

"I am gay, Brandon. There's no rumor about it." Nick had to stop himself from laughing. "So what. If they'd ask, I'd just tell them." Rolling his eyes and shaking his head, Nick added. "Queer as a three dollar bill."

"Don't you dare." Brandon growled.

Nick glared back. Brandon was way out of bounds. "Don't I dare, what?"

"You can't tell them that." Brandon pleaded. "Ever, never. Don't."

"Because I'm with you, right? Guilt by association. That's it, isn't it?" The truth hit Nick hard. "You're ashamed of us." He hissed. "I am not and will not be ashamed of who I love. Are you embarrassed by me? Is that it?"

Jumping to his feet, Brandon almost shouted. "You're fucking with my life, Nicky! I'm a cop, cops aren't gay!" He turned to the kitchen and tossed the can. It ricocheted off the wall and clattered to the floor.

"Lots of cops are gay." Sick of reasoning with Brandon, Nick yelled back. "You're fucking gay… or you fake it really fucking well!"

"In San Francisco, New York, Miami, some big department maybe, but not here." Brandon gripped his skull like he was trying to force his brains back inside. "Just rein it back. Don't be so…"

Nick stood and stepped in to Brandon's personal space. "So what?" The question was quiet and deadly. Brandon better not say what Nick suspected he might.

"I don't know," swallowing, Brandon shrugged. He looked lost. Nick didn't much care. "Just not so..."

Nick finished the sentence for him. "So gay?"

Crushed, Brandon studied the floor. "Yeah."

Nick wanted to kill him. This was insane and he was sick of it. "I am fucking gay and so are you!" With an unintelligible growl, Nick stalked to the bedroom. Done, he was done with Brandon's crap. No way would he let anyone run his life like that.

Brandon followed. "But nobody knows that!"

"Bullshit!" Nick yanked his suitcase from under the bed. Without looking, he tossed it on the covers and tore it open. "How can you be so threatened by what you are?"

"Because the two things that I am don't mix. I can't be both. Can't you just put a lid on it while you're at the station?"

"Put a lid on what?" Damn near tearing the closet door off its hinges, Nick grabbed his clothes and threw them into the bedroom. Since he hadn't planned on being more than a week with Brandon, it didn't amount to much. He shoved past Brandon to collect the stuff in Brandon's drawers. "And what are you saying? You'd choose being a cop over being with me?"

"That's not what I'm saying." Adrift in the archway, Brandon almost whined. "I'm just asking if you could not be so out when you're with me."

"It's exactly what you're saying." T-shirts balled in his fists, Nick yelled back at Brandon. "I threaten your precious little career and you'll choose it over me. I get it. I'm just a toy you have off on the side when it's convenient for you. Fuck that!" He pitched the shirts back toward the suitcase. Jabbing his finger into Brandon's chest, Nick got right into the cop's face. "I'm not going to be forced into the closet because of your fear. Nobody's going to think you're gay, just because you've got a gay friend."

Brandon gave a step back. "But you're staying with me, here. They got to be thinking."

Shit, he needed one of those shirts. Nick randomly grabbed one and yanked it over his head. "If my staying with you is such a threat," sans socks, Nick shoved his feet into his combat boots, "it's a good thing I'm gonna go stay somewhere else."

"That's not what I meant, Nicky!" Brandon roared back at him.

"Yes, it is." All the anger at Brandon came out in trying to zip up the case. It took Nick three tries to get the zipper moving. "Just my presence contaminates your little, narrow world." He spun. "Ever since I came here, you've been shoving that in my face. I'm fucking sick of it! I can't live like that, Brandon. I don't know how the hell you can live like this. I'm a nervous wreck and it's only been two weeks. This is insane."

"It's not insane! It's my life!"

Low and ominous, Nick hissed out the last of it. "Your life is insane."

"How the fuck can you say that? You're so freaking perfect?" Finally, Brandon went on the offensive. Well, too freaking late for that, Nick snorted to himself. "I'm out and that's the way the world is? Haven't you ever been afraid, Nicky? Haven't you ever been threatened for being what you are?"

Nick shoved Bandon to the side. "Hiding isn't the answer!" He spat before stepping into the bath.

"It's my answer!"

Not even paying attention, Nick tossed his things into the small bag sitting on the toilet tank. The stuff didn't deserve the abuse. Nick was too pissed to care. "Well, maybe your answer sucks!"

"Fuck you!" Brandon screamed.

"No," Nick was so mad, he could barely see straight. "I don't think so."

"Nicky, what the hell are you doing?"

Nick stated the obvious. "Leaving." Whatever he'd missed he could pick up at the drug store.

"Why?"

"'Cause, apparently, I fuck up your perfect little life too much." Nick glared at Brandon from the door of the bathroom. "Know what? I'm glad I found that out now."

Voice hovering somewhere between authoritative and pleading, Brandon stated. "You're not leaving."

"Watch me." Nick growled

"Nicky, you son of a bitch," Back to yelling, Brandon ordered, "don't you dare!"

"That's the second time." Nick advanced, and Brandon backpedaled into the living room. "You know what, I dare. Fuck you, I dare."

Begging, Brandon dogged his steps. "Don't walk out on me, Nicky!"

"Why? Give me a good reason to stay." This was Brandon's last chance. If he could come up with three little words, maybe Nick might consider staying—might. "You're fucking sick and paranoid. My mental health deserves better than that. I don't want to end up a head case… you're good enough in that department for both of us."

"You walk out, I'll never forgive you." Those weren't the three words. The three words that Brandon seemed unable to say.

"You'll never forgive me? Forgive me?" Nick tugged the suitcase off the bed. Bathroom junk tucked under his arm, he headed towards the door. "Think again, closet boy. I'm not the one who needs to be forgiven. You're the one who's asking me to change everything I am." He fished his keys off the breakfast bar as he passed. "You knew the package when we started this relationship. I don't expect you to be out… flipside is, you don't push me in. I'm sorry I got all messed up in your life, but it happened. Know what? Now you get to explain why I'm going to be at a hotel. Yeah, Nick and I had a screaming bitch fight. If that ain't gay, I don't know what is, baby. I ain't gonna broadcast it, but you're going to have to figure out what lies you're going to tell now."

"Fuck you, Nicky!" Brandon roared, "It's not fair to do that to me!"

"No, fuck you!" One hand on the door, Nick yelled back. "This whole trip hasn't been fair to me. I've been living from one lie to the next for you and I'm sick of it. Life has dealt you some shitty stuff recently, but you're throwing crap on everyone who wants to help. That's it. I'm done. Goodbye." He yanked the door open. Out in the courtyard, Nick could hear the kids from apartment five playing in the pool.

"Where are you going?"

"I have no fucking clue." He hauled his stuff out the door. With one last glare, he added. "And even if I did, I wouldn't fucking tell you." Then he slammed the door behind him. Nick drew in a ragged breath. The last time he'd walked out on someone was Jake. That had been in Vegas… home, where he knew people. Nick had no clue where to go. One thing was certain, he wasn't going back in that apartment. He just had to make it to the car and drive away. After that… well he'd figure it out somehow.

Chapter Twenty-Three

Brandon stared into a glass of soda and wished it was a beer. The tisk, tisk across the table caused him to look up. "Honey, you know me. There ain't nothing about my life I'm ashamed of." Roberta, her blond hair pulled back by a red bandana, smiled at him. Absently, she flipped the ends with her fingers. The movement set large gold hoops swinging. After all those messages, Roberta finally caught him at the station. She insisted on meeting him at a dive coffee shop in the crappy part of town where she generally trolled. There were better ways to spend an evening. Brandon hadn't been able to come up with any of them as an excuse.

"I do what I do, and you and I, we play our little cop and working girl games." Roberta leaned back and spread her arms along the back of the booth. "But there is this kinda respect between you and me. And, you know, I came into it, and I had my reasons, and maybe, baby, some of them weren't good reasons, but they was reasons, and I was old enough to know what I was doing and why." Another smile flashed. Brandon really wished he had a beer or maybe something harder. "Now I tell you, I respect you and I know you're gonna do right, 'cause you're a good man… even with all this messed up in the closet, outta the closet, I don't even know which closet, lifestyle you got going on." Reaching out, she tapped the back of his hand with one outrageously long nail. "But you respected me and you never made fun of me. And you was so sweet the first time with your 'yes, ma'am,' and 'no, ma'am' and that's even when you already knew I still got my boy bits down there."

Two days had slipped by since Nicky walked out. Each minute he was gone eroded another little bit of Brandon's composure. "Would you just fucking get to the point?" He snapped at Roberta. Fucking returned her calls and she's *got* to meet him. Won't tell him why. Brandon almost blew her off, but she was one of his street contacts. One he hadn't cultivated in a while. Like plants, if you didn't give 'em a little attention once in a while, contacts withered and died.

Plus, it got him out of the station. Nicky still assisted the investigation, fiddling with the last bits of whatever he did with the programs and machines. What Nicky wasn't doing was talking to Brandon. Brandon'd tried with a, "Hi," that morning and rated a glare. That pretty much settled things as over. Nicky didn't want to be with him any more. He needed to accept that and move on. Brandon didn't want to move on.

"Now here I am saying how wonderful you are and you just go and talk trash like that." Brandon jerked his attention back to Roberta. Today she'd dressed down: a baby doll T-shirt and red pedal-pushers. She fluttered an outrageously manicured hand in front of his face. Her nails matched her pants. "Do people kiss that mouth? I mean, honestly, can you suck dick good enough to make up for all that negative, nasty attitude?"

No returned phone calls. Not knowing where he was, what he was doing, nibbled away at Brandon's mind. Without his sleeping pills, Brandon wouldn't have even seen the insides of his eyelids the past two days. On top of that, now Roberta handed him attitude. "Bite me, Roberta."

"Honey, I call it like I see it." She purred. Her hand went up the moment Brandon opened his mouth. "And before you start up again, I needed you to come meet someone. Hopefully they ain't got scared and run away."

"Who?" Well at least they were getting to the point of this little shindig.

"A couple of girls." Sliding out of the booth, Roberta added. "Their guy, he thought he'd dump them in the real bad part of town… you know, scare 'em some. Maybe some of the other girls on the street would rough 'em up, they'd get in trouble, go hungry, then he come get 'em back. But that boy didn't count on it being Roberta's turf, uh-huh." Brandon guessed she assumed he'd follow. She walked through the diner, garnering the stares of a few patrons.

Abandoning his soda, Bandon stood and jogged to catch up. "What, you bucking for a heart-of-gold award?" He growled at her back.

She turned to look at him over her shoulder. For once that evening, she didn't smile. "You fifteen, sixteen and you've been on the street for a while, I'll mess your ass up you try and take my money." As Brandon made it to her side, Roberta glanced over to a table at the back. Two girls, little girls with long black hair and round brown faces, huddled in a corner booth. Both wore overly large T-shirts bearing slightly obscene slogans and probably scavenged out of a working girl's closet.

"Honey," as she dropped a hand on Brandon's shoulder, Roberta's voice went soft, "these, they just babies. If that one," she pointed to the slightly smaller of the pair, "has had her first period, I'll give my tits back to the doctor. And they naive little babies at that. Nobody, I mean, nobody, messes with babies on my street. So they been with another girl, she's been sick so they helped her keep things going a bit. But they been there a few days now and money is money. We ain't social services. So Praise the Lord you finally got back to me, or I would have had to cut them loose before they talked to you."

The small girl, wearing a pink halter with decals of fried eggs where an adult woman's tits would be, looked up at them. Her eyes were huge, like one of Shayna's dolls. "They know something, huh?" She couldn't be more than a year or two older than his own daughter.

"You always so bright. You see right through all the street talk I've habituated myself to." Roberta sauntered to the table and dropped into a chair. A wiggle of her fingers motioned Brandon over. "You know, I actually got some college." Pushing out the other chair with a platform pump-clad foot, Roberta grabbed her tits and shook them. "These titties and the drugs, they don't come cheap and answering phones ain't gonna do it, though." When Brandon sat, she smiled at the wide-eyed children. "So I told these girls you're gonna take care of them. You're gonna do that for me, right?"

Brandon sighed. "I'll do my best." God, he hated seeing this shit. Kids fucking turning tricks. Runaways come off a bus and some guy grabs them and tells them he'll be their friend. Or he sends one of his girls, maybe sick or pregnant, out to troll.

The promise earned him another pat, this time on his thigh. "Now I know I'm not going to say their names right." First Roberta pointed to fried-egg T-shirt girl and then to her companion. "This is Thom and this one is Malis. Thom don't have much English, but Malis speaks some." Roberta reached over and flipped his earring. "Girls, this is my friend, his name is Brandon. Okay?"

"We go with him?" Malis seemed suspicious. Brandon couldn't blame her for that. He certainly wasn't dressed like a cop. Most officers didn't wear Harley logo T-shirts and biker boots, or sport multiple piercings in their ears or eyebrows. Of course, if he dressed in uniform, they probably would have run the moment they saw him. Maybe they thought Roberta sold them out to a pimp.

"Finish your ice cream first, sweetie." The motherly tone boggled Brandon. Where Roberta had developed maternal instincts… well, Brandon was fairly certain hormone shots didn't give you that. "We got time."

Malis didn't touch her sundae, although the girl named Thom dug into the whip cream with a vengeance. Staring hard at Brandon, she asked. "We no go with you?"

"Later, baby." Roberta shushed her.

Brandon rested his elbows on the table. Smiling, he asked. "You go with a lot of men?"

"We go," the girl looked at her hands, "sometimes."

"Do they give you money?"

"No." Malis looked up at him like Brandon'd lost his mind.

Of course not, they were kids. No pimp, even stoned out of his gourd, would let them handle cash. "Do they give somebody else money so that you will go with them?" She just stared at Brandon. "Do men give money to have sex with you?"

"Oh, yes." She smiled. It was strained. "We go, you pay. You pay *Ba`Ngoa-i*." The name clicked something in the back of Brandon's brain, but he couldn't quite make it link up to anything else. "*Ba`Ngoa-i*, she say we be good, we go work in café."

Brandon rubbed his temples with the heels of his palms. He couldn't even imagine Shayna, with her fashion dolls and princess fetish, having sex with men. Hell, he freaked when Dian told him their girl was going to start taking the bus to school. "I'll take care of them for you, Roberta." I'll take care of them for their folks. What Hell must they have lived in for them to send their kids halfway around the world on their own? "We'll call Social Services and see what we can do."

"See, you're good people." Roberta purred. "And, honey, now that's only part of it though."

"Part of it?" Brandon looked from Roberta to the girls and back again. "What do you mean?"

Wiggling into her seat, Roberta pointed to Malis. "See, now as I understand it, Malis here is Cambodian." She batted her eyes and shot Brandon a pout. In response, he cocked one eyebrow. It was obvious Roberta enjoyed being the center of attention. "Now, I don't know where this girl gets it, 'cause I don't have enough of any of their languages to really know what the Hell they's talking about. From what Malis says, Thom is Vietnamese." A coaxing grin flashed. "That right, Thom is from Vietnam?"

Malis answered. "Phái." Brandon assumed that meant yes. The body language wasn't there, but the tone was. Thom hadn't stopped shoveling ice cream into her mouth. The spoon hit the bottom of the glass with a clink. Flicking her gaze up to Malis, Thom reached out and snagged the other sundae. Then she began to devour it.

"Now somehow Thom gets mixed up with all these Cambodian girls." Roberta circled her hands around on the table. "Thom, she has some Cambodian, I guess. So she and Malis they kinda become friends." Now it was mystical waving between the two. "And," Roberta slapped one palm on the table, "they're here in the US and they think they're gonna go be maids or movie stars or something." Her left hand swatted invisible, ludicrous thoughts near her ear. "I don't know and I don't think they really know. But they get here and they're put in this house. And they got these really hard-looking Vietnamese kids to guard them so they don't run away. Now Thom, she pretends like she stupid and not Vietnamese. She hears these two boys talking about… well no, you tell them sweetheart."

Somewhere between disappointed and relieved, Malis asked. "We not go with him?"

"First, sweetie," Roberta coaxed, "you tell them what Thom heard."

"Okay, Thom, she Vietnamese."

Brandon grunted. "I got that."

"Thom is name in Vietnam and Khmer, my country." Malis went to take a bite of her treat and realized it was gone. With a glare to Thom, who didn't respond, she continued. "So they not know she Vietnam. They make us in house with men, bad men. They Vietnam. All time they talk. Thom talk me. Boys say they hurt Vietnam boy with gun. They say they go to store and he outside and they hurt him bad."

"What do you mean," Brandon leaned in, trying to not seem too anxious. He didn't want to scare her, "hurt him bad?"

Leaning in, Malis whispered, "They make him dead."

"Tell him about the car, baby." Roberta pushed the girl's bangs off her forehead. Once again Brandon wondered where Roberta got the motherly shit from.

"The one boy, the one he say hurt other boy sometimes he nice to us." Her voice was still soft, almost so soft Brandon couldn't hear. "We not to go outside house. He take me outside sometimes. He like me I think. He show me his friend car. I wash for friend and he give me candy."

"What did the car look like?"

"It small with lights all over." Placing her hands flat on the tabletop, she took a deep breath. "It look like this table."

That didn't quite add up in Brandon's brain. How could a car equal the Formica monstrosity between them? "Like the table?"

"The color," Roberta jumped in, "it was like the color of this table?"

"And on glass," the girl's hands rose and fell in a long wave, "*Rorng* but no Khmer."

Twice in one night; language barriers were a bitch. "I don't understand."

"Here, baby," a piece of scratch paper came from inside Roberta's pocket, "she drew it for me."

Brandon unfolded the drawing, smoothing the edges down and pinning it between his fingers. An undulating serpent, with a narrow body and dog like legs, crawled across the paper. The face wasn't more than a gaping mouth with eyes. Unlike the dragons in Chinatown, the only ones Brandon was familiar with, the thing sported a beard that stretched back to its tail. He tapped the picture and stared at Malis. "This is what it looked like?"

"Phái."

Shit, Ray could help with this again. They'd need to thoroughly interview Thom. Malis as well, but Thom would have understood what the gang actually said. He'd call Ray before he called Social Services. Hopefully, the girls would have at least some clue as to where they were living. Even if they could get the police close to the area, a stakeout might spot the people Vivian turned them on to. This would give the task force bigwigs a hard-on to beat all hard-ons. And Brandon would be the one blowing their minds.

A bump at his shoulder startled Brandon out of his plans. "Next time, closet boy," Roberta leaned into Brandon's body and purred in his ear, "when I call you, call me back. If I'm tracking your sorry ass down, I mean business."

CHAPTER TWENTY-FOUR

A summer monsoon hung over Riverside. Bruised gray clouds pissed down the back of Brandon's neck. Across the street the lights from an L-shaped motel complex twinkled through the drizzle. The overblown ambiance reminded Brandon of some B-grade, fifties romance. This was about the point where the hero usually got the girl or got offed. Brandon preferred getting laid to being killed, but he didn't expect either to actually happen. He checked his pager to make sure no one hunted for him. Technically, Brandon was on duty. Brandon had clocked out on lunch nearly an hour earlier. He should have headed back to the station twenty minutes ago. Instead, he leaned against his bike and stared at a door on the first floor.

Nicky's room.

It wasn't that hard for Brandon to find where Nicky holed up. A half-assed tail got Brandon to the right part of town. Then it was merely a matter of looking for a Miller-Meteor Endloader Hearse in various parking lots. That big, midnight-blue monstrosity stuck out like a neon sign. Especially since most people didn't want to park their cars anywhere near the classic meat-wagon. Cop savvy combined with good old fashioned con work wheedled Nicky's room number out of the desk clerk.

Nicky was already at the station when Brandon arrived on shift that afternoon. Ray made it down sometime after four, meeting with the senior detectives. Various briefings and debriefings ate up the afternoon. A few Brandon was privy to. Most he wasn't. At six, he watched Nicky head out for the evening. As long as Nicky pulled eight hours, he didn't have a set schedule. Six thirty and Brandon set out for the motel. He didn't know why, he just knew he had to.

From behind him a familiar voice laughed out, "Well, lookie what the dog left out in the yard."

Brandon turned. A see-through poncho laced with glitter covered Roberta from head to mid-thigh. Tonight, without conceding to the weather, gold-toned platforms graced her feet. Pink hot-pants and a white wrap shirt finished off the over-the-top outfit. "Oh crap." He breathed.

"Oh, crap my ass, boy, you gone off the deep end and done turned stalker?" She waved toward the motel. Brandon noted that her nails matched her shoes. She clucked her tongue against her teeth and chided, "Hanging out in front of cheap hotels. I'd worry that I was ruining some big time cop business, but I ain't never seen an unmarked Harley."

"Get lost, Roberta." He growled and shifted. "It's none of your business."

She rocked herself back on one leg and cocked her hip. "Why are you out here, getting soaked to the skin, and not with that fine boy of yours?" Batting her eyes, Roberta offered him a smile.

Brandon didn't smile back. "I said get lost."

"No, not tonight." Another shift got Brandon another hooker pose. "I'm bored, it's raining." Roberta rolled her eyes. "I ain't leaving until you come have coffee with me."

"I'm not in the mood." Looking back towards the hotel, Brandon shook his head. "And we had ice cream just the other day."

"Well, let's see." The outrageous manicure came into view. "We can go find someplace to sit down out of sight and where you can buy me some coffee or we can stand here on the street." Roberta ticked off points on gold-tipped fingers. "See, everybody in those pretty black and whites, they all know me. How many of them know you, baby? Here you are, hanging out on the street talking to a transsexual hooker… wonder what they'd all think."

"That is a low card to play."

"I know, but like I said, I'm bored and you ain't got no better place to be or you wouldn't be here. Come on, right down the street. That's the kind of place you boys in blue all use like second homes. If anyone sees us there they'll just assume its business. Your kinda business, not mine."

Mouth open to respond, Brandon caught sight of a white Jetta pulling into the lot. It parked next to the Hearse. Nicky hopped out of the passenger side. Slower and using a magazine as an impromptu umbrella, Ray got out of the car. Brandon could see Nicky laugh. He said something to Ray. Ray must have answered because he headed towards the front of the Jetta and met Nicky there. Maybe they said more things. Brandon couldn't tell. All he could see was Nicky opening the door to his room and Ray following him inside.

"Oh, Lordy." Brandon didn't even turn to the sound of Roberta's voice. All his will seeped out through soles of his boots. When Roberta hooked her arm through his and tugged, Brandon didn't resist. "Oh, baby, come on. You need that coffee now." She led him like a child down the street. He didn't even know where she was taking him. Nicky and Ray, his mind played those last few seconds like an endless porn loop. Ray and Nicky, why? It didn't make sense. She steered him through a doorway and a jumble of tables. Finally she stopped. With another, "Lordy," she shoved Brandon at a booth.

"So that's why you standing in that parking lot, moping?" Roberta undulated her six-foot-plus frame into the caramel confines of the opposite bench. One filmy shirt draped, elbow cocked on the laminate top, the other draped across the back of the seat, her Asian pattern platforms hung off the end. Fluorescents caught the sparkles imbedded in her nails as she waved Brandon into his seat. "Sit." When the waitress came Roberta ordered. "Coffee, you take yours?"

The girl's name tag said Joy. Every bit of joy looked long beaten out of her. Brandon couldn't even dredge up a smile as he dropped into the booth. "Black's fine."

"Sure is." Not even Roberta laughed at her joke. She shrugged. "He's paying and you can just bring us one of those pot thingies and lots of cream 'cause we got stuff to talk about."

"Don't tell me," Brandon stared at the table, "the hooker with a heart of gold?"

"Look, closet boy," one long finger snaked out to tap his nose. "I'm just a person, a real person who makes her money on her back. So don't you go get all high and mighty on me. If I didn't already know you, I would have just left your ass out on the street. 'Cause while I'm in here, I ain't making money. But I got an investment in you. I ain't never called that card 'cause I save my favors up for when I really need them. Someday I might need to call your sorry white ass and have you take care of something. The way you're living, it's just gonna drive you insane. And I ain't spent all this time cultivating you to have you up and blow a gasket on me."

Ray wasn't Nicky's type. And Ray had a boyfriend… they'd bought a house. What the fuck was he thinking, people cheated all the time. Enough domestic violence calls, and a cop figured that out. Roberta's words finally filtered through his thoughts. He looked up at her as the waitress set their coffee, a nicked steel carafe, and a bowl of plastic creamers on the table between them before wandering off. "You have an investment in me?"

"Yeah. I do." Roberta's smile was genuine and warm. "And I don't want to see you end up like these desperate fucks that come after me. Wifey and kiddos at home, and they out hitting the streets looking for my dick, but wanting the tits so they can pretend."

Guys like that were losers. Brandon lifted his mug then set it down without drinking. "I'm a cop, that ain't gonna happen."

"Baby, you don't think I know some of the dirty laundry of this shithole town?" Six sugars and three creams went into her coffee. As she stirred, Roberta scolded. "You think y'all are above it? Wanna know which councilman wears women's panties and likes it down and dirty?" Her spoon, dripping with coffee, came up to threaten his nose. "Who on the police force likes to suck dick? They out there baby. And they's messed up as hell and I don't want you to be one of them." She dropped the spoon and picked up her mug. With a smile, she took a deep draught. Speaking over the lip of the cup she added, "You treat me right. You don't ask me things I can't tell you. The biggest thing, baby, you treated me like I was just another girl on the street."

Why would he treat her different from any other hooker? "You are just another girl on the street." Nothing made sense, least of all Nicky and Ray.

"No, baby," Roberta caught his chin with one long nail and forced him to look at her. Brandon guessed she was pretty enough. As a guy, Robert might even have turned him on. But under the fake lashes and makeup lurked a pretty decent human being. Brandon figured it was the same for most working girls. "I'm a girl with a dick. A lot of cops don't get past that and they think that means I ain't a person, that they can do anything they want."

"Gee thanks for telling me how special I am."

"Now spill." She tickled his chin with her fingers. "I ain't in this for a lousy cup of coffee. Get it out."

Brandon shook his head. "I don't think so." The conversation wouldn't, couldn't go there. "Sharing my personal life with a hooker. No."

"Okay, look, who else you got to tell." After another gulp of coffee, Roberta poured more sugar in her cup. Brandon's stomach rolled. "You gonna hang with all the boys in the locker room and use the *she* instead of *he* routine so you get some sympathy from your gang-bang brothers?" The spoon clinked the edge of her mug as it circled. "Oh, don't look shocked. Y'all are just one big gang with badges. But you know you could do that and it'll never get out, 'cause you can't tell no one what's really going on. I know you, not well, but better, I bet, than any of those meatheads you work with."

"You know me?" Disbelief warred with sarcasm in Brandon's voice.

Carefully, she set the spoon down beside her cup. "I wouldn't even have to have our history and I'd know you. What do you think it means to be a big, black teenager who everyone is saying you so smart. And you're going to your room thinking about slitting your wrists because you ain't a five foot two waif with tits to die for and hair down to your ass? We don't care who you are inside, it's what we need you to do. It is your duty to be strong and marry some girl 'cause we need more men who can be role models for the kids." Brandon stifled the laugh that bubbled up. "Now what did I say that was funny?"

"Nothing." Remembering his own coffee, Brandon gulped it down. Lukewarm and bitter, no wonder Roberta put so much crap in hers. "Kids, role models. It's nothing."

"Oh, baby, you didn't do that to some girl did you?" Brandon didn't even have to answer the question. She must have read the truth in his face. "How many kids you got?"

"Just one. Back in my trying-to-convince-myself-I-wasn't phase."

"Uh huh." Brandon found himself smiling in response to Roberta's grin. She rested her chin on her palm and drummed out a tune on the table with her fingers. "I can see it. I bet you were one of those boys who always wanted to be a cop, huh? Were you one of those cute little explorer scouts?"

"Naw." That was laughable. Boy Scouts were dominated by Christian groups and he'd been raised as a lax Jewish kid. At least until his mom died. It wasn't until his dad married Edith that they'd got back to their roots… his dad did. Brandon never really thought about it much beyond a vague sense of identity. "I was too dark and angsty to be one."

"Oh, I can see that." Roberta leaned back, staring at him with huge brown eyes. "So you were out in the rain stalking a hotel room?"

Brandon sighed. "Nicky." She was right, who else did he have to talk to about this? No one.

"That's your boy's name," she coaxed. "Nicky?"

"Yeah. Nick, Nicholas." Pushing the cup away, Brandon scooted to the corner of the booth and mimicked Roberta's heels over the end position. "He ah, moved out… well, he never was moved in, but he was staying at my place."

"Y'all had a fight?"

"You want a prize for that deduction?" Brandon snapped. "Yeah, we had a fight. Shit, he ah, the other guys found out he works for gaming control." When she looked at him like he'd sprouted horns, Brandon realized Roberta wouldn't know what that meant. "He's a Nevada State Agent responsible for like, rigged games and shit. And we're working an angle on that kid that was shot, that there were illegal games in that place. Well, the other detectives convinced the sergeant to bring him in and help with that, and so he's been around the station a lot."

"That's hard isn't it?" Relationship sympathy from a hooker, Brandon tried to fathom how low he'd dropped. Of course, Roberta probably knew most cops better than their wives. She came into contact with more of the boys in blue than their families would. "'Cause they don't know? And he's out, huh?"

"Yeah." Brandon stared out the window. "And he just doesn't, I guess, cover, you know? Nicky doesn't think about it. So yeah, people are talking about, well, maybe he's a little light. And what the fuck am I supposed to say? I got all in one guy's face because of it, but still here's this guy staying with me in my one bedroom and everyone thinks he's gay. I told Nicky to ease it up so he gets all pissed off. And now he and Ray are hanging out."

"Ray?" Again that *I'm here for you* tone. "That's who he was with tonight?"

"Ray's a shrink, over at the campus. He and I," Brandon paused, searching for the right way to phrase it, "shit, date's not the right word."

"He's your ex?"

"Yeah, but he's Vietnamese. And we're dealing with all these kids who we can't really communicate with. I mean, most of them speak English, but we can't get into their heads. My bright idea was to have Ray talk to them."

"And then Ray started talking to your Nicky."

"Yeah, and looks like they really hit it off." Toying with the tongue of his belt, Brandon added. "Nicky and I, you know, had a fight. It wasn't just that. Lots of stuff's been going on recently. And basically, Nicky told me if I was going to be a paranoid idiot, then he'd just move into a hotel so I didn't have to pretend we weren't sleeping together."

Again she prompted him. "And…"

"And, I went over there tonight, I don't know, maybe to see if I couldn't fix it. And there's Ray going into Nicky's room."

"So you gonna just let your ex-boyfriend steal your new boyfriend?"

"Look, Nicky wants a life." Brandon shrugged. "He wants to hang out, go to parties, clubs, and whatever, but he wants to be open about it. I ain't open about it. No romantic dinners. No holding hands walking down the street. It's just not gonna happen. Time he figured that out. Ray's a good guy. He'll give Nicky that. Nicky deserves that."

"He told you that?"

"No, no he didn't. I just know. I can see it."

"You can see it? Boy, you can't see anything but the back of that door you been staring at for years. You in the midst of a fucking pity-party. Y'all did a stupid ass thing, and you don't want to try and fix it because it's just too damn hard. You'd have to admit you fucked up. Well, baby, news to you, you fucked up. Don't you dare fuck it up more. 'Cause if you don't go and tell that boy why you all put out, he is gonna leave your sorry white ass. And then you'll deserve it. Get your head outta your ass and go over there and crawl. Beg. Whine. Whatever you got to do. 'Cause the only time I ever seen you not bouncing like a freaking crack-head was when you were around that boy. He's good for you in ways you don't even understand."

"You have no freaking clue what you're talking about." He could feel the heat rising up his neck. "What, you think you know me? You're life's so fucking good that you can give me advice?"

"See, you're mad… that means I'm right."

"Fuck." Brandon muttered and tossed back more nasty coffee to mask his agitation.

Roberta stared at him for a bit. Finally, she asked, "Do you love him?"

"He's Nicky." Drawing little patterns in the wet ring left by his cup, Brandon tried not to think too hard. "He's like my best friend."

Slower this time, she repeated. "Do you love him?"

"Yeah." He ran his hand through his hair. "Yeah, I love him."

"Have you told him that?"

"Nicky knows how I feel."

"So you haven't told him." Roberta added a few tisks to punctuate the statement. "Look detective, sometimes people need to hear the words. Your Nicky needs to hear you say it."

"So you're a shrink now?"

"No, baby, I'm a hooker. For some guys that's the same thing." Roberta's laugh echoed through the diner. Brandon dropped an inch down in the booth in case anyone looked. "Like I said before, I like you. You're good people. I don't want to be reading about you in the paper. How you ate your own gun and everyone is calling it a 'cleaning mishap' 'cause no one wants to say another cop blew his goddamn head off."

He snorted. "That ain't gonna happen."

"That or you'll be one of those liquored up, washed up officers. You know the ones, they drink so heavy, even when they sober you can smell the booze in their sweat."

"What," Brandon stared at the stained ceiling, "if he doesn't want to hear it?"

"What if he does?" That woman could convince a frog to fly. "What if that's all it took? Is it worth it, baby? This not saying anything 'cause you might get hurt?"

"I don't think…"

"Don't think, do. Just go. Knock on that door, tell that sweet brown thing you can't live without him. Turn off the brain and just do it." Flipping her hands like she was shaking them dry, she ordered, "Go now, coffee's on me, 'cause you need to run." When Brandon hesitated, Roberta pointed to the door and ordered, "Get! Before I decide to go all hormonal on you. Don't think I can't whoop your little bubble butt."

Brandon slid out of the booth. "Yes, ma'am." He smirked. Knocking one of her platforms with his knee, Brandon added, "Thanks."

"Somebody's got to save your white ass." Shooing him off, Roberta grinned up at him. "You go on. And don't you be telling no one that I'm nice or nothing."

At least now, if anyone asked, he could stretch the truth and say he had to meet an informant. "I wouldn't dream of it." The last he saw of Roberta, she was dumping another six sugars in her coffee. Damn shit would rot her teeth out. He stepped out of a muggy diner into a muggy evening. If anything, the rain came down heavier. As he trudged toward the hotel, Brandon wondered where the theme music was. He needed to know if he was heading towards the big happy -reunion moment or crashing into oblivion. A weight lifted when Brandon realized that Ray's Jetta was gone. Crashing into a make-out scene… he didn't even want to think about that.

Brandon's resolve almost failed him at the door. From deep in his memories, he dredged up a recollection. An old patrol officer, Wise or Wisse or something, wearing a rumpled uniform and blue circles under his eyes. You knew it was lunch when he came back weaving. His wife had left him. His girlfriend had left him. One day he drove out to the desert and shot himself… *accidentally*, twice. Brandon was not going to be him.

After a deep breath and then another, Brandon knocked on the door. He counted to ten and no one answered. Well, hell, maybe they'd stopped by to pick something up and then headed out. Palming his face, Brandon tried to keep the world from crashing down around him. There was always tomorrow. Brandon reminded himself of that as he turned away. Crash and burn music it was.

Behind him the door snicked open. He turned to find Nicky in jeans and nothing else. Water dripped from his hair and beaded on Nicky's shoulder. Oh crap, now he'd actually have to say something. Jamming his hands into his pockets, Brandon mumbled out a, "Hey, Nicky."

Nicky stared. "Are you stalking me or something?"

Fuck, technically he was. Avoiding an admission he didn't want to make, Brandon asked his own question. "Can't I just talk to you?

"Go home, Brandon." Nicky growled.

He should ask how Nicky'd been. Or maybe, he could tell him how lonely it was at night. Instead, Brandon's mouth opened and an accusation framed as a question spilled out. "What were you doing with Ray?" That's not where he'd wanted to start this conversation.

Another long, hard stare answered him. "Having dinner." Nicky crossed his arms over his dark chest and leaned against the doorframe.

Brandon shuffled uncomfortably. "Why?"

"Because eating alone in this dump sucks." Like he couldn't believe Brandon had to ask, Nicky rolled his eyes and looked away. "And, I don't know, maybe because I need to be with some other gay guys who actually act like gay guys."

"Goddamn it, Nicky, this is so hard for me."

That snapped Nicky's attention to him. "So hard for you? For you!" He spat. "Fuck you, Brandon! You drag me into a case, get me fucking assigned to it, in the middle of fucking Riverside so I can't even go home. You fuck up our relationship, not once but twice in as many weeks. You try," his tone dropped to a low-voiced hiss, "every moment I'm here, to get me to drag myself into a closet I've never been in. What the hell is hard for you about this?"

"Can't I," Brandon didn't want to have this conversation in the parking lot, "come in and talk to you?" Really, he didn't want to have the conversation at all, but he needed to have it. It galled him that Roberta was right.

"No, I'm pretty good with seeing you miserable in the rain." Nicky sneered. "It fits somehow. Little wet puppy at my door begging to come in."

"You're really getting off on this, huh?"

A tight, sarcastic sneer told Brandon he'd hit it dead on. "Immensely."

"Please." If he had to, he'd beg. "I don't want to talk about this out here."

"Too bad." Nicky shifted, staring at Brandon. Water dripped into Brandon's eyes and he brushed it away with the back of his hand. "You want to say something to me, you can say it from out there."

"Look," he swallowed his pride, "I'm sorry I overreacted.

Nicky laughed. "You think? You're the one who seems to have a problem with me being gay. No one else at the station seems to give a rat's ass except you."

It was time to come clean or at least a reasonable facsimile of it. "Look, I got into it with another detective," Brandon paused hoping for effect, "about you. I got my ass chewed by my Sarge because I called it like I saw it. He pissed me off, what he said about you. I've never stood up to anything like that. I blew." A deep breath and Brandon continued. "It scared me. I realize you want to have a real queer lifestyle, not be stuck with some guy who acts like he's straight. I don't know if I can give that to you, Nicky."

The sneer dropped into a sad smile. "Brandon, there is no one way to be gay." Nicky uncrossed his arms and ran one hand up through his hair.

"Fuck, it… I've really got us both fucked up, huh?" Brandon had never been that close to an apology before. It felt weird.

"Just a little."

Brandon tried again. "Can I come in now?"

"Depends," Nicky held up his left hand, index and middle fingers spread in a V, "do you know the two words?"

Forgiven, he was forgiven. He saw it in Nicky's eyes. "Sorry?" Brandon whispered, just in case he got it wrong.

"Well that's close enough to one of them, I'll let the other slide for now." Nicky stepped away from the door and walked toward the bed. Motioning for Brandon to follow, he added, "Get your ass in here before you get sniffly or something." Nicky flopped onto the mattress.

Gingerly, Brandon eased himself onto the edge. He reached out and ran his hand along Nicky's arm. It felt so good to touch him. "Look, I keep thinking." God, he didn't think he could miss someone so much in just two days. The hurt of not having Nicky around was damn near physical. "I'm going to be thirty in two months, I'm still a closet case and I don't see that ever ending." Not so long as he was a cop, and Brandon figured that would be until he died. "Before you met me, you lived the same kind of life Ray does. Not really, but you know, out, open, not looking over your shoulder. Going on dates and dinner and movies and shit." Nicky's skin tickled his fingertips. It was electric. "I can't give that to you, Nicky. So I'm looking at you two together." The admission made Nicky raise his eyebrows. Realizing he deserved a lot of shit for that, Brandon continued. "I saw him bring you back here, and I wondered what the fuck I got that you want?" He pulled his hand back and rubbed his thighs through his jeans. "Nothing. I ain't got nothing to offer a guy like you."

"Brandon," leaning over, Nicky stilled the nervous stroking with a touch of his hand, "the first time I met you, you told me you weren't out."

"Actually, I think I told you sometime after that."

"Well, yeah," Nicky chuckled, "we were kinda screwing our brains out the first few hours. What I mean is, I knew going into this, that that was part of it. It's real hard sometimes to deal with. I think you'd be happier if you'd let that fear go, but it's not my life. And whatever your life is, I like being part of it."

"You want to come home?" Brandon didn't dare look up.

"Are you asking me to?"

"Yeah," sandwiching Nicky's hand between his, Brandon nodded, "come home with me."

"On one condition."

"What?"

"Don't make me hide, too." The pressure as Nicky squeezed his grip reassured Brandon in a thousand little ways. Nicky would try it again. Brandon promised himself he'd be better, try not to be so paranoid. "I'm claustrophobic. How you survive in that closet, I have no clue."

"Okay." Brandon looked at Nicky. Night-black eyes smiled back at him. Nicky was better than he deserved. "The investigation is almost over anyway." He said that more for his own benefit than Nicky's. "We'll wrap it up and things will go back to how they were between us."

"Probably not, I've seen enough of what you're going through." Brushing against Brandon's earrings, Nicky sat up and moved in close. Brandon could smell the hotel soap. Somewhere under it, hiding, was the scent of Nicky. "Look, one of the reasons I left early is to talk about it with Ray." Even if Nicky holding a heart-to-heart with his ex disturbed him, having Nicky that close again comforted Brandon. "Honestly, I never thought about *why* you are like you are. I just assumed you'd just have the normal fears about coming out. Ray told me about some of the cops he's known and how they treated him. The bigots. The assholes." Nicky pulled him in and pressed their temples together. "It must be really hard working with guys like that."

"It is." Brandon drew in a ragged breath. Nicky would never really know, but at least he tried to understand. "It really, really is."

Chapter Twenty-Five

Double rows of white laminate desks marched across rosy-brown carpet toward the front of the room. Chalkboards and whiteboards held scribbled schematics of various buildings. Detailed planning for the bust started days ago. Photos from the ground and the air littered the tables. The recon team brought surveillance video from the day before, and an officer messed with the video player up front. Tape marked floor plans of the target houses spread across the back parking lot. Rehearsals of the entry team had been in progress when Brandon and Nicky hit the station. Hours of preparation for a few minutes of action. The goal was to saturate the house before the occupants knew what hit them. The motley assortment of uniformed and plainclothes officers filled the briefing room to near bursting. A tense buzz vibrated through the room. Out of the crowd, a third maybe were task force members. Brandon recognized many of them from meetings over the past four weeks.

Besides Riverside regulars, Sheriffs from two counties and even a couple Feds were present. SWAT teams from Riverside, Indio, and San Bernardino made appearances as part of the plan. The possibility of something going bad jumped exponentially with the presence of the gang. At each stage, the investigation grew beyond the borders of the city. While it was still Riverside PD's show, they didn't have the authority to bust a house outside the city limits. And the girls – the ones like Malis and Thom – human rights violations needed the reach of the good ol' US of A. This would be round one. From here, who knew where the Feds would take it. Round one was good enough for Brandon.

He shifted over as Nicky dropped into the seat next to his. "This is what it's all about, huh? Why you get so jazzed about the insanity?" Nicky teased. "Maybe I'll call my boss after this and tell him I'm not coming back… Riverside's too exciting."

Laughing as Brandon's shoulder's tensed, Nicky added. "Naw, I do miss *my* job." He looked up and Brandon turned slightly to catch Weaver at his other shoulder. The older detective popped Brandon's bicep with his fist before settling his bulk in another chair. Nicky leaned in over the desk and propped his chin on his fist. "Sitting with the cool kids today?" It hit Brandon. God, it was almost a month, an entire month of being on the task force and being with Nicky. Sometimes it boggled Brandon how such a large portion of his life could be compressed into a small amount of time.

"I figure if I hang out with you two, some of that dumb beginner's luck following this idiot around," Weaver slapped Brandon's back, "might rub off on me."

Luck his ass, Brandon worked the case hard. "It ain't luck." Glowering at his partner, Brandon rocked his chair onto the back legs and crossed his arms over his chest. Damned if he'd let Weaver steal his thunder. "It's having the right contacts."

"It is luck," Weaver's derisive huff said it all, "*and* having the right contacts."

Leaning in, Nicky whispered. "Is it the luck of the Irish or the swish that you want?" Weaver choked and Brandon had to stop himself from popping Nicky one. But he'd made a promise. He wasn't Nicky. Nicky wasn't him. Luckily, so far his lover had kept his promise to hold things low key. Now Brandon just had to work on the not being overly paranoid part. Not the easiest thing in the world when he'd lived it for nearly a decade. Brandon squelched it down and settled for a nasty glare. It felt completely ineffectual and a little juvenile.

"Actually, I'm going to say it and then I'm going to hate myself." With a heavy sigh, Weaver twisted to face Brandon. "Thanks to you, Carr, they've managed to pinpoint a couple of the hubs to their little shithole operation."

Suspicious, Brandon prodded, "What do you mean thanks to me?"

"You gave the force the people we needed to solve this. There's no way, with our resources, we could have gotten that deep into the computers so quick. Your bud, Nick, the shit he does with those machines, fucking amazing. And the shrink, I'm not much into those witch doctor, mental health guys, but he got through to them. The Vo kid, the two baby hookers, even the convenience store clerk; they all came through. We got warrants based on a lot of that crap. The info spun us off into a dozen different locals." A tight smile cracked Weaver's face. "Nobody's ever going to say it. People are going to steal your thunder. You'll get hosed on the credit. You will know though. That's what you take to your bed every night, got it? When everyone else has forgotten, you'll remember, Nick will remember, and I'll remember."

Brandon stared. That was the most direct, hell, the most encouragement, he'd ever heard out of his partner's yap. As he opened his mouth to snark back, the door banged open.

A booming voice heralded the entry of the lieutenant in charge. "All righty now, people." Beaming from one dark ear to the other, he swept into the room. He clapped his hands and the room snapped to attention. "We're all here to get ready for a walk in the park tomorrow." With a nod to the Feds in attendance, he continued. "We know where we're going. By now you know why we're here or y'all don't belong in this room." Nervous laughter rolled across the crowd. "What we've found is that our players are into a little bit of everything. Minor in drug trafficking, maybe, but in no way rivaling the Hispanic or African American gangs around here. However, they seem to be moving a ton of remarked and mismarked computer equipment." The man nodded towards Nicky, and Brandon felt a surge of pride.

"They act as guard dogs for human trafficking. Hopefully, when we hit that, there'll be a few bigger fish smoked out. Obviously this little gang didn't bring 'em over, but they have contacts who did. We've got names of contacts from the computer investigation. Some confidential informants have come forward and given us details that correlate with other avenues we've uncovered. Y'all did good." He spread his hands. "So, I'm turning you over to your various assignments for core briefings. Remember there will be observers with us. So, my task force junkies, get your assignments. Take off. Go home.

Sleep if you can. We're hitting them at five in the morning so we'll need you here by three for staging. We want to get those bangers when they've only had a couple hours sleep."

Breaking out into smaller groups, Brandon found himself with Nicky, and some of the gang unit he recognized. They'd been assigned to a team headed by a Riverside regular named Schafer. Black uniform and tactical patches on his sleeves told them he was a SWAT veteran.

"While we'll go in first and do a clear, there's too much space, too many locals, and not enough men for SWAT to do it all." Riverside SWAT numbered twenty-four officers, and only eight of those lived, breathed, and ate SWAT. The rest could be called up on an as-needed basis. "So here's the drill. Hold onto each other. Three man teams, each man holding the belt or shoulder webbing of the man in front. Don't let go. We assume it'll be active shooter conditions. They want to take us out rather than go down themselves. We have unarmed LEO personnel on this team," a nod to Nicky acknowledged his status, "and he will be assigned to a two man protective team." Schafer reached out and slapped a rookie and his training officer on the shoulders. Brandon couldn't argue with that decision. The rookie was too green to go into the hot spot. Still, he would rather have Nicky with him.

Looking the rookie dead in the eye, Schafer hammered his point. "You are to stay back and not involve yourself until we have cleared the target of suspects. Our warrant specifies we are looking for the usual drugs, paraphernalia, and weapons. However, computer parts, software, CD burner towers—whatever the hell those are—blank disks, labels, anything that can be used to repackage and remarket computer goods." A jab in Nicky's direction spelled it out. "That is what this gentleman is for. Our target is pegged as the hub of the black market tech operation. If you do not know what it is for, whether it can be used in the manufacture, reproduction or illegal distribution of computer parts, you ask him." Schafer smiled at Nicky. "So how big are the parts we're looking for?"

"Well everything from your standard computer case," Nicky marked out a six inch by two foot, by three foot box in the air, "to micro-processors... so about the size of a postage stamp."

Big grins spread across the faces of the team. Schafer rubbed his hands. "Okay, men, you know what that means. We got authority, between the drugs and the tech, to justifiably search anywhere and everywhere." After that bit, their briefing proceeded uneventfully. Reviewing safety protocol and determining who went with who took up some time. Split off from his partner and Nicky, Brandon got hooked up with a set of uniforms. Arguably, the patrol officers were a bit more up on their tactical maneuvers. Often detectives didn't hit a scene until the shit had already hit the proverbial fan.

Brandon checked and rechecked his gear once they were done. Detectives, however, traveled light so he had to scrounge a few things to gear himself up. Gone were the days of a twenty-pound duty belt rigged for every contingency. Schafer hustled Nicky off to find him a Kevlar vest, which took the better part of an hour. By the time he was back, Brandon was packed and ready to ride.

Wind whipped the words out of their mouths on the Harley. That pretty much killed conversation. Back at home, Brandon tossed his bag on the couch and began another comb-through of assorted stuff. Vest, radio, and tactical helmet had all been issued to him for the raid. His own pistol would be his only sidearm, but Brandon figured he'd wear the military surplus BDUs he kept for low-key club wear. Extra pockets would come in handy for clips and such. The uniformed officers carried rifles instead of their normally issued shotguns. The department frowned on shooting your own...far more likely with the scatter pattern of a shotgun.

Nicky landed on the couch next to Brandon. "Aren't you excited?" Equipment rolled off onto the floor. Nicky vibrated like a crack-head. Well, Brandon knew how he felt. He remembered his first big bust. He'd been jittery and high-strung for days before his first raid.

Still, it bugged him. He needed to back it down and Nicky amped him up. "Well, yeah, but I know I need to relax."

Brandon masked his irritation by bending down to retrieve the wayward things.

"How can you relax?"

Things were as good as could be managed. Brandon stuffed the kit back into his duty bag. "I usually have to relax myself." Well, there was always sleeping pills. Maybe he'd dump a couple of his prescription sleeping pills into Nicky's soda and make him crash.

"Relax yourself?" Leaning in, Nicky whispered, "Any particular methods?" Nicky smelled like adrenalin. It drifted off his skin and danced through Brandon's senses.

Jeans going tight, Brandon shifted to relieve the pressure. He could think of ten other things he'd rather do to relieve the pressure. Any one of those ten would probably relax him. "You mean, like the good old one-handed massage?"

Lazing into the corner of the couch, Nicky grinned at him. "You know you did good today?" He nudged Brandon's knee with his own.

Brandon would much rather have the one handed massage than a compliment. It drove him nuts how Nicky's moods could shift so quickly. "Like how?" he growled.

Nicky reached across and walked his fingers up Brandon's arm. "You didn't completely freak out when I fucked with Weaver." God, he liked it when Nicky touched him. The touch almost made up for the earlier shit. A few more minutes of contact and Brandon might forgive him.

"I completely freaked out," his growl didn't even convince himself, "but bit my tongue."

Up and across, Nicky straddled Brandon's lap. A hard cock to match his aching prick rubbed against him. Nicky rocked forward, brushing his lips. Slow, but demanding, Nicky nipped along Brandon's jaw. He blew in Brandon's ear and the cop shuddered. "Oh, that's what the muffled screaming next to me was all about?"

"Bite me." Brandon grumbled. When Brandon slid his hands over Nicky's ass, his lover bit his ear. "Ow." Brandon yelped, bucking against Nicky's hips. It rubbed them together.

Nicky and biting… one of his things. "You insisted."

Brandon groaned as Nicky sucked on the bruised skin. "I'm going to have to work it out of your system, huh?" Brandon grazed his knuckles along Nicky's spine. "Or I'm not going to get any sleep?"

Nicky arched into the stroke exposing his lean, brown neck. "Pretty much." As he moved, his hands snaked down and tugged Brandon's belt loose. He popped the buttons on Brandon's fly. One warm, strong hand worked under Brandon's shorts and stroked him. Nicky's palm caressed his prick.

"You're so bad for me, Nicky." He managed to get it out without sounding too desperate.

"No, baby," Nicky gazed down at him. His eyes were positively predatory. "I'm good for you." Brandon was so hot for Nicky when he got like that. Well, Brandon was hot for him damn near anytime. That kinda look burrowed into his core and set Brandon's nerves screaming.

Brandon hissed. "You're good to me."

Nicky put his hand on Brandon's chest. "That too." With Brandon's cock wrapped in his hand, Nicky slowly jerked him. Brandon fumbled with Nicky's jeans. The button and zipper were almost beyond him as distracted as he was. Still, he managed to get it all undone. Then Brandon slid his hand under the denim. Nicky was so hot and hard. Warm silk slid in his grip. Nicky hissed and squeezed Brandon's cock. "What say we head for the bedroom?" With that, he released Brandon's cock and slid off his lap.

"What's in the bedroom?" Brandon struggled to stand.

Backing towards the bedroom, Nicky beckoned with his hands for Brandon to follow. Pulling his shirt over his head as he turned, Nicky added. "Condoms, lube." Nicky paused, tossed the shirt somewhere into the bedroom, and stared at

Brandon over his shoulder. "Rope." Then he resumed walking, or at least trying to. He had to stop twice to take off his boots.

Brandon was off the couch. "You had me at the condoms and lube." Shirt, boots, jeans; it all came off in the rapid, awkward dance toward the bedroom. "The rope just makes it special."

"See, rope," Nicky stepped over to the dresser and began pulling lengths of colored rope from his duffle, "plus headboard equals tying up." He sorted through them. Brandon shucked his shorts as Nicky added, "Now, aren't you glad I bought you a bed with a headboard."

"I thought you were just being nice to me." Brandon flopped on the bed, his hands folded behind his head and waited. Nicky moved about the room collecting bits. So sexy, Brandon could watch him like that forever. Lean muscles moved under that warm skin. "I didn't realize you had ulterior motives." When Nicky turned and smiled back at Brandon, his heart raced. It wasn't because of the sex or that Nicky was hot… Brandon couldn't get a bead on why Nicky's smiles hit him so hard.

Three sections of silky black rope dangled over Nicky's forearm as he walked to the bed. Another, much longer bit of red cord looped over his shoulder. The rope fascinated him so much that Brandon barely took note of the tube and box Nicky dumped on the nightstand. "I always have ulterior motives." Only one other thing held Brandon's attention. That dark V of skin flashing where Nicky's jeans gaped sent shivers up his back. The head of Nicky's cock poked over the waistband. Brandon wanted to reach out and yank the material off his hips.

Instead he watched Nicky take each length of black cord, fold it in half and lay it on the bed. Against the red sheets the effect was dramatic. "Why do you always do it like that?"

"Like what?" Nicky raised his eyebrows and slid the red rope off his shoulder.

Brandon swallowed. "So slow and, I don't know, so…"

"Ritualistic?" Nicky finished the thought for him. Soft thuds sounded as the ends of the rope hit the floor. Nicky ran it through his fingers, gauging the length and folding it into fourths. "Isn't that all part of it? The sensuality of the rope, the anticipation; aren't those just as important?"

"I guess."

Nicky sat on the edge of the bed. He ran his hand over Brandon's bare thigh. "It's like a form of meditation in sex." Moving from Brandon's leg to his arm, Nicky wrapped his hand around Brandon's forearm. With the other hand, he grabbed one of the sections of black rope. "Ritual submission." The loop draped over Brandon's wrist and Nicky fed the ends through it. Then he pulled it tight. "Letting me own you." Using the cord to hold Brandon's arm, Nicky caught his free hand. He brought the two together and looped the rope over that wrist. Then he wound it over and under three times in a figure eight pattern. Once that was done, Nicky wrapped a few turns around the center, tightening the rope. He tied it off and pushed Brandon back. "Lay down."

A little awkward, Brandon scooted down and managed to lay on his back. Nicky's fingers walked along his sternum. Brandon tensed and Nicky laughed. "What are you planning?"

"For me to know," Nicky grinned, "and you to experience." He dragged the red rope up Brandon's body. The nap caught Brandon's skin and gave him chills. When he got to Brandon's chest, Nicky let the rope pool. He reached down and took hold of Brandon's bound hands. Pulling them up, Nicky looped the red cord over where the black met between Brandon's hands. He slid the ends through the loop and then back under and through itself again to make a knot. With the rope as a lead, Nicky pulled Brandon's arms above his head.

Brandon couldn't see exactly what was happening, but it felt like Nicky was tying him to the posts in the headboard. "Kinda thought the bed was a little fem when I saw it." His fingers brushed the wrought iron bars. "I get it now. There was method to your madness."

Nicky rocked back. He stared down at Brandon and teased. "Yeah, you'll get it." Once the rope was secure, he threaded the ends around the back of the bed. They ended up along the outside edge of the mattress on opposite sides of Brandon's body.

Brandon's prick ached. It stood damn near straight up and begged for a touch. Nicky ran one finger in the pre-cum pooling on the crown. Little shocks wicked down the shaft and through Brandon's balls. "Shit." Brandon hissed. "What are you going to do with the rest of the rope?"

"You," Nicky covered his throbbing head with one hand. Chiding with words and actions, he growled, "ask too many damn questions," as he squeezed. "If you don't stop, I'll have to gag you." Then he smirked. "Maybe I should just gag you anyways." Brandon groaned. "That sounds like a yes to me." Nicky slid off the bed. Two steps got him to the chest of drawers. Nicky's small black duffle sat on top, the one filled with various ropes.

Brandon rolled his head and watched Nicky's butt flex under his jeans as he walked. The movement twisted his arms and pulled his shoulders. Brandon savored the feel of being tied up. He jerked his bound arms a couple of times. Not because he had any desire to get free, but just to remind himself of the binding. The rope bit into his wrists. Not hard, but definitely enough for him to feel it. Another moan rose through his chest. Brandon didn't even try to stifle it.

A chuckle sounded from Nicky's general vicinity. After rummaging in the bag, Nicky came up with a line of red and black braid. He turned and rested his ass against the dresser. One end of the thin rope held in his fist, Nicky looped it, brought it up to hang over his thumb. The other end dropped to the floor. Wrapping the rope tightly over the folds, Nicky advanced on Brandon. A small loop was left at the beginning. When he reached the opposite end, Nicky threaded the end used for the binding through the top loop. Finally, he tugged the smaller loop, drawing the other loop tight over the ends of the rope. The two ends he tied together before dangling the whole mess over Brandon's face. It left something that looked vaguely like a hangman's noose.

Nicky crawled up on the bed and straddled Brandon's chest. He held the rope gag down. Unable to resist the pressure against his lips, or the want in his hips, Brandon opened his mouth. Threading the long end under Brandon's head to pass it through the loop, Nicky licked his lips. "Now, where were we before you had to be gagged?" Some knotwork by Brandon's ear snugged the rope-bit down. "Oh, yeah." He smirked. "Tying you up."

Wriggling back down, Nicky stopped at Brandon's hips. He thrust, grinding his crotch against Brandon's cock. The denim and zipper scraped sensitive skin and Brandon sucked in his breath with a hiss. With every bump, Brandon got a fleeting taste of skin. He shuddered. He wanted to beg Nicky to fuck or suck him or anything that was more than what he got. All he could manage was a strangled gasp around the rope gag.

Apparently satisfied with the reaction, Nicky edged off Brandon. He sat down on the bed and drew one of the remaining black cords through his fist. Again a loop folded at mid point started the tie. Nicky slid the fold under Brandon's thigh. He passed the ends through the loop, under the cord again and knotted it. Then he pushed Brandon's leg up so it was bent at the knee. Another figure eight tie between thigh and calf bound his leg. "That," Nicky purred, "is called a tower tie." He moved to the other leg and repeated the process.

Brandon raised his head off the bed. Looking down his own body, he could see his swollen prick straining between his bent legs. The position canted them out away from his pelvis. He was open and vulnerable to Nicky like that. It made him tremble. He didn't like to give up control, but he needed to. Nicky knew that. And Nicky was the only one he'd go this far with. Pure and simple, he trusted Nicky. He trusted Nicky more than he trusted himself sometimes.

Running his hands over Brandon's inner thighs, Nicky devoured him with those dark eyes. He eased off the side of the bed. The spot he chose forced Brandon to strain to see him. With a wicked smile gracing that strong-featured brown face, Brandon had no doubt that's what Nicky intended. Both hands slipped into his jeans. He cupped his crotch under the denim and his eyes drifted shut.

Crap, Nicky had to be playing with his cock and balls. Brandon wanted to see it. Nicky likely knew that and was torturing him with the tease. After a few minutes, Nicky opened his eyes. Nicky used the back of his wrists to push the denim off his hips. The beautiful, porn star sized prick revealed itself. Brandon groaned. He loved Nicky's prick like nothing else. Long and broad enough to spread him good. It was as dark as the rest of him. Veins laced the shaft. The thick red head throbbed and a crystal bead of cum glistened at the tip. Nicky shucked his jeans.

He stepped out of the denim pooled at his ankles and reached for the nearest end of red rope. That he forced behind Brandon's knee. Letting the rope scrape Brandon's skin, Nicky pulled the end back toward the headboard. It forced Brandon's leg up and back, straining his hip joint. Although intense, it wasn't truly painful. Nicky caught Brandon's foot with his hip, holding him in place. A wrap around the center of the tower-tie, instead of around the knee itself, meant the joint wouldn't be unduly strained. A quick release knot tied Brandon back.

Nicky's cock bobbed enticingly as he walked around the bed. It was hard for Brandon to follow his progress. Every move strained his joints or tugged at another muscle. Still, he tried. Besides the sexy man circling him, the feel of the ropes was a reward. No one other than Nicky could keep him helpless like this. Even Weaver, his partner, who he trusted with his life… well, he didn't trust him like Nicky. He didn't just rely on someone to assist him; Brandon put his entire well being into Nicky's hands. This was absolute blind faith. And he had that faith in Nicky.

Nicky slid the other end of rope behind Brandon's opposite knee. Again, he pushed and tied Brandon's leg back. Brandon's hips rolled and lifted his butt off the bed. The binding held him spread wide. His cock pulsed against his belly. Brandon closed his eyes and shuddered. A few twists reminded him of the ties. Not that he could forget. The physical sensation, like a lover's rough kiss, against his skin made him ache. His tongue toyed with the coiled rope between his lips. He could be as much of a slut as he wanted like this, because, after all, Brandon wasn't in control. What did Nicky think when he watched Brandon like this? Did he like how Brandon just gave into his feelings? Considering that Nicky usually got rock hard when he tied Brandon up, Brandon figured it turned Nicky on.

Brandon jumped and hissed as cool liquid hit the skin between his balls and his ass. His eyes flew open. Nicky had one leg up on the bed. The other hung off the edge. He smiled and dropped the lube somewhere beyond Brandon's line of sight. Sheathed, Nicky's prick reared up from the thick black fur between his legs. Anticipation frayed Brandon's nerves until he almost shook. Nicky slid his fingers through the gel and teased Brandon's hole. Slowly he tickled the opening. It felt so good, even if it wasn't enough. Brandon squirmed. Caught up in the rope, that was all he could manage.

Forever ticked by as Nicky teased him with light touches. Time, responsibility, and fear ceased to have any real meaning. Brandon stared at Nicky… his Nicky. Brandon would kill anyone who tried to take Nicky from him. That realization scared the hell out of him. He wanted to be with Nicky. He wanted a future with Nicky.

Finally, Nicky knelt between Brandon's legs. He took his slicked cock in his hand and pressed it against Brandon's ass. With Brandon trussed, Nicky didn't even have to hold him. The only contact was that thick head brushing his hole. Nicky pushed, fighting the resistance with nothing but his prick. The only place he could fight was with the muscles of his ass. Brandon's body tried. Slow, but insistent, Nicky's cock breached Brandon, forced him open. Brandon gasped as Nicky slid home. He was so full.

Brandon's bonds prevented him from reaching out. Only where their bodies joined did Nicky touch him. Nicky rammed into Brandon, rocking him. The ropes pulled at his arms and legs. With his hips tilted up, Nicky nailed him on every thrust. He moaned into the gag. The slap of Nicky's hips against his ass drove that big cock deep inside. Muscles trembling, Brandon lost himself in the sensation. Heat ate through him. He was nothing but a mass of nerves.

Nicky grunted out Brandon's name. The word, how he said it, so desperate and needy, sent chills racing into Brandon's dick. It felt like the skin of his prick would split at any moment. Nicky's pounding became frantic. When he reached down and grabbed Brandon's cock, Brandon screamed. The gag muffled the sound. His senses churned. His entire being collapsed into his balls. Brandon yelled out at each stroke. Then the fire burned up through his cock. Jet after jet of white spunk splattered his chest and chin. Brandon trembled. He would have collapsed, but the ropes held him tight. A few more thrusts and Nicky tensed. The cock in Brandon's ass got hotter and thicker. "Brandon." Nicky hissed as he came.

Panting, Nicky dropped forward. His arms landed on either side of Brandon's chest. Nicky smiled and reached to undo the gag. As the knot gave, the bit rolled from Brandon's mouth. His tongue was dry and he swallowed trying to get some spit going. Otherwise, he was completely relaxed. Brandon stared into that dark-eyed gaze. He took a deep breath. "Goddamn, Nicky." What was there to fear when Nicky was with him? "I love you, you bastard." The words were wrapped up in a contented sigh.

Then it hit him, what he'd said. Oh Shit. Brandon swallowed hard. Nicky came closer, almost nose to nose. His eyes were so intense, Brandon could hardly stand it. He shuddered as Nicky cupped his face in his hands… held him, stared at him. A soft and deep smile lit up his face. When Nicky kissed him, Brandon felt just how much Nicky needed to hear him say it.

CHAPTER TWENTY-SIX

Across the car, Brandon sat staring out the tinted window. A rifle, barrel pointed toward the roof of the Crown Vic, rested on his knee. Other than the sleeves of his black T-shirt, Brandon's upper body was encased in a bulky flack jacket. A gunmetal gray riot helmet rested between his feet. Black military surplus BDUs, combat boots, and the high and tight haircut made him seem rather sexy and dangerous. Well, Brandon always looked sexy. The dangerous part added a decidedly delicious edge to Nick's thoughts.

Six people in total jammed the sedan; five rather large men and one petite district attorney named Sajani Shakya. All of them wore riot gear similar to Brandon's, even Nick and the attorney. Badges tucked into a clear pocket on the front let everyone know they meant business. Nick never realized district attorneys were issued badges.

Headlights barely cut through an early morning haze. Every so often Nick caught a glimpse of the SWAT van in front or the cars behind. The vehicles were stuffed with cops, all of them outfitted in raid gear. Adrenaline and anticipation, cut with a healthy dose of fear, ran thick in the car. It sharpened Brandon's cologne, gave it a heady undercurrent. Nick shifted and hoped the DA didn't catch a gander of his woody. Brandon had teased him earlier about bust-rush. Now Nick understood what he meant.

Shakya sat between Nick and Brandon reviewing the warrants. At least that gave them some breathing room. The three men up front knocked shoulders and knees. As they neared the target house, the radio crackled. "Team four is almost to the target," echoed through the unmarked. Nick wasn't sure, but he suspected someone in the lead vehicle sought information. "Is there any change in status?" Lookouts positioned just after midnight watched the various locals for activity. Like any good paramilitary operation, they required surprise. Surprise required up to the minute information.

"No, no change in status." The lookout hissed back, her voice muffled in an effort not to call attention to her position. "The house is dark; there are two cars in the drive."

Shit, it was really happening. Brandon grabbed his helmet off the floor and Nick's nerves jangled in response. How everyone else maintained such calm demeanors escaped him. "Ten-four that," broke over the air. "Has there been any activity?"

"Negative. Nothing since around the time we came on scene." The officer's disembodied voice reassured. After a pause she added, "Thirteen forty-five, one Asian male and an elderly Asian female entered the target. No other activity since that time."

"Ten-four. Thanks for the update." Nick snorted. Shakya looked up from her papers. Pausing as he buckled the helmet's strap under his chin, Brandon glared at him. Shaking his head Nick brushed off his outburst. Really, he'd never thought that cops would be so damn polite to each other over the air. Brandon's constant use of expletives and prime time TV skewed his expectations.

They pulled up to the curb in a rundown neighborhood at the outskirts of town. To the left squatted a gray stucco apartment complex. Dead grass, bars on the windows, and a six-foot iron fence surrounding the property gave it the look of a maximum security prison. Chain link and beaten dirt defined most of the yards. Security gates covered every door and window down the street. Nick had never seen so many big, ugly dogs. Almost half the houses had a pooch the size of a pony chained in the front.

Silently, the SWAT team filed out of the van. They looked like science fiction warriors with their bulky padding and covered in black from head to toe. Using hand signals and whispers they directed the other officers and their teams. Two men, keeping low and moving fast, dragged steel cables toward the target property. A three-man team split off from the group and headed over the wall into the back yard. The units of non-SWAT officers followed the black-clad cops headed for the front of a two-story bungalow.

Nick, the attorney, and a group of four uniformed officers with a sergeant named Smaels, hung back by the cars. It was their job to coordinate with the other takedowns. If anyone suspicious tried to intervene or run, the cops could jump in. Once the house was clear, then Nick and Shakya would assist with the search. Until then their main job was to stay out of the way.

The lead officers hooked the cables to the security door. Close in behind them, a cop stood ready with a handheld battering ram; a two and a half foot, forty pound section of solid metal pipe. He crouched, gripping the tool by handles at the back and mid point. Cops fanned out along the walls. The team leader raised his fist. Maybe two heartbeats passed and the man jerked his arm. Tires squealing, the van sped off. Cables went taut in a moment of resistance. Then the security door broke from the frame and went spinning through the yard. It landed on one of the cars in the drive and the whoop of an alarm sounded.

Ram held at hip level, the officer stepped up. Two quick, heavy strikes and the front door cracked. Almost simultaneously, another officer stood, broke out a window with a metal rod, and tossed in a canister. Blinding light flashed through the widows and a deafening bang shattered the morning. Twenty other car alarms joined the wail of the first. Smoke rolled out of the door and officers rolled in. Following the SWAT lead, Brandon's team disappeared inside.

The choppy purr of a helicopter buzzed overhead. Nick realized he was holding his breath, willing Brandon to come out safe. At either end of the street, patrol cars converged. They'd keep the road clear and assist with crowd control. The officers at the vehicles spread out. Anyone who ventured out of a residence would be herded back in until the raid was over. Almost oblivious to the chaos, Shakya sat in the back seat making notes and flipping through papers. How she could be so blasé about the proceedings baffled Nick. Agitated, Nick walked toward the back of the Crown Vic where one of the cops, Jamision according to his name tag, stood relaying information over his walkie-talkie. He nodded to the officer, rested his butt on the trunk and pulled out a pack of clove cigarettes. Waiting sucked. Worrying about Brandon sucked. He was stuck with both for the time being.

Rriitt, rriitt… bullets chewed the ground at Nick's feet. Each burst of automatic fire jerked Nick's tendons like strings. His body reacted before his mind actually processed that they were being shot at. The universe went thick as he stood and turned. Someone yelled, Nick thought it might be the district attorney. Collapsed thunder erupted next to his ear. A slow motion world twisted as the black barrel of a gun spun past his face. Fine scarlet mist drifted in its wake. Chewed red, Jamision's mangled hand slammed against his arm. Blood spattered his shirt. The scent of copper mixed with sulfur and burnt skin clogged Nick's lungs.

Voices screamed in his head. *Run! Find cover!*

Every step weighted with lead, Nick ran. He could hear the yells of cops when they returned fire, but he couldn't see them. Gunfire, backed with the drone of the helicopter overhead, became a drill in his skull. Adrenaline pulled his senses like taffy. His body dragged in the air; it took him hours to breathe. Uniformed cops dove behind fences or cars or just hit the ground. Staccato shots ricocheted through Nick's veins. Heavy, hard, a weight smashed into his back. Gravel scoured his skin as the force drove Nick to the ground.

He was dead.

Hot in his ear, a somewhat familiar voice yelled, "Keep down! Stay low!" Sergeant Smaels scrambled over Nick. "Move or die!"

Nick forced out air and his lungs yanked it back. Not dead, it took a moment for that reality to penetrate Nick's brain. Smaels knew what he was doing. If Nick stuck with him, he might remain in the not-dead-yet contingent. Crawling, praying, Nick shot across the street behind the officer. His vision narrowed to the blue butt in front of him. Focus. Stay alive.

Gray cinderblock loomed ahead. Too far ahead, they'd never make it.

Exposed targets highlighted on a field of play. Each inch equaled a mile. Every moment Nick didn't feel a bullet bloom in his back was a miracle. Smaels slid the last few inches to cover. Spinning he grabbed Nick's lapel. Torn fabric screamed as the sergeant hauled Nick in. He landed hard on top of a hibachi. Charcoal dust bloomed around them. Cinders mixed with sweat and blood, gagging Nick.

The screaming crack as high velocity projectiles dug into the brick stung Nick's ears. Glass-fine shards of concrete lacerated their skin with the bullets' speed. Smaels pushed Nick down, forcing him into the small space where wall met a concrete-slabbed front yard. His body, his vest, became Nick's shield. "Ball up," the cop hissed, "get under me as much as you can."

"I though they said this area would be clear." Nick had to yell to be heard.

"We're cops, not freaking superheroes." Smaels shoved harder. "Somebody missed something." And they could die because of it.

Another round of shots sprayed. They rang against the abused hibachi. Concrete shrapnel spattered and splintered, pain cracked Nick's skin. He huddled against Smaels. They both reeked of fear.

"You hurt?" The sergeant screamed the question.

Two breaths and Nick remembered his bloodied shirt. "Not mine!" Although his bum shoulder hurt like hell and the small of his back felt bruised. He wiped his face with the back of his hand. It came away with thin smears of fresh blood. Okay, not all of it was his. The concrete probably cut him.

Static crackled at Smaels' shoulder. "Okay!" Shouts, 10-codes and *officer down* wailed over the channel. "Scared?"

Pinned behind the low wall, Nick nodded. Water replaced blood in Nick's veins. Somewhere, out there, in that insanity was Brandon. "Shitless!" He hugged his knees to his chest.

For a moment, Smaels stared at the slowly brightening sky. Dawn was only minutes away. Smaels rolled his head toward Nick, a tight smile broke his face. "Me too!" he hissed.

Chapter Twenty-Seven

A thick layer of smoke, remnants of the flash-bang grenade hung in the house. Filtered through thick layers of his facemask, the scent still seared the inside of Brandon's mouth and nose. Graffiti covered every wall. Most of it was poorly done and obscene; at least the parts Brandon could read. Red Latin letters spelled out what Brandon assumed were Vietnamese words. Beer cans and trash littered the floor. He tried not to step on any of it as he led his team through their assigned rooms. Hartley, from Narcotics, cursed under his breath as his foot knocked over a pile of trash. Roaches scuttled away to be crunched under their boots.

One team peeled off to the opposite side of the house. SWAT moved up the stairs leading to the upper floor. Brandon's team moved quickly and deliberately through the rooms. Each doorway was checked and rechecked. Brandon set his back to a spray-painted wall. Franco, Hartley's partner and the third man on the team, mirrored his move. Shouts sounded somewhere off to Brandon's left, somewhere not where his team was. Brandon fought the urge to check. His life, and those of the men with him, depended on staying focused. With an indrawn breath, Hartley kicked the door with his boot and, weapon held in firing stance, dove through. Brandon and Franco funneled in behind.

"Down!" Franco yelled. "Hands where I can see them." Sleepy, stunned and looking frightened, eight women huddled in the room. They might be virtual slaves like Thom and Malis. They might be gang associates, girlfriends and such. Most likely the group was a mixture of both. Officer safety came first. Everyone was treated as a potential suspect.

"On the ground!" Brandon barked his order. "Lay down." He grabbed the nearest girl and forced her face-first onto the filthy carpet. When Hartley repeated the move with a second woman, the rest got the picture. They fell to the floor, hugging each other or with hands over heads. Brandon dug plastic restraints from his pocket. While Franco covered them, Brandon and Hartley set about securing the women's wrists.

Brandon looped the flex-cuff over his prisoner's wrists. The rip as he yanked the threads through the roller locks seemed louder, more metallic than it should. He looked up. Franco glanced at Brandon and then at the door. He heard it too.

Gunfire.

Gunfire outside.

Emergency chatter started on the radios. Automatic fire. Cool and efficient, the dispatcher's voice cleared the channel. "All units at target four be advised, we have shots fired and at least one 10-53." Shit, they'd shot a cop. "Possible sniper. Location unknown at this time. All non-essential traffic clear this channel."

Brandon's gut turned to water. Nicky was outside. Nicky was out there and someone was shot. "Fuck!" Brandon stood. He turned to the door and stopped. Six unrestrained suspects lay on the floor. No matter what was happening anywhere else, Brandon's responsibility was in that room. The brutal truth of being sworn, the job came first. Helpless, he shoved down the panic, packed it into a little corner of his mind. Cops who panicked died. Mechanically, he went through the motions of cuffing the remaining women.

Franco's eyes were wide. Hartley shook. Brothers were in trouble outside and they had to remain inside. "Come on!" Brandon barked. "We got a house to clear!" Hartley remained with the detainees and the other two officers moved into the next space.

Each room after that was hell. Brandon pretended the voices over the radio didn't exist. Exterior gunfire became background noise. Everything had to be pushed away. Brandon couldn't allow himself the luxury of thinking. Just move, check, clear, and move again. They hit the kitchen and cleared it. Then Brandon sent Franco back for Hartley. That's when it got really bad.

Squatting with his butt on his heels and his gun held ready near his shoulder, the few seconds of being alone ate at Brandon. Rancid smells emanated from garbage cans brimming way past full. Flies buzzed around a sink full of unwashed dishes and stagnate water. Brandon could single out every sound. Each individual footfall on the upstairs floor registered. The steady whooph, whooph of a helicopter gave him something to count between bursts of gunfire. At least one fully automatic rifle was in use. That probably belonged to the perp who shot at the cops. Intermittent staccato bursts from small arms fire answered. He laughed at the irony. Most of the big guns were *in* the house. That's where the bad guys were supposed to be.

Fragments of *what if* tore at his mind. What if Nicky was pinned down? What if Nicky was shot? What if he were dead?

A vision of Nicky, eyes open and staring, swam into Brandon's mind. Flat, lifeless, and filmed-over dark eyes looked out at nothing, a thin line of red dribbled from the corner of his mouth. He lay in the dirt with blood pooling around his head. The vest might protect his center, but Nicky hadn't been wearing a helmet. There'd be nothing between that strong-featured face and a bullet. Wails heralded the approach of emergency vehicles. The sound confirmed Brandon's nightmare.

Calm down Brandon reminded himself. Nicky was a big boy. He could take care of himself. Except, of course, for when somebody tried to kill him. Dredged-up memories of hours spent pacing the corridors of a hospital emergency room assaulted him. Nicky had lain there, barely breathing, for more than a day. He'd looked like fucking Frankenstein with all the stitches and staples they'd used to patch him back together. Trying to wipe away the memory, Brandon palmed his face. His eyes and cheeks grew hot. He sucked in air and blew it back out. Why was it so hard for him to breathe?

Footsteps sounded in the room behind him. He looked up as Franco and Hartley herded the gals into the kitchen. Once more he shoved the fear back. Until it was clear, they'd have to keep their prisoners inside. They couldn't risk it. The officers made them squat along the interior wall. That was as safe as they could manage for the time being. Not long after, the other squad joined their group. They had two men in custody. Neither looked over eighteen, but both wore the hardened faces and low-slung pants of gang bangers.

Radio channels were cleared for the hell outside. Brandon managed a quick check-in. Raising his hand held unit to his lips, Brandon whispered, "Teams Tango three and two." Inwardly he groaned. He felt so stupid as he said it. SWAT commanders suffered delusions that they were actually in the military, lacing their missions with combat babble. "We've cleared and we're 10-15 with ten possibles." Brandon wiped the sweat from his eyes with the back of his arm. "Holding in kitchen of target four."

"10-4." The dispatcher paused. "Teams Tango two and three proceed with suspects through rear yard. Be advised, officers standing by. Head left when you hit the alley behind residence. Vehicles will be in position where alley intersects street to take custody."

Shit, they were on the move. "10-4." It was goddamn hot in the kitchen anyway. No one wanted to hang in that stink. Nodding to the other cops, he hissed, "We're out of here. Take 'em out the back. Plans say there's a wall at the rear of the property. Hit the alley, head left."

"Got it." The other team leader acknowledged. One of his men scuttled to the door. A cautious check of the yard and he motioned another man out. Hartley and Franco pushed, pulled, and prodded the suspects to their feet. Brandon kept watch through the door, back into the house. As he scanned, he noticed the black forms of the SWAT team easing down the stairs. Another couple of girls, dressed only in T-shirts and looking all of thirteen, followed the lead officer. Like all occupants of the house, their hands were cuffed behind them. The next three officers held a hogtied guy between them; one at each shoulder and the last holding his feet.

Bringing up the rear, the final officer wrestled with an elderly Asian woman. She cussed and spat as he manhandled her down the stairs. As they headed down the hall to the kitchen, Brandon covered them. Just because they thought the house was clear didn't guarantee it. The SWAT officer stepped through and dropped to one knee next to Brandon. "You get 'em out?" It was as much an order as a question.

The two girls looked ready to piss themselves. "Yep." Brandon slid between them, grabbing their elbows to hurry them along. At a crouching run, Brandon hustled the pair through the door and into the yard. They dropped down a set of broken concrete steps. Off to one side, Brandon noticed the carcass of a mongrel dog. Glassy eyes stared out at nothing and blood stained the dirt under its massive head. If Brandon had to guess, the rear SWAT team took it out for officer safety. The drone of several helicopters washed over the early morning. Gunfire was louder, more insistent. Broken glass, dog shit, and rocks crunched under his boots. A quick glance told him that while one of his two prisoners wore jelly sandals, the other didn't have shoes. Without breaking his stride, Brandon swung the barefoot girl over his shoulder in a fireman's carry. The dead dog probably outweighed her by ten pounds.

Hartley crouched next to the rear wall. Five feet of cinderblock tagged with spray-painted scrawls stood between them and the alley. He caught the first girl around her waist and lifted her. Two sets of hands reached from the other side. With her arms bound behind her back, it was awkward as all hell, but somehow they managed. Then they hoisted the other girl up and over. By that time the SWAT folks were at the wall. One SWAT team member dropped to his knees and assumed the cover fire position. Brandon and Hartley jumped up and straddled it. Hogtie guy got bundled over the wall with little problem. The Asian grandma… she was a pill. Biting, kicking, and screaming, it took six men to get her over.

Finally, Brandon dropped into the alley. He was quickly followed by the last of the SWAT team. They hustled all the suspects to a waiting van. The plan had been to process any prisoners at the scene. With the clusterfuck in progress they'd punted with plan B. The other squad, Hartley, and Franco clambered in with the suspects. Thank God the vehicle was full so Brandon didn't have to make an excuse to stay behind. Hartley slammed the door and the van took off.

Now Brandon could panic. He still didn't let go completely, but he did allow himself the luxury of quietly freaking out. Nicky was out there, somewhere. God only knew what had happened, but Brandon's mind called up the worst. Guns drawn and moving in a ragged formation, the officers worked toward the corner. A line of patrol cars blocked the intersection. Brandon sidled up next to a senior officer. "What's the word?"

"You from the inside team?" When Brandon grunted, the officer ran it down. "We have men pinned all over the street." A burst of gunfire sounded and everyone ducked. The black and white served as a shield. Brandon crouched at the bumper and stared down the empty street. Two people huddled behind the Crown Vic they'd arrived in. From what Brandon could see, neither appeared to be Nicky. But he couldn't be certain. "They had a lookout in one of the other houses. Once he woke his ass up and realized what was going down, he opened fire. Snipers are in position on two roofs. As soon as they get a clean shot, they're cleared to take him out."

Tense seconds ticked by. Brandon scanned the cops scattered near the vehicles; maybe four officers, not including those he'd arrived with. Nicky wasn't among them either. Fear burrowed into his chest and made itself comfortable. Sweat slicked his palms, ran down his neck, and glued his shirt to his back. His knuckles were white from gripping his pistol.

Soft, but so clear, a whisper came over the radio, "I'm clear." One loud, crisp shot echoed. "He's down."

Another flurry of activity as SWAT booked off to search the sniper's local. Until it was clear, nobody moved. The delay sapped more strength out of Brandon. He couldn't stand the wait, the not knowing.

Off to Brandon's left, he saw movement. A uniformed sergeant, Smalls or Snails or Smaels, peered over a low wall. Brandon swallowed. He and a rookie were the ones assigned to Nicky. Smaels reached down to assist someone. Then he and

Nicky jumped the wall and ran toward the patrol cars. Nicky held his arm tight against his side. Blood stained his shirt.

Brandon forgot how to breathe.

Everyone dropped as two shots reverberated through the neighborhood. Nicky and Smaels plastered themselves to the side of a truck. From where he crouched, Brandon could see part of Nicky's arm. Lots of dark splotches mixed with a few bright red blots across his shirtsleeve. Fuck, fuck, fuck. Nicky'd been shot and Smaels must have tied it off. Why else would he be bleeding? And he was so fucking pale. Brandon could see him shaking from thirty feet away. Don't let him bleed out.

He scuttled around to the very end of the cars. There wasn't more he could do than watch. They were too far away. His vision narrowed until the only thing he saw was a bloodied arm. Smaels whispered something to Nicky and he nodded back. When he turned his face, Brandon caught a line of red trickling over Nicky's cheek. No, shit no! He'd spent too much fucking time bringing Nicky back to lose him now.

Frozen by duty, Brandon couldn't move. Procedure said to stay put unless someone was at risk. Training had drilled it into his skull. Still, he scoured the area for something to use as a shield so he could go get them. He had to get to Nicky. He couldn't let Nicky die. Fuck him, all of the riot gear was with the SWAT team. Brandon looked back to see Smaels ticking a count off on his fingers. When he reached three, Nicky and the sergeant darted into the street. Smaels huddled, protectively, over Nicky. Shit, he was fucking hit! Smaels treated Nicky like he was fucking hit.

To hell with procedure. Brandon dashed into the street. Grabbing Nicky he spun and ran back towards cover. "Where are you hurt?" he hissed.

"I'm okay." Nicky panted.

Smaels dove behind the car and Brandon slid behind him. Pulling Nicky down, Brandon shoved his hands under Nicky's vest. "Where the fuck are you shot?" His hands roamed over a familiar neck, chest and arms. He couldn't find it. Where the fuck was the wound?

Sounding baffled, Nicky protested, "I'm not shot!" Brandon figured he might be in shock. Damn, he was pale enough for it.

"Don't you dare do this to me, Nicky!" The sharp edge in his voice startled Brandon. "I almost fucking lost you once." All the blood was on his left sleeve. Over and over, Brandon checked. How could he apply pressure, stop the bleeding, if he couldn't find it? Damn near hysterical, Brandon hissed out, "I can't go through it again!"

"Brandon!" Nicky caught his hand. "Brandon!" With his other hand, Nicky grabbed Brandon's jaw. Forcing Brandon to look at him, he repeated. "I'm okay. It's not my blood. I just fell and hit my shoulder. I may have hurt it again."

Not quite convinced, Brandon mumbled. "You're okay?"

Nicky smiled. "I'm fine." His voice was soft and reassuring.

"You sure?"

"Completely."

Brandon let out an explosion of breath. He pulled Nicky to him, almost into his lap. "I kept thinking I was going to get out here and find you hurt or worse." Brandon's voice broke as he hugged Nicky tight. "I can't take that again. It almost killed me the last time." He buried his face into Nicky's neck. The chinstrap of his helmet and the straps of Nicky's vest bit into his skin. Brandon ignored them both. "I was so worried. So scared." If he could have held Nicky any closer, Brandon would have. "I don't want to lose you. I just want you safe."

"Ah, Brandon," pushing against Brandon's upper arms, Nicky tried to pull away. Nicky grunted, "You're squeezing me."

"Yeah." Brandon refused to let him. He wouldn't ever let Nicky go. "So what?"

Nicky swallowed. Brandon felt Nicky's Adam's apple bob against his cheek. "There's people watching." he whispered.

Brandon froze and hissed out, "Fuck." He slid his gaze to the side. Smaels stared at them with open-mouthed amazement and the other officers' eyes were wide. Only the ones farthest away didn't seem to have noticed. Shit! Shit! Shit! But even as he was cursing himself, it hit Brandon. Fuck 'em. Nicky was safe. Nicky wasn't hurt, or at least not badly hurt. Nothing else mattered but that. Brandon pulled Nicky into his chest and hugged him tighter. "To hell with them, as long as you're okay."

CHAPTER TWENTY-EIGHT

A slight breeze brushed Brandon's back as he sat watching people; mostly guys. For once that week, the evening seemed cooler, not quite so hellish. The abundance of old growth trees surrounding the backyard took responsibility for some of that. Brandon sometimes forgot there were places as tranquil as this in downtown Riverside. He didn't get into the historic district much.

Things were winding down, getting back to normal. Jamision would be in the hospital for a while; his injury might be enough to bust him out. The doctors couldn't be sure of how much nerve damage was done by the bullet. Fortunately for him, the DA was red-cross certified and had kept him from bleeding out. After his little outburst, Brandon had spent most of Sunday hiding in police work. Awkward didn't describe the half of it. So far no one had said anything. It was only Monday though. Scenes and suspects were still being processed. It might take months before they knew how successful the raids had been. Hell, Brandon and Nicky finally left near midnight Sunday, while bags of evidence were still being hauled out.

All things considered, the brass announced it to the press as a triumph of police work; tallying up arrest numbers, evidence seized, and only one injury. The biggest news, feisty Asian grandma had been identified as the infamous *Ba`Ngoa-i*, the madam from the *Tin Tin!* and wanted in connection with several con schemes and prostitution counts. Like any good cop, Brandon realized success could only truly be measured once the assholes were in jail. Still, there were some small triumphs. Malis and Thom were in a shelter, a good one with some Christian group. Roberta had paged him. Brandon had called her right back and gotten the news.

Jeff had been right. The only two people, so far, that acknowledged Brandon's part were Jeff and Nicky. Give it a week or so, the excitement of the bust would die down. Then

Brandon figured the rumors would start. Five cops knew he was gay and they'd start talking. One guy's suspicion, Brandon could talk that down. Five witnessing him fall apart over Nicky… there was no way he could deny it now. Brandon took a swig of his beer and stared glumly across the lawn at Ray's guests.

It felt odd to be among so many other gay men and not be cruising. A decent smattering of Ray's work contacts and neighbors rounded out the crowd. People gathered in knots around a patio bar and on the back porch. The interior of the bungalow was wall-to-wall bodies. A quarter million dollars worth of built in cabinets and hard wood floors: Ray and Colton's two-bedroom, nine hundred square foot slice of the American dream.

A voice at his shoulder startled Brandon. "How does it feel to be here?" Ray asked as he dropped into a chair.

"Downtown?" Brandon was perplexed.

"No," Ray drawled out the word, chiding him with it. "Among the out crowd?"

Brandon swallowed and looked back through the door at Nicky. He leaned against the kitchen counter, gabbing with someone Brandon couldn't see. Black jeans, combat boots and a button-down black shirt with the sleeves rolled up, Nicky oozed sex appeal. When they'd arrived, Ray insisted on introducing them as *my old flame Brandon and his boyfriend Nick*. It was almost enough to make Brandon turn tail and run. Only Nicky's vice-like grip on his arm kept it from happening. That, and if he didn't lay claim to Nicky, the guys would have lined up three deep trying to hook up. No one was going to get between Brandon and Nicky.

To think he could have lost Nicky, again. He'd just been overwhelmed and reacted. Maybe that was the easiest way. If he'd made a decision and planned it out, Brandon knew he would have backed down. There was no other option now. Five guys, including a sergeant, witnessed him go all gushy over Nicky. Once you stepped out, the door locked behind you. Another glance toward the kitchen and Brandon caught Nicky staring at him. He took a swig of his beer. Nicky smiled, pushing open the back screen and heading toward where Brandon sat. "Really fucking scary, actually." he admitted.

Ray chuckled. "See, I always knew you were too smart to be a cop."

"Shit," Brandon rolled his eyes. "Thanks Ray."

In a softer tone Ray added. "It gets easier." He nodded to Nicky when he joined them.

As he pulled another chair closer to Brandon, Nicky asked, "What gets easier?"

"Coming out."

"Ah." Nicky settled into his seat. His knee bumped Brandon's. For once Brandon didn't feel compelled to scoot away. "Lots easier." Nicky agreed. He leaned in and rested one hand on Brandon's thigh.

Such an intimate touch in a pretty public place; Brandon had to stop himself from making sure no one saw. "And better?" Please, God, let it get better. If he suffered through the angst much longer, Brandon knew he'd go nuts.

"Sometimes," Ray shrugged. "Sometimes it gets worse for a while." Considering the ice in his glass, Ray seemed to think a bit. Then he added, "Some people won't react well. They might be embarrassed that they didn't know or because they said things in your presence that they realize were bigoted. Others are just full of hate."

Worse, holy shit he didn't think he could handle worse. "And why is that better?"

Nicky squeezed. The gentle pressure comforted Brandon. Nicky would be there for him. "Because you don't have to go through your life worried that someone's gonna find out." He smiled. "They already have, it's out there, everyone knows. There's no lingering dread of being outed by someone else. Whatever happens… it isn't going to hurt you because someone knows now and can threaten you with bringing it up. No blackmail." Nicky reminded him.

"I don't know if I can deal with all this, guys." Brandon sighed through another swallow of beer. "I mean, how should I handle letting everyone know?"

Ray stood. "Look, I'll leave you two to work it out." A glance back at the house let them know why. "I'm going to go circulate." As he walked off, Ray added, "Good luck."

"Thanks, Ray." Nicky waved before turning his attention back to Brandon. "You don't have to let everyone know, not at once." Again he adjusted his chair so that they sat facing, knees touching knees. Earnest, Nicky offered his thoughts. "There's no rule book that says you have to come bursting out of the closet singing show tunes. Little by little, slow and easy is okay." He leaned in, hands resting on Brandon's legs. "Take it one day and one person at a time. Soon you won't have to worry, people will let others know."

"Oh, great," Brandon rolled his eyes, "rumors. That's fucking worse."

"No," Nicky slapped his leg, "because people will come to you and say, 'Hey, so-n-so says you're gay,' and you can just look them in the eye and say 'yeah, I am.'" He spread his arms as though it were that simple. "And a lot of people will just be okay with it."

And a lot of people wouldn't. "What about those that don't take it so well?" Brandon growled. "What about them?"

"There's prejudice out there. But they know you." A reassuring rub up his leg had Brandon almost convinced. "Probably some will just be shocked and get over it after a while. There may be people who just go cold, drift away. Most of the people who have issues with you being gay will fall into that category." He shook his head and chewed on his bottom lip for a moment. "Others, well there's an outspoken minority who will make a big deal about it. You just have to ignore and avoid them."

"Nicky, what am I going to do?" Brandon looked up. The moon loomed huge between the tree branches. "I'm going to freak the first time it happens."

"You'll be fine." Brandon had to be testing Nicky's patience with all his doubts. He knew it. Still, Nicky didn't stop being supportive. "You'll do fine. Shit, you save peoples' lives, stare down guys with guns, you can handle this. Honestly Brandon, you don't actually have to 'come out,' you just don't have to 'be in' any more. Think, at least when someone asks you what you did this weekend you can say, 'I hung out with Nicky,' and you won't have to worry about whether they think I'm a guy or a gal. It won't matter what other people think."

Brandon rubbed his hands over his face. "What about my parents? What should I tell them?" His dad would blow. Edith already thought of him as the black sheep, a jerk who walked out on his wife and daughter. "Fuck, my ex is going to freak. Oh God, Shayna."

"Don't rush." Nicky's gentle laugh cut through some of Brandon's panic. "Wait until the timing's right. Someday I'd like to meet your parents, but, you know, if the first time it's as your best friend Nick… that's fine." How did Brandon ever find someone so understanding? He didn't deserve anyone as good as Nicky. "You know them. I don't. And, you know what, nothing says you have to tell everyone. I want to be part of your life Brandon. All of it. I'd like to meet your daughter. Maybe, someday, if we get that far, I might like her to call me, maybe, her Uncle Nick."

Teasing, Brandon bumped Nicky's knee. "Not Daddy Nicky?" As soon as he said it, Brandon realized he wasn't terrified of the thought. And it was scary not to be scared.

"Brandon, when you're ready for that, I'm ready for that."

"What?" He tried not to sound panicked.

"I told you once, I think we deserve wonderful." God, Nicky was so intense. For once Brandon wanted intense. He wanted committed and serious, not just a few fucks and it's been fun. "That, for me, would be part of wonderful."

Fantastic as it all sounded, Brandon couldn't quite accept it. "I don't think I'm actually ready for that."

"Yep, you're not." Nicky agreed. "But I'm willing to wait for it. Brandon, you're someone I've been looking for, for a long time." Settling back into his seat, Nicky watched him intently. "Just remember to talk to me. Don't shut me out and we'll figure out how to make things work."

Things went quiet for a while, neither talking. It felt good just to be in Nicky's company and not be afraid of discovery. Brandon occasionally glanced at Nicky. He seemed lost in his own thoughts. Thoughtful; Nicky was thoughtful and strong. He was brave in that just-doing-what–needed-to-be-done way. There were so many things Brandon admired about Nicky.

"Shayna will like you."

"Yeah?" Nicky looked up and grinned.

"Yeah, I think so." It was Brandon's turn to lean in. He didn't want to hurt Nicky, but he had to be clear about things. "Before, before the rest of them know, I need to know how…"

Nicky rocked forward to meet him. They weren't more than a foot apart. "What?" His tone said he might already know the answer.

"Babe, if she doesn't get along with you."

"Shh, don't." Pressing his hand against Brandon's lips, Nicky whispered. "I understand. You're her daddy. She comes first." He ran his palm across Brandon's cheek and over his shoulder.

"Actually," Brandon snorted, "she hasn't had me as a daddy for so long, I don't even know how to deal with it." How had he let it get to that point? He'd never wanted to be a weekend father. Hell, Shayna was lucky if she saw him half that often. So much had happened in nine years, Brandon wasn't sure he could undo a lot of it.

"Well then," Nicky's tone went business like, "first you have to become her daddy again." Gently, he teased. "Then we can work on the whole two daddy issue."

Brandon held up the hand that didn't have a beer in it. Catching his pinky with his thumb, he wiggled the remaining fingers. "Three."

"Three?" Nicky seemed confused.

"Well, yeah, she has Frank," Brandon was certain he'd told Nicky that his ex had re-married. "Dian's husband."

"Oh, yeah, three." Standing, Nicky stretched. He smiled down at Brandon, "What a lucky girl, huh?" They probably ought to head home. Nicky had to leave now that the investigation was over. His own job beckoned. Tomorrow they'd make sure Querida could handle the drive; check oil, brakes and such. The day after that, Nicky headed back to Vegas. Through a stifled yawn, Nicky asked, "Will Dian fight you?"

"What?" Brandon pushed back his chair and stood up. "Fight me?"

"If you want more time," Nicky's hands slid around Brandon's middle. "Will she fight you?"

"No, I don't think so." The panic welled up again and Brandon fought it down. He didn't have to be scared anymore. The secret was out. Hesitant, he wrapped one arm over Nicky's shoulder and slid his other hand across Nicky's ass. "Well, I can't really say, 'cause I don't know how she'll take the issue of, well, me and who I am. But, she and Elaine, my stepmom, are always pushing for me to be involved." A little bewildered, Brandon shook his head. "Kids, Nicky, you really want to get involved in that?" The comments Nicky'd always made about his friends' children… well it made Brandon suspect the opposite.

"With you?" His bright eyes erased some of the doubt. Nicky pressed his forehead to Brandon's own. "Yes. I want to be with you, Brandon," he reassured, "whatever that means. It wasn't what I planned for my life, but like my Gramps always said, 'Life has a habit of switching blueprints on you when you're not watching.'" A low chuckle rumbled in his chest.

"Shit, Nicky, I don't know." Brandon pulled him closer. "I don't know if I can think that far ahead."

"Don't. Just realize that's not going to be a problem." It felt so right for them to be together like this. No matter what any one else thought, he and Nicky were meant to be. "Difficult, everything with us is a little difficult, but not a problem bigger than just making us work."

Brandon brushed his lips against Nicky's cheek. "We'll make it work. I promise."

ABOUT THE AUTHOR

JAMES BUCHANAN, author of over ten novels and single author anthologies, lives in a 100 year old Craftsman in Pasadena with her SexyGuy, two demon spawn and a herd of adopted pet dogs, cats, rats and fish. Between managing a law practice with SG, raising kids and writing books, James volunteers with the Erotic Author's Association and Liminal Ink as well as coordinates the newsletter for the ManLoveAuthor's co-op. James has spoken and read at conferences such as Saints & Sinners and the Popular Culture Association. In the midst of midlife crises, James bought and learned to ride a Harley – it went with the big, extended-cab pickup. James has been a member of CorpGoth since 1993 and been known to wear leather frock coats to court. If you don't find James at the computer working on her next book, you're liable to find her out on the bike.

Visit James on the web at:

http://www.james-buchanan.com/

http://eroticjames.livejournal.com/

http://groups.yahoo.com/group/eroticjames/

If you're a GLBT and questioning student heading off to university, should know that there are resources on campus for you. Here's just a sample:

US Local GLBT college campus organizations
http://dv-8.com/resources/us/local/campus.html
GLBT Scholarship Resources
http://tinyurl.com/6fx9v6
Syracuse University
http://lgbt.syr.edu/
Texas A&M
http://glbt.tamu.edu/
Tulane University
http://www.oma.tulane.edu/LGBT/Default.htm
University of Alaska
http://www.uaf.edu/agla/
University of California, Davis
http://lgbtrc.ucdavis.edu/
University of California, San Francisco
http://lgbt.ucsf.edu/
University of Colorado
http://www.colorado.edu/glbtrc/
University of Florida
http://www.dso.ufl.edu/multicultural/lgbt/
University of Hawai'i, Mānoa
http://manoa.hawaii.edu/lgbt/
University of Utah
http://www.sa.utah.edu/lgbt/
University of Virginia
http://www.virginia.edu/deanofstudents/lgbt/
Vanderbilt University
http://www.vanderbilt.edu/lgbtqi/

Stimulate yourself.
READ.
www.manloveromance.com
THE HOTTEST M/M EROTIC AUTHORS & WEBSITES ON THE NET

Printed in the United Kingdom by
Lightning Source UK Ltd., Milton Keynes
142010UK00001B/9/P

9 781608 200160